Gone for a Soldier

The Owen Family Saga

Also by Marsha Ward

The Man from Shenandoah

Ride to Raton

Trail of Storms

Spinster's Folly

Gone for a Soldier

The Owen Family Saga

Marsha Ward

WestWard Books
❧•❧
Payson, Arizona

Gone for a Soldier
© 2014 Marsha Ward

Cover Design by Linda Boulanger
www.telltalebookcovers.weebly.com
Interior Design by Marianna Robb

ISBN 13: 978-0-9883810-3-2

WestWard Books
P. O. Box 53
Payson, Arizona

PRINTED IN THE UNITED STATES OF AMERICA

For the readers, without which writers have no reason for being.

With grateful thanks to Becky Rohner, Julia Griffin, Connie Wolfe and Justin Knudsen for their suggestions; to C. Michelle Jefferies, Carol Crigger, Bill Markley, Patricia Nipper, and C. David Belt for their endorsements; to Taffy Lovell and Deb Eaton—who won naming rights for several characters—for the use of family and other names; and to all those who have encouraged me to keep writing.

Notes and Disclaimers

Since the Shenandoah River flows south to north to empty into the Potomac River, locals refer to points south on the river as *up*, and points north as *down*. Thus, one would go *up* to Harrisonburg from Mount Jackson, and *down* to Winchester. It's an elevation thing.

You will encounter words and phrases used differently here than in our century. *Dear* in one instance means *costly*. *Make love to* means *pay court to*, except where it doesn't. You will know the difference. I use the term *secesh* early on as an adjective. It was slang for *secessionist*. Waynesborough, Spottsylvania, and Harper's Ferry are spellings used in those times. Many people did not adhere to established spelling norms, although they considered themselves literate.

For purposes of story, the details of some military encounters may not align exactly with the historical record. I have, however, made such attempts as were possible after almost two years of intensive research, to use existing accounts with as much accuracy as possible in regards to troop movements, skirmishes, battles, and the like in this novel.

Where I have had characters enroll in military units, they are actual companies in actual regiments and brigades. Their commanders are genuine, in most cases.

The notable exception is the cavalry company raised by the character Roderick Owen. It is entirely fictitious, although I have inserted the "Owen Dragoons" into actual encounters with enemy forces.

The Families

The Owen Family of Shenandoah County, Virginia
Roderick Owen, farmer, horse breeder
Julia Helm Owen, his wife, whom he calls Julie
Rulon – age 20, sometimes called Rule
Benjamin – age 19
Peter – age 17
Carl – age 16
James – age 14
Marie – age 13
Clayton – age 11
Albert – age 10
Julianna – age 8, also called Jule or Anna

The Hilbrands Family of Mount Jackson, Virginia
Randolph Hilbrands, merchant
Amanda Hilbrands, his wife
Mary – age 14
Ida – age 13
Sylvia – age 11
India – age 7
Eliza – born late in 1861

The Allen Family of Shenandoah County, Virginia
Theodore Allen, wealthy businessman and landowner
Louisa Allen, his wife
Merlin, their son, who doesn't play much of a role
Ella Ruth, their daughter – age 16, who does

Other Characters of Importance

Ren Lovell, corporal in Rulon's company
Owen Leoyd, private soldier in Rulon's company
Garth Von, private soldier in Rulon's company
Vernon Earl, from whom Rulon learns a valuable skill

Chapter 1

Rulon — April 19, 1861

Rulon Owen hadn't intended that crisp Friday in April to be momentous.

In fact, when he'd saddled his horse in order to do an errand in Mount Jackson for his ma, he hadn't given much thought to anything but stealing a few moments to see Mary Hilbrands.

She was only a little bit of a thing, a girl with dark hair and eyes that shone like . . . well, they kind of smoldered nowadays whenever she looked his way. Those smoky dark eyes gave him a shaky feeling that spun his head in circles and tied his gut into knots that . . .

"Whew." Rulon realized he'd let the horse slow to a walk while he'd been off in a reverie, somewhere not in Shenandoah County, as far as he could tell. He got the horse loping again, and wished it was already a year from now. Mayhap folks wouldn't get their tails in a twist about them keeping company once Mary turned sixteen in May next year. He was almighty tired of Ben and Peter, and especially of Pa, accusing him of trying to rob the cradle because he'd taken such a shine to the girl. Yes. He'd concede that she was young, but when she spoke his name, his knees felt like they was composed of apple jelly.

Ma sides with me, he thought. *Pa was the true cradle-robber of the family when the two of them wed. Him twenty-four. Ma barely sixteen.*

He wasn't likely to throw his opinion on that subject in his father's face any day soon. Firm. Formidable. The entire county used those words to describe his father. Rulon shook his head. Receiving back-sass from his offspring did not sit well with Roderick Owen. But at age twenty, Rulon hadn't taken a lickin' for a long spell. *Maybe Pa's gone soft in his old age. That's likely, now that he has nigh onto forty-five years pressing him down.*

Rulon rode on, wondering what to do to get his father off his back on the subject of Mary Hilbrands. *It's time I ask Ma to say a word to Pa,* he determined at last. *She won't let him ride me once I begin to court Mary in earnest.*

He slowed the horse to a walk as he entered the town. Ahead, he spotted his brother Ben pulling sacks of grain out of a wagon parked in front of the mill where he'd taken employment over the winter. Glancing up, Ben saw Rulon, and stopped to raise his hand in greeting, a big grin splitting his face.

Rulon drew rein and halted. "Brother Ben." He clasped the outstretched hand. "What makes you so happy today?"

"I am put in a smilin' mood from seein' you with that enraptured look on your face. Can't wait to thrust your hand into the cookie jar, huh?"

Rulon snorted at Ben's fancy.

Ben kept on talking his nonsense. "Oh yes, indeed. You're an enchanted man, spellbound and smitten, ready to do that girl's bidding."

"Speak for yourself, brother."

Ben laughed and said, "Give my best to Miss Mary," then smacked Rulon's horse on the rump, which caused it first to shy and then to run.

After a block atop the runaway, Rulon regained control of the animal. "Heartless boy," he grumbled, his face hot with humiliation. He settled the horse down to a sedate walk once again as he proceeded on his errand.

As he came in view of Mr. Hilbrands' store, he saw a crowd of excited men, some coming, and some going. Some were running. *Running!* What was amiss?

He drew up and dismounted. As soon as he had his feet on the ground, a friend of Pa's shoved the newspaper from Harrisonburg into his hands and bid him take it home. Slapping him on the back, the man ran down the street.

Rulon watched the man's hasty departure, then looked at the immense black headlines of the special edition. **WAR**. He read the subtitles interspersed with the text on the front page. **Ft. Sumter surrenders. Lincoln calls for troops. Via. Conv. votes to secede. Ratification vote in May. Counties raising Companies. Defend the Homeland.** His heart went cold at the urgency of the words. It soon rebounded, and began to beat at a rate he'd not experienced many times in his life. He looked up from the paper, his breath as quick as his heart rate, and made a decision. Feeling the cogs of his life shuddering to a halt and then changing direction, he strode into the store to put his plan into action.

80

Rulon hadn't stepped far into the store when he found himself surrounded by a torrent of men: men shouting at each other, men who flung their arms about with great abandon, men who thumped their fists into their hands. A woman whom he recognized as the baker's wife stood hunched in a corner, as though she were protecting herself from the volume of noise in the building. Two of her daughters hid behind her, clutching brown-paper-wrapped loaves of bread to their chests. The girls looked exactly alike, so they had to be her twins.

He spotted his Mary at the side counter, holding her hands to her ears. Excited at the prospect of getting her approval of his newly minted plan, he grinned at her and waved the newspaper, hoping she would look up and see him. She did so as he approached, and smiled at him, but kept her hands over her ears.

Pushing, shoving, elbowing his way, he got to the spot, leaned over the counter, and asked, "Will you have me if I speak to your Pa today?"

She shook her head. His heart constricted. He thought it had stopped. He drew back and searched her face.

Her countenance softened. She must have realized what she'd done, because she shouted, "I cannot hear you."

Rulon's heart began to work again. He held up a finger and went to the end of the counter. He moved behind it and pulled Mary toward the back room. When he figured she could hear him, he tried again. "Sugar, do you have any objection if I ask your Pa for your hand?" He couldn't resist planting a quick kiss on her earlobe. Then he stood back and awaited her reply.

Her eyes widened, and a small smile tugged one side of her mouth upward. The other resisted movement, and he wondered if fear had taken root in her heart.

"Please say you don't object, Mary. I'm fixin' to ask him,

today. Right away."

"Why, Rulon? We pledged to wait for all that weddin' talk until I'm sixteen. I'll only be fifteen the end of next month."

He showed her the newspaper, pointing to the headline. "We are in a precarious situation. It's to be war, Mary. Abe Lincoln is drivin' us to that, and I'm leavin' soon."

Mary read the banner and on down the page. Her half-smile fled. Her eyes grew even larger. She put out one hand as though she would grasp onto his shirt, then pulled it away and tucked her arm behind her back. "You're leaving?"

"It's my duty to defend my home, Mary. Give me a better reason. Give me the right to defend *you*."

He saw tears in her eyes, filming the gaze that was fixed on him as though she were already memorizing his features before he departed.

She breathed deeply. Once. Twice. Then she spoke. "You may ask Papa, Rulon."

At her answer, his heart began beating as rapidly as a tattoo rattling on a drumhead. He leaned in and brushed a kiss onto her cheek. "I'll go seek your pa's favor now."

He backed away and into the store, relief mixed with anxiety. What was Mary's father likely to think about marriage talk today? Was all this ruckus good for business?

As Rulon rounded the counter, Chester Bates, a friend of his father, clapped him on the shoulder and spun him around.

"I see you've heard the news. There will be a place for you in the Mount Jackson Rifles, I dare say."

"Hello, Mr. Bates." Rulon nodded a greeting to the man. "Isn't that an infantry outfit?"

"It is, and the finest company in the Valley."

"Thank you for thinkin' of me, sir, but I have my heart set on joining a horse troop."

Frank disappointment showed on the man's face. He tipped his hat. "Good luck. I haven't heard anyone speak to raise one here."

"I'm obliged for the good wish, Mr. Bates." He spotted Mr. Hilbrands coming in the front door with a broom. "Excuse me, sir. I'm on a quest."

Mr. Bates quirked his sandy eyebrow as he followed Rulon's

gaze. A grin overtook his face. "Ah. Good luck on that adventure, young man. I reckon Randolph's not thinkin' about marrying off his daughter just now." He stuck out his hand.

Rulon shook it, and struggled to make his way across the room.

☙

Mr. Hilbrands had such a dark look in his eye that Rulon thought he was about to twirl the broom above his head and bring it down on some miscreant's shoulder. However, the time was now, or it would never happen, so he pressed forward through the throng and got within speaking distance of the man.

Rulon tried to speak loudly enough for Mr. Hilbrands to hear him above the hubbub in the room. "Sir, may I have a word?"

"Not now," the man answered.

"I only need a moment," Rulon said, feeling his confidence ebbing away.

"I'll speak to you when I've dealt with this turmoil," the man said, his dark brows drawn together.

"That suits me, sir. Do you need assistance?"

"Not this minute." Mr. Hilbrands raised the broom above his head, in a startling imitation of Rulon's imaginings, and thundered at his neighbors, "This is a place of business. I have work to do, customers to tend to. If you can't moderate your voices, take your discussions to the street."

Rulon had never heard such a speech from his prospective father-in-law. He wondered about the timing of his petition. How would it be received when the man was so worked up by the interruption of his commercial enterprise?

However, when the subdued men about the room had lowered their conversations to a reasonable level, Mr. Hilbrands was evidently satisfied by his efforts, and turned to Rulon, bearing a smile on his face.

"What can I do for you, young man?"

Rulon gulped, trying to think what to say right off. Every thought, every carefully planned sentence had fled from his brain.

Mr. Hilbrands arched an eyebrow, and Rulon hastened to find words to start his own speech.

"Nice . . . nice day, sir."

5

The eyebrow inched higher.

"You must be aware that your daughter Mary and me have been keepin' company for some time," he began, feeling like a veritable dolt. Of course the man knew that. He'd sat in the parlor his fair share of time to accompany them.

Mr. Hilbrands nodded. "Yes, indeed. Go on."

Rulon swallowed. "Sir, Miss Mary has agreed that we should, um, wed before I go to serve my country in this comin' squabble."

Both eyebrows rose toward the tin ceiling. The black, forbidding look had returned to Mr. Hilbrands' features.

"We had planned to wait another year to ask for your permission to marry, but sir, the state of affairs demands, um, requires a change in our circumstances." Rulon felt like his tongue was dragging through molasses with each word, forcing him to speak so slowly that he wasn't sure the man's patience would hold out much longer.

"You want to marry my daughter? Now? Before you traipse off to make war with the Yankees?"

Rulon squirmed. The man made his proposal sound somehow improper and self-serving.

"I reckon that's about the size of it, sir," he admitted, casting his gaze down to the tips of the man's shoes.

"This is a surprise, and not a welcome one, young man. My daughter is still of tender years. I think it a mite unseemly of you to talk marriage at this time. Hmm."

"Please consider my request, sir," Rulon said, feeling like a beggar. "Mary's wishes are in accord with mine."

Mr. Hilbrands eyed Rulon and stroked his thin moustache. "This will require discussion with my wife," he said, his voice also conveying that he did not favor such a turn of events. "She must have an opportunity to give her opinion on this matter."

Rulon felt his heart plummeting to the pit of his stomach. He gulped anew and screwed up his courage for a final feint. "When might you give me an answer, sir?" He had so little time before other Virginia patriots stole a march on him and whipped the enemy. He might lose out entirely.

Mr. Hilbrands looked even more startled, if possible. "I will speak to the missus today. I suppose you want a speedy reply?"

Rulon nodded.

Mr. Hilbrands raised his chin. "You may expect our answer on Sunday morning, then, before the Sabbath service."

"Yes, sir. Thank you, sir! I will see you then, sir." Rulon turned on his heel and marched out of the store. Only then did he recall the errand Ma had given him to purchase a pound of sugar. He squared his shoulders—feeling very foolish—turned around, and re-entered the mercantile.

℘

Rulon arrived in the barnyard of the home place an hour later, and shouted "Pa!"

"I'm here," a voice called from inside the barn.

Rulon dismounted and shoved his hair out of his eyes. When had he lost his hat? He pulled the horse along, wondering how his announcement would be received.

"Pa," he repeated, almost breathless, as he halted beside a horse tied securely in a stall. Rulon paused to swallow in an attempt to ease his dry throat.

"Hmm?" Pa bent over an upraised hoof, his hammer held in midair as he evidently waited for Rulon to speak.

"Charleston's secesh boys fired on Fort Sumter last week. The Federals gave up the fort. Ol' Abe Lincoln called on Virginia for troops. What an insult he gives us!" He stopped to get a breath, then continued, his words tumbling over each other. "The Virginia Convention voted to secede, but there'll be a ratification vote in May. We're going to war, Pa. The counties are raising new companies in case we're called to fight. Of course we'll be called up."

"What?" His father spit a mouthful of nails into his hand. "Where'd you hear that secession news, boy?"

Rulon held out the newspaper, forgotten in his rush to impart what he had learned. "The Hilbrands' store. I was—"

"Hold on there." Pa let the horse's hoof down easy and straightened up. "You was makin' love to his daughter. She's too young for you." He took the paper Rulon still offered him and let it dangle at the side of his leg.

Rulon's belly tightened. "I was fetchin' the sugar Ma asked me to bring her," he replied. Knowing he was on the edge of anger over the subject of Mary's youth, he needed to move away and

7

cool down.

He stepped back to his horse, wrapped his fingers around the side of the stirrup, and gripped it so hard his hand went white. When his breathing had slowed, he released the stirrup and dug the parcel out of the saddlebag. He held it up where Pa could see the proof. Trying not to bite off his words as he lowered the packet of sugar, he said, "Miss Mary an' me, we've had an understanding for quite a spell."

"She's barely out of the cradle. You leave her be."

Rulon took a deep breath and held it for a moment before he said, "That's up to Mary's pa. I've asked him for her hand."

"You've done that? Asked Rand?" Pa shoulders seemed to sag slightly. "Have you given this plenty of thought, son? Miss Mary is still a schoolgirl."

Rulon measured his words. "I can't help but think of her night and day. I know she's young, but she's coming up on fifteen. She wants to wed me, and she's got a right strong opinion on the matter."

"You can't wait till you whip the Yankees?"

"No, Pa. I reckon I'll take my chance for a bit of happiness before I leave."

His father shook his head in resignation. "I can't blame you for that wish, Rulon. I expect you considered that wartime is risky?"

"Yes, Pa. That figured into my decision."

Rod sighed. "If you're set on this course, bear in mind to give the girl her happiness, too. Treat her well, and with respect. You're committin' for a lifetime, you understand?"

"I never thought otherwise."

"You keep them marriage vows in mind while you're away." He looked off into the distance, as though remembering another time. Then he slapped his leg with the newspaper and turned to Rulon again. "Temptations to break them will present themselves. They always do."

Rulon chewed the inside of his cheek.

"You won't get diseased if you avoid those temptations. That's not a thing you want to bring home to the wife."

Rulon shifted his weight from one leg to the other, then back again, wondering how they had gotten onto this subject. "I don't intend—" He stopped, his voice strangled in his tight throat.

"Then don't give in to mankind's carnal nature." Pa turned away and lifted the horse's hoof. "Don't do it."

❧

When Rulon came in the house before supper, Pa sat near the fireplace, reading the newspaper brought from town.

Rulon took a seat on a stool, uneasy about striking up a conversation that could wander onto the previous topic. "Pa, are you about finished with the paper?" he asked, drumming his fingers on his knees.

Pa looked up. "Not quite. What has you all-fired curious to read the news?"

Rulon cleared his throat, not once, but twice. Pa continued looking at him. Rulon glanced at his father's face, then away, and cleared his throat a third time. When he could no longer fail to respond, he said, "I'm seeking a cavalry company to join." He swallowed, avoiding his father's eyes entirely now. "I figured the paper would have word about a company or two being formed."

"Cavalry, you say?"

"I been raised up with horses all my life long, Pa. I reckon it's natural I go to war ridin' one."

Pa nodded. "Good reasoning. Take a look, then." He held out the paper.

Rulon devoured the columns of print, moving his forefinger down each article. In a few moments, he flicked the paper with his nail in disgust. "There's nothing." He looked up to see his father watching him intently.

"Nothing in our county?"

"Yes. I cannot fathom it."

"There are several infantry companies forming up, one right over in Mount Jackson."

"I don't admire the thought of trudging along on the ground. I prefer to ride."

Pa shifted in his chair. "Did you take notice of the mention of the Harrisonburg Cavalry?"

"Yes, sir. It says they're called to muster on the twenty-second of next month. Weren't they formed a couple of years past?"

"That's right, after John Brown raised his ruckus. Valley folks

9

feared his cock-eyed scheme to raise a rebellion among the Negroes would take root in the wrong minds." He put out his hand for the newspaper.

Rulon passed it over. "I recall the alarm that put into the ladies hereabouts. I'm glad Ma is made of sterner stuff than Mrs. Hilbrands. Her fit of the vapors is legendary."

"Would you consider enrolling with the Harrisonburg troop?"

Rulon ran his hand through his hair. "I doubt they'd let me enroll, Pa. I'm not from Rockingham County, and I sure haven't drilled with them none."

"Their captain is Tom Yancey."

Rulon stared at his father, not making a connection between his comments.

"The Yanceys are kin of ours. Not close kin, but cousins, none the less."

Rulon straightened. "I'd forgotten."

"Family ties should count for something. I'll write a letter, if you'd like."

"It might go down better if I do it."

Pa considered that, and finally nodded. "You have the right of it. Let me go over the family connection." He rose and got the family bible down, brought it back, and opened it to the center section.

As Pa and Rulon explored the kinship between the two families, Ben came in and sank heavily onto the hearth, mumbling under his breath. He rubbed his head hard with both hands. "When are you goin' to geld that colt, Pa?" he finally interrupted.

"Throwed you again?" Rulon asked, smirking.

"No, I flew off on my own," Ben said, looking askance at Rulon.

"You should leave the horse-breaking to James. He has the knack."

"He's a baby."

"He still has the knack and you don't."

"How's he do that?" Ben rubbed his head again.

"He was born to be a horseman," Rulon said, then went back to his talk with Pa, who appeared amused at Ben's misadventure.

Before long, Rulon knew all about his relationship to Captain

Yancey, and let Pa go back to reading his newspaper.

"Ben," Rulon said, standing up and putting a hand on his brother's shoulder. "Come set on the porch with me until supper's ready. It's too warm in here with the fire." He cast a glance at his father, but he had resumed reading. "*I* don't have old man's bones," he muttered in a soft voice.

Ben acquiesced, and followed Rulon outside. "You called Pa an old man? You're a brave soul, Rule. By the way, I found your hat fetched up against a blackberry thicket along the road as I came in from town. I left it hanging in the stable."

"That was kindly of you," Rulon said with a snort. "It wouldn't stay in your hand long enough to bring it to mine?"

"The colt needed working."

Rulon nudged a chair out from the wall with the toe of his boot. "I can't figure why there's no cavalry company forming up hereabouts," he mused as they settled into their seats.

"Cavalry? You won't see much action riding a horse around the country."

"I reckon I will. A horse will get a body to the heart of the action quicker than a footsore man can march there."

Ben cuffed Rulon on the arm. "A horse will get shot out from under you. Then where will you be? Afoot, brother. A mere camp dog."

"I'll take the risk. I like horseflesh between my legs."

Ben chortled. "You like—"

"Don't you dare say it." Rulon waggled his finger under Ben's nose. "The haughty Miss Allen can't be pleased that you prefer the mud-slogging infantry," he added, deftly turning the conversation in another direction. "You'd rather come home to her with brogans full of muck than clean boots?"

"It doesn't seem likely that I'll be comin' home to her at all, except in a brotherly fashion." Ben's face lost all humor. "Miss Allen's pa has forbidden her to consider a match with me."

Rulon raised an eyebrow. "An Owen boy ain't good enough for him?"

"This Owen boy don't have any property. That's all that matters to him. Property and possessions."

"That's hard luck, Ben. What does the lady have to say?"

Ben rubbed his nose with a knuckle. "I've a notion the lady is wavering a mite. I'm plannin' to see her tomorrow night. With a little luck, maybe I can talk her into elopin'."

"You'd go that far?"

"I ain't content without her."

"I reckon I know that itch." Rulon tipped his chair back, balancing on the rear legs.

"Are you makin' any headway in scratchin' it?"

Rulon sat silent for a time. He pinched a crease in the leg of his trousers and adjusted the fabric. "A mite," he said finally.

"You randy dog," Ben said, and whistled.

Rulon smacked him on the side of the head, growling in his throat, "It's not what you think, brother."

"Ow! Spare the brainpan. It's had enough abuse today." Ben slapped away Rulon's hand. "You're always a-sniffin' around the girl. What else can I think?"

"Good luck in your quest with Miss Allen, brother." Rulon leaned farther back in his chair. "We're heading for war. Soon enough we'll have other battles to win. Through the cavalry, of course."

Ben started to sweep his boot toward the legs of Rulon's up tilted chair, but Rulon forestalled him by settling it back to the floor, then grinned at his brother in triumph. "I'm fixin' to write a letter to Captain Yancey to offer my sword to the Harrisonburg Cavalry."

Ben's guffaw exploded onto the soft evening air. "Your sword? Where do you reckon to get a sword to offer?"

"It's a metaphorical sword, you dolt. What will you offer? A bedroll?"

"I'm goin' to offer my own self, and see no impediment to being accepted. The Mount Jackson Rifles are taking enlistments soon."

"You'd best work fast on the girl's pa, then."

"Don't I know it!" Ben's voice took on a note of despair. He rubbed his hands up and down his thighs. "If she won't go away and marry me, you and me will have to beat back those Yanks quick so I can come home and change the man's mind."

∞

Rulon had just passed the fried potatoes down to Ben when he leaned back from the table, looked around at the family, straightened his shoulders, and cleared his throat with emphasis.

"Got somethin' to say, brother?" Ben asked, his eyes twinkling in the lamplight.

"I do," Rulon declared. He fiddled with his fork, then laid it on the table and got to his feet. "I'm fixin' to wed Miss Mary Hilbrands."

"Scratchin' your itch," Ben muttered.

Peter was next down the table from Ben. "Maybe in a year or two," he jeered.

Rulon sat down and picked up his fork. "No. We'll do it as soon as Mr. Hilbrands gives me his consent."

Pa spoke. "How long do you reckon before he has an answer for you?"

"He said he'll talk to Missus Hilbrands and let me know their decision before church on Sunday." Rulon wagged his head. "I hope Mary has occasion to converse with him and make her feelin's known. He had a reluctant spirit about him."

Ben chuckled. "Miss Mary don't have enough age on her to have an opinion, brother. She ain't but a year older than James, and he's a veritable baby."

"Am not," James countered from across the table.

"Are too." Peter dived into the fray, grinning widely.

"Always stirrin' up trouble," Rulon said, glaring at Ben, who gave him a triumphant look.

"Quiet," Pa thundered, slapping the flat of his hand on the table top.

After a moment, once silence had been achieved, Ma spoke up. "Rulon, when did you ask Mr. Hilbrands?"

He looked down the table at his mother. "Today when I was in town. After I read the news, I figured I'd best not wait longer."

"What news?" demanded his sister, Marie.

"War news. Abe Lincoln asked for troops to put down the rebellion in the cotton states," he said. "I'm going to enlist in a troop of cavalry, if they'll have me." He picked up his fork, held it for a moment, then stabbed it into his potatoes. "I want Mary to wed me before I go."

"Oh Rulon," said Ma. "You're too young."

"Ma." The distress on her face disturbed him. "I aim to marry her in any case. Better now than later." Or *never*, he dared to think.

"To go for a soldier," she said, her voice low.

"I'm almost too old," he huffed.

"Can I go, Ma?" Albert was only ten.

"No!"

"They'll need drummer boys. Or fife players."

"You don't play drum or fife, either one." Carl reached out and attempted to deliver a blow to Albert's ear, but Albert ducked as Pa pounded the table again.

"Food's getting cold," Pa declared. "Discussion's over."

Rulon raised his fork and shoved a mouthful of potatoes past his lips, wishing he hadn't even begun to broach the subject. *What an unruly bunch!* The sooner he was off on his own, the better.

Chapter 2

Ben — April 20, 1861

Ben waited in the darkness of the lane that led up from the north fork of the river. Before him on a rise stood the grand house, the centerpiece of the prosperous farm owned by Miss Ella Ruth Allen's father. Behind him, tied to a low-hanging tree limb, his horse nickered softly and stamped a hoof.

Ella Ruth was late in arriving to their tryst, but that was to be expected. Ella Ruth was late for every occasion.

He smiled momentarily at her habitual tardiness, and then adjusted his leaning position against the smooth tree trunk. If he had his wish, he would scoop her up and run away to the nearest place he could marry her, but she hadn't yet agreed to elope with him. He hoped his powers of persuasion would be sufficient to the task tonight. If not, he only had a few more days to win her over to the idea.

Hearing footfalls on the lane, he pushed away from the tree and straightened.

"Ben?" Breathless. Timid. Hopeful.

"I'm here," he called, keeping his voice low.

The footsteps slowed. Hesitant. "Where? I cannot see you."

She was close, so close to him that he could smell the scent of the rose water she wore. He moved forward. "Here," he said, bringing the girl into his arms.

"Oh Ben," she sighed, snuggling against him, her head fitting into the hollow beneath his chin. "I worried you wouldn't come." Her anxiety showed itself in a constrained giggle.

"You can depend on me," he told her, repeating a phrase he'd said many times before in his attempts to woo and win her.

"You always say that," she said, a bright little chuckle in her voice.

"I want you to remember it. I want you to know I am true to you. There is no one in my heart but your dear person."

"Oh Ben," she repeated. "It's Poppa you need to convince, not me."

He sighed. "Don't I know it." He held her, rocking her slightly. "What's the secret? How do I make him see my worth?"

"I cannot advise you on that point."

He heard the despair in her voice. "Ella Ruth, what does your ma think? Does she influence him?"

"Oh no! Momma doesn't meddle in Poppa's affairs. She wouldn't dream of telling him to let you—" Her voice choked.

No help in that direction. Ben sighed again. "There has to be a remedy. Does your brother have influence?"

"Merlin keeps out of Poppa's business."

Gall rose in his throat, and he couldn't speak until he had cleared it away. "My pa always told me life wasn't fair, that I should buck up and realize it for truth. I reckon I didn't know what he meant until now."

"Don't you get disheartened, Ben. I adore you. Poppa will have to see, sooner or later, that you are not merely a farmer's son, but a person of real substance, real importance. Like I do." Her voice rose to a squeak.

Marveling at her remarkable speech, he patted her hair, then stroked her cheek. "I won't lose heart, but time is growing short. War is coming, the papers say. I expect I'll go fight for the Confederacy."

"Oh no. You can't. You would have to leave me." She snuggled tighter against him.

"That's the way it is with war. All the more reason to redouble my efforts. When can I talk to your pa again?"

"Not for days. He's on a trip for business."

"Humph." Ben pondered on the problem, still stroking Ella Ruth's cheek until she stayed his hand.

"Ben."

"Hmm?"

"How much do you care for me?"

He shook his head, drew all his focus together to answer the question. "There ain't a measure large enough, girl." Moonlight fell upon her brow. It gave him an idea. He took her chin between fingers and thumb and gently turned up her face so he could gaze directly into her eyes. "You are the sun, the moon, the stars to me.

No man ever loved a woman more."

Ella Ruth giggled. "I wish Poppa had a romantic soul. He couldn't help being moved by such tender words." She shivered. "He's a businessman."

"A very wealthy businessman."

"Yes." She sighed. "Can't you make a pretty speech about business, Ben?"

His chuckle sounded rueful to his ears. "I could tell him about mill stones and sacking flour and the best method to repair a sluice. However, I don't own the mill."

"Tell him about all your pa's nice horses."

"They don't belong to me, neither."

"Don't you own anything, Ben?"

He drew her close. "I own the love I bear you."

"Oh Ben. Such a pretty speech. And all for naught." Ella Ruth turned her head and sighed against his chest.

Disappointment in himself and his prospects surged through his veins. He really didn't own anything of substance, anything that a wealthy businessman would count as property. Despite the momentary negative thrust of his thoughts, he knew he had to press on and gain the prize. "I will put my mind toward finding a solution, my darling," he murmured. "All is not lost."

"Yes, Ben."

He stood quietly for a long moment, rocking her again in his arms. He didn't dare kiss her and excite his yearning. Not right now. Instead, he rocked her.

She said nothing, evidently content to be enfolded in his arms.

When he could not bear the silence a moment more, he whispered, "We could go up to Staunton and find a judge to marry us."

Immediately she began to shake her head against his chest. "I couldn't. I just couldn't. That would be wanton."

He tightened his hold a fraction. "Oh girl, I am wantin' you to marry me. Don't you want to?"

She wiggled his embrace loose enough that she could look up at him. "Of course I do. I want a lovely wedding in the church, with six bridesmaids, and roses heaped alongside the pews and under the altar, and my poppa giving me over to your keepin', and my momma's special cake afterward. That's my dearest dream."

"Not me?"

She tilted her head to one side. "Not you what?"

"I'm not your dearest dream?"

She giggled and gave his chest a little shove. "That's my dearest dream of a wedding, silly boy. A girl must keep hold of her fond dreams."

And a boy has to damp down his passions, he thought, choking back his disappointment at her refusal to consider his suggestion. The company he intended to join, raised by her own cousin, was going to war soon. He didn't dare tell her that tonight and chance a quarrel.

"Once Poppa admits what a wonderful catch you are, we will have that lovely wedding, with all our friends and family to witness our happiness." Her eyes sparkled. She walked two fingers up his shirt. "Ben, you'll look so handsome in a frockcoat, with great long tails, just like in the novels."

"I've never seen such a coat," he said, dubious that a piece of raiment like that was to be had in the entire county.

"We can have it made to order in Boston, and shipped here by special coach."

Ben drew a breath and nearly choked at the thought of the expense. He turned aside and coughed. Ella Ruth took such wild fancies into her mind at times. "Girl, you do realize Boston is in another country now?"

"Oh, you men say that, but it's not important. Poppa can get anything."

Sometimes he simply wanted to shake sense into her, but knew it would do nothing to advance his cause. "Never mind," he crooned into her hair. "First things first. When will your poppa return from his trip?"

"I don't know. I'll have to ask Momma tomorrow." She stirred. "I can't chance being out too much longer, or she will suspect I'm meeting you." She raised her face and gazed into his eyes. "Kiss me, Ben, before I go back."

He knew it was folly to arouse the ache that kissing her would unleash, but such a frank appeal could not be denied. He bent to the task, trying for a brief encounter, but the soft curves pressed against him worked their charms, and he yielded to a second kiss. Fortunately for his resolve, Ella Ruth pulled out of his embrace and patted him on the cheek.

"Be good, Ben," she bid him. "Think of me, not of any other girls."

"I am not acquainted with any other girls," he murmured, half stupefied. "Only you. Only you."

She slipped away, turning briefly to blow him another kiss, then she was swallowed up amidst the trees surrounding the house.

Ben exhaled until he thought his lungs surely were as bereft as his arms, then slumped over to support himself with hands on shaky knees as he took in air once more. If a whirlwind had caught him and flung him against the side of a barn, he figured he could not have felt more battered than he did by his emotional and physical upheaval. How could one little girl do this to him?

He slowly straightened and went toward his horse, not sure if he even had the strength to haul himself into the saddle. "Brownie," he said, patting the animal's neck, "don't you let me drown crossing the river."

∞

Rulon — April 21, 1861

Rulon stood just below the bottom step of the stairway leading up to the door of the church, clasping his hands behind his back. He heard his shoe tapping rapidly against the brick. He simply could not control the foot as he waited.

"Young man!"

Rulon swung around at the sharp tone he heard in Randolph Hilbrands' voice. It sounded like the man intended to give him ill news. "Sir?" he said, hoping his face bore a conciliatory aspect.

The man descended the steps, a frown bending his thin moustache in a downward curve.

A chill raised the hairs on the back of Rulon's neck. Had he lost Mary? He couldn't feel his hands.

Mr. Hilbrands stopped on the step above where Rulon was standing, and stared down at him. He took a quick breath. "My daughter wants to be your bride," he said, a fierce look on his face. "She says it must be now, before you enlist. I told her that was a fanciful notion."

Rulon didn't dare say a word. He couldn't hear himself

breathing.

"She is most persuasive in her reasoning. She is young, but she seems to have a firm grasp of what she is fixing to do. Given the circumstances, I am giving consent."

Rulon felt himself toppling, and slid his left foot back to maintain his balance. His ears rang with the man's words. *I am giving consent.*

"Tha-thank you, sir." He struggled to stand upright, instead of sagging as he felt inclined to do. In point of fact, his knees begged to kiss the steps, but he conquered the impulse after a long moment, and thrust out his hand to seal the bargain.

Mr. Hilbrands solemnly shook it, but added, "Her mother is not convinced as yet, but may come around in due course. You would do well to spend time in that effort."

"Yes, I will, sir. Thank you again." Rulon left off pumping the man's hand, expecting to take his leave and go to Mary's side to ask her to marry him.

Mr. Hilbrands forestalled him, saying, "Come to the house after the service to speak to my daughter. You will want to tell her that I spoke to the minister. It appears there are several weddings taking place due to this war fever. He does not have any open days until May 11th. Will that suit?"

Rulon hoped his mouth wasn't gaping as Mr. Hilbrands' words swirled in his brain. May 11th. That was an age away. He gulped. "Yes, sir. That suits just fine. Give Mr. Moore my thanks."

"He'll want your coin for the service. Two dollars."

Rulon gulped again. Two dollars. That was four days' wages hereabouts! He'd never thought of any cost involved in getting wed. Two dollars! What would Pa say?

80

After he had spoken to Mr. Hilbrands, Rulon entered the church, found his place in the family pew, and craned his neck to look at his intended, but Ma's hand on his shoulder drew his attention to the proceedings at hand. The Sunday service had stretched to three hours, an interminable length, which gave him ample time to think on the moment of his encounter with Mary and its solemn significance.

Now he knelt before the girl in the gloomy parlor of the

Hilbrands' home, his gut tied in knots.

"Mary?"

Dust motes danced in the sliver of light streaming between the drawn drapes. His throat felt dry as the dust lying underneath the table against the far wall. Which girl had stinted in her dusting duties the previous day? Perhaps his arrival had caught Mrs. Hilbrands so unaware that she had forgotten the sad state of her parlor.

Where *was* Mrs. Hilbrands? Should he and Mary be alone? They'd never kept company in this room without another person as chaperone.

Rulon fought his increasing panic, grateful that at least he was kneeling. The position gave his knees no chance to knock together. He knew he was squeezing Mary's fingers too tightly, and willed his grip to loosen, his shoulders to lower from their hunched position near his ears.

What was he doing here? How had he come to be proposing marriage to this girl who he knew to be so pure and tender and full of hopes for the future? What was their future to be? Only days before, his thoughts had centered only in somehow quenching the fire that arose in him whenever he was in Mary's company . . . touched her hand . . . or merely thought about her. The swell of her bosom drove him insane with desire, and his constant thought up to now had been how he might coax her to be alone with him, to let him touch . . . her flesh.

He swallowed.

And now? Now war was upon then, hovering over their lives like an inky thundercloud. It changed everything: every path, every hope, every desire. His desire. *Oh God, help me to have solemn thoughts on this holy day, this portentous day, this . . . engagement day.*

He cleared his throat, glad Mrs. Hilbrands had *not* had the opportunity to throw open the drapes. If Mary saw his countenance, surely she would see the doubts that must be covering it as he rethought his rash decision. He must be mad.

"Mary," he tried again, his ears catching the tremor in his voice. What a shambles he was making of the affair! Hearing how his voice trembled, she might now tell him "no," guessing how much he doubted. Could she know that he was driven more by the burning in his loins than by a burning in his heart?

No, that wasn't right. Not right at all. *I love Mary more than life! I'm sure that's the truth of the matter.*

What would Ma think of him and his carnal desires? The truth was she'd never feared to lay down the law in their home, to broach a subject he'd quaked to speak about to his pa. She did not hesitate to tell her sons to keep their pants buttoned until they were duly wed.

Well, if I can carry off this speech properly, I'll soon be duly wed and she can set her mind at ease where I'm concerned.

"Mary," he said again, thinking, *I've been doin' this all wrong. Think on how much you love the girl.* He pursed his lips and let out a long sigh. "I can scarcely bear the thought of goin' off to fight, of leavin' you behind, without makin' you my wife."

Ah! This is fearsome work!

He bowed his head, closing his eyes to block out distractions while he tried to regain his courage. He breathed deeply, feeling a need for a larger volume of air in his lungs, then opened his eyes again, focusing on Mary's blue and gray striped skirt. The cloth shivered beneath his gaze. The realization that she was trembling as much as he, finally steadied him.

He looked up. Mary's face lay half in shadow, half in light as the sliver of sunlight illuminated one cheek, one side of her fair brow, one half of her raven-dark hair. She was biting her lip.

Rulon took another deep breath. "My tenderest feelings are toward you," he declared, voice steady at last. "My bosom swells with joy at the mere glimmer of hope that you bear me similar feelings." *Where was this flowery turn of phrase coming from?* He brushed away the errant thought. "Will you marry me, my sweet girl?"

"Yes."

Even though her answer was but a whisper, he heard it. Joy swelled his chest as he had just claimed it would, to such a degree that he felt he would suffocate. The next thing he knew, he was smothering both of Mary's hands with kisses, and oddly, her fingers were wet.

To his horror, he took note that the moisture came from his own streaming eyes. What shame! If his brothers ever heard of this—that he had cried like a mewling babe because a girl—

No. He would own up to his seemingly womanish response if he ever had the occasion to do so. Mary had given him her answer, and bolstered by thought of the consent he'd won this morning from her father—reluctant though it had seemed—he reckoned he was justified in shedding a few tears of elation and triumph.

"Rulon," she whispered, her voice quivering slightly, "my heart is yours, and ever has been." She inhaled quickly, twice, then said, "I saw you talkin' to Papa this morning. What did he say?"

"He gave consent," Rulon began.

Mary cut him off. "Thank the Good Lord!" She removed one of her hands from Rulon's grasp to dash the tears from her brimming eyes.

"He was somewhat reluctant, but did not seem inclined to demand a long courtship. He knows our time together is short with war comin' upon us."

"Papa can be sensible when he puts his mind to it."

Rulon stroked the hand that Mary had allowed him to keep in his. "Your pa said he spoke to the minister about a ceremony."

She inhaled sharply. "He did?"

"Mr. Moore is available on May 11th. Three whole weeks away!"

"Only three weeks?" Mary shook her hand out of Rulon's and covered her face.

Rulon rocked backward at her strange reaction. "Sweet girl, three weeks is a lifetime to wait."

Mary peeked over her fingers. "Oh Rulon. I have only three weeks to get ready for my wedding day. I wonder what Mama will say?"

&

Mary — April 21, 1861

Mama had plenty to say, Mary discovered soon after Rulon took his leave.

She had swept into the parlor almost before the front door had closed upon the man, dragging Mary with her by a tight grasp on her arm. She thrust her onto the same chair upon which she had sat when Rulon knelt before her, then dropped into the seat opposite.

"You are too young to be a wife," she said right off.

Mary attempted to turn away that argument, pointing out that her own grandmother had married at the tender age of thirteen.

Mama compressed her lips and wagged her head. "The society was much different in that era. I am raising you to be a lady, and ladies do not wed before a proper age."

"Mama, this is war time. Rulon is enlisting soon. If I let him go without, if I don't marry him now, perhaps I will miss my chance entirely." The idea that Rulon could die brought waves of sadness crashing upon her, almost knocking her against the back of the chair upon which she perched.

"I do not recall hearing any proclamation of war. Mr. Hilbrands has not imparted any such news to me. He would have done so, had there been a need."

"I read in Papa's newspaper that war with the North would commence soon." Mary offered up the news as further evidence of her need. "The headlines were the largest letters I've ever seen. The editor said Virginia will surely secede and join the other states in the Confederacy. Mayhap they won't even wait until the convention vote is ratified in May. Mama, I have to marry Rulon before he leaves the county."

"You do not have to do any such a thing," Mrs. Hilbrands stated, but her voice had dropped in volume and firmness. "I suppose—" She stood abruptly, and headed toward the door.

"Mama?" Mary got to her feet and called out her strongest argument. "We have an appointment to be wed. With the minister."

The door slammed.

Mary stood rooted in place for a few seconds, then began to pace the room.

Would Mama try to convince Papa that wedding Rulon was a bad notion? Did Mama have some unspoken objection to her marriage into his family? Her parents had known Rulon's folks for years. Her father and Mr. Owen were friends of long standing. The man had a fine reputation as a farmer and horse breeder. Mary stopped in mid-stride. Did Mama dislike Mrs. Owen?

No. That couldn't be true. When she came to town, Mrs. Owen often traded her eggs and cream for goods in her parents' mercantile establishment. Mary had never heard of any discord in their bartering of goods. Mama always conversed with her in a familiar manner.

Mary continued pacing. What could be causing her mother's opposition? Rulon and his family were upright people, God-fearing people. Perhaps a bit, oh, irregular in their thinking about slavery being unjust, but she knew a few other folks in the county had similar feelings. That was such a small thing. There could be no logical impediment to a match between their families.

Growing weary of her mindless tours about the room, Mary sat, hands in her lap, shoulders bowed. Impending war and Rulon's proposal had certainly turned her world on its ear. She had known for months that she wanted to marry this particular man, but had thought the event was a few years in her future. Now he was set on going to fight, and the time to wed was here and now. In three short weeks, in fact.

Joy flashed through her, causing her heart to beat at a furious pace. As quickly as it had come, the elation was replaced by anxiety brought on by the thought of her mother's unanticipated resistance. *How am I to prepare for my wedding alone?* She clasped her hands, twisting them against each other. *Mama, Mama. I need you.*

≈

Rulon — April 21, 1861

Ma met Rulon at the door of the kitchen. She didn't say anything, just waited for him to speak first, her face aglow, yet strangely reserved.

"I done it, Ma. Mary accepted my proposal to wed." Tiny moths skittered around inside his belly.

Ma beamed. "I knew she would, son. She bears you a great affection."

"Don't she, though. It half puts a man on his guard, thinkin' about the future."

Ma patted his arm. "You have a grand future, son. At least, we all have the hope of that." As she spoke the last few words, her voice dropped almost to a whisper, her fear plainly exposed.

"Ma, everything is goin' to be just fine. We'll whip those Yankees in a fortnight and be home before planting time is done."

He jerked his chin for emphasis.

"That is my prayer, Rulon. Come. Sit. Tell me your plans. When will the happy day occur?"

Rulon took his accustomed place at the table, then picked up and fidgeted with the salt cellar. "Mr. Moore's first open date to hold a wedding service for us is May 11th." He looked up at his mother. "That's three weeks off."

"Only three weeks!"

"Mary said that too, 'only three weeks.' What does it mean?"

"There's so much work to do, son. Mary needs to come up with a pleasing and serviceable dress. Then she has to plan and do the decorating, make a party and write notes to invite folks. Bake a cake and whatever other refreshments she wants. Weddings don't come off without a passel of work."

Rulon took the salt spoon out of the cellar and examined it. He put it back into the salt. "That didn't enter my mind, I reckon. I only been worrying over two things. The first is earning the two dollars I need to pay Mr. Moore, and the second . . ." He paused and leaned his chair back on two legs. "I've been mulling over what to write in a letter to Captain Yancey up in Rockingham County. I figure I've got only one chance to convince him to take me into the Harrisonburg Troop before it leaves."

A deep furrow appeared between Ma's brows. "The fighting. Is that all you men think about?"

"No. No." Rulon let the chair return to the floor. "But Ma, I don't want this little squabble to be over before I can take part."

"I reckon there's time enough for you to join some other company, if it really is to be war. Armies don't form up overnight, son."

Rulon put the salt cellar back on the table and nudged it into place. "Didn't we beat the Mexicans in short order?"

"It took a while, a long while. Those were hard times."

He shrugged. "I own I don't recall a great lot."

"I don't wonder, you bein' nothing but a little sprout at the time."

"Pa don't talk about it much."

"No, he don't, and thankful I am of that." Ma wiped her hands on her apron. "What will we need to do for the pair of you and the celebration? Will the girl marry from her father's house or the church? Will there be a shiveree or a proper party? No question that I'll fix a place ready for her when you bring her home to us."

Rulon shifted in the chair, uneasy that he'd not thought of any such details, nor even where Mary would live when he left for war.

"Ah, we didn't get to that stage of talkin', Ma. It's early times yet to worry on that."

"Humph. You want to wed in a hurry so you can go to war, but don't take the time to converse with your gal about your plans? Spoken like a man who don't have to do the work."

"Ma." He made more than one syllable of the word. "We was . . . we was busy."

"Less spoonin' and more talkin' would suit." She arose and squinted at him. "I reckon it never occurred to your mind to think beyond the needs of your body. A man needs to use his brain as well as his other parts when he's fixin' to wed."

"Ma!" he said again, this time to her back as she turned it to leave the room. "You speak the most outrageous— We wasn't spoonin'." The rush of warmth to his face was echoed in his "other parts" as he thought of Mary. And spooning. And earning two dollars. His ardor deflated. This business of getting married had more complexity than he'd suspected.

Then there was that other business. He had to write that letter. Sighing, he got up and fetched the ink bottle, steel-nibbed pen, and a few sheets of paper. Then he set about the task, thinking about each word before he wrote it down, hoping his plea would convince the captain to accept him into the troop, worrying if his spelling was acceptable.

Chapter 3

Rulon — April 22, 1861

As soon as he awoke the next day, Rulon rushed to waylay Ben before he rode into town to his job.

"Have you heard of any work at the mill?" he asked as they washed.

Ben glanced up, startled. "You can't have my job."

"I don't want it. I need day work. I have to earn two dollars to pay the minister."

"That's the cost of takin' a bride? I will keep that in mind." Ben ran a hand over the fine-haired stubble on his chin. "I don't believe I'll shave today." He looked at Rulon, who had already lathered his face. "How about down to the Columbia furnace?"

"I was hoping for work closer by."

"I know they was hiring Negroes for day labor from Mr. Meem. When Virginia goes to war, that furnace will be hopping to get enough pig iron smelted for the Tredegar Works in Richmond." Ben wiped his face dry, then chuckled. "You didn't know I knew that. I keep my ears open at the mill."

"Good for you, brother," Rulon mumbled, paying close attention to shaving under his nose. "I reckon I will look into it."

"You'll have to stay at the iron plantation. It's too far away from the place to ride out there every day."

"I'll take a bedroll. Do we still have any of that jerked venison?"

"How am I supposed to know that? Ask Marie. She knows what's in the larder."

"I will do that." Rulon took a towel from around his neck and used it to wipe away the last bits of stray lather. "Thank you for the information." He grinned. "A few days of work, and I'll have the money to put into Mr. Moore's palm."

"Generosity becomes you, brother." Ben buttoned his shirt.

"Ha! Any amount will be worth havin' the girl as my wife."

"Ease up, Rule. Think on somethin' else, for a change."

Rulon snorted. "Like breakfast? The smell of that bacon does make a man's mouth water."

Ben laughed as they finished up and followed their noses.

∞

"Marie, do we have any jerked venison?" Rulon asked his sister after breakfast.

"I do believe there is a bit down in the cellar," she answered. "Why do you need it?"

"I'm off to look for a job at the Columbia furnace. I reckon I'll stay over and work it, if I get on."

"That sounds reasonable, but don't Pa need you today?"

"The seed is all in the ground, and he's finished shoeing the horses, so I figure I'm free for a spell."

"You haven't asked him?" she asked as she opened the trapdoor to the cellar.

He fidgeted with his hat. "No. Do I have to account to him for all my comin's and goin's?"

"You do if you're fixin' to go off that-a-way," she said, her voice getting muffled as she descended the ladder.

"Little sis, you're too nosy."

Marie's head reappeared after a moment. "Do you want this, or shall I feed it to the hogs?" She held up a tied bag, but out of his easy grasp.

"I want it."

"Then keep a civil tongue in your head. Apologize."

"I'm sorry. You're growin' taller every day."

"Rulon! I mean say you're sorry for callin' me nosy. That's Julianna's domain."

He laughed. "You have the right of that. I am sorry I called you nosy. I'll speak to Pa. Now, can I have the jerky?"

She grabbed the ladder with the hand holding the bag and held out her other hand for a boost up the last rungs. Rulon gave her the assist. She pushed the trapdoor into place and turned to face him. "Here it is. You'd best start mindin' your tongue real close if you think to take a wife. You can't call *her* names."

He raised his eyebrows. "I don't intend to, unless you mean 'Darling' and 'Dear' and 'Sugar' and the like. I plan to use them real often."

"You are incorrigible!"

"Am not. Where's the respect due me, sis?"

"For what?" she scoffed. "Bein' born first? That's purely happenstance. I've got more sense'n you. I most likely was busy tendin' to the Angel Gabriel's fire, or I would have come first of all."

"You don't say." Rulon shoved the bag into his pocket and grinned at his sister. "You've got a lively imagination, I'll give you that."

She stuck out her tongue. "Off with you. Talk to Pa. I don't want him stomping through the kitchen with muddy boots because he's cross with you."

He grinned again and took himself out of the house to speak with his father.

❧

Rulon topped the hill and pulled up his horse so they both could rest for a few minutes before making the descent. The trip up the hills from Edinburg had been grueling for the animal, and he dismounted and pulled a bottle of water from his saddlebag. He took a long drag, then used his hat to water the horse.

The village around the Columbia Furnace spread before him on the floor of the valley. Beside Stony Creek, the limestone and frame buildings lay, and back farther, against the hill, he saw the furnace itself. He wondered where he would locate the foreman, at the headquarters, or at the works.

He decided whoever did the hiring would more likely be in an office. He stowed his damp hat under a strap on his saddle to let it dry, climbed aboard the horse, and tongue-clicked it into movement.

At the office, he was directed to speak to a Mr. Harvey about employment.

"Yes, I reckon we'll be needing more workers with this war talk," the man said. "I can hire you today to fell trees for charcoal, or next week to drive a team to Edinburg. The teamster pay is higher, but you say you want day work?"

"Yes, sir. That suits my circumstances better."

The man looked Rulon over. "Well, it appears to me you have

the shoulders and arms to handle the saw and axe work. The pay's fifty cents a day, and I'll put you on a gang tomorrow. Did you say you're from Mount Jackson?"

"Thereabouts, yes sir."

"I reckon that's too far to ride out every mornin'. If you brought a bedroll, I can let you make a camp over yonder." He gestured to a copse of trees.

"That will suit me fine, sir. I come prepared."

"Good, then. Take care of your animal, and I'll have a piece of paper for your X when you return."

"I can sign my name, sir."

"Interested in office work? No? All right. Come back around the front when you're ready and you can meet the gang boss."

"Thank you, sir. I'm obliged."

ຂ

Rulon — April 27, 1861

On Saturday, Rulon rode back home with two dollars in his pocket and sore arms, shoulders, and back. He could scarcely wait to see Mary and tell her about his week, but first, he needed to clean up to make himself decent for the visit.

When he'd washed up and put on clean clothing, he picked out another horse and saddled it.

Peter approached with a frown on his face. "Take me with you."

"What task would take you to town, boy? I already asked Ma if she had needs. She said 'no'."

Peter ducked his head and mumbled something so low Rulon couldn't make it out.

"Speak up, boy. I haven't got all day to set here waitin' for you to talk at me."

"You know what I want," Peter replied, all but shouting.

"You reckon you're a man and should do the duty of a man to defend his home?" Rulon swung aboard his horse. "Nah. Ma won't have it."

"I am a man, Rule!" Peter swiped a hand across his dark-stubbled chin. "Anyone can see it."

Rulon's horse turned, and he brought it around before he spoke again. "Needin' to strop a razor each day don't make you a man. You barely celebrated seventeen years."

"I reckon the ability to raise a beard will help when it comes time to sign the paper."

The horse started to rear, and Rulon got it under control, then dismounted to check the gear.

As he calmed the horse, he threw a comment over his shoulder. "The matter has been decided. Ma don't want you to go." He lifted the saddle and found he'd been careless with the blanket. A fold in the material had caused the animal discomfort. He smoothed it out, restored the saddle to its place, and turned to his brother. "Despite the whiskers, you can't pass muster with that baby face." He buckled the cinch.

"Can too."

"Can not." Rulon ruffled his brother's hair. "The company clerk will take one look at you and spy you out for a fraud."

Peter jerked his head away. "Rule, you surely take the joy out of a man's life."

"A man?" Rulon snickered. "Don't call yourself a man again in my hearing, baby boy."

Peter planted his fist next to Rulon's eye.

Rulon probed the spot as he held Peter off with his other hand. "That is going to raise color, boy."

"No more than you deserve," Peter blustered, trying to swing again. "Bear the mark as a sign of your unbridled tongue!"

"That I am obliged to do." Rulon gave the young man a healthy shove away from him. "You still ain't goin' to town with me. I got business where you ain't wanted." He mounted and trotted off before Peter could recover and answer back.

&

Rulon — April 27, 1861

Mary reacted predictably, Rulon thought, recoiling at his swollen eye, then bringing him a cold compress to apply to it.

"Who did this to you? Was it that bunch of rowdies who hang out at Fletcher's? You weren't drinking? Oh, Rulon, how could you?"

He took her hand, mostly to keep it from fluttering around his face. "No Mary. Peter did it. He socked me when we was foolin' around."

"Why would he do that? Your brother is a beast."

"No he ain't. I called him a name, and he felt justified."

"Why were you quarreling?"

"Mary, Mary." She was becoming overwrought, and he sought to quiet her with a little kiss on her temple.

"Don't you kiss me. Answer my question."

"Humph. He wants to enlist. I said he would be caught out for lyin' about his age."

"You were doing a noble task, then, preventing him from—"

"He didn't think so. When I called him a baby, he hit me."

Mary sat back on the sofa. Her face became stone. "You were goading him?"

Rulon shrugged his shoulders. "That's the way it is with brothers, Sugar." Remembering she had none, he added, "Don't sisters tease and josh each other?"

"Not to the point of violence, we don't."

"You never hit Ida?"

She looked horrified.

"Pushed her? No. Pinched her, then?"

"Well, maybe I've pinched her a time or two, but only when she well deserved it!"

"Boys ain't so dainty. Our bodies are larger than girls' are, for the most part, and we flail our arms around some. From time to time, somebody's liable to get in the way of a knuckle."

"You won't be doin' that with me?"

He drew her into an embrace. "No." He kissed her. "No. I'm no woman beater." Her lips tasted of honey.

Mary freed her lips long enough to ask, "You reckon I'm a woman?"

"No question," he muttered on an exhaled breathe. "No question at all."

"Um," she murmured, permitting him a second kiss before she pushed him away.

"We have plans to make, Rulon. There's so little time to get this weddin' together. Papa gave me a bolt of fabric, and I had another piece that goes with it, so once I borrowed a pattern from Lucy Hayes I started cuttin' out my dress. It's goin' to be so lovely, Rulon. You will just adore it."

Rulon doubted he could 'adore' any dress, but kept his mouth shut on that head. He could certainly adore the figure within it.

Sister Ida says she'll help me bake the cakes." She took a deep breath. "Mama seems so listless. I cannot get her excited about helping with the preparations." She counted on her fingers. "Rulon, May 11th is just two weeks away," she said, a little wail in her voice.

He bent and kissed her cheek. "We'll get it done, Sugar."

She drew in a breath, then looked around. "Papa said we should have the ceremony right here in the parlor. It will take less time and effort to decorate it rather than the church, and besides, we won't have to pay a rental fee."

Rulon nodded at the sense of that. It was enough botheration that the minister was charging money to read the words over them. He remembered something and said, "Ma told me to ask if there is to be a party afterward. I reckon she wants to pitch in any way she can."

"That is so sweet of your mama. I will send her a message. We shall have a small celebration. Perhaps only our families and close friends. Sweet cake and punch will suit for the refreshments. I don't reckon we need to hire a band. What do you think, Rulon?"

"No," he said, fervently shaking his head at the thought of more expense. "I don't think that's needed."

She considered. "You are right. A band wouldn't fit in this room anyway."

"No band. No," he agreed. Right now he didn't care about music. He wanted to kiss her again. Taste that warm honey again.

Mary looked up at him, trouble drawing her brows into a frown. "You're determined to enlist on the 22nd next?" Her voice quivered.

"That's when the troop is mustering." He tapped her nose lightly with his forefinger. "It's only for one year."

She sighed. "One year. A very long year."

"I'll write you every day."

"You'll be riding around the countryside. Most likely you won't find a place to post a daily letter. Instead, promise to write me every week."

"Every week, I promise," he agreed, focusing on her trembling lips and wanting them pressed against his.

"Here is some good news. Mama has resigned herself to our

weddin'. Papa gave her to understand that it is right and proper that we marry now. When she finally agreed, she said she would have India's belongings moved into the nursery and Ida's things moved into Sylvia's room so we can have my bedroom to ourselves."

Rulon sat up straight. "No. We're goin' out to the farm. Ma has already fixed up a spot for your necessaries and clothes and such."

Mary looked at her hands, folded together in her lap. "Oh, I couldn't. Mama is so set on her plan." She looked up, appeal in her dark eyes. "We must allow her some small victory in exchange. After all, she did give in to Papa's reasoning."

"But you'll be my wife. You should live with my family while I'm—"

Mary's eyes filled with tears, and she took a shaky breath. "Rulon, don't say that. You're quarreling with me." She hid her face with both hands.

He ducked down, trying to move her hands aside. "No, sweet girl. I ain't. It's the normal way of things to go to your man's place." He shrugged one shoulder. "Well, in usual circumstances, you'd have your own house, but—"

"But you're going away. We don't have time to set up housekeeping. Please, just stay here with me until you have to—" She began to sob on the word "go."

"With all your sisters?" he mumbled, suddenly alarmed at the notion of sharing a house with the girls.

Mary sniffed. "They won't be in the way. Our room is in the back of the house."

At her words, so innocently spoken, but so evocative of intimacy and a door closed against the world and prying eyes, Rulon felt his blood warm. He swallowed hard. *It's time to leave.*

Mary undid his resolve by leaning forward and kissing his cheek. "Then it's settled? You'll be with me here?"

He groaned, and moved her face so that her lips met his. "I'll be with you anywhere you wish," he whispered against them. "Ah, Mary." He shuddered, acknowledging to himself that he'd reached his limit of endurance. "I have to go now."

"What?"

He exhaled. "I can't stay here." He managed to get to his feet, and reached for his hat. "You rouse my senses, Mary," he explained in answer to her questioning look. "I can't bear to touch you without—" He gritted his teeth before he said more than he should to her. "I'm not in a proper state," he finished, knowing that his words hadn't reached her understanding. She had no knowledge of his condition. She was a babe, young and innocent of the ways of men, of married folk.

"You'll come again soon? We have more plans to make."

"When I'm able," he whispered. "When I can do so." He jammed his hat on his head, fled the parlor, and barged through the front door.

&

Rod — April 27, 1861

Roderick Owen sat in his favorite chair, enjoying the peace of the evening now that the young ones had all gone upstairs. He stared into the fire, listening to the soothing crackle of the flames for a while before he bestirred himself to go to bed.

Julia came and stood behind Rod's chair, her hands resting on his shoulders. "The day is fast approaching," she murmured.

"The day?" Rod looked around, craning his neck in an attempt to see his wife.

"Rulon's weddin' day. The ceremony will take place in two weeks. The eleventh of May. That is a Saturday." She straightened his head and her fingers began to knead his neck. "My baby boy is now a man." Her voice seemed sunken into her throat.

"He'd like to presume that of himself." He captured one of her hands underneath one of his. "There's a heap of impetuosity in his nature."

"Don't he come by that naturally!" Her free hand wandered up the back of his neck, spreading his hair between her fingers.

He shivered at the touch. "Woman, what do you mean by that?"

"Husband," she returned his bantering tone. "Who was bent on eloping instead of facing my brother to ask for my hand?"

"Jonathan is formidable."

"No more than you."

"I have grown into my fearsome posture."

She chuckled. "How do you reckon Jonathan arrived there?"

36

He pulled her around the side of the chair and lifted her onto his lap. "You are my daily breath, Julie. I don't take a step without thinkin' on your beauty and grace."

She took his earlobes between her fingers and stroked them. "Husband, what news are you tryin' to ease into breakin' to me?"

He sighed, a long exhalation. "You know me too well, wife." He enfolded her in his arms and drew her close, nuzzling the top of her head. "I am fixin' to raise a cavalry company."

She struggled against him, squirming until she was in a position to see his face. "You wouldn't! Can't you be satisfied that you went off when you were young and played at war in a foreign land?"

Her irritation pricked both his conscience and his pride, but he could choose to address only one or the other. He chose to be properly abashed, but to lay his actions to pressure.

"Chester Bates brought the idea to me. It seems sound."

"You'd blame your friend for the notion? Roderick Owen, you are a scoundrel."

"I . . . am a scoundrel," he agreed, tilting his head to the side. "But I'm your scoundrel, and my native land's scoundrel. I can't let the Yankees invade my home."

In a flash, she turned into a melting woman and sank heavily against his chest. "I had hoped to avoid losing you to this squabble," she murmured, her voice catching.

"Oh Julie, Julie." He felt the softening of his sinews that her distress brought upon him these days. Tenderness had not been native to his nature, but over many years, he had learned a hard-won lesson. Tenderness betwixt a man and his wife was well worth cultivating. "I cannot pretend to know what is in store for me. I cannot lie on that point to ease your feelin's." He kissed her hair. "Know this, woman. I will love you beyond any power that death has to separate us."

She wept in his arms, soft sobs she surely was trying to keep within the bounds of their chair. He could only whisper endearments and hold her closer to his soul.

Chapter 4

Mary — May 1, 1861

Mary sat in a small room off the kitchen where light from the sun illuminated the purple fabric in her lap. The tip of her tongue peeked out from between her lips as she concentrated on taking small stitches to join two pieces of the material together. Her sister Ida sat across her, sewing a seam into another two pieces of fabric.

"This is such tedious work," Ida said with a sigh. "Why can't Papa buy us one of those sewing machines?" She batted at the golden curls against her neck. "It is so warm today."

"Those machines are too expensive, Ida. Papa cannot afford to buy us one." Mary bent over to bite off the end of a thread. "Besides, he cannot procure one soon enough. You know I have a limited amount of time to finish my dress. Keep stitching."

Ida took one stitch, then stopped to ask, "Why is Papa allowing you to marry? You're not even fifteen yet. Mama wants you to wait until this war is over."

"That is my affair. Mama already agreed that I can wed, and there isn't any time to spare. If you don't want to help me with this skirt, go see if India brought home the lard for my cakes, and send her in here. Her stitches may not be pretty, but they will serve."

Ida put her work in her lap. "I think your beau is selfish. He is going off to war, but first, he wants to get married and do those things to you, those things Papa does to Mama."

"Ida!" Mary felt a flush going up her neck.

"Disgusting!"

"What are you talking about?" The heat of the flush was spreading throughout her body, and Mary shifted her position on the hard chair.

"Lizzie Sue told me all about it. She said—"

"That meddling little gossip? You cannot pay any attention to what she says, Ida. She doesn't know anything." She herself didn't know anything, just that Rulon's kisses—when she allowed him to kiss her—drove her to distraction with feelings she had not experienced before he began coming around and they had come to an understanding.

"Yes she does. She's told me many things that are true."

Mary noticed her sister's idle hands, and waggled her finger at them, relieved to find something to divert her thoughts from Rulon. "You are talking about this so you don't have to help me."

Ida smirked. "You're going to do those disgusting things with Rulon."

Mary sniffed in pretended disdain. "I cannot imagine what you are talking about."

"You had better find out quick. Ask Mama."

"You know she won't discuss anything like that." Mary had tried to broach the subject.

"What won't I discuss?" asked Mrs. Hilbrands as she entered the room.

"Nothing, Mama," said Mary. "We were only talking nonsense."

"I can imagine." Mrs. Hilbrands turned to her younger daughter. "Ida, did you dust the parlor this morning? I swear there is dust laying on all the surfaces in the room."

"I'm sorry, Mama. Mary has been hounding me to help her finish sewing her skirt."

"You must not neglect your chores. Each one teaches you how to manage a household one day."

"Yes, Mama. Shall I go now and dust?"

"That is wise, daughter."

"Mama," Mary protested, but her mother cut her off.

"You must manage your dress by yourself, Mary. We cannot quit our tasks merely because you are going to be wed. Against my advice, I might add."

Ida arose and made a face at Mary behind their mama's back. Then she left the room with a flounce of her skirt.

"You could have chosen to wear your Sunday dress, after all, instead of making a new one."

"I deserve to have a new dress when I make such a large change in my life."

"I would rather you wait until you are sixteen."

"I cannot wait. We have discussed this time and again. I am determined to become Rulon's wife as soon as may be."

"That young devil will be the ruination of you. He is only thinking of his own interests."

Mary stood. "I will not listen to this talk against Rulon. I believe I will go sweep the porch now." She put down her unfinished skirt and left the room, feeling like crying, but holding her chin high. She *would* marry Rulon, and he would *not* be her ruination.

❧

Rulon — May 7, 1861

"You'll be needing a horse."

Rulon turned from scooping oats out of the grain bin to see his father leaning against the door frame. Since Pa almost never leaned against anything, Rulon wondered how long he'd been standing there surveying him.

"I reckon I will. What will you take in trade for the bay?"

"You've worked the farm since you were old enough to lift a shovel or hoe weeds in the field. I figure that labor is plenty in exchange for the bay and her tack."

Rulon felt his throat constrict with sudden emotion. "I'm obliged," he managed to get out in a husky voice.

"You sure it's the bay you want? The sorrel is well mannered."

"The bay has spirit and don't spook easily. I reckon she would make a good battle mount."

"That's canny thinkin', son. I agree. She will be steady under fire."

Rulon nodded. In a matter of days, he would leave this farmstead to live in town with his bride. Soon after, he expected to be doing some kind of patrolling, or picket duty, or whatever it was a cavalryman did to defend his country. That is, if he ever got a reply to his letter. If he wasn't acceptable to Captain Yancey and the Harrisonburg Cavalry troop, he would have to start his search all over again. He found himself chewing on the inside of his cheek.

"What has you worried, boy?"

"I ain't heard from Harrisonburg yet."

"Give it time, give it time. Yancey's bound to be a busy man. A lawyer, I hear. It's likely he's wrapping up his business."

"You're right. But getting married also has me perplexed." He shook his head. "The tasks Mary has been doing make my head swim."

Pa chuckled. "The ladies like everything fancy, son. Take a deep breath. Enjoy your day. It will be here before you know it."

"I wish I could believe that. It seems a lifetime away."

Pa nodded his head in understanding. "The day will come. By the way, your ma says there is another item you'll be needing. My ma passed down her weddin' ring to me when she died. It was intended for your ma to wear, but she already had the one I give her when we married, and she preferred that one. She said you should have it to put on Miss Mary's finger. She'll give it to you when the day comes around." He raised his eyebrow. "I wouldn't have given a geegaw like that a thought, so I'm pleased she recalled the little ring."

"Such a lot of to-do." He whistled.

Pa came over and clapped his hand on Rulon's shoulder. "Silken entanglements, boy. All these arrangements for fancy ceremony and parties and such sometimes seem unnecessary, but they keep the ladies happy. That's what matters, after all. Keep the wife happy, and you'll have a happy life." He tightened his grip briefly, then removed his hand.

"That's the sum total of your fatherly advice?" Rulon grinned wryly. "No words of wisdom for, other matters?" His face felt hot as he said the words.

Pa stared at him for a long time, and Rulon noticed a pink tinge on his father's forehead.

"Words of wisdom?" Pa cleared his throat. "Be gentle." He paused for a long moment, then added, "Work out the rest yourself." He turned away, then looked back over his shoulder. "Treat the bay gentle. She's a lady, too."

He was gone in a moment, and Rulon was left alone to chew on both his cheek and the words that still seemed to hang in the air.

∞

Julia — May 8, 1861

When Rulon came into the house at noon for dinner, Julia had been so intent upon the project she was doing with the girls that she was caught at what had remained a secret for some days.

"Ma," he said, his rising voice reflecting his surprise.

She stood and tried to put the work in her lap off to the side where he could not view it, but knew he had seen what they were up to. Marie had similarly shoved worsted material down on the floor beside her, but Julianna wasn't so wise, and only froze with her needle caught in grey fabric.

"Is that a uniform? I haven't even heard back yet from Captain Yancey. Why would you—"

"The answer is 'yes,' and it doesn't matter if you go with the Harrisonburg Troop or some other company. I reckon you're a-goin', and we have to put the best shine on the matter." She knew she sounded a bit defensive, but couldn't help defending her action in preparing a proper send-off for her first born. "I know you are set on bein' a cavalryman in this tussle, so you'll go as the fine-lookin' son of Roderick Owen of Shenandoah County, with a grand new suit of clothes, even if it is a uniform." She stood as straight as she could, hoping she didn't dissolve into tears and shame herself.

"We're beholden to Miss Mary for keeping silent about the material your ma purchased," Rod said from behind Rulon. "It was difficult for Randolph Hilbrands to find the braid, but he persevered, and found it in a shop down to Richmond." He walked over and held up the decorative sleeve resting in Julianna's lap. "The outfit will serve you well, wherever you end up."

The other boys crowded into the room behind Rulon, who stood slack-jawed, half-blocking the doorway.

Ben crossed over behind Marie and picked up the pants she had been working on. "Ha! A gold stripe down the leg? This is too fine for you, Rule."

Rod swung around, saying, "That's enough, Benjamin."

Julia pursed her lips as she looked around. A swirl of male voices surrounded her. Did boys relish fighting all their lives? Her sons' excitement filled the space in the room, and she had to raise her voice to be heard over the hubbub. "Marie, is the table laid?"

"Yes, Ma," she answered. "Julianna, come help me serve."

Julia followed her daughters to the kitchen. How had her family become so firmly entangled in this war?

⅓

Mary — May 10, 1861

Mary stood in the garden, halting for a moment before she resumed her pacing beneath the bower made of lilac bushes. Was everything ready? She had gone over her lists time after time, but felt that she had neglected a detail, some tiny particular that would put a finishing touch on her preparations. She stepped out onto the path again.

Is Rulon this nervous tonight? He had come to see her, but she had refused to let him enter the house, too distraught to entertain him without knowing all was ready for the next day.

She was getting married tomorrow. No. She couldn't be ready for this huge step. Becoming a married lady. Bearing a ring on her finger. Hearing folks call her "missus" instead of "miss". This was momentous. She wasn't ready.

She wanted to flee. She could run away, down the Valley Pike to hide in a crag in the mountains. Somewhere that Rulon wouldn't find her.

Rulon. What was she thinking? Was Rulon the right man for her, the right husband, the right—she shuddered—lover?

I don't even know what that means. She made a turn before she got out of the shadow of the lilacs. *Ida's foolish prattle has unnerved me.* Her talk of "disgusting things" that went on between married folk was truly unsettling. *What does Rulon intend to do to me?*

She tried to calm herself, to curb her distraught state. *Rulon loves me. He would never give me injury. I'm sure he will want to kiss me, though.* But what would come after the kisses? What was she expected to do? It was far too late to attempt to coax her mother into giving her pertinent information. What had she committed herself to do?

She wrapped her arms around herself and began to cry. Stumbling to the bench, she sat and put her face into her hands and sobbed until she had exhausted her tears and herself. Then

43

she dried her eyes and walked back to the house to try to get into bed without any foolishness from her sisters.

ଛ

Rulon — May 11, 1861

Rulon swung down from the horse with great care, mindful of the clothing he'd borrowed from his father to wear on this much-anticipated day. Peter took charge of his horse, tethering it to the hitch rail in front of Randolph Hilbrands' home.

Ben pulled up beside Rulon, dismounted, and gave him a knock on the shoulder.

"What's that about?" Rulon said, brushing off any dust Ben may have left behind.

"Cranky, are you? I didn't expect crankiness on this fine weddin' day." Ben looked him over and guffawed. "You did a fine job with those buttons. Lined 'em up right nice." He doubled over with laughter.

Rulon looked down. He'd mis-buttoned the suit coat. Alarmed that his nerves were so evident, he re-did the job and scowled at Ben. "Your day will come, little brother."

"He won't have to button his own coat. Massa Allen will give the job to a slave." Peter ducked as though he expected Rulon or Ben to throw a punch.

Rulon peered at his brothers. "Rowdy troublemakers," he pronounced them. "Try and keep at least one civil tongue between the two of you."

"Oh, we'll be good, big brother," said Ben.

"Yes indeed. Best behavior," Peter agreed, grinning.

Rulon groaned. "I am not convinced."

The two younger brothers turned to look at one another, their upturned mouths reflecting their merriment at Rulon's expense.

"I'll hammer you both into the ground if you disrupt my wedding," he warned them.

"I reckon you'll be too busy with other matters," Ben said, laughing out loud now.

"Not that you'd know anything about caring for a woman."

Ben cocked his head. "Maybe more than you."

Rulon drew back his fist, then caught himself and muttered a mild oath. He wouldn't spoil his own marriage day by tussling with his brothers. Instead, he turned and strode toward the door, hopeful that the first sight of Mary would change his unease to gladness.

Mrs. Hilbrands opened the door to Rulon's knock and bade him enter, a small unchanging smile pasted on her mouth. As he hung his hat on the hat rack, he wondered if he should try to charm her, call her "Mother Hilbrands," or perhaps kiss her on the cheek, but in the end, his terror left him meekly following in her wake without any attempts on his part to ease the tension. Perhaps the sight of the lingering yellow and black color around his eye had contributed to the lack of warmth in her welcome.

He heard Ben and Peter coming through the door behind him, laughing. They shut up as they closed the door. Were they being respectful or did the oppressive atmosphere affect them as much as it did him?

When he entered the parlor, the first thing he noticed was the drawn drapes, heavy barriers that forbade the sun to shine upon his marriage. He wondered if the darkness was a sign, an ill omen of some sort, and his anticipation deflated.

The furniture had been shoved up against the walls, making room for the families and their guests to stand to witness the proceedings. Candles in heavy pewter holders stood along the mantelpiece, ready to be lit.

"Wait here," Mrs. Hilbrands said, then left him in the dim room with only his brothers to attend him.

"It's a mite somber in here," Ben said, and going to the nearest window, he tied back the drapes. Peter joined in, as Rulon protested in vain.

"Don't make trouble for me," he implored his brothers, thinking he sounded like a feeble old woman as he untied a pair of sashes to let one of the windows fall prey to the darkness again.

"The missus don't like you?" Peter asked, cocking an eyebrow.

"Well enough, I reckon," he said. "It's the weddin' she don't like."

"As long as the girl is satisfied she's getting the right Owen," Peter said, smoothing down his hair. "I'm closer to her in age. By rights, I should be standing up with her today."

With an effort of will, Rulon refused to rise to the bait. "How far behind us was Pa?"

"He climbed in the wagon and set out just after you rode off. He should be driving up the street any moment," Ben said, and craned his neck to peer out the window opening to the front of the house. "Yes, there they come. Don't Ma look fine in that getup?"

Rulon was too occupied with adjusting the tail of his coat to go over to the window to admire his mother's finery. Where was the minister? Had Mr. Hilbrands changed his mind? Where was Mary? He pulled at his binding collar.

The knocker fell on the front door with a boom, causing Rulon's heart to jump. From the sound of the greeting, one of the Hilbrands girls answered, and soon his parents and his siblings came into the parlor, trailed by the Bates family. To his relief, Mr. Hilbrands accompanied them, bringing the minister along at his side. However, Mrs. Hilbrands kept her whereabouts a secret, and Mary was nowhere in sight.

Mr. Hilbrands greeted his guests, planted the minister before the fireplace, and called out into the hallway for a lamp to light the candles.

Mary's younger sister, Ida, brought a light, and as she performed the task with the candles, Mr. Hilbrands left the room.

"Such comings and goings," Ben commented behind the mask of his hand.

"Hush," Rulon whispered, adjusting with a shrug or two the position of Pa's coat upon his shoulders.

Just then, Mrs. Hilbrands came back and stood in the doorway, looking somewhat pale as the light of the now brighter room fell upon her countenance. Ma went and greeted her, patting her cheeks with hands encased in lace mitts. *Where did Ma dig those up?*

Rulon counted his siblings. Carl, James, Marie, Clayton, Albert, Julianna. The entire Owen clan had come to either tease him unmercifully or make merry. *They had better behave*, he thought.

Mrs. Hilbrands looked toward Ida and motioned with her head. The girl promptly left the room. Then the woman made gathering motions with her hands, and the guests pressed toward the door.

Rulon didn't know whether to remain where he was or go along with the crowd, but the minister nudged him, so he chose the latter.

People spilled out into the hall, and Rulon edged up to the parlor door. Youthful female voices began to sing a song about "this happy occasion," as Mary's three sisters descended the stairway, carrying more lighted candles. At the top of the stair, Mr. Hilbrands stood with Mary on his arm.

Rulon sucked in his breath.

His bride wore a right pretty dress, light colored with purple flowers on the top, and purple with white flowers on the bottom. The skirt was wide enough to fill the area between the bannister and the wall. On her head, a circlet of purple blossoms of some kind crowned her dark hair.

"Mary." His shallow breathing allowed only a whisper of her name before he choked with emotion.

Her gaze rested momentarily upon him as though she had heard him say her name. Her simmering look pierced his soul. Then she lowered her eyes, took on a shy aspect, and made her slow way down the treads, leaning on her father's arm.

He found himself being pulled backwards, stumbling, to his place alongside the minister. Ben pinched his arm, and he remembered to stand tall, but was scarcely able to draw breath.

His family formed an aisle. The girls came forward, still singing, until they stood at the front, at one side, lined up next to Mrs. Hilbrands. Mr. Hilbrands brought Mary toward him, stepping carefully, stopping before the minister with Mary on his far arm.

The girls stopped singing.

The minister opened a book and began intoning words that Rulon paid no mind to. Mary was half hidden beyond the bulk of her father's body. Why didn't the man step back? Then Mr. Hilbrands said "I bring her," and granted Rulon's wish that he leave Mary's side.

Rearranging the couple, the minister kept talking, but Rulon only heard sound. All he could absorb was the fact that Mary now stood beside him, hands clasped together, looking at the carpet, her elbow brushing the sleeve of his coat.

After an interminable time, the man before them said something incomprehensible, then smiled and nodded at Rulon.

Ben toed him in the ankle. "Your answer," he hissed.

Rulon woke from his stupor and said, "I do."

Mary echoed him in her turn.

Mr. Moore took hold of Mary's left hand and looked expectant. Rulon felt Ma's ring come sliding across his palm. Ben. Rulon got it between his fingers, turned and put it on Mary's finger.

The minister said something about "man and wife," and smiled again. Ma gasped in the background. Mary turned to him, eyes glowing.

Peter chuckled. "Kiss her, or I will."

Rulon inhaled. Was it over? He felt an elbow in his ribs, and decided it was. He turned to Mary, looked at her upturned face, then kissed her.

She smelled of soap, and the purple blossoms, and another scent he didn't try to identify. Instead, his brain asked the most vital question. When could he carry her up those stairs to seclusion and privacy?

℘

After a party that lasted far too long, Rulon accompanied Mary up the stairs. She led the way down the hall, holding his hand tightly. She opened the door to their sanctuary and entered. He closed the distance between them.

He took her in his arms, covering her face with kisses, moaning, "Mary, Mary." He felt the fabric of his father's best trousers pressing against the evidence of his lust. Yes, it was lust, he admitted with almost his last coherent thought; frighteningly powerful in its hold on him. He kicked the door shut, too far gone to bother to secure the latch.

Mary pulled away from his frantic kisses long enough to do the job, then he gathered her back, intent only upon fulfilling his need.

They bumped against the bed. He laid her upon it and shed the intolerable trousers with such abruptness that a few of the buttons flew from their moorings and scattered on the floor. He lifted her purple skirt and moved undergarments aside to the extent that was necessary for his purpose, all the while crooning her name, over and over, a paean to wedding and bedding the girl as so often he had craved to do. Daytime or night, his imagination had driven him toward this moment, and he reveled in the commencement and completion of the connubial act.

After, her clothing restored to its accustomed place, Mary lay in his arms, trembling and sniffling against his shirt.

A thread of guilt needled into his consciousness. Pa had advised him to be gentle. He had not been. What if he had injured Mary?

He looked down and asked, as tenderly as he could, considering he was still breathless, "Did I hurt you?"

"No," she whispered, her voice too shaky for him to believe her denial.

"Mary? The truth, girl."

"Yes. A little. I didn't expect . . . that."

He groaned, covering his eyes with his hand. At length, he mumbled contrite words. "I beg forgiveness for losing all control, for overtaking you with my lustful yearnings." He shook his head, abashed at his behavior. "I'm a cad."

He felt the negative movement of her head against his chest.

"I am. I was thoughtless."

Mary stirred again, then planted a hesitant kiss on the side of his chin.

"I wanted you," she said. "I didn't know all that meant."

He removed his hand from his eyes, turned and kissed her hair, then settled her head into the hollow of his neck.

She continued. "I didn't know what 'coming together' signified."

"Your ma never—"

She snorted. "Mama doesn't talk about, ah, carnal acts."

He barely heard the last two words, her voice was so low. He reckoned it had cost her considerable effort to speak them. "She didn't prepare you?"

"It gives her the vapors to mention the subject."

"Ah, Mary."

"It was your right, Rulon. I know that much."

He lifted her chin and kissed one eyelid, tasting the salt of her dried tears. "My right don't include being rough. I regret I caused you pain."

She seemed to think on that for a while. Then she spoke hesitantly, her voice very soft. "Pa looked at me peculiar one night when I was goin' on and on about bein' woman-wed soon. He said, 'Mind he don't injure you.' I laughed at him."

He rose up on an elbow and stared down at his wife. "I did."

"No!" Her eyes went dark, then narrowed. Her hand cupped his cheek. "I am your woman now." Her little finger moved across his mouth, light as a butterfly. "I have waited so long to say those words." She swallowed. "A slight pain now is nothing in comparison to the longing I have felt to be your wife."

Rulon watched the movement of her throat, wishing for nothing more than to kiss the skin above her pounding pulse. He bent his head and did so. Her hand crept around to the back of his neck.

"Do it again," she murmured.

He took note that her respirations had begun to flutter faster. Her pulse beat more strongly against his lips. "What?"

"Show me I am your woman," she managed to say.

Chapter 5

Ben — May 13, 1861

Ben was about to follow Pa from the supper table when Peter mentioned offhandedly that he had fetched the mail from town and Rulon had received a letter.

Ben let Marie take away his plate and utensils, then said, "That's probably from the Harrisonburg company captain." He took a toothpick from the supply at the center of the table. "Why didn't you leave it off for him at Hilbrands' store? Hand it over, boy. I'll see he gets it tomorrow."

Peter put on a truculent countenance. "Who says I have the letter in hand? Who says I didn't deliver it directly into his greedy palm?"

Ben eyed him as he worked the toothpick around his teeth. He stopped long enough to say, "I thought the lad was on his honeymoon."

Peter quirked an eyebrow. "I sent Ida to knock on the door with my message. It took him long enough to come downstairs." His smug grin disappeared when Ma bopped him on the head with a wooden spoon.

"Mind your thoughts, son," she said above his howl of pain. "Keep 'em out of married folks' business."

Ben chuckled, and she turned on him.

"The same goes for you, Benjamin. Have an ounce of respect. If not for Rulon, at least for that young wife."

"Don't you be a-chastening me with that thing," Ben protested, putting his arms up for protection. "I've taken a mite too many whacks from it." The fingers of one hand explored around his head. "Yup, I have lumps aplenty from that ol' spoon." He said as an afterthought, "I meant no harm to Mistress Mary."

Ma waggled the implement in his direction. "You're not too old to take another lick if you don't curb your tongue and shackle your unruly thoughts," she said.

"Rulon don't mind a bit of rough talk," Peter said, rubbing his head.

"I mind," Ma said, her voice firm as she gestured with the spoon. "I mind on my own account, and that of your sisters here, and because I don't want you growing up rough and godless. The Man Upstairs has put his bounds on loose talk, and I won't have it around my table, nor amongst my children."

"Yes, Ma," Ben said.

Peter muttered something, and Ben gave him a poke.

"Yes, Ma," Peter blurted out, then turned and cuffed Ben in the arm.

"No fighting at the table," Ma said. "If you want to wrassle, go out on the porch."

✺

Rulon — May 13, 1861

When Rulon surfaced from his indulgent weekend, he became aware that he and Mary were expected to eat meals with the Hilbrands family, particularly the evening meal. In addition, he was expected to wear his finest go-to-meeting clothing for the occasion. When he asked about the seriousness of the request, Mary's solemn face and raised eyebrows gave him his answer.

"But sweet Mary, I've outgrown my good trousers. That's why I borrowed Pa's for the wedding." He grinned in an abashed manner. "I have to get those buttons sewn back on so I can return them to him."

"I can do that before we dine," Mary said, picking up her sewing basket.

"Why is your ma so set on having grand suppers, anyway? I'll be wearing the same clothes I wore on Saturday, my best shirt and Pa's trousers. She wants the coat, too?" At his wife's nod, he made a face. "Your folks saw all that at the weddin'. If they want something showy, I reckon I can't provide it, unless I'm to wear the uniform."

"I'd rather you didn't, but I don't expect this attitude to last for long," Mary said as she threaded a needle. "Ma will grow fatigued of putting on airs and washing the tablecloth and napkins every week. I don't rightly know why she thinks she has to make a great show for us, anyway. The truth is, we usually have

52

an oilcloth on the table."

"Just like at home." He handed Mary the trousers and buttons.

Mary looked at him, a little smile playing around her mouth as she tilted her head.

He backed away. "I'd rather look at you in all your finery." As he dropped his hand, it slid across the edge of his belt buckle, and he let it linger there. "My wife." He watched the spread of happiness across Mary's face. "It gives me great satisfaction to say them words," he said, a little huskily.

Mary looked up with a full smile. "It gives me great satisfaction to hear you say them." She shook a finger in his direction. "Now don't you get any ideas, Mister Rulon Owen. I don't have time for sport if I'm to get the buttons back on these trousers and you dressed like a fat holiday turkey for my mother to admire."

Rulon hooted with laughter and went back to where she sat to give her a quick hug. She returned it with relish, gave him her cheek to kiss, and went back to work on the buttons.

∞

Well into supper, Randolph Hilbrands cleared his throat. "Mr. Owen."

Rulon had taken notice that Mr. Hilbrands had begun to address him in that manner since the wedding. He looked up and gave the man his attention.

"I understand you received a letter today."

"I did, sir."

"Daughter Ida says it came from Rockingham County."

Nosy little chit. "Yes, sir, it did."

"Mr. Owen, may I know who sent you the letter?"

That's where Ida gets her nosiness. "Sir, it's from my cavalry troop's commander, Captain Yancey, who is kin to me."

"Ah, a military matter."

Although the man made a statement, a slight upturn to his voice made Rulon aware that it really was meant as a question.

"Sir, he welcomed me to the Harrisonburg Cavalry and gave me a date to report for duty." Rulon figured he may as well give the man what he wanted. He was, after all, paying for Rulon's and

53

Mary's keep. "It's May 22nd, as I reckoned it would be. I will leave here on the 21st in order to arrive early on the appointed day." He glanced at Mary. Their discussion of the matter had been a mournful one.

"Ah," Mr. Hilbrands said again, evidently satisfied with the answer. "Have you a hat?"

"My everyday one is all, sir."

"That will not do." Mr. Hilbrands arose and went to the sideboard, where he opened a door and drew forth a round box. He brought it to the table and reseated himself. "Now this is an acceptable hat for a cavalryman," he said, lifting from the box a slouch hat decorated with a black plume and held up on one side with a pin. Holding the headgear in reverent hands, he murmured, "It is after the fashion of the one worn by Colonel J.E.B. Stuart himself. I imagine he will be your ultimate commander."

Rulon gulped. "I reckon that's a mighty fine hat, sir," he managed to say. "Much obliged."

"The best available." He put the hat to one side on the table and looked up. "You will require armaments?"

"Yes, sir. Whatever I can bring."

"I have a pistol I want you to carry." Mr. Hilbrands took one from the hat box and laid it on the table.

"Thank you, sir. I'm much obliged."

"I would extract your promise to bring it home, but I know I cannot."

Rulon looked at Mary. Her face had gone white. "Sir, if you don't mind, the ladies."

"I know of their tender sensibilities, man. I live with a passel of 'em, don't I?" Rand scowled and his face reddened.

"My wife—"

"My daughter knows she could lose you." Mr. Hilbrands's scowl deepened. "I reckon that's why she was so insistent in the matter of your somewhat hasty marriage."

Mary made a little sound of distress, and Rulon reached for her hand under cover of the tablecloth. He bent his head close to her ear and asked in a low tone, "Have you had your fill?"

She nodded, and he stood up and looked at Mary's mother. "Excuse us, Mrs. Hilbrands. My wife and I are going to retire.

With your permission, ma'am?" He glanced at Mr. Hilbrands' annoyed countenance. "I am very much obliged to you, sir, for the gifts of the splendid hat and the pistol. However, my wife is unwell. Goodnight, sir." He hoped that was sop enough to deflect Mr. Hilbrands' anger as he gave Mary his arm and beat a formal but hasty retreat.

୧

Rulon lay on his side, watching the rise and fall of Mary's bosom as she slept. His ardor spent for the time being, he only marveled at the mysteries kept hidden beneath the cloth of her nightdress. For a girl everyone told him was too young to be his wife, she was undoubtedly woman enough for him.

He regretted that he would have to leave her soon. The letter Peter had shoved at him earlier that day wiped out all his wonderings about their future. Captain Yancey had replied to his question and had agreed to take Rulon into the troop, but only on the strength of the family connection. The captain stated in no uncertain terms that he had to prove himself a worthy cavalier.

He could ride. That wasn't a problem. He could shoot a shotgun, rifle or pistol, as he had proven countless times. Since he had been old enough to hold a weapon, Pa had taken him along to hunt meat for the family. His ability to shoot with better-than-average accuracy wasn't a question in his mind. The question causing him disquiet was, could he kill a man?

He felt sweat break out along his upper lip, upon his limbs and his brow. Could he ride into battle, take aim at a human being, and squeeze the trigger? He ran a hand over his forehead and down his face.

Mary stirred and he froze. She mumbled something he couldn't catch and threw an arm over his body. Then she resumed her slow, regular breathing.

Rulon let out his breath and returned to his thoughts.

Could anyone who was already a member of the Harrisonburg Cavalry kill another man? As far as he knew, none of them had had occasion to meet an enemy on a battlefield. They likely had only drilled for the happenstance. Training. That was what he lacked. Training. How did one train to kill an enemy?

He swallowed. Captain Yancey's letter had given the date on

which he was to appear at the Harrisonburg Cavalry's camp in that town. Next week. So soon. So soon.

He was to bring what arms he could gather, along with a good horse and tack, and whatever personal effects he would need to sustain his needs as a military man. He had the horse and tack as his father's gift, two changes of clothing, and the fine uniform his mother and sisters had sewn for him. Mr. Hilbrands' hat was a mite outlandish, but the pistol was a timely gift and would serve him in good stead. He supposed he would have to acquire powder and lead balls, but perhaps the company would provide that. He knew so little about the details of war.

He was to enlist for one year.

He gulped. A year! He would be gone from Mary for a year. Would she forget him during that length of time? Would his caresses be gone from her memory when he returned? Would time dim her recall of the fervor of their entanglements, flesh against flesh as he had convinced her was right and proper?

He carefully placed his hand over hers as desire returned. Dare he wake her? Dare he not? He brought her hand to his lips, and at his soft kiss, she awoke and turned to him, eyes hooded and dark.

"Rulon? I am glad you're here. I dreamed you had gone."

"No, it's not time to leave you. Not yet." His voice sounded a little uneven, perhaps hesitant, to his ears. "Not for several more days."

"You are troubled." She got her hand loose and touched his cheek.

How do women know these things? "A little. I'm worried that I'll show myself a coward in battle."

She made a small sound, a disbelieving sound. "Not you. You're strong, like your papa. Did he ever run from anything?"

She sounded sleepy, and Rulon regretted awakening her.

"No. Not to my knowledge."

"I like your papa." She closed her eyes and smiled a bit.

"I reckon he's a good man. Go to sleep, little wife. Morning will come early."

"It always does," she agreed, and turned her head away, sighing herself into sleep.

ॐ

Rulon — May 21, 1861

It's here at last, Rulon thought when he awoke on the day he was to leave for Harrisonburg. He looked at Mary's face in the dimness, lightly touching his arm, peaceful in sleep. *This ain't going to be easy.* Last night they had spent a considerable time finishing off their honeymoon before sleep overcame them. He had intended to leave this morning without further connubial contact, but the sight of Mary's slightly parted lips, and the curl of hair that lay across her throat aroused him.

He put out a finger to brush her cheek. She was awake in an instant, although her eyes opened only partway, like her lips. Her hand went around the back of his neck, and Rulon heard himself moan as his resolve slipped away.

Later, he thought, *It's still early. If I don't stop to eat, I can make camp tonight and arrive in good time tomorrow.*

Mary climbed out of bed as Rulon dressed. She had removed her nightgown, and held it so it covered her, but she dropped it, approached him, and put her arms around his neck.

"Woman, I can't take the time—"

"I know that. I'm searing myself upon your memory," she said, her voice a little flirty, and at the same time, a little desperate. "You go win this war and come back to me and . . ." She ducked her head.

"And what? There's no doubt what I'll do when I return." He hugged her fiercely. Excitement filled him, but it wasn't a renewal of lust. It was a prickling anxiety to begin the new adventure, to beat back any Yankee threat to his country.

"I don't mean 'and we'll have another go.' I reckon something is different about my body." Mary backed out of Rulon's embrace and touched her white belly. "I believe . . . it might be possible . . . that I'm increasin'." She didn't give him a chance to draw her to him again, but bent out of his grasp, picked up her nightdress, and draped it over her arm as though it were a shield.

"Mary," he whispered, his hands dangling. He gulped. Was he a father already? "When will you know for certain?"

She shook her head, biting her lip. After a moment she could speak again. "I don't know. I don't know. Perhaps a month, two months? I don't know. You will be home soon, won't you?"

He had no idea how to answer her. The reckless youth in him yearned to answer yes, but the unknown stretched before him like a dense cloud he could not penetrate. He tried to nod, to agree, but could not. "I will try," was all he could force past his lips before he enfolded her in his arms for the last time today.

Today. The last time today. Not the last time forever. He shook off that spectral thought and turned away to finish dressing. He heard Mary's clothing rustling as she dressed in silence. *My wife. The mother of my child? God strengthen you, Mary.*

❧

Rulon cleared the outskirts of Mount Jackson and put the horse into a steady gait. Did he have time to bid his kinfolk farewell? His early morning dalliance with Mary had put him behind schedule, but he might have a moment to spare. Should he share Mary's incredible supposition with his ma? No. It was just that as yet, a supposing, a feeling not proven. Still, canny women had canny senses, and his Mary was . . . What *was* Mary?

A little bit of a thing. The young girl he'd yearned for, all right, lusted after, and won because the Yankees were raising an army. Had times been different, would he have been able to marry her so quickly? Would she have consented to become his wife, to bare her heart and soul, and so readily give him her body to satiate his needs?

Surprisingly, she had taken to the marriage bed with an avid desire he had not expected. Was that a woman's way in order to become with child? Was that what Mary had craved from him? A babe? Had his lovemaking pleased her, or was it a sham to collect his seed?

Rulon pulled up and dismounted, breathing heavily. Where had he picked up this doubt? He surely didn't need to be unmanned when he was on his way to who knows what encounters with men who would take away his rights as a Virginia citizen. He scrubbed his clean-shaven face in his hands. He removed a flask of water from his saddlebag and took a swig of the liquid. He swallowed, put the bottle away and straightened his shoulders. *Mary was pleased to become my woman. Those eyes did not lie. She rejoiced in being with me.*

Half afraid of the tug that drew him back to Mount Jackson, he mounted and gigged the horse forward, onward toward Harrisonburg.

A mile or two more and he saw the bend in the road ahead where lay the turnoff to a lane that he could find on the darkest of nights. At the end of the lane, his family would be going about their daily tasks, perhaps thinking about him, perhaps not. Rulon cleared the bend in the road and reined the horse into the wide path. He had to be quick. Harrisonburg wasn't far away, as the crow flies, but he would need most of the time left of the day to make the trip on horseback.

Julianna saw him first when she turned from feeding the hogs. "Rulon!" his younger sister shouted, then dropped her pails and ran toward him, braids flying, spindly legs showing beneath her swirling skirt, skinny arms outstretched to him.

He dismounted before she reached him and caught her in his arms, noting the tears streaking her face.

"Why are you goin' to fight?" The anxiety in her voice caused it to come out high and thin, and he hugged her tighter than before.

"Our country needs me," he answered, muffling his answer against her sunbonnet.

"What if you die?" she wailed.

He couldn't reply. When he raised his head to take a last look around the place, Ma was there with Marie beside her, their grave faces bringing a lump to his already tight throat.

Then Albert, the mischievous scamp, came running down the lane, with Pa and the rest of the boys walking behind him. Ben was the only one missing. They had made their farewells in town.

He had to hug them all, even Pa. Then Ma began a prayer, and they quit their hats, joined hands right there in the lane, and listened to her heartfelt plea for a short war and safety for the troops.

As Ma spoke the "amen" and the family joined in, Rulon was reminded that he hadn't left Mary with a prayer. Mayhap he should have, instead of bedding her one last time. Devotion to God should be in their marriage, as it was in his parents' union, he reminded himself. He climbed on the horse, pledging to be a better husband when he got the chance. *If I get the chance.*

�

As Rulon approached Harrisonburg in late afternoon, he kept his eyes open for a place that would make a good camp. He would need water for the horse. The river lay nearby, rippling its way north to the Potomac.

The Potomac! He would be there in a few days. The federal armory stood on its bank at Harper's Ferry, and he'd heard a whisper that it was now in the hands of his countrymen.

A glow of anticipation began to grow in the pit of his stomach. Across that wide river, his enemies gathered. He imagined a city of tents occupied by rough men eager to put a musket ball into his forehead.

His fingers touched the supposed spot. With effort, he lowered his hand as he admonished himself to quiet his fear. *Don't go borrowin' trouble, boy. You may soon have a baby to support, a child to raise up. Keep your thoughts on gettin' home to Mary, to Mary and your son.*

His son! But could the babe be a girl? No. He was sure that if his seed had taken root in Mary's body, he had made a son. There was no doubt in his mind. The elation rising in him, the warm conviction, assured him on that score.

His thoughts jumped to Mary, with her winsome smile and raven hair. How bold she had been this morning, tossing all convention aside with her nightdress to, what was it she had said? *To sear herself upon my memory.* He shivered. That moment was not to be forgotten. She had achieved her end.

Soon a fine meadow that stretched off the road a ways drew his attention. The lowering sun glinted on water beyond. Beside the meadow stood a barn and other outbuildings. Near to a chicken coop, a house—white paint gleaming on half the boards— occupied the space at the head of a lane.

He reined the horse off the road, followed the path, and halted in the dooryard.

"Hello," he called. "Is anybody home?"

A full-bearded man stepped out of the barn and approached. "Hallo," he said, his deep voice easily pushing through the mass of facial hair. "What might I do for you?"

60

Rulon doffed his hat. "I was seekin' a camp spot for the night and noticed your fine pasture over yonder. Might I bed down alongside the river?"

"Going for a soldier, are you?"

Rulon nodded. "I am. Enlisting tomorrow."

"It will be my honor to have your company on the place. You are . . . ?"

"Rulon Owen, Mount Jackson."

"Mr. Owen. I am Helmut Strauss. You will sup with us tonight, if you please."

The man offered his hand, and Rulon gave him his.

"Many thanks, Mr. Strauss." He looked around the farmstead. "Have any chores I can do?"

"I was milking cows, Mr. Owen. Come. Get off your horse and take him to the well. When you have seen to his needs, you may lend me a hand with the last few animals."

Rulon dismounted with a sigh. "You're mighty gracious, Mr. Strauss. I'm obliged for your kindness."

"We must do all in our power to repulse the threat to our lands, Mr. Owen. I am in your debt."

Chapter 6

Rulon — May 22, 1861

When he had spent an hour helping around the Strauss farm, Rulon enjoyed a hearty meal laid on the table by Mrs. Strauss, and after a bit of conversation with Mr. Strauss, he bedded down beside the murmuring Shenandoah.

He was up early so he could don his finery, but no earlier than Mrs. Strauss, who turned aside his protest that he could eat a johnnycake from his saddlebag for breakfast, and plied him with sausage, fried potatoes, and eggs, which he washed down with large amounts of creamy milk. He took his leave soon after, stuffed to the brim with good food, and with a parcel of sandwiches from the good woman, to boot.

A short ride brought Rulon into Harrisonburg. It was not difficult to locate the place he was to enlist, as a row of several tents stood in the town's courthouse square. He dismounted and asked a passing man where he should enlist, and was directed to one of the tents. He hitched his horse to a nearby post and ducked inside the flap.

"Mornin'," a cheerful voice welcomed him as he entered. "You the man from Shenandoah County?"

"That's me. Name is Owen, Rulon Owen. I live near Mount Jackson." He took off his hat, wondering if the plume was too ostentatious.

The other man got up from behind his camp desk, pulled down his jacket, and extended his hand. "Pleased to make your acquaintance, Owen. Ren Lovell. I'm from Hilton Crossing up the pike about two miles."

Rulon took the proffered hand and gave it a firm shake. "I'm glad to know you, Lovell. Mayhap I should clarify. I moved into town when I wed a little more than a week ago."

"Felicitations, I'm sure." The man was slightly taller than Rulon, and slender, with bright yellow hair and a full moustache.

He wore a short jacket with golden bars slashing the front, brass buttons holding it closed, and pants not unlike his own. His unabashed smile showed off a crooked front tooth and two dimples just beyond the facial hair. "Must have been hard to leave the new missus."

Rulon grinned back. "You have the right of that. I don't want to miss the doin's, though. I believe the wife understands."

"Don't you be certain of that. The ladies may nod and smile, but they don't comprehend the issues or our need to whup the enemy."

"They do pitch in, regardless. Mount Jackson is buzzing like a bee tree. The ladies have taken over the Union Church for sewing circles."

"They will do such. Are those ladies the ones who made your outfit?"

"No." Rulon felt as though the uniform marked him as an outsider. "My ma and sisters made it up for me. Wanted me to make a good showing for the family."

Lovell chuckled, said, "Nothing but the best for the honor of the family," as though he understood perfectly Rulon's discomfort, then reached back to his desk and snatched his cap, which he seated on his head. "I'm to take you to meet the captain. He'll want to size you up before we commence drilling today."

"Drillin'? What do you do in the drills?"

"We run the horses around a bit, and get more familiar with Hardee's tactics." Lovell smiled again. "That's in a book the captain always totes around. I saw you tying up a horse. Yours? How are you armed?"

"The horse is mine. I brought a pistol I acquired not long ago. Gift of the wife's father."

"Uh huh. What is it?"

"A cap and ball five shot."

"That'll do to start," Lovell said. "Drop your gear in the corner and I'll make you known to Captain Yancey."

"It'll be fine to meet him at last. He and I are kin. Second cousins, my pa reckoned it." Rulon put down his saddlebags and followed Lovell out of the tent and down the row to a larger tent near the center. A guard stood beside the hanging flap, carbine on his shoulder.

"Captain in?"

The guard gave Lovell a smirk. "I'm a-standing here, ain't I?"

"Tell him the new man came up."

"Go ahead in and tell him yourself." He eyed Rulon from top to toe, then returned his gaze to the feather adorning the hat. "You the new boy from down in Shenandoah County?"

Rulon nodded slowly, then Lovell tapped him on the arm and held the tent flap open. "Let's go."

Unsure about what kind of welcome awaited him from his cousin, Rulon straightened immediately upon entering, side-stepped to let Lovell enter, and then stood stiffly to his estimation of attention.

ॐ

The man in front of Rulon looked up when he and Ren Lovell entered the tent. He was clothed in a military uniform with a dozen or more gold buttons up the front of the coat and copious amounts of braid adorning the sleeves. Even seated in his camp chair with one leg crossed over the other, he had an erect carriage. Several papers covered his lap, and others had spilled onto the floor around him.

"What do you want?" he barked.

"Captain Yancey, sir. Rulon Owen, come here from Shenandoah County, has reported to enlist, sir," Lovell said, snapping off a salute. "He is fixin' to sign the paper, sir. I was told to bring him here when he arrived."

Rulon imitated Lovell's salute, but the captain gave him little notice after the first cursory inspection.

"Is he outfitted?"

"He has a pistol, sir."

"Humph. I expected more from Shenandoah County than a pistol, that, that uniform, and a fancy hat." He pointed his pencil disparagingly at Rulon.

Rulon shifted his weight forward and began, "Sir, I—"

"Shh," cautioned Lovell. He spoke to the captain again. "He reckons he's your cousin, sir."

"I allowed him to join the company on that foundation," Thomas Yancey said. "It won't buy him special favors."

"No sir," Lovell said.

"Dismissed."

Lovell threw Rulon a glance and motioned with his head toward the tent flap. Then he saluted, about faced, and dragged Rulon outside while he was trying to execute another salute.

Lovell maintained his hold on Rulon's jacket until they were clear of the tent and the guard. Then he let go and grinned. "You should see your face."

"Whew." Rulon let out a breath, not sure if this would be an everyday occurrence or not. He brushed his hands down his uniform. "I don't look as fine as he does."

"Not many of us do. When we get to Harper's Ferry, I reckon we'll get you outfitted with the uniform pieces you're missing and the gear you'll need, if you didn't bring anything more from home."

"Saddle and saddlebags with my personal necessaries is what I brought." Rulon felt his face go hot. Was the intense labor of his mother and sisters all for naught? He followed Lovell back to the tent where they had met.

"You'll bunk here with me'n Owen," Lovell said when they'd made it back.

"Owen? I'm Owen. Rulon Owen."

Lovell grinned, showing the ubiquitous dimples. "He's Owen Leoyd. What are the chances you two would end up in the same outfit, let alone be tent-mates?"

"What's he like?" Rulon asked, sitting on the blanket covering the one cot out of the four in the tent that gave the appearance of being unclaimed.

"You met him over yonder, guarding the captain from the Yankees."

"Hmm. I reckon we'll get along all right."

"He's not as easy-going as me, but there's no evil in him. I can't say the same about the other fellow sleepin' here. He's over to the hospital, playing sick." Lovell aimed a kick at the leg of the nearest cot.

"He's not sick?"

"More like he's perverse," Lovell responded with some heat. "He'd as soon stick you with a knife as shake your hand."

Rulon arose with haste. "I'm not takin' his cot, am I?"

"No. That's unused."

"What's he doing in the company?"

Lovell wore a sober face for the first time in their short acquaintance, and swore briefly. "He's the surgeon's pet, some kind of kin. The doc wouldn't leave home without the rooster fart, so he dumped him on us."

Rulon caught himself before he laughed at the man's epithet. After he could speak without chortling, he asked, "When do you reckon he'll show his face here again?"

"If I had my druthers, never." Lovell took a deep breath, apparently trying to return to happier thoughts. "Likely tomorrow before we leave. The other doctors won't keep him long before sending him on his way."

"I reckon I have to meet him one time or another."

"Too bad you can't add 'never' to that."

"What does the man look like? I don't want to come upon him unaware and get on his bad side."

"He don't have a good side, Owen. Stick close to me, and I'll endeavor to point him out before you're obliged to meet him here in the tent."

Rulon nodded slowly.

Lovell pulled a paper from a stack and put it on the table before Rulon, accompanied by a pen he had dipped into an inkwell. "Sign here, Owen. This says you're bound in service to Virginia for one year."

"I can read," Rulon muttered as he took the pen. He bent to the task, then straightened and handed back the pen. "The fight will be over long before a year comes around. What then?"

Lovell tilted his head to one side and scratched under his chin. "I reckon the boys in charge will let us off, unless we're needed to guard the border."

"Let's hope ol' Abe Lincoln sees the right of our argument before then."

Lovell sanded the paper, then stowed it under a paperweight. "Time for our final drill, Owen. Keep your eyes open. You have a lot to learn today, because we'll be on the road tomorrow."

☙

Rulon — May 23, 1861

The next morning, Rulon awoke to the touch of a pinching

hand over his mouth and the prick of a knife to his throat under one ear.

"Get outta yore cot, sissy boy. We're packin' up to move outta here."

Rulon scarcely breathed. The knife's tip moved fractionally. Then it lifted a bit, but still made contact with his skin as it traced a line across his neck toward his other ear. Lovell hadn't been joking about the danger of this man.

"Von! Leave the man be!" Lovell's voice barked. "Put that hog-sticker away and prepare to strike the tent."

The man named Von growled an obscenity and removed the knife. "He's not our kind. Look at that damn feather," he added, gesturing toward Rulon's fine hat. But he finally backed away, left the tent, and made his noises outside.

"Whew!" Lovell expelled a gusty sigh. "I couldn't be sure he would obey me," he said, approaching to eye Rulon's neck.

By this time, Rulon had arisen and was dressing in haste.

"He didn't leave you any permanent damage," his new friend observed. "The sooner we can put him on a patrol against the Yankees, the sooner he'll be able to do what he loves best."

"What's that?" asked Rulon, dreading the answer as he struggled to recover his dignity.

"Killin' folks."

❧

As soon as the tents had been struck and stowed into a baggage wagon, the men of the Harrisonburg Cavalry were mounted and on their way to war. They made a steady progress down the Shenandoah Valley, passing through town after town where crowds gathered to cheer them on. Bands played rousing marches. Dogs nipped at the heels of the horses.

At last, Mount Jackson loomed before the troop. Rulon's stomach knotted with tension as he spied his father-in-law standing in the road before his store, hat uplifted. And there . . . there stood Mary—upright, graceful, her raven locks gleaming in the sun.

Her eyes swept the rows of horsemen, then found him. At last he was glad he was wearing the uniform and hat she could identify. She locked her gaze upon him as though to plumb the depths of his very being. She raised a white handkerchief aloft. It fluttered in the slight breeze before she brought it to her lips and bestowed a kiss upon it.

Rulon devoured the sight of her, the slender figure clothed in a summer dress of some purple stuff. She did so love the color. As he looked at her, she launched her body forward and, braving the mass of horseflesh, came to his side.

He feared for her safety, but she smiled up at him, reaching up as she kept pace with his horse, offering up the handkerchief into his hand. He took it, pressed it to his own lips, and tucked it into the front of his coat, right over his heart.

Her hand touched his lightly, and he moved to enfolded it, but she pulled free of his grasp and threaded her way among the horses to the side of the road. She had not been quick enough to prevent him catching sight of the tears beginning to fill her dark eyes.

Oh Mary. Tears? Did she fear for him? For herself? Was she ill? Ah, how heavy a burden it was to leave her behind again and go off to face an uncertain future at the hands of an unknown, uncaring foe. Would a Yankee musket ball claim his life? Make Mary a widow? Make his child an orphan?

He turned in the saddle and searched through the people standing along the way, but Mary was gone from his sight. Perhaps she was shielded from his view by larger citizens. Mayhap she had fled into the store to hide her emotions.

His heart felt as though a hand were wrapped about it, squeezing it tightly and painfully, as he rode with the troop out of the town, onward toward Harper's Ferry.

&

Rod — May 26, 1861

One evening, Rod kept his sons at the table after supper, and produced a sheaf of papers and a lead pencil.

"Boys," he said, "Rulon has gone into the fighting. Benjamin will leave soon, and so will I. I'm raising a company of cavalry."

"Pa, you didn't tell us," complained Peter, running his finger in a circle on the oilcloth covering the wood table.

"You didn't need to know," Rod answered. "But now things are moving along, and I reckon it's time to lay out the plan on what's what in running the farm for your ma."

Carl groaned and let his head fall forward. "Pa," he said as he raised it, "we know when to plant and how to milk the cows and butcher the hogs and break the horses, and—"

"I reckon you all think you do, but there's a good chance you could forget a thing or two of vital importance, like saving sufficient seed, and watching the mares for signs of their season so you get the best stud to cover her at the right time." He turned to his third-born. "Peter, I'm putting you in charge of the crops. See that you don't forget to harrow after you plow."

"Pa," Peter said with a snort. "I've done that plenty of times."

"See you don't forget. Carl, you're to manage the cattle herd and the hogs. Keep track of the weather when you go to butcher, and mind that Granny sow. She's vicious. If she weren't such a good breeder, I would have eaten her long ago. Clay is to help you." He looked at the younger son. "You're a good milker, so don't take any guff from Carl."

It was Carl's turn to whine "Pa," and he took full advantage, while Clay played with his folding knife and grinned.

"James," Rod said, pointing his pencil down the table. "You are to oversee the stable. I know you're young, but you have more horse-sense than many grown men of my acquaintance. I've written down instructions on breeding the dams. I want you to keep the lines as pure as you can, so watch that stud I bought from Kentucky. He'd have his way with every mare on the place, if you'd let him."

"Rod," Julia called from her chair.

"I'm not tellin' him anything he don't already know, Julie," he remonstrated. "Albert, you are to help Peter. Make sure the seed don't rot from planting at the wrong time. Help your ma with the pumpkins in the kitchen patch. She don't have to heft them when there's a strong boy on the place."

Albert grinned at the compliment. "Yes, Pa."

"I've made lists for the chores that need to be done at certain times, and in correct order. Mind you all study them out and help each other when you're not busy with your own tasks. Am I understood?"

"Yes Pa," came in a chorus from both sides of the table.

Rod nodded, and passed around the pieces of paper. "You

may as well keep them all together in the farm journal, in case someone takes sick or has an injury and another one of you needs to fill in." He took a deep breath and looked at each boy in turn. "I'm putting my trust in you all to do your duty and support your mother."

"Jerusalem crickets! I feel left out," said Ben.

Rod narrowed his eyes at Ben while he considered if that was a profanity, or crude talk instead. Ben looked so innocent in his disappointment that he decided to let it go without any further notice. He looked down the table again. "You have your work cut out for you. Get a good night's sleep. I'll start easing you into your tasks tomorrow."

❧

Rulon — May 28, 1861

Garth Von brought out his knife a few days later as the tent mates cooked their rations for supper. He got Rulon's attention when he growled "Owen!" and began to stroke his bewhiskered neck from side to side with the thin blade.

Rulon tried—with little success—to suppress a shudder as he dropped a slab of pork into the kettle. What was wrong with the man? Why did he bear him a grudge? He'd not known of Von's existence a week ago. Surely he had done nothing inside of that interval to merit such menacing behavior.

Von continued to mimic slitting a throat for several minutes, eying Rulon all the while.

Rulon's stomach curdled with fear. He stepped back from the fire and fought the sensation, yet it sat heavily upon him. Was he a coward? He squirmed at the notion. He thought not, but he had never encountered such unwarranted ill will on the farm.

Sure, he had tussled with bullies, town boys with too much time on their hands. They were easily met, and usually beaten, at least after he began to get his growth and put weight on his spindly frame. This situation felt different, like pig iron cast from a defective mold. The man was certainly contrary, but there was something more, besides.

"He's mad, you know," Owen Leoyd muttered for Rulon's ear as he broke a loaf of hard bread over his knee and handed him a chunk.

Madness. Was that what glittered in the man's eyes, flitting away for a time, then returning, doubled in intensity?

Rulon felt the hairs on his neck raise, and knew it wasn't due to the night air.

Von lurched forward, and Rulon threw himself backward, smacking up against Ren Lovell, spilling his tin cup of coffee.

But even as Lovell cried out in protest, Rulon saw that Von's movement wasn't an attack. The man thrust his knife into the kettle and stabbed the pork several times.

He looked up and cackled at Rulon's discomfort. "That's what I do to sissies," he crowed, and stalked away.

Equal parts of shame and humiliation served to dampen Rulon's appetite as he apologized to Ren. *Hell's bells!* He was a coward for reacting to the man's erratic acts.

Chapter 7

Mary — May 30, 1861

Mary locked the door of her room before she undressed and changed into the shift she wore at night in the summer heat. She noticed that the touch of the fabric irritated the skin of her bosom that had been so tender of late.

Did I bump into something? she wondered. *I can't recall doing so.* She sat on the bed and began braiding her hair. Every time one arm or the other brushed against her breasts, she felt the annoyance of pain.

She must take a look, see if she had bruised herself.

She swallowed. A proper young lady did not look at her body. She kept it covered, always.

She swallowed again. *Except when Rulon asked me to disrobe so he could gaze upon me.*

The request had disturbed her, but she had finally come to terms with it and acquiesced. Several times. Over and over and over. She felt herself warm and swallowed again. She had done that to please her husband. That was permissible.

I have injured myself somehow, she temporized. *I must discover where.*

She took the lamp to the looking glass and set it down. She took a deep breath. Her mouth had gone dry and now she couldn't make saliva to swallow. Holding her breath, she took the shift from her body. She breathed out. She examined her form in the glass. She lifted the lamp aloft to cast a wider pool of light. She held her breath again and looked closely at her breasts, careful not to touch them. They looked larger than she had imagined they were, but they had no bruise upon them that she could see. It was evident that she had not run against anything that had injured her flesh.

She let out the held breath in a shaky sigh. Mortified that she had been gazing at her own body, Mary placed the lamp on a chest of drawers and blew out the light. She stumbled to the bed, frantically replacing the shift. Whispering a prayer for forgiveness, she got into bed and covered herself with the bedclothes, although the night continued warm.

She lay in the bed, clasping the quilt to her chin. Tears stung her eyes. Why had she done that? Why had she looked upon herself? A tear slid down her cheek. Would God punish her for that sin? She trembled. What if she was . . . what if Rulon had truly left a child in her belly? Would God strike out at that child? Cause it harm for her sinful glance? She sobbed, letting her tears soak the bedding. She couldn't believe in a vengeful god who would punish a baby that way.

Perhaps there was no god. No! No! That would mean there was no one to watch over Rulon, to keep him safe. She could not believe that, either.

Growing so hot that she began to perspire, Mary flung aside the bed covering, keeping only the sheet on her body. That was better. That was sensible.

The bed seemed so empty now that Rulon was not here to fill it with his vitality and strength. How she missed him! A scrap of contrariness arose in her and she ventured to touch one breast. It remained tender.

Something was happening to her body; that was sure. Was this a sign that she truly was increasing? Who could advise her?

She quickly ruled out speaking to her mother. Mama never talked about such matters.

She had no close friends who were married ladies.

In despair, she realized she had no one with whom she could counsel.

She lay quietly, thinking of Rulon's last embrace on the morning he had left. How she wished he were here to comfort her! Certainly her own mother had not been the tenderest soul of late. But Rulon could be as tender as a mother when she needed that of him. Perhaps his mother had played a part in shaping a gentle part of his being.

His mother. Mother Owen. Mary inhaled deeply. *She can advise me.*

Mary covered her mouth with her hand, then thought how foolish that movement was. The audacious thought had come from her brain, not her mouth.

Mother Owen. She was a forthright, courageous lady if there ever was one. Did she shrink from discussing matters of . . . anatomy?

There was but one way to discover if she did or did not. Mary had to ask her.

∞

Mary — May 31, 1861

The next day, Mary sat in the back room of the store, sorting skeins of embroidery thread by color, when her father entered and looked down at her. When she glanced up, her heart froze at the sight of his frown.

She had difficulty getting any words through her suddenly-dry throat. "Papa?" she finally forced out. *Has he some news of Rulon?*

He shook his head with an effort. "Rest easy, daughter. My mind was elsewhere."

"May I help, Papa?" What was causing him such a concerned look?

"You must not worry yourself, Mary." He forcibly thrust his hand through his dark hair. "Your mother is not as excited as I had hoped she would be about her condition."

"What do you mean, Papa?"

"Perhaps you shall have a brother by and by," he said. "That is my hope."

Mama is increasing? That certainly would account for her irritable attitude of late. "Felicitations, Papa," she said, a bit staggered to think that her parents partook of the same delights that Rulon and she had discovered together. She banished the thought, unable to lend it credence. Mama would not take delight in intimacies.

Papa extended his hand, in which he held a letter. "The missive is addressed to you. I'll leave you to read it in peace."

As her father left the room, Mary examined the folded paper, her hands shaking. Yes, it was from Rulon. She recognized his script from the notes he used to leave her in the fork of the elm in the backyard of her father's house. She got the letter open and smoothed it across her knees.

Berryville, Berkeley Co. Va.
Twenty-fourth May, 1861
My pretty wife,
We have arriv'd at camp. I only have a momunt to scribbl this note Thank you for the token which I will wear over my heart until I see you again.
The wether looks like rain. We hope it holds off until nite. The fellows in the company are mostly of the regular sort. I will get along with them.
A trumpet is soundin. Corp'rl Lovell tells me the call is ment to get us on the march. I must post this now. I will rite to you later. Tell the little one his papa lovs him. Mary, my sweet Sugar, I see yor face each nite in my dreems.
Yor husband
Rulon S Owen, Private
Co. I, 1st Reg't Va. Cav.

Mary sobbed as she clutched the note to her bosom. Rulon was well. He loved her. He hadn't written that, but she could feel the strength of his esteem from the words he used. She briefly touched her skirt where it covered her abdomen, hoping there was a "little one" there to whisper to, hoping it was the son Rulon seemed to expect.

After a while her tears dried, and she tucked the note into her bodice, listening—for the rest of the day—to the crackle of the paper every time she moved around, going about the tasks that earned her keep while her husband was at war.

&

Ben — June 5, 1861

Ben took his noon break alongside the creek behind the mill, eating the first of two sandwiches Ma had packed that morning. He had just begun to wash it down with a bottle of milk he'd retrieved from the creek when small hands crept across his face from behind him and covered his eyes.

"Guess who," demanded a voice he knew so well that he choked as desire rose in him.

Keeping himself very still, he said softly, "Marie? How'd you get here? Did Pa bring you into town?"

"No! Guess again."

"Julianna? You sound so grown up." He put as much incredulity into his voice as he knew how.

"No-uh," said the girl, exasperation making her draw out the word.

He put the bottle on the ground beside him and placed his hands over the top of the ones touching his face. "I do not know any other women but my ma and Ella Ruth Allen." He heard the huskiness of his voice. "Ma is busy weedin' the truck garden today. I conclude that you are . . ." He brought the hands to his lips, kissing first one, then the other. "My love. My all. My Ella Ruth."

A long and satisfied sigh answered him. Then the hands were tugged free of his grasp and Ella Ruth dashed around, planted herself in his lap, and put her arms around his neck. "I'm not your Ella Ruth yet, Benjamin. You have to get Poppa to let us marry."

He groaned as he bent forward and found her mouth, muttering, "Lordy, lordy, don't tempt me so."

She let him kiss her for a while, then shoved him back.

"Ben, Poppa is home from his trip. Come to supper tonight and plead your case to him."

Ben felt his eyebrows rise. "He'll let me come to supper?"

"I haven't asked him, but I'm sure he won't mind. I told Momma I would invite you, and she shrugged her shoulders, so I do not feel she will object if you arrive about six o'clock."

"That's some progress, at least," Ben muttered. "I'm obliged that you've been working on your ma to change her opinion of me."

"Momma does not hate you, Ben. She quite likes you, in fact. She is concerned that you don't have property. You must be able to support a wife, after all."

"Sweet girl, you do remember I'm goin' off to fight the Yankee hoards?"

"Oh Ben, that is so tiresome. Don't talk about that anymore."

He took her face between his calloused fingers and held it still. He gazed into her eyes. "Ella Ruth. The Rifles are leavin' this month. You know that, but you persist in disbelievin' that I'm obliged to go. If I come to supper, it will be to ask for your hand on the spot, and to tell your pa that we're going to be married as soon as may be. There will be no fancy weddin'. It'll be only you, me, and our folks." He swallowed. "Or it will be nothin' at all."

Ella Ruth drew in a sharp breath. She let it out slowly, shakily. When at last she spoke, she said, "Benjamin, you do not mean that. You cannot rob a girl of her dreams."

"If you truly want me, girl, the time has come to act like it. Now . . . or never." His throat felt as though it burned as he uttered the ultimatum.

She stared at him, frowning slightly. "You are serious," she finally said.

"I never have been more."

She gave a little shake of her head. "This talk is so unlike a gentleman, Benjamin. You are mistreating me." She got off his lap.

"No. I am offering you my heart, my life." He felt himself quivering from the strain as he arose. "But you must take them now, or you must leave them alone."

She raised her chin. "I don't like this talk, Benjamin. When you can treat me nicely, you may see me again." She turned her back and picked her way across the yard toward the front of the mill.

Ben exhaled. The girl would not see reason, could not see that life was spiraling out of her grasp, that she must bend her will to the times or they would break her. He felt as though his heart were cracking into pieces as she slipped around the corner.

80

Mary — June 7, 1861

Several days after Mary had determined to speak to her mother-in-law, Julia Owen came into the store with a basket of eggs. Mary headed off her father and beckoned her mother-in-law to the side counter.

"Mother Owen," she said, hoping her smile was bright and cheerful, and not the wan greeting she was afraid might be seen on her face. "This is a good lot of eggs. You must be delighted with your hens."

"Hello, Mistress Mary. They are laying well. I'm mighty pleased to see you. I received a letter from Rulon a few days ago.

He is unhurt and busy. Have you heard from him?"

Mary dropped one hand behind the counter and started to touch her stomach, but thought better of it. She couldn't keep up that action every time Rulon's name was mentioned. What if she did it where others could see?

"Yes, ma'am, I mean Mother Owen. He wrote about the men in the company and the trumpets. He sounded very excited."

"Young men are excited by fightin', it seems. Are you well? You look a little green around the gills."

Oh, I'm feelin' . . ." Mary hesitated, then lowered her voice to a whisper. "Ma'am, may I ask your advice about a delicate subject?"

Julia looked perplexed, but nodded.

"It is a somewhat personal question, a very personal, delicate question."

"Mary girl, you may ask me anythin' you have a mind to." She looked around the busy store. "Would you prefer that we speak in the back room, or the garden?"

"Thank you. The garden is a peaceful place." Mary removed her apron and came around the counter. "The eggs will be fine sittin' there for a few moments. I promise not to take much time. I—"

Julia took her arm. "Let's go to the garden, my dear."

Once they had settled themselves on a bench under the elm tree where Rulon used to leave notes for her, Mary began in a soft voice. "Mrs. . . Mother Owen. I cannot speak to my mama about this. You appear to be made of sterner stuff than she is. I must ask . . . please advise me . . . how am I to know—"

"If you are to have a babe?"

"Yes!" Mary's relief left her limp. Rulon's ma would not shy away from the difficult topic.

Julia smiled and took Mary's hand in her own. "You have a vital young husband. You are young and in good health. You undoubtedly have come together in the good Lord's way, if Rulon's dash up the stairs on your weddin' day is any measure."

Mary felt herself blushing at the mention of her husband's haste. She nodded.

"It's not been a month since that time, but mayhap your visit did not come around?"

"My visit?"

"The monthly. The accursed nuisance of womankind."

"Oh. I understand. I did not think to notice."

"Pay heed if it don't appear." She looked Mary over, top to toe. "You may feel a strangeness, a difference in your being?"

Mary slowly nodded, feeling wonderment at her mother-in-law's knowledge.

"Are you overly fatigued?"

"Yes, ma'am."

Julia placed her arm across her own chest. "Do you have soreness in your bosom?"

"Yes. Certainly that."

"Do odors offend you?"

"Now that you mention it, ma'am, yes, there are particular odors I cannot bear to smell."

Julia smiled. "It is early to know for sure, but it appears I am to be a granny."

"Pardon me?"

"You are likely increasin', my dear girl. You will give me a grandchild."

Mary sighed at the woman's confirmation. She said in a shy tone, "Rulon hopes for a son."

"Of course he does," Julia said, then laughed. She added, "Every man upon this earth thinks only of sons." She sobered, her smile fading. "Daughters can come later, but sons are highly valued for the first of the offspring. For some reason, begetting a man child is a proof of manhood. I don't pretend to understand it. Men are strange creatures."

Mary stared at the woman. Unlike her own mother, Mrs. Owen wasn't afraid to speak about anything. She herself knew only a little about a man's pride, but did know it was a thing she dared not meddle with. Her own father had exhibited a longing for a son not many days ago.

Swallowing, Mary asked a final question. "Will there be other signs to mind?"

"There are many. You may have difficulty keeping food down. Experience aching in the back." Julia patted her chest. "These will swell, increase in size. You will need to alter your bodices. Then, of course, you will need to let out your waistbands, as your belly will gradually enlarge to accommodate the growin' child. You must have seen that in your mother."

Mary lowered her head. "We were not encouraged to take notice, ma'am."

"Your ma is a mite squeamish on that head, but since she is with child, you might take heed, this go-around."

Mary gasped. Mother Owen knew everything. "I only learned that a little while ago. She has been so irritable, and treated Rulon in a miserable way."

"As long as you treated him well, I reckon he didn't even pay heed to that."

"Mother Owen, how you do talk!"

"No offense meant, my dear. I did mean treating with him in more ways than just the one. Always feed your man well. Tend whatever wounds he may carry, be they physical or to his spirit, with gentleness and a good try at understandin' his pain. Listen to his complaints, and soothe his soul. Those are the secrets to happiness in a marriage."

"I will remember your words for when he comes home."

Julia nodded. "Store them up. This fight can't last many months. Mr. Lincoln must be given to understand he cannot invade our homeland. We will resist firmly."

Mary let go of Julia's hand and clasped her own hands together. Rulon would return soon. They would have a child to raise up together. She looked at her mother-in-law and remembered something.

"Mother Owen, this isn't your homeland. You weren't born in Virginia."

Julia Owen raised her chin. "This valley is my home, girl. I married my man here, and bore my children in the house he built for me. This," she nodded, "this *is* my home."

Mary felt a slight rebuke in her words, but forgave her the bluntness of them, glad that Mother Julia Owen was like a rock, the firm foundation that had nurtured Rulon to manhood. Mother Owen would be a loving granny to her child. What kind of grandmother her own mama would be had yet to be determined.

ᔍ

Mary — June 12, 1861

Upon arising one morning, Mary barely made it to the

washbasin in time to empty bile and not much else into the ceramic vessel. Her stomach heaved past the point where there was anything left to expel, and when the cramping tightness in her abdomen had ceased, she sank back to the bed, shaking with weakness. Mother Owen had mentioned that one symptom she'd likely have was an inability to keep food on her stomach, but she had yet to eat anything today. Was this some other illness? She touched her face to check for fever, but there was none.

When she felt steady, she approached the basin for the purpose of emptying it into the slop bucket, but the smell made her gag. *Oh-h-h.* She retreated toward the bed. Who could she get to take this vile, odorous mess away? Ida wouldn't do it. Of that she was sure. Perhaps she could bribe India with a sweet from the store? For now, she would have to leave it in place. The smell was insufferable. She could not bear to approach the basin to deal with it herself.

Brushing her hair away from her face, she made an attempt to make herself presentable for the day, but she hardly felt presentable. Instead, she felt queasy, and several times had to restrain herself from renewing the debacle at the basin.

She couldn't work at the store in this condition. What if she had an accident at the counter, or on the merchandise, or, worse yet, on a customer?

At last she gave up the attempt to dress, and crawled back into bed.

It must not have been much past eight o'clock when a quick rap on the door woke her up. Who was disturbing her hard-won sleep? She took a tentative breath and said "Come in," hoping the effort to use her voice wouldn't roil up her stomach.

Her mother entered, moving so rapidly that the scarf she wore in a vain attempt to cloak her condition fluttered aside, revealing a thickness in her waist and a roundness at the front of her skirt.

"What is this nonsense?" she asked. "Why were you not in the kitchen preparing breakfast? We had poor fare for your father's meal this morning. He works so very hard to meet our needs."

"Mama," Mary wailed. "I'm sick."

Mrs. Hilbrands laid the back of her hand on Mary's forehead. "There is no fever. What ails you?" She turned her head back and forth, sniffing. "What is that horrid stench?"

"I vomited," Mary confessed. "Please, get someone to take it away. I cannot bear the odor."

"You are— He—" Gasping, Mrs. Hilbrands put her hand to her mouth, then removed it so she could speak. "I told you not to marry. He has made you, gotten you, left you with child. How could you, daughter?"

"Beg pardon? How could I do what?" *Questions. Why is she asking so many questions when my stomach is reeling?*

"Engage in carnal intercourse with that boy." Mrs. Hilbrands looked as though she thought she herself had broken all the Ten Commandments by speaking of it.

"We are wed." Mary wanted to vomit again, and threw off the covers so she could swing her limbs out of the bed. "It's the way of married folk."

"And in this house!" She pointed at the bed, accusation written on her face.

"You wouldn't let me leave. Mother Owen had a place for me, but you—" Mary couldn't finish her thought, and she scurried to the basin to vomit again.

When she had finished, Mary begged, "Go away. Please, go away, and take this basin with you."

Rulon — June 15, 1861

Rulon had spent the last three nights on picket near the Potomac River and had just come back to the camp. As he rubbed down his horse, thinking of nothing but getting into his blankets and catching a few hours of rest, Ren Lovell approached and gave him an envelope.

"I thought you might like to have this, Owen. It got here with a packet of dispatches after you left."

Rulon took the letter and stuffed it into his pocket. "I'm obliged, Lovell."

"Go get breakfast before you sleep. We might all be hauling our tails out of here later today."

"Where are we bound?"

"The general is moving his headquarters. I'm not certain if we're going along or staying put. The colonel likes being in the thick of the fray."

"I wish we were better armed."

"We're supposed to get sabres soon. Not that I'm convinced they're good for anything. Not when some Yank troop is shootin' lead balls at us." Lovell grinned wryly.

"How soon can we expect carbines from Richmond?"

Lovell snorted. "Maybe in a month. Maybe longer. There is a good deal of confusion in the armaments department. I swear old Beauregard gets all the arms shipments before any thought is given to us here behind the Blue Ridge."

Rulon made polite conversation as long as he could stand to do so, itching to get away so he could pull out the paper burning a hole in his pocket. He was almost certain the letter was from Mary. He'd caught merely a glimpse of the script on the face of the envelope before he'd put it away, but those rounded letters could only have been written by a young female, and he doubted his sisters would think about writing to him.

When he finally found a moment to himself, he snatched the letter from its hiding place and tore it open. He forbade himself the assurance of looking at the signature, and instead started at the top.

Mount Jackson, Chenandoah County, Va.

Tenth of June, year of Our Lord one thousand Eight hundred sixty-One

Dear husband,

I cried from relief to receev your lettr Thank you for writin altho it must needs be in hast. All are well here.

I have discover'd the cause of my Mother's late ill humor toward you. She is ~~breeding with child~~ increasing. How much fun we shall have raising our children togethr.!! That is, if I am to have a child. I do not kno at this time if my suspicions are true. I only kno the joy that corses through my bosom when I think of the possibility. That thot warms my being.

Yor Mother was in the store three days back and sends you her greetings. I was able to converse with her for a few moments. She seems assured that the signs I told her that I have been having are good ones concurning carrying a child. She is hoping along with me that I will soon kno for certun ab't the matter.

I pray you will take caution in all your ~~manuvrs~~ ~~manoeavrs~~ whenever you move about in sight of the Yankees. Hold the memry I left you close to your heart always.

The wife you love,

Mary Margaret Hilbrands Owen

(That is the first time I have writ my name down to you in its entirety)

Rulon stood very still. Merely reading Mary's words about the memory she had branded upon his soul aroused him, and he fought to curb the need it brought before it engulfed his body. A handful of tents had been pitched behind the hill on the Winchester road. He knew who inhabited them, but with Mary dancing around the notion that they really would have a child, he felt a strong compulsion to renew the pledge he'd made to himself, and he supposed, to God, not to take himself off to seek relief there.

Von and a few others of his acquaintance in the company were not so circumspect. Their boastful talk would drive him mad today if they had been with the harlots last night.

Clamping his teeth on his lip to divert his pain elsewhere, Rulon put the letter away and went to eat whatever the cook had prepared.

Chapter 8

Ben — June 15, 1861

Ben signed his name, then took the uniform that had been made by the ladies of the town especially for the men of the Mount Jackson Rifles, which they also named "Allen's Infantry," in honor of he who was their captain. Ella Ruth's own cousin. He swallowed the bile that arose upon thinking of her name and their last encounter.

He went behind the church and found that he was not the only man in the company with the same idea for privacy. He chuckled wryly, then shucked his ordinary clothing and dressed himself in the finery befitting an infantryman. He stowed his regular clothes in a haversack that had been provided to him for the purpose of trucking some of his accoutrements about. After that, he went to find his mother.

"Don't worry for my sake," he told her, holding her hand and stroking it. "This won't last long. The shine won't be off our tent pegs before you'll see us come marchin' down that road and home."

Ma seemed a bit assured by his joke and made a little noise he took for a laugh, but the sound was very faint among all the conversations going on in the square. She looked around.

"Did your girl come?"

Ben scowled. Up to just a few minutes ago, he had attempted not to think about Ella Ruth's absence. Now Ma's innocent question brought a flood of pain. "She won't be comin'. She rejected my offer of marriage." The words cut deep.

Ma squeezed his hand and said in a low voice, "I'm sorry, son." Her face showed her deep concern as she tried to comfort him.

He tried to grin to reassure her that he didn't care anymore. The grimace he produced hurt his lips. "Never mind, Ma." He patted her hand. He'd tried so hard not to remember the gash in his soul as he had prepared for this day.

He inhaled and mentally shook himself. Never mind, indeed. He had much better things to occupy his thoughts from now on.

"You behave, now," Ma said. "Go to church services as often as you can. I hear Mr. Jackson is a godly man. You hold him for your example."

"Old Jack?" Ben saw the question on his mother's face. "I hear tell that's what the men call the general, Ma. 'Jack,' from his surname, Jackson."

"That's a mite disrespectful, don't you reckon?"

"If that's the worst he's called, he'll be mighty lucky, Ma." He turned as he heard a bugle call. "Hear that sound? I have to go now. Give my regards to Pa and the young'uns. Tell Peter his time will come, and not to hurry into anything." He let go of her hand, gave her shoulders a quick squeeze, and moved away, forming up with his squad in a line.

Then they marched away, followed by a baggage wagon full of tents and the accoutrements they could not carry on their persons.

ஐ

Julia — June 15, 1861

"Mama, where is Peter?"

Upon hearing Julianna's question, Julia looked down the table. She had only just become accustomed to seeing a gap where Rulon had sat for so many years. Now Ben's place beside it would also be empty, for only a short time, she hoped. But Peter? Where was he, indeed?

"Rod, did you send Peter on an errand?"

He looked up from his plate of stew, frowning. "I did not, Julie. I figured he went into town with you and Benjamin. He wasn't in the buggy with you?"

"No. It was only Ben and me. Belle is a well-mannered animal, so I figured I would have no difficulty driving her home myself." She took a moment to think when she had last seen the missing boy. Trepidation sent a chill racing along the nerves of her arms. This morning . . . this morning after breakfast Peter had given her a fierce hug before he returned to his chores. She had thought it had something to do with comforting her in the face of Ben's imminent departure.

Her nails dug into her apron as her hands formed claws around the fabric. "No," she said, deep in her throat. "No, he wouldn't." She felt the weakness brought on by blood leaving her head and raised her hands to support herself against the possibility of falling, bringing the apron clenched within them.

"Julie!"

She heard her husband rise, utensils clattering to the table, striking his plate, and the legs of his chair scraping the floor. Hurried footfalls. Then his hand was firm upon her shoulder.

"Julie." He breathed heavily. "One of the horses didn't come up to water this afternoon, the one we call Brownie. I thought perhaps it got loose from the pasture." He stood beside her, his breathing easing toward normal. "I was going to send one of the boys to look for it. No need for that now. He took the horse."

"Where would he go?" she asked, her voice muffled in the apron. She wanted to enfold her runaway son in her arms, redo the embrace she had shrugged off with such haste this morning.

"Ma." It was Carl. "Pete's been studyin' the newspapers. I reckon he—" His voice faltered and she heard him take several gulps of air before he continued his story. "I saw him cut something out, then tuck it in his shirt. I made him show it to me. It was a mention of the Shenandoah Rangers forming up. I thought he was going to pull a prank on somebody." He sniffed. "It's a cavalry company. That's why he needed a horse."

Her head drooped farther toward the table. The Shenandoah Rangers? She knew nothing about that outfit. Who would know? Who could she ask?

She got a hand loose from her apron, reached out, and clutched her husband's vest instead. "Rod," she whispered. "Will General Meem know anything?"

"I'll make inquiries, wife. There's aught we can do tonight. Eat. You'll want the strength." He patted her shoulder and shifted his weight. "Eat!" His command was directed to the children. Then he said in a weary voice, "I'll speak to you after supper, Carl."

⁂

Rod — June 17, 1861

Rod cut short his day's work to ride into Mount Jackson to see what he could learn about his missing son. On the way, he encountered Chester Bates, who was headed into town on a different errand.

"Rod," said his neighbor. "Fine day. Have you given thought to my idea?"

"I have." Feeling grumpy, Rod didn't expand on his answer.

"It's been two months. Have you made any progress?"

Rod sighed. "I have. Several men have volunteered." He thumped his thigh. "I told Julie first thing."

"Well, at least you gave her warning. When does the company enlist?"

"Any day now. First I have to find my boy Peter."

"Find him? That sounds like he's run away."

"He has. We think he's joined up." Rod pursed his lips in anger. "Julie's fit to be tied."

"I can imagine. Do you have any notion where he's gone?"

"None, except that Carl thinks Peter may have taken a shine to joining the Shenandoah Rangers. Have you heard anything about them?"

"Shenandoah Rangers?" Chester scratched his head. "The name sounds familiar. I'll think on it."

"Let me know right quick if you remember," Rod said, his tone a bit brusque. "If Julie takes it into her mind to prevent me from going to the war over this affair, I'll be in the brine with the pickles."

After bidding Chester goodbye at the edge of the town, Rod made the rounds of places that would have information: the store, the drinking establishments, and the telegraph office. Monday was a work day, so there were few people hanging around, and none of them was interested in a military company formed anywhere else than in Mount Jackson. Rod decided that Monday probably wasn't the best time to expect a full crowd.

As he left the telegraph office, he spied Chester coming up the street toward him. He seemed anxious to waylay him, and spoke as soon as he arrived.

"Rod," he said, puffing from the exertion of his hurry, "I

recalled where I heard the name of that company. Sam Myers, the man who used to run the Columbia Furnace. He raised the Shenandoah Rangers over to Edinburg. If they haven't rode away yet, Peter may be down there."

Rod felt his breath leaving his body in a sigh. Peter was as nearby as that? He looked at the sun. His search had eaten up the afternoon, but if he left now, he could get there by dark.

"Chester, can you get word to Julie that I've gone to Edinburg?"

"I'll tell her myself."

"Much obliged, friend." Rod clapped Chester on the arm in farewell. He made haste to where he had tied his horse, mounted, and rode off toward the north.

He arrived in Edinburg as night fell. Since it was too late in the day for him to go about searching for Peter, he was obliged instead to seek a meal and a place to sleep. He found a small tavern that served food, and dug into his pocket for the price of the victuals. The talk in the tavern of the brave Rangers having left the town disheartened him.

When he finished eating, he asked the proprietor about lodgings, and was directed to ask at the livery barn. He spent an uneasy night on a pile of hay, wondering what Julia would say about his failure to bring back their son.

The next day, his fears solidified into reality. The Company had indeed gone to war, and Peter with them.

≈

Rod — June 18, 1861

When Rod rode down the lane late that night, a lamp burned in the kitchen window, casting a checkerboard patch of light across the dooryard outside the house. Julia's disappointment lay ahead of him at the moment when he would give her the bad news. Wrapped in an unfamiliar sense of failure, he dismounted in front of the barn, struck a match and lit the lantern hanging inside the door, then cared for the horse.

He paused before he closed the barn door. The scores of feet between the barn and the house stretched through the darkness like a gulf of bitterness. Julie waited up for him in the house. He was sure of that. She wanted to know if he had brought back her boy. Surely she had looked out when she heard the approach of his horse. Surely she already knew that only one horse had come down the lane and passed through the stream of light. Surely she already knew he had failed her.

Rod's heart sank to his toes as he stepped away from the barn. It seemed that his boots tripped him time and again. Was he so old that he could no longer walk that distance without faltering? He stopped, struggling to purge feebleness and pain from his body, regret and despair from his soul by an act of will. Julie would need strength from him, comfort from him, solace and peace. He shook his head. He couldn't give her the latter two gifts. She would have to get them from God.

After a long time, he moved forward again. Julie waited. He couldn't put off speaking to her any longer.

Upon reaching the house, he opened the door, noticing a squeak in a hinge. He would have to oil that tomorrow.

Julia was not in the kitchen. Rod took the lamp from the window and carried it into the parlor. She sat in his chair in front of a fire that had sunk to embers. When he approached, he realized that her head lay against the wing of the chair. She had fallen asleep while she waited for him to come home.

His first reaction was relief that he wouldn't have to dash her hopes tonight. He set the lamp on the hearth and adjusted the guttering wick. Then he knelt before her, wondering if he should scoop her up and take her to bed or leave her in the chair for the night. She looked comfortable enough, but he needed her beside him to comfort his own soul.

He must have made a noise, perhaps cleared his throat unconsciously, because before he could rise and pick her up, she opened her eyes. Focus came slowly, but then her eyes sharpened with recognition.

"Rod?" She put out a hand and touched him lightly on the breast of his shirt. "Is Peter—"

Before she could ask, he shook his head and said, "No, I failed you, Julie. He'd already left before I got to Edinburg."

Her eyes softened, and he thought she would begin to weep, but she surprised him by saying quietly, "Such an impetuous boy. So like his pa."

He could only shake his head.

She continued. "You're wore out, husband. Did you eat? I saved you a plate of supper."

"I couldn't eat it this late, wife. I am bone-weary. Come. We need sleep."

Chapter 9

Rulon — June 27, 1861

Troopers from Company "I" had followed a Yankee patrol for an hour before they lost sight of the enemy and pulled up in a grassy meadow. An older member of the troop, Vernon Earl, was ordered to dismount and puzzle out the direction the patrol had taken. As Rulon awaited the command to move out, he dozed in the hot sun, gratified to catch a few moments of rest.

He started awake when someone slapped his leg and a gruff voice said, "Ho, Owen! You've slept long enough. Get down and lend the old man a fresh set of eyes."

His sergeant was the speaker, and Rulon hastened to swing off the horse, responding with a "Yes suh" that was half drawled and half garbled from drowsiness. He glanced around to find the man on whom they relied in such situations. Vernon Earl had learned his tracking skills over a lifetime of hunting game in the Blue Ridge Mountains. However, his sight had recently begun to give him trouble.

"Mind where you step!" the old man warned as Rulon approached. "Don't bend the grass."

Rulon stopped. What was he supposed to do for the man? He slapped at a whining mosquito, which put him in mind of an old bite now itchy. As he scratched it, Earl called to him.

"Tread there and there," he said, pointing with a grizzled forefinger. "Look down. Notice the hoof prints?"

Rulon took a step where the man had indicated, then glanced downward. He saw nothing resembling what Earl had mentioned. "No."

"Well, they ain't none. The horses didn't come this-a-way." He began to walk ahead at an angle, head down, and Rulon followed.

When he caught up, he asked, "What are you looking for?"

"Bent grass. Clumps of overturned sod. Horse apples." Earl chuckled. "If you ain't keerful, you'll find the horse apples first with your boots."

Rulon lifted a foot surreptitiously and peered at the bottom. It appeared damp from mashing down the grass where's he'd been stepping, but to his relief, it was not coated with horse dung. However, when he put his foot down again, he spotted a place where faint variations made him think perhaps the grass had been disturbed. When he took a step closer, he found sod scattered about in a regular pattern, on a line heading off towards a wooded area.

"Mr. Earl." Once he had the man's attention, Rulon pointed out the patch. "Is this what we seek?"

Earl knelt on one knee and examined the overturned sod. He stirred a clump with a finger to break it up, then bent over and smelled it. When he arose, he said, "That's it precisely, boy. You have a good eye."

Rulon felt a prickle of pride, but had no idea what the man had been about when he had worked with the clod of earth. He determined to discover the man's secrets by helping out at every opportunity and thereby learn the tracking skill.

ജ

Julia — July 10, 1861

After spending a long day spinning yarn, Julia sat down to write a letter to her eldest.

July 10 1861
Owen Farm
Dear son Rulon,
We are well here on the farm. Yor father is raising a Cavalry company that will leave soon to Defend us. Ben marched off with Allen's Infantry. Peter ran away with the horse we called Brownie to join a cavalry company raised in Edinburg. Ben so cottoned to that horse. He will be mortified if any harm comes to it.

I am sorry to tell you that Peter left without our Blessing and a proper Send Off. He always had a streak of the willful, as you well know from Celebratin your nuptials with that Colorful eye. I will say no more of Peter's escapade. He will learn Discipline in the Army, no dout.

We had an excitement a few days ago when a large meteor, as the scientific men told us, came down from the sky and exploded with a great noise and shower of light. Not knowing the origin of the heavenly display at first, we imagined that we were under a surprise Yankee bombardment, and of corse went down to the Cellar for safety. After an hour's wait and no more Shells sent, as we supposed, we emerged to find that no Federal Army had come upon us. When we later learned the True Origin of the great sound, we felt chagrined and foolish at our actions and the time wasted. However, we safely escaped the supposed attack, and count our reaction as a fine drill for an actual event of that sort.

You may imagine how little Julianna carried on with a nervous fit for quite a time, but I hardly blamed her, as I was equally frightened by the great sound and show of light.

I must tell you that your dear wife has high hopes that she will have happy news to relate to you soon. I am overjoied at the prospect.

Be firm and stedfast at all hazards, dear son, and uphold the Good Owen Name. Your father and I bear you a great affection.

Your mother
Julia Helm Owen

When she had finished the task, she went to give the letter to Rod so he could post it on his next visit to town.

"Husband, it pains me that you are going off to fight a young man's war," she said, as she settled into her chair before the fireplace.

"Don't give in to your nerves, Julie," he said. "You know I can't keep away from this scrap."

She made a scoffing noise. "You don't have to relish it so."

"Am I relishing war? Not so. My intent is to keep you and my young'uns safe, to the best of my powers."

She wanted to go over to Rod's chair, curl up in his lap, gain comfort from his touch, but those young'uns were seated around the room, and she could not bear to display to them so much of her need. She must make a strong show before them.

"I've written to Rulon," she said instead. "I told him about the Great Noise." She dangled the envelope from her hand. "I wonder if cannon fire is louder than that meteor."

Her husband looked over at her.

She read concern for her in his eyes. It ever was there, his steadfast devotion to his duty toward her. At other times the look added affection, and at special moments, frank ardor heated the mixture to an explosive glance that quickened her vitals. But for tonight, the gaze contained concern and duty.

"It has been many years since I've had experience of cannon fire." He took the envelope from her, letting his index finger rest upon the back of her hand. "I'll take this to town on Friday."

She nodded, releasing the paper. So few folk understood her man as she did. He had just told her he cherished her. It was her turn to relish something in her life, and this bit of byplay between them would do nicely.

"Ben, bring the Bible," Rod said. "Time for devotions." He looked toward Julia.

She noted that his glance now contained more than merely the concern it had held. The crickets had barely begun to chirp. She laid her hand over her heart and felt the increase in its speed. A weeknight? She smiled to herself, trying to get her mind focused on godly pursuits to end the day.

∞

Mary — July 12, 1861

Two months had passed since her wedding day, and Mary was at last satisfied that she was with child. The totality of the evidence was overwhelming. She was quite queasy. She couldn't stand many smells about the house, especially the odor of her own vomit. Her breasts remained tender and felt huge. A part of them had changed color, and the whiter areas were laced with dark blue veins. Her body felt ungainly and somehow different. Most convincing of all, she had not been visited by the women's curse.

Once she had gained enough equilibrium to go to work and ensconce herself in the storeroom, she pulled a piece of paper from a sheaf and prepared to write to her husband.

She sat for a long time, pen un-dipped in the ink, trying to decide how to break the news. Did she dare to write in plain language all that was happening to her? What if the letter fell into enemy hands? This letter wasn't going to be a state secret, but it was private between herself and Rulon, and precious to her. What if one of the soldiers in his company got his hands on it and read out the words? Did men in such close quarters tease each other in such a way? She had to suppose they might, judging from the observations she had made of Rulon's brothers.

What a perplexity. She wanted to share with Rulon the wonderment of the changes in her body, the puzzling moods that sent her into a spiral of emotions, the yearnings to hold the babe she now sheltered inside her body.

What if he didn't care? What if his war work was too much of a burden upon his mind and he had no time for dithering about her?

In the end, she took the safe road, and wrote him a short note.

12 July, 1861
Mnt Jackson, Shen. Cty, Via.
Dear Husband,
If you are able to come home this winter, you will notice changes in my person, as you will have a child after the turn of the year. I am as well as can be expected.
Mama is dificult. I reckon she gave no thot to being with child at her advanced age. She is past 30, after all. I hope she is breeding a boy, for it surely is her last chance.
I have no dout you left me a boy. Yor mama smiles and agrees.
Be safe, dear Rulon, I pray you. Hold this letter to yor heart and you will feel all the affection I put into it.
Yor own Mary

After she wrote and sealed it, she wished she had put in more of the feelings she was experiencing daily. Not the unhappy things like throwing up her food, but the more positive ones, like filling out her bodices more, and the euphoria of knowing she would bear him a child. No matter. It was a safe letter, and she hoped he would read between the lines to discover the full meaning of her words and sense her deep emotions.

&

Rulon — July 16, 1861

One night after a very exciting day on patrol and in camp, Rulon wrote to Mary.

16 July, 1861
In Camp at Berkeley Co. Va.
My dear Mary,
Our troop has been much engaged in traveling about the county, traping the Federal boys when they venture out from Martinsburg to hunt, which causes them to Hate us. Today we got word that J.E.B. Sturt is now Colonel of our regiment in fact, having receeved that comission of rank. I may have told you Harrisonburg Cavalry is assigned as Company I in 1st Regt. Va. Cavalry. This is a Large regimnt, haveing twelve Companys in all on this Date.

Col. Sturt insists on drills every Morning and Parade in ev'n. He also takes the Companys out himself to Patrol, which can be exciting when we come up amongst the enemy. Have no fears, Mary, as He has always brung us Through without incident. He does not permit Us to retreet, if on Foot, with our backs to the foe, but must March backwards to where we left the horses. If mounted, we may only trot away, for he says we are to reserve a Gallop for the Charge. The Col stirs every mans blood with his bravery.

Dear wife, I hope You find yorself well. I delited to lern in your last lett'r that you hope for the best. I had a note from Ma in which she said you now have further news for me. which I am anxious to receev. I assure you that I carry each of yor letters against my heart until I am handed the next one.

With fondest remembrance of your kind soul,
Yor husband,
Rulon S. Owen, trooper
1st Regt. Va. Cav., Co. I

After he had signed his name, he re-read what he had told his wife. Perhaps he should not have mentioned about Colonel Stuart taking them into the enemy lines, but the deed was done, and he didn't have time to re-do the letter.

He sealed the envelope and gave the flap a quick kiss, feeling foolish as he did it, but it comforted him that Mary's fingers would touch the spot. Perhaps she would bring the paper to her own lips before she opened the flap. Thinking that was almost as good as feeling her lips under his.

He gave in the letter to be posted, and trudged back to his lonely cot.

𝕏

Ella Ruth — July 19, 1861

Ella Ruth breezed into her father's office one afternoon, glanced at the three other men whose buzzing conversation resembled a dispute, shrugged her shoulders, and approached her father anyway.

"Poppa, you really must send for this," she said, waving a sheet of paper under his nose. When his look held a stormy aspect, she seated herself on his lap and put her arms around his neck. "Please, Poppa? If you put in the order now, I will have it back from Paris before it goes out of style."

She watched as her father's neck and face went from the normal pink color to a glowing scarlet. Perhaps she should not have interrupted his little meeting, she mused. Business was, to him, important, but she was also important, was she not? Did not he enjoy pampering her as much as her heart desired? What a pity Ben would not do so.

"Daughter!"

To her surprise, the word exploded from her father's lips, and he put her off his lap with firm hands.

"I am engaged, as you can see," he added, his voice elevated and angry. "We are not to be disturbed!" He gave her a little shove back toward the doorway.

Under the impetus of his push, Ella Ruth stumbled out of the room, chagrined and confused. Poppa had never treated her in such a manner before. True, she had burst into his meeting, but he always had delighted in giving her whatever she had asked. Why was his behavior so odd today?

She decided to listen to the conversation spilling quite clearly through the still-open door. The loudest voice went on and on about "nothing ventured," while another voice agreed with every point. Her father and the third man countered with "risky" and "ships boarded," and "cotton prices."

After several minutes, her head began to hurt because the argumentative exchanges held no meaning for her. However, they seemed to hold significant meaning for Poppa, and they had turned his outlook sour. Perhaps it was in her best interest to pay better attention to his concerns. She must make a beginning another time, when her head had ceased pounding.

Was all of the nonsense because of this war Ben had insisted was going to change everything? Something had certainly changed Poppa.

She went up the stairs to her room to rest. That surely must cure her headache. She sighed as she opened the door. She missed Ben. Her plan had been to convince Poppa that her ultimate happiness depended upon becoming Ben's bride in a magnificent ceremony this September, which would have entertained her with a great many delightful activities this summer. Now she had nothing to do with her time.

She sat at her dressing table and stared at her reddened face in the mirror. She no longer envisioned a blissful summer of shopping and parties, a splendid wedding with many attendants, and a bright future as Ben's wife. Ben had left her flat, going off to take target practice against the Yankees. She sighed and tested her forehead with the back of her hand. Had she a fever? No. Evidently not, notwithstanding her flushed cheeks. She touched her lips. How she missed Ben's kisses. A chill raced down her spine. Why had he gone in such haste, without even coming around to say goodbye?

Upon several moments of reflection, she considered that in all fairness to Ben, she *had* treated him with a teensy bit of disdain at their final meeting behind the mill, when he had offered her his name, his hand, his heart. In that moment, those had not been enough. She had thought she needed the pomp, the dress, the flowers, the crowd of friends to admire her good fortune and her conquest. Her heart lurched, leaving a tightness in her chest.

She leaned her elbows on the table. What would Momma say about leaning on them? No matter. She didn't care if they became rough and red. She cupped her cheeks in her palms. The longer she stared at herself, the more desolate she felt as she realized she had been wrong. Of what worth to her was the lacy dress hanging in her armoire when she had lost the man she loved?

She thought back to how Poppa's recent rejection had made her feel: confused, chagrined, put out, unappreciated, even unloved. Her cheeks grew hot beneath her fingertips as shame overwhelmed her. She had rejected Ben's offer because it didn't come with the elaborate trappings she had always dreamed of. She had rejected *him*. How must he feel?

She knew now. Confused. Unappreciated. Unloved. She had wronged him. She had broken his heart.

Oh, Ben.

Ella Ruth put her head down on her crossed arms and sobbed.

Chapter 10

Rulon — July 21, 1861

Orders had come down from General Johnston's headquarters to keep eyes on the enemy army led by General Patterson that had invaded the Valley. For the last few days, Rulon's company had been engaged in riding in countermoves against the Federal troops.

Near Winchester, a patrol became a skirmish when four members of Company "I" encountered enemy soldiers willing to fight. After dashing at each other a few times with no significant injury on either side, the Federal patrol withdrew and must have come across an artillery battery as they retreated. Soon after, the foursome from the Harrisonburg Cavalry found themselves targets of a Yankee bombardment.

Rulon hunkered down in a ditch alongside Owen Leoyd while artillery shells explored the air above them.

Leoyd said, "Them shells always whistle that-a-way when they miss you. If you don't hear 'em, they're gonna get you, so bless the noise of 'em."

"Obliged for the advice," Rulon replied, covering his head at the sound of a particularly close whistle.

"We'd best leave here," Leoyd commented. "That was a mite too near for my taste. Can't you get rid of that feather?"

Rulon grunted. He'd grown fond of the embellishment on his hat, especially since their colonel sported one so like Rulon's on his own headgear. How long was his plume going to be a source of merriment and ridicule for the fellows in the company?

He didn't have time to dwell for long on the good-natured abuse he'd received. During a brief lull in the fire, he and Leoyd beat a retreat to their horses, and found the rest of their comrades to continue the patrol.

When they returned to their bivouac, Ren Lovell announced that the company was to make all haste to Manassas Gap to cross the Blue Ridge. "General Beauregard is in a bad way. McDowell is on the move, and he's got a right smart lot of soldiers with him. We're ordered to battle, boys."

After that, the company rode toward the fray through fields alongside the infantry-clogged road.

"Pull down that fence, Owen," Ren called out. Both Rulon and Owen Leoyd dismounted, cast a wry glance at one another, and took the rails down so the company could advance. Dodging sleeping infantrymen in the way, crossing ditches, and riding over uneven ground ate up the miles, but sapped their strength, as well. Rulon tried to keep behind Von, as the man's ugly temper had simmered over into vile curses at nightfall when he realized that the baggage train with rations had not kept pace with the cavalry.

Finally, after thirty-six brutal hours in the saddle, the men of the regiment dismounted alongside the Bull Run.

"Line up for rations," a fellow called out, and Rulon stumbled over to do so. Head pounding from the dust and confusion, he procured the raw makings of his meal and found a fire on which he hoped to make it palatable. After he ate, he found a spot of grass, lay upon it, touched the handkerchief Mary had given him to his lips, and fell immediately into stupor.

About daylight, he awoke to the sound of musketry and bugles, and rushed to follow the order to saddle his horse. Then he washed the sleep out of his eyes, watered and fed the horse, and ate a hasty breakfast.

Captain Yancey ordered the company into line alongside the others, and Rulon sat his horse as Col. Stuart and a small detachment crossed the Run on a scout. After a while, they returned, and Rulon watched a trooper ride toward General Johnston's headquarters. He figured the man would report the findings of the scouting party.

The day grew hot as the din of battle increased on their left. They had received no orders, so they sat on the earth in the sun beside their horses, listening to the wood-shrouded struggles around them, and dodging wayward artillery shells.

"Ah!" cried a man from the Howard County company, as a shell burst in their column. The horses scattered, riders futilely pulling on their reins and swearing profusely.

Marsha Ward

"Anyone hurt?" called their captain. By some lucky happenstance, neither men nor horses were injured.

One time, they were allowed to seek water for their horses. Soon, however, they formed back into company lines, but waited in vain for any action. He could see the restlessness of their colonel. After the noon, he began to send messengers off, and Rulon turned to Ren.

"Where are they goin'?"

"Humph. If it was me, I'd be sending word to the generals that we're a-sitting over here with our thumbs up our butts and nothing to do."

Rulon hadn't heard such coarse talk from Ren before, and figured he had as bad a case of nerves as any other man around.

"We have to wait, then?"

"I reckon so. We're the pawns in this chess game, Owen. We do what we're told."

Rulon eyed the man. "We're not the knights?"

"Mayhap we are. We still have to await the hand of the general to move."

Garth Von growled an excited curse, then added as he pointed a finger, "He's staff, ain't he?"

Rulon turned to see a mounted officer coming from the woods at the gallop. At the sight, he got to his feet and looked to his horse, hoping the officer brought orders.

Evidently he did, as he saluted Col. Stuart smartly and gave him a message.

"Boots and saddles," Ren said as the bugle sounded. "We're in action at last."

Rulon had never seen such chaos, nor before felt such a rush of energy as he experienced several times over the remainder of that day. Although worn out from the long ride out of the Valley through the pass, the cavalry companies nevertheless feinted and parried with Federal forces the rest of the day, capturing some here, some there, breaking away when necessary, but mostly pressing forward, as was Colonel Stuart's wont.

General Early's brigade came up and Stuart sent the general a message. Early's soldiers waded into the battle with courage and speed. Then Rulon's company dashed into another skirmish. Upon returning with prisoners, he noticed that a sixteen-gun artillery battery commanded by Lieutenant Beckham had become attached to their flank. After each cannonade from the guns he worried for his hearing, but the fire was most welcome, as the shelling drove the Federal troops into cover and prevented them turning the left flank.

They were on the move again once the company had secured the prisoners. As they rode around a house, Col. Stuart sent another messenger. Beckham's guns then opened fire upon a Federal regiment drawn up in front of a wood, and the enemy began to retreat. Troops from Early's brigade took over the chase while Beckham's guns continued the cannon fire, but when the enemy moved out of range, the battery fell silent. Rulon only had time to attempt to shake the ringing sound from his ears when his company moved on the chase once more, with Beckham's battery following.

Rulon and two others soon dropped out from following the Federal flight when they were detailed to the rear accompanying a squad of captives. He learned over the campfire that night that the very last of Stuart's chasers followed McDowell's army a full twelve miles.

He said to Ren Lovell, "The Colonel surely does cotton to the chase," to which Lovell replied with hoots of laughter.

"They name Jeb Stuart 'the dashing cavalier' in some parts," he said when he could talk. "He does love the chase, and all that it brings."

"Glory?"

"Yes."

"Honor?"

"Of course."

"The attention of the fairer sex?"

"Not as much as you'd think. To some degree, though."

"Is he a married man?"

"Yes, and reputed to be happy in his union."

"Good for him." Rulon thought of his little wife, of the privations of the day's campaign, and of the relief he now felt at being safely delivered from any harm he could have met on the field of battle. He needed to write to Mary again soon to let her know he was hale and hearty.

ॐ

Rulon — July 22, 1861

Rulon's first opportunity to write home after the battle came the next day in camp, when he snatched a moment to pen a letter.

22 Jul 1861
Fairfax C-H, Va.
Dear Wife,
I rite in haste to inform you of my good health following the rout of the Federals at Manassas junction. We are all well in the Company except for one poor fellow who met His Maker upon the field of honor, and another who suffer'd two wounds. Now we have moved forward to picket posts at Fairfax court-house Upon our journey here we come upon much salvagable goods that will stand us in Good sted. We feast'd upon Yankee provisions, and I tell you, wife, it is good to have a full belly again.

I picked up a picnick-basket droped by some fair Yankee ladie come to watch us Confederates get our come-uppance. Instead, we sent the Federal boys flying back to Washington City, making as quick a retreat over the same ground as it took them two or three days to advance. Mr. Lovell and I enjoied the ham sandwiches therein, after which I gave the basket to a farmwife. She was happy to receive the striped tablecloth and napkins, along with silver tableware. We don't have a use for those fancies in the cavalry.

Our Colonel Sturt covered himself with glory in the late campaign. The men of a few companies feel he works them too hard, but I'm glad of his spirit and daring. I have lerned a good deal from his example.

Mr. Earl, the old tracker, tells me I have sum talent in the skill. I continu to lern what he teaches me. He says I may soon track for a patrol on my own. I reckon his prais gives me prideful feelins but I trust not to exces. I want yor pa's hat to fit my head when this war is won.

Mary, I look forward to coming home to you soon, sinse the Federal Yankees know we are fighting men and will keep our country.

Until that happy Day,
Yor husband, who holds you most dear,
Rulon S. Owen

When he had given in the envelope to be dispatched at the next opportunity, Rulon wondered when mail from home would catch up with them. Surely by this time, Mary had discovered if she was with child or not. He yearned to know if it were true. He hoped she was carrying his babe. If he should be taken by a shell or a musket ball, a child would be a comfort to Mary, and to Ma and Pa, as well. He whispered a silent prayer that he would not be taken from her, and went to curry his horse.

℘

Ella Ruth — July 22, 1861

Ella Ruth regretted her sporadic fits of crying over the last two days. All the thinking and the tears had given her a tremendous headache. Even so, excitement bubbled in her stomach. In an effort to cheer her up, Poppa was taking her with him to Harrisonburg. She planned to shop to her heart's content.

The day began too early for her taste, but Poppa insisted on an early start to avoid the likelihood of meeting with enemy troops on the move. The Yankees were said to be tucked in safely down the Valley in Martinsburg, unlikely to come up to battle against the steadfast Virginians holding the line, but Poppa seemed cautious lately.

She climbed into the buggy with his assistance. "It is mighty kind of you to include me in your trip, Poppa," she said with a smile as she settled into the seat and adjusted her hat and veil. She turned to look at the servant getting on a horse behind the buggy. "Will Thomas be able to keep up with your prize team?"

"He rides well enough." He lifted the lines and clicked his tongue at the horses. Once they were on their way, he said, "I will not be able to accompany you for shopping, but Thomas will be with you to carry all your baubles."

"Poppa! I will be just fine alone. I do not plan to buy more than five or six 'baubles,' as you put it. I must have a new hat, however. This old veil is too thin for the sun."

"You won't go unaccompanied, daughter. I cannot allow you

that liberty."

"Pish and tush." She looked again at the old black-skinned man following them. "He does seem to know how to ride. If you insist on him coming along, I suppose I shall endure it."

"Thomas is reliable, Ella. You will treat him well."

"Of course I will, Poppa! To hear you speak, one would think I was heartless."

He glanced over at her, but said nothing.

"I'm not heartless. I treat everybody well."

"Then what of your tears the past days?"

Ella Ruth sniffed. He knew she had been crying over her lost love affair. "You should have permitted me to marry Benjamin. If you had been agreeable, I would not have rejected him when he surprised me, when he told me out of the blue that we had to marry right away, without any friends around us. I was caught off guard, and yes, I did treat him badly. I'm sorry I did."

"You've had the household in quite an uproar, daughter."

"I miss Ben. I was wrong to turn him down so precipitously." She turned away. "Don't make me think about it now. I am on the point of crying again."

After the day-long drive, Poppa got them situated at the finest hotel the city offered, although it seemed to be teeming with people. As a result, she was obliged to sleep on a cot in the same room with Poppa, and Thomas was sent off to take a spot in the stable. How scandalous to share quarters with her father at her age!

During the evening she kept to the room reading a lady's fashion magazine while Poppa met with a business partner. Growing restless, she went to the window, lifted aside the drapes, and peered out. A group of men carrying torches had gathered opposite the hotel, and she shivered at the ominous looks on their faces. What had occurred to give them such long jaws?

After a while spent gazing at the men, she was no more enlightened on the matter, and let the drapery fall closed. She picked up her magazine once again and tried to find the most delightful items with which to make a shopping list.

However, she could not concentrate on that simple task. She had been so thrilled to accompany Poppa on this excursion to town, but now disturbing thoughts of Ben intruded. Where was he these days? Was he well? She supposed he was somewhere down the Valley, guarding the river against a Yankee invasion. She hoped he was getting enough to eat. How the man liked to eat!

She put down the magazine, unable to keep to her task. Poppa seemed to be worried these days. Did he entertain thoughts that Mr. Lincoln's army would come up the Valley and wreak havoc upon his business? Everyone prattled on about how the Yankees would try to overrun Virginia, but with men the likes of Ben on duty, she was sure that could never happen.

He always talked about how much he loved his native land, Virginia. Surely no one would stand stronger against the enemy threat. Her stalwart Ben! How hard he had worked at the mill, throwing about those bags of grain like a common laborer. She adored how his muscled arms were built like iron. How could a girl have any fears when Ben guarded the border, protecting her?

A chill disturbed her reverie and she wrapped her arms around herself. She could not help remembering the look on his face before she had whirled in anger and left the yard behind the mill on that horrible day. She felt as though a leaden casing wrapped around her heart. Ben wasn't standing guard for her. She had ruined their bond with her foolish pride and fancy dreams.

Perhaps it was just as well when Poppa came into the room, his face a thundercloud.

He said right away, "I'm sorry to spoil your outing. We leave before the crack of dawn to return home."

"But Poppa—"

"Not a word, Ella Ruth. There's been a battle. The war has come into Virginia."

She inhaled sharply. Ben!

"There, there," he said, softening his countenance as he approached. "We're not in immediate danger. We'll arrive home in time if we leave early enough."

"Poppa, I'm afraid." She heard how thin her voice sounded, and it frightened her still more.

He put his arms around her and she nestled into them. Poppa wasn't as strong as Ben, but he would do, for now.

ಬಿ

Ella Ruth — July 23, 1861

The journey home began even earlier in the day than had the one to Harrisonburg. The buggy moved through a ghostly mist that swirled as high as the tops of the wheels and obscured Ella Ruth's sight of the hills and gaps that she knew lay out there in the semi-darkness.

She sighed. Mist nearly always made her feel giddy, a bit excited, especially if she were on her way to meet Benjamin. But such was not the case today. *Today,* she thought, *today is not the same.* Today the mist caused her an unfamiliar sense of unease, a chilling sensation that all was not well, that the mist was not friendly, would not hide her escape from the house to meet Ben.

Ben. Perhaps she would never, ever see him again. That was entirely her own fault. She might never see Ben because— She drew a quick breath.

Please don't let Poppa hear me if I cry, she thought, struggling against the emotion sweeping through her body. Grief, hard as granite and bitter as quinine, ripped at her insides, tearing open a hole in her heart that only Ben could fill. She had nothing upon which to lay the blame but her own stiff pride.

Only that stubborn pride would get her through this moment, mask the trouble in her soul from Poppa, keep her alive in the unfulfilling future she saw stretching before her, endless and sterile. A future without Ben.

"You're quiet this morning." Poppa's voice broke into her solitary thoughts. "Disappointed not to spend my money on a new bonnet?"

She shook her head. "I suppose I'm tired," she answered, knowing it to be partly true. Her brain and bones and sinews reeked of tiredness. Was she disappointed that her shopping party had been terminated so abruptly? No. Not really. Her overwhelming pain stemmed from the grief, and yes, anxiety, on top of it all.

Poppa had mentioned a battle. Ben had gone for a soldier. Had he been involved? Was he wounded? Had he been . . . She couldn't even bear to think of the word. Ben, so alive, so vital.

She shifted on the seat cushion. He would not be dead. She

would not entertain the notion. She glanced sideways at her father. Perhaps engaging in conversation would rid her of this pall.

"You're a mite quiet yourself," she said, struggling to put a tease into the words.

Poppa looked over at her. "I have a few things on my mind," he said. "I don't fancy ruination, daughter."

Ella Ruth did not answer. Poppa seemed too preoccupied to pay mind to her. So be it. She would be silent and endure the ride home as best she could.

When the sun finally lifted above Massanutten Mountain, the mist began to burn away, revealing first the treetops, then more foliage, then entire trees, glistening with dew, green and tall and comforting, and at last, the pike.

They were alone on the Valley Pike, she and Poppa. The wheels chattered slightly on the rock surface. The clip-clop of hooves behind them reminded her that one other person accompanied them. Thomas. She wondered if he was annoyed at Poppa's early start for a second day in a row. He was growing older, with grizzled white patches on his head where there had always been black kinks before. Older folks sometimes complained of rheumatism and such. No matter. It was his duty to obey Poppa's directions, even if they were tiresome at times. Like this morning.

Presently, another vehicle approached, coming toward them in some haste. Poppa moved the horse from the center of the road to allow the wagon van to pass their buggy. The wagon had canvas sides, rolled down and tied, and several dark, blotchy stains on the material caught her eyes, but not before the appalling sounds of moans came to her ears. Hideous, terrible moans.

"Poppa, what is th—"

"Cover your ears!"

Her hands flew up to do so. What was causing that noise?

"Ambulance wagon," he muttered as the din faded in the distance. "Do not look next time," he added.

Those blotches on the sidewalls. Her heart shrank. Blood. Of course they were blood. An ambulance carried wounded men to the hospital. Were they going all the way to Staunton? She looked back, unable to restrain herself. How many of the wounded would be alive when they arrived?

Was Ben among those poor boys in the wagon?

She asked herself the same question each time they passed another ambulance, until the flood of them moving south up the pike had her sobbing, biting her veil to bits with the anxiety of not knowing the answer.

Chapter 11

Rod — July 31, 1861

Captain Roderick Owen of the Owen Dragoons mounted his mare, spur jingling as he swung his leg over and found the stirrup, feeling slightly chagrined that he was getting into the action so late. He figured all that was left was a clean-up, or some kind of defensive movement to enforce upon the Yankees the notion that everything was over but the shouting.

Julia came over and leaned against Rod's leg. "You come back safe, husband," she murmured in a voice stripped of emotion, as though she had spent it all. "We have that grandchild a-comin'."

"That will be a joyous day." He rubbed the thigh of his other leg.

"Peter?"

He barely heard her thin voice above the pounding in his chest.

"I'll see about finding the boy after I join the regiment," he said, putting his hand on the side of her head, lightly, briefly. "If I can locate him, I'll send him home."

"They won't shoot him for desertion?"

"Nah, not that. I'll do it proper, get him discharged for being underage."

"Will they do that? Send him home?"

"I reckon. The government didn't make a call for young'uns." He cleared his throat. "I don't see this to-do extendin' for much longer, but he may yet have a chance to join in."

"No." Julia's voice found an emotion at last as she wailed the word. "Rulon and Ben are enough to send," she finished, head down, pressed tight against Rod's trouser leg. "And now, you."

"Julie," he began, but couldn't find any words to comfort her. Finally, he drew on the ancient faith. "Put the future in the Good Lord's hands, woman. He will see us through."

She let him loose and backed up, firming her shoulders.

"Indeed," she said, with one last sniff, and made a "get along with you" gesture.

Rod rode down the lane without looking back, knowing if he did, he likely wouldn't leave his wife and home. But the pull of war was strong, and he gave in to it, even knowing what he knew of conflict, and blood, and the rancid taste of conquest.

⁊

Rulon — July 31, 1861

Rulon sat his horse in a driving rainstorm, grateful for the Federal overcoat he had acquired after the late battle. A biting wind added misery to the wet weather. Staring across the Potomac River, he could see the fortifications of the enemy capital. Soldiers drilled in the rain on a parade ground off to the left. Around the city, flag snapped so smartly on their poles he imagined he could hear them. Vidette duty often sent him within close proximity to the Yankees. In fair weather, he enjoyed acting as a sentinel for his country. This foul weather made the long hours of observation more challenging.

The wind shifted, and he adjusted his hat and collar to deflect the water attacking from a different angle. The skin of his neck seemed warm to the touch, even with the rain cooling the air. He shrugged off the notion that he might be taking sick. He didn't have time for that nonsense.

"Owen, we're moving back," said Owen Leoyd.

Rulon reined the horse around to follow the other man, and experienced a momentary dizziness. It wasn't enough to unseat him, but did give him another fleeting thought about taking ill. He shook it off as before. Too many of his comrades were sick. He couldn't let down the company and the regiment by joining them.

Leoyd led the way to a thicket about a mile away. There the two men dismounted and sheltered as best they could as the storm beat its fury upon them.

After a while, Rulon noticed himself shaking. He hunched into the greatcoat, putting his hands up the opposing sleeves so he could rub his arms inside the wool, and then chafed his hands together. When his teeth began to chatter, he began to feel concern.

"You ailin', Owen? Don't you make me sick or nothin'," Leoyd said. He had mentioned repeatedly how much he enjoyed using Rulon's last name as much as possible as sort of a joke, seeing as how it was his own first name. He didn't seem like he was joking now, though, as he added, "I don't cotton to taking a fever from you."

"It's the cold wind," Rulon replied. Several of the men in the regiment had been so sick they'd been discharged and sent home, and a few had even died. Rulon did not intend to be among either group.

At last the wind died down.

"We should keep our eyes peeled for the relief vidette," Leoyd said. He squinted into the rain. "They should be along before sundown." He chuckled wryly. "It's not dark yet, is it? Hard to tell with all this bad weather."

Rulon shook his head. "I reckon it's early yet. Shouldn't we take another look across the river?" He could barely get the words out for the tremor in his jaw that made his teeth click together.

"Nope. The Yankees are still over there, all right. I don't figure they're going to be doin' any marchin' in this rain."

"I s-suppose you're r-r-r-right," Rulon stammered.

Leoyd squinted in his direction. "You better git seen by the doc when we git to camp. I don't like the look of you."

"You n-n-never did."

"Well, yeah, but you look kinda mealy-mouth an' green just now."

"I'm fine. N-n-never b-b-better."

"Don't lie to me, Owen."

"Leoyd?" A low voice called from behind them.

"Over here," he answered. "'Bout time you boys showed up."

After a few verbal jabs back and forth, the new vidette took over the watch, and Rulon and Owen Leoyd made their way to their mounts and started back to camp.

"Doctor," Leoyd muttered after a few miles.

"If I don't f-feel better t-t-tomorrow, I'll c-c-consider your adv-v-vice."

❧

Rulon — August 1, 1861

Even with his heavy wool coat pulled up over his blanket,

Rulon shivered all night and awoke feeling like he'd been stomped underneath a herd of stampeding mules. His face ached, his shoulders ached, and he knew the signs of a galloping fever when he felt them.

Someone in the tent was tending the stove, from the sounds of a chunk of wood settling into the ashes, but the heat might as well be going up the chimney, for all he felt of it.

"You've had a chill all night," Ren said quietly. "I recommend you get over to the hospital. I'll cover for you at roll call."

"I'm f-f-fine," Rulon protested, opening his eyes to find Ren staring down at him.

"I can't make you go," Ren replied, "but we're better off if you go be sick with the other fellows instead of staying here with us." He rubbed lather onto his face. "No offense meant."

"None t-t-taken. Do I appear to be sick?"

Ren quirked an eyebrow. "I'd say yes. No spots on you, but I'm not a medical man. Let the doc look at you."

Rulon got up and dressed as quickly as he could. "Still rainin'?" he asked, looking at his still-soggy hat.

"Not so much as yesterday. If you need help, I'm almost finished shavin'."

"I'll make it, thank you kindly."

When he arrived at the hospital tent, an orderly had him wait for almost an hour before the doctor appeared to ask, "Symptoms?"

"Ch-ch-chills, f-fever, aches. P-pain in my j-jaw now."

"You had that stammer all your life?"

"Sh-showed up yesterday with the ch-chills."

"Hmm. Any spots?"

"Haven't looked."

"You a drinking man?"

"On s-special occasions, yes."

The doctor got a bottle and tumbler, filled the glass half full of amber liquid, and thrust it into Rulon's hand. "This is a special occasion. Drink it down. If it doesn't help or you get further symptoms, come back tomorrow or the next day."

Rulon looked at the doctor, then at the tumbler, then did as directed, got up, and went back toward his tent, his gullet burning, but his body warmer.

Ben — August 2, 1861

When Ben's company had gone into camp following the battle of Manassas, he was persuaded that he ought to write home, and hunted up a pencil and paper to accomplish the task.

Dear Ma,

I reckon you will be pleased to heer that Me and the other fellows in the Company hav been fending off the foe as admirably as we can. Our Company is called "G" in the 33rd Regiment of Virginia Volunteers of Infantry. We are, as I had supposed, fightin in the Brigade of "Old Jack". We Took part in the big Battle at Manassas junction after we rode the rail cars over hill and thru vale. I tell you, it was mighty fierce sittin atop them cars and feelin the wind pushin aganst us so hard it like to blow us away before we got to the station at M. We lost a few boys in the fight. I will mention, not to worry you, but to inform, as there is naught to worry you in the tale, that I receev'd a slight injury to my limb from a ball hitting upon a drummer boy and coming through him to smite me. I'm O.K. The Surgeon took out the ball and gave me a piece of cotton Lint to press on the scrape, and I'm right as rain now. I can't say the same for the unfortunate drummer boy.

The sting of the gunpowder smoke gettin in our eyes and up into our noses and choking our breth was the worst part of the battle. That, and the bellowing of the Yankees long guns as they spoke out real sharp and threw their shells acrost the fields and into our lines. When we could no longer bear to receev the shells in our ranks, we broke over the crest of the rise called the Henry House Hill and battled our weigh to the long guns to silents them. When the task was done and the shelling ceased, I wondered woud I ever hear right again.

"Old Jack" has a new name, giv'n him by a General what was shot dead soon after he spoke it out. The story goes this general Bee saw our troops drawn up Firm upon the ridgeline and said somethin like "There stands Jackson like A stone Wall," and he's been called Stone Wall Jackson ever since. He don't much like it, as I hear.

Give my affection to Pa and the young'uns, and accept my kiss upon your brow in grateful thanks for all you done for me thruout my years. I hope you have good news from Rulon and that he is well. Tell the rascal Peter to stop hounding you to go to war. There's plenty of fightin to go around, but I hope his time don't come soon to protect his native country. We bigger boys are risin to the task.

Your faithful son Benj'n

Chapter 12

Rulon — August 4, 1861

By Sunday, Rulon knew he was in trouble. With no appetite, he had grown weak over the last few days, and yesterday he had fallen from his horse. This morning he awoke with a swollen jaw and a tingling near his ear. Although he ached from the fall, he hadn't landed on his head, so the swelling puzzled him.

He sat on the edge of his cot, hand to his ear, dizzy and faint.

"Owen, what's wrong with your face?" Ren squatted down to get a better view.

"Swollen jaw."

"Hmm." Ren got up and backed away. "Mumps! You've got mumps."

"No."

"Yes. Get out of here."

"I reckon you're right," Rulon admitted. He pushed himself off the cot, caught his balance, and pulled on his trousers. Ren threw him his overcoat, and Rulon picked up his hat. As he shuffled toward the flap of the tent, Ren called to him.

"Wait. This came yesterday." He picked up an envelope from his camp desk and held it out. "From your wife, I imagine."

Rulon reached over to get the letter, and thrust it into his pocket. All the movement made his head swim, and he stopped for a moment to get over the feeling.

"Need help getting to the hospital?"

"I'm fine," Rulon said, his voice so weak he barely recognized it. He turned cautiously, lifted the flap, and stepped into a chilly wind.

&

Mary — August 5, 1861

Mary looked up from the list she was filling for Mrs. Bingham to see Miss Ella Ruth Allen hovering around the dry goods. She cast a furtive glance toward Mary.

When Mary had finished with the baker's wife, she noticed that the girl was looking her way again, but another customer claimed her attention, and she forgot about her for a time.

Sighing when she had finished filling the order, Mary straightened her shoulders and looked around the store. Ella Ruth was still in the same spot, fingering cloth and glancing her way every three seconds.

"May I assist you?" Mary called.

Ella Ruth took a tentative step in Mary's direction. She picked up speed, and was practically running when she reached the counter. She inclined her head as though the motion accompanied a curtsy, and said, "I am Ella Ruth Allen. Perhaps Benjamin has spoken of me?"

"Mary Owen, at your service. What may I get for you, Miss Allen?"

"Oh, you do not understand. I am not here to purchase anything. I only want—" She turned her head away sharply, sniffed, then collected herself. "I wish to know if you have heard from Benjamin."

"Benjamin?"

"Benjamin Owen. You know who he is. Your husband's brother?"

Now the situation came clear. This was the girl whom Brother Ben loved. Rulon had spoken of his sibling's difficulties with obtaining permission to marry the girl. Mostly as a contrast to his own happiness. Mostly between their bouts of intimacy. Mary felt herself grow warm. She wondered if her face was glowing.

"I cannot think why Brother Ben would communicate with me," she said, dodging the girl's searching gaze. "Have you not heard from him?" She knew her words would sound cruel, so she had softened her tone as much as she could to deflect any implied criticism. "Perhaps he is not in a place where he can write."

Mary watched in fascination as the girl's face seemed to crumple into what looked like a dried-apple doll's face.

"I, I, I would not marry him," she said, her voice breaking. "I was too full of pride. Now he is gone, and it is too late. I am so sorry. Tell him I am sorry."

"Brother Ben will not write to me," Mary repeated. "There is no cause for him to do so. If he has been able to write home, Mother Owen will have his address. You must petition her for that." Mary reached across the counter and patted Ella Ruth's hand where it gripped the edge of the counter. "I cannot help you, although I wish I could."

Her own happiness felt like a betrayal of this grieving girl, but that was nonsense. She barely knew her, and what she did knew of her selfish nature boded ill for any future with Ben. He had taken the rejection of his offer of marriage very hard, and had gone away with the taste of bitter ashes in his mouth.

Ella Ruth grabbed Mary by the wrist. "I cannot approach the woman. You must ask her for me. Please." She finally seemed to notice that she was detaining Mary, and released her arm.

The gasping way in which the Allen girl said the word "please" told Mary what a price she was paying in asking the favor. She was used to getting everything her own way in life. She had spurned Brother Ben. Perhaps she should pay for her foolishness a while longer.

But Mary knew she couldn't poison her babe by harboring rancor. She cupped her swelling stomach behind the cover of the counter, and nodded her assent. "I will ask Mother Owen for news the next time I see her. If she has any, I will pass it along to you."

How desperate was the countenance of the contrite girl! Mary almost felt sympathy for her plight, but not quite yet. Ella Ruth must prove her worth by coming to fetch any tidbit of information Mary might glean.

"Be here in a fortnight. I will give you any information I possess," she said, and tried softening her demand with a smile.

"Thank you." The girl pressed Mary's hand between hers. "Thank you," she said again, this time in a whisper.

As the girl left the store, Mary wondered if she would actually come through the door again.

Rulon — August 6, 1861

After two days in the hospital tent, and several draughts a day of quinine mixed in water, Rulon still hadn't shaken off the chills and fever. His jaw ached, and now his ear was beginning to ring as though a troop of spur-jingling cavalry kept passing through his head. Worse still, he hadn't mustered the strength to read Mary's letter.

Feeling like a mewling new-born calf, Rulon struggled to sit up, determined that he would open the envelope at the very least. Once that was accomplished, perhaps it would be easier to read out the words she'd sent him.

When he had worked the flap loose, he saw that the letter was three weeks old, dated on the 12th of July. The first line told him Mary had confirmed her hopes that she was carrying his child. Joy surged through him, momentarily giving him the strength to sit longer and finish the letter. Further down the page, his heart lurched with additional gladness as he read that she was sure the child would be a boy. How could she know that, he wondered? He supposed her assurance came because he had so strongly and repeatedly expressed his wish for a son. She believed it because he wanted it. Dear sweet Mary.

Exhausted from the effort of reading the letter, Rulon lay back on his cot, his eyes wet from emotion. Yes, he had said he wanted a son. He didn't know much about young'uns and how they formed in the mother's womb, but he imagined the outcome was fixed by now.

A young'un. A child. He was going to be a father. He sucked in a long breath. He hadn't been much interested, as his brothers and sisters came along, in the months of progress toward what women called "the happy event." His happy event. Would this fussing and fighting be over in time for him to be there when Mary brought forth his son?

He thought about Mary. What was she going through? What would she endure when the time came to birth his child? He'd never wanted to know about the birthing part of the child-bearing process.

Would she suffer during her travail? The word itself brought to mind adversity. Burdensome toil. Pain. He shuddered to think about what women must suffer in delivering the young of mankind. Ah, Mary. She was such a little thing. She surely would be inconvenienced by giving birth. Might she die?

But Ma hadn't— He cringed. His mind would not even go toward relating the totality of such events with his mother. She was Ma! She never even—

After a long moment of the blankness of avoidance, he had to admit that she and Pa must have done some measure of . . . getting together, else they would not now have their sons and daughters.

He wiped his feverish face. He must be hallucinating to be thinking of carnal knowledge in the same context as his parents. But no. He was lucid. This was real. He held Mary's letter here in his hand, and he returned to worrying about her in the coming travail. It was true Ma had not died in birthing ten children, but he had heard her mutter something daunting about "the valley of the shadow of death" before Julianna put in her appearance.

He would have to redouble his prayers, make a greater effort to live a stalwart life in order that God would bless Mary in her hours of pain and labor and giving birth.

When she had successfully come through that time, he was going to be a father.

What kind of father would he be? Strong and autocratic, like his own? Of a willy-nilly persuasion who sought the fashion of the moment, like a man he knew in New Market? Stern, but fair to his children? What if this young'un was a daughter, instead of a son? Could he be kind, but firm, to keep her safe from predators? Predatory males, like, like, himself?

He thought long and hard about the concept that the coming child could be a tender daughter who needed a father on hand to protect and cherish her. He had to make it through this illness, this war against the Yankees. Son or daughter, it really didn't matter now. Sometime early next year, he needed to be home to welcome the new little one into his heart and home.

"God, let me live to see my child," he whispered. "Don't let me die in camp because of the mumps." Annoyingly, his eyes leaked as he said the words, and he had to wipe them furtively.

He didn't know if mumps was a fatal disease. The doctor had said it was usually one of the ailments a child went through, but hadn't added whether or not children died from it, like they often did with the measles, which thankfully, he'd survived. How he'd avoided contracting this mumps illness up to now was a mystery to him.

The doctor had mentioned one other thing, and Rulon thought on it now, wondering if he should include a special appeal to God about it in his improvised prayer. He finally decided that given the risk, he would take a chance on annoying God with the plea.

"Dear God," he started again, whispering as before. "Don't let my parts swell up."

The doctor had told him to take notice if his "testicles" became swollen, and to let him know if they did. Rulon had asked for a translation of the unknown word, and was horrified to be told what it meant, and that he might lose the power to engender children should the ailment spread to that site.

"Please," he added, knowing his vanity had partially prompted him to ask this boon, but hoping such a thing was important to a God he had been taught was the Father of All. Mary wanted several children, and the thought that a misplaced childhood disease could rob her of that fulfillment had been causing him a good deal of anguish. "Thank you for any mercy you can spare to Mary an' me," he concluded his appeal, and turned his head so his tears would be less apparent to the other patients in the tent.

ॐ

Mary — August 9, 1861

"Mother Owen," Mary greeted her mother-in-law later that week. "Welcome. That is a fine basket of eggs."

"And here is a can of cream," Julia said, indicating the metal armful Albert bore into the store.

"Cream! That is priceless these days," Mary said. She patted the counter, and Albert hoisted his burden onto it, then moved off to explore the inventory.

"How are you, my dear?"

"I feel better on some days than others. Today has been a good day. Do you suppose the sickness will lessen in time?"

"Most times it does, Mistress Mary. How long has it been, now?" She ticked months off on her fingers. "Almost three months gone. I predict a spate of better times a-comin'."

"That will be most gladsome." Mary gave in to the desire to covertly pat the place on her abdomen that would be expanding more each future day. "Are all well in the family?" she asked in order not to neglect the social niceties.

"As well as can be expected, I reckon. We miss those not

present, but are doing our best to carry on with the chores." Julia lifted her hands in resignation. "Mr. Owen apportioned the tasks to the boys, but we miss Peter's help. The scamp!"

"Have you had news from your sons?"

"Rulon has had the most time to send a letter, and I have received his. I have not heard from Ben or Peter. Or Mr. Owen," she added.

"I am sure you will hear from all of them, given time," Mary said, hoping her words would comfort her mother-in-law. "You might be surprised to learn that I had a visitor on Monday."

"Not the monthly?" Julia's face grew grave.

"Oh, no. No. I mean Miss Ella Ruth Allen came into the store to speak to me."

"That girl?"

"I know she rejected Brother Ben's offer of marriage. It appears she has repented of her pride. She seemed very contrite for her actions."

"What did she want with you?"

"She asked for news from Brother Ben. I reckon she also wants to obtain his address for correspondence."

"Hm. I wonder if he will welcome that from her."

Mary shrugged her shoulders. "I agreed to ask you for an address, once you have one to share, of course. If she has the gumption to attempt to correspond after turning him off, I figure she deserves the chance to ask for forgiveness, at the least."

Julia sighed. "Mary, you have the right of it. When Ben deigns to write, I will bring you the particulars."

"Thank you, Mother Owen. I knew you would rise to your good reputation."

"My good reputation?"

"Miss Allen was afraid to approach you. I told her how good you are. Perhaps one day she will have the courage to speak to you herself."

"You're a caution, daughter Mary. Talkin' me up that-a-way. I'm plain Julia Owen. She has no reason to fear me."

"I'm hoping she will come to know that, ma'am."

Chapter 13

Rulon — August 10, 1861

Throughout the week, Rulon suffered a great deal of pain from his ailment. He began to write a rough journal of what was happening to him in case he didn't survive the disease, and got Ren to promise he would send the account of his illness to Mary in that event.

He wrote of fever coming and going, of nights of torment spent pacing beneath a tent upon which drummed incessant rain, of keen pains darting through his jaw and each tooth, of muscles and nerves jerking and quailing at the pain, of tremors, then more pain that the doctor could not ease.

One night he found that sitting alongside the stove with his mouth full of cold water brought a small amount of relief. Finally, the pain, fever and swelling abated, and he looked forward to being discharged the next morning.

He awoke while it was yet dark and screamed in agony. The other side of his jaw had risen in the night, and all the pain, fever, and throbbing were back. One of the men assigned to nurse the patients came running with a light, and tried to shush him.

"Quiet, man. What ails you?" He held up the light, then swore when he saw Rulon's cheek. "That must pain you a mite."

Rulon tried to tear his jaw off to relieve his distress, but the nurse tied his hands down and summoned the physician.

The doctor swore in his turn. "It's four o'clock in the morning. Keep silent!"

Rulon clamped his teeth shut, shame crowding him into desperation. He thrashed on the cot. He could not endure this torture further. He wanted to die.

"Oswald, bring me the laudanum."

"Should you waste it on him?"

"Do as I say." The doctor flung out his arm, indicating his disgust. "Dying men shouldn't deal with all this noise."

Sometime after the doctor administered part of a tumbler of bitter liquid to him, Rulon began to drift in a half-lit world of haze and buzzing. Then he went into a dark place and knew no more.

When he awoke to full sunlight, he vowed to comport himself with more order despite the pain, and apologized to his fellow patients. When he was allowed to go relieve himself, he discovered that his worst nightmare had become reality. Harboring icy despair at his predicament, he asked to speak to the doctor.

After an examination, the man said, "The swelling is not severe. Time will tell if there is a diminishment in your vigor. You have a wife?"

Rulon could hardly bear to speak. "Yes," he finally said through gritted teeth.

"Children?"

"One coming soon," he managed.

"That's good. You'll have one child, at least. Bear up, man. Another two weeks and you'll be in the field again." The doctor gave Rulon a pat on the shoulder, a curt nod, and then hurried off.

Rulon lay down, the pain in his soul vying with the pain in his jaw for supremacy.

৪১

Rod — August 11, 1861

Having arrived at his duty post, Rod wrote home to Julia.

11th Aug'st 1861
Outside Charles Town, Via.
My dear Wife,
I take pencil in hand to inform you of my safe arrival to the place of our posting. The Men of the Owen Dragoons have covered themselves with glory in the past week, firstly, in arriving without incident, and secondly, in defending the Bord'r with dispach and zeel.

We have been assigned to tear up rails and Ties from the Baltimore & Ohio Rail Raod so that the Enemy does not have Use of it to invade our Land. Deer Wife, yu shoud see the hearty manner in wich my boys attack there task. Altho we do not ride as much as sum woud like, whatever we are commanded to do is honorabl, as I tell the boys.

Do you heer from our Sons who are servin the Comnwelth of Virginia? My hope is that they will bear themselves well and bring honor to the Owen Name.

My devoshun to you is without ceasin. Embrace the young'uns for me, and acept a kiss upon yor brow from

Yor husband,
Capt'n Roderick Owen
Commanding, Owen Dragoons
7th Reg'ment Via. Cav.

ဆ

Mary — August 14, 1861

Mary sat at the table one evening, picking at her food. Nothing appealed to her. Some of the odors made her gag. The stink of the cabbage was insufferable. She passed the dish to Ida as quickly as she could.

Ida thrust an elbow into her side. "Don't throw up on me," she warned in a hiss.

"I'm not sick," Mary hissed back.

"You look green. Excuse yourself."

"I'm not ill," Mary repeated, a little louder.

"Mary," her mother's voice broke in. "Are you ailing? If that is the case, it would be best if you left the table."

"I am not ailing," Mary reiterated. "I merely do not have a strong appetite this evening." She laid her fork on the oilcloth. "Was there a post today?"

"No letters," Mr. Hilbrands announced.

Mary felt her blood congeal in her veins. No letters. No word from Rulon again today. Weeks had passed since she had received a message from him. She hadn't read of any battles since the big one at Manassas. What was going on? Was he ill, injured, dead?

"Did the Rockingham paper arrive?" Perhaps that weekly newspaper carried additional information about Rulon's company that the papers from New Market and Woodstock did not.

"I expect it tomorrow, daughter."

She felt like screaming, pulling on her hair, falling to the floor and drumming her heels on the carpet. That would get her nothing but a reprimand from her mother. Every day Mama found a new fault to point out, a new action that didn't suit her fancy, for which she spoke to Mary as though she were a naughty child.

I wish I had never pressed Rulon to let me live with my parents, she thought. *How much better it would be to live at the Owen farm.* But the die had been cast, and she knew her mother would not let her move from the house now.

She held her breath for a moment, then let out a sigh. "I believe I am ailing after all," she said. "With your permission, I'll retire."

She scooted back her chair and escaped the room as quickly as she could. *Oh Rulon. Please be in good health. Please come home soon.*

৪৩

Peter — August 18, 1861

After thinking for a long time about how to couch his first letter home, on a bleak Sunday Peter finally decided he knew what to write.

18 August 1861

Der Pa and Ma,

I greet you with tha hope that yu are all well at home. I regret that I took off in such a great hurry and was neglectful about sayin my goodbyes. My intent never was to hurt you. and I hope you will be forgivin of my tresspass. I reckon a man is obliged to be about the busines of defending his country from the invader.

The Rangers have been put into the 7th Virginia Cavalry Regim't commanded by Colonel Angus Wm McDonald. He is an older man, but spry enuf despite a bad case of rumitizm. I hav been took into several brawls with the Yankees from which I emerged unskathed except for a paltry sabr cut upon my side wich is healin nicely. I wil bear a pretty scar to show my future wife as proof of my valor in battel.

Not havin much else to report, I will end. again beggin your forgiveness for the manner in which I took myself and the horse Brownie off from the place. Give my affection to my brothers and sisters. Tell Marie I miss her shortbread. We count ourselves lucky if we eat twice a day, and then our meals are beans and hardtack biskets.

I send you my deepest regards and love,
Yor son Peter

ɞ

Mary — August 19, 1861

On the 19th of August, Mary had conquered her stomach enough to show up for work in good time, and was removing the dust cloths covering the goods set up in the windows when she heard a tap on the front door. She looked out the glass pane to discover Ella Ruth Allen outside, an anxious expression on her face.

Mary unlocked the door and opened it a crack.

"We have not yet begun the day," she said after giving her a brief greeting.

"Please, won't you admit me? Father is on his way to the courthouse and agreed to let me come to buy a trifle if I didn't delay him but five minutes. I haven't a moment to spare. Please?"

The young woman's use of the word 'please' twice impressed Mary as to the urgency of her errand, and she bade her enter. "What trifle did you have in mind to buy?" she asked, turning to the wares.

Ella Ruth raised her shoulders, evidently in a protective motion, as she wrung her hands. "That was a subterfuge," she finally said. "I came for news of Benjamin. Do you have any word? An address where I might write him?"

Mary studied the pinched face, and put out her hand to lay it on Ella Ruth's. "You must compose yourself," she said.

Ella Ruth's face blanched. "Ah!" she wailed. "He is gone?"

"No. No, no. I merely mean that Mother Owen has not heard from him as yet. However, you may take comfort that his name has not been published on a list. Come back on Monday next. Perhaps there will be word this week."

Ella Ruth sighed raggedly. "Thank you for your kindness. You are a dear girl. I am sure your husband is happy in his choice of a bride." She cast her eyes down, then up again. "Are you well? You seem a trifle pale."

"I am as well as may be," Mary replied, with a small, secretive smile she kept from blossoming further with strong effort.

"What do you mean?"

"I am to have a child," she answered, and could not restrain her lips from their upward course.

Ella Ruth looked stricken. "If only, ah, if only I had not been prideful, I might have been even now carrying a child of my own. Benjamin's child."

Mary wondered if Ella Ruth realized how unseemly her thought was. She and Brother Ben were not married, and she should not talk of such things.

Ella Ruth spoke again. "I wish you every happiness, Missus Owen." She clasped her entwined fingers in front of her face, and seemed about to burst into tears.

Mary said nothing for a moment, then decided she must be gracious. "You're very kind in giving me that sentiment, Miss Allen. You may yet rejoice in a happy interval of your own. Rulon tells me this conflict cannot last for long. He and Brother Ben and the rest of the family will surely return soon."

"I can only pray for that glorious day," Ella Ruth squeezed out in a choked voice. "Thank you once more for being my intermediary. My go-between," she hastened to explain. She looked out the window. "I must go now. Poppa will be waiting."

"Do not forget your trifle, Miss Allen," Mary said, fishing out a stick of peppermint candy from a jar and wrapping it quickly in brown paper. "Here now. Take it. You have need of a smile."

Ella Ruth nodded as she accepted the parcel, then slipped away and closed the door quietly behind her.

Chapter 14

Julia — August 21, 1861

Clay brought mail from town, and in it was a letter addressed to Julia. She took it, looked at the inscription, and hugged it to her heart. "Your brother Ben always makes his letters with fancy doodiddles," she said to the girls, and sat down at the kitchen table in the middle of her work day to read the letter from her boy.

Marie and Julianna crowded around, and Clay hovered in the background as she read it aloud.

Julia smiled at Ben's description of riding atop a railroad car, frowned at the mention of a slight wound, wondering if he was making light of a more serious injury, and wept a bit for the mother of the unfortunate drummer boy. Beside her, the girls sniffed in sympathy.

"Stonewall Jackson," she murmured, thinking it a fitting name for the dour professor from the Virginia Military Institute. She had heard of his fondness for lemonade, and wondered if she ever would have occasion to serve it to the man. However, he would surely not be in the Valley for any cause except to do battle, so cast aside her notion as a flight of fancy.

As she folded up the letter to put it away, she recalled Mary's visitor, and the request for Ben's mailing address. She hesitated. The girls did not need to know of the foibles of romance at their young ages, so she arose and said, "Back to your chores, daughters. We have had a pleasant interval, but there remains work undone." She also shooed Clay out of the kitchen so she could be alone.

When her children were out of the way, she wrote out the directions on a scrap of paper, and tucked it behind a wooden box sitting on the mantelpiece. When she went into town later in the week, she would give Mary the paper.

ॐ

Mary — August 26, 1861

The next Monday, Miss Ella Ruth Allen showed up bright and early at the Hilbrands' store.

Glimpsing the wan, earnest face as Ella Ruth came through the door, Mary smiled to herself. This time, she had good news to impart. Not only had Mother Owen given her a slip of paper with the particulars of where it was that Brother Ben could receive mail, she had also allowed her to read the letter he had sent to his mother.

Although he mentioned that he had received an injury, he had made light of it. She wasn't about to mention it to Ella Ruth and get her all a-flutter with worry. If Brother Ben was willing to enter into correspondence with the girl, he could apprise her of the facts himself. Mary put on a bright smile to greet her visitor.

"You must have good news for me," Ella Ruth said as she approached, her anxiety showing in a pinched look of anticipation.

"I do indeed," Mary replied.

"Missus Owen has received word?"

"Yes. A letter came to her." She placed the scrap of paper on the counter. "She wrote out this address for you, and wishes you all success in the delivery of your correspondence."

"You were right," Ella Ruth breathed as she picked up the paper. "Missus Owen is a good woman."

Mary moved her head slightly, as though to say, "I told you she was," but she had no intention of speaking the rebuke out loud.

Ella Ruth smiled at last and Mary saw the comely face that had attracted the notice of Brother Ben.

"Have you any leather pocket books, the kind with writing paper inside, and perhaps a leaden pencil attached? I would like to purchase such an item."

Mary raised her eyebrows at the request. Surely she didn't intend to send a gift like that upon her first contact with Brother Ben.

Ella Ruth must have guessed her concern, for she said quickly, "I wish to write a note as soon as possible. If Benjamin is disposed to renew our . . . friendship, I shall dispatch the wallet to him on a later occasion." She ducked her head. "If he is not, I shall use the paper for other letters."

"I will ask my father," Mary said, and went in search of Papa. He found a pocket book which, when Ella Ruth saw it, placed a smile of satisfaction upon her lips.

"That will do splendidly," she said, somewhat more shyly than Mary had supposed her response would be. Mr. Hilbrands supplied the price, which Ella Ruth paid immediately.

When her father had gone about other business, Mary asked if her customer had other wishes, since she had not left once the money had changed hands.

Ella Ruth asked, her voice low, "Might there be a private place where I can write a letter? I do not dare write it at home and post it through my father."

"Certainly. You may use the desk in the back room. Just pass through here and follow me."

Mary showed the way, and was about to turn to leave the room when Ella Ruth put out her hand and touched her belly. Shocked, Mary said, "Ah!" and stepped backward. Ella Ruth pulled away her errant hand.

"I do beg your pardon," said the girl, speaking rapidly. "I have not had any experience of children, or ever been near a woman who is increasing. I so want to bear Benjamin's child."

Mary looked at her, stunned. She finally said, "But you hurt him sorely. He may not even—"

"I know my folly," Ella Ruth cried out. "My pride may have prevented any happiness I could have in this life. I may never have the chance to marry him." She put forward her hands in a supplicating gesture. "Do forgive me the indelicacy, Mistress Owen. Ah! How I wish to bear that name. You are fortunate."

"Yes," Mary agreed, still shaken by the intimacy of the cupping hand upon her skirt. "I married a good man, and I am bearing his child. I wish you every fortune, Miss Allen. Now I must return to my duties."

"Thank you." The girl inhaled sharply. "I hope that you and I may become friends. I hope we may share a name someday."

"Perhaps," Mary said, and turned away before the prospect that the tears stinging behind her eyelids could slide down her cheeks to reveal the reality of her loneliness. Rulon had not yet had the opportunity to touch her as Ella Ruth had. How long would it be before he could return from war and do so?

❧

Ella Ruth — August 26, 1861

Once Mary left her to herself in the back room, Ella Ruth crossed her arms on the desk and rested her forehead upon them. At last, after all the waiting, she had received the directions to which she could write to him, and she had no idea what words to put on the paper.

Whatever she wrote, it must appeal to his sense of fairness, and must convince him that she had undergone a true change of heart. She knew she had done wrong by him, but it wasn't enough to convey only that important message. She had to somehow soften Ben's heart toward her, for she knew she had caused it such pain that he would guard it most carefully against further hurt from her.

"I was so unbelievably heartless to you, my love," she whispered. "I refused to acknowledge how the world would change."

She raised her head and took up the pencil. There was plenty of paper in the pocket folio. She would simply have to try setting down what was in her heart, and if the first try did not suit, she would make another attempt . . . and another, and another, until she had it right.

She took several deeps breaths, licked the tip of the pencil, and poised it above the top of the sheet of paper.

Her fingers seemed to have no bones, and she dropped the implement. It rested where it had fallen, rebuking her for such absurd folly.

She hung her head. This was a senseless endeavor, foolish and vain. He would never forgive her.

Before despair could overcome her, however, a stubborn voice arose in her head. "You must try," it said. "You cannot give up before you make an attempt."

She recognized the inner voice. It was an echo of what she had heard throughout her life: her father's voice, encouraging her and her brother to take hold of every advantage in life.

The lesson had been taught. It had been received. It had become ingrained. Now it was time to execute the plan she had formulated. The tenacious Miss Ella Ruth Allen, daughter of a bull-headed and very successful businessman, straightened her shoulders, picked up the pencil, and went to work.

It took her three tries before she was satisfied with her labors. She had either written a letter that would cause Ben's heart to melt with compassion, or it was the wrong approach entirely, and he would reject her overture and cast her aside as she had done with him. However, she had made the attempt. Now she would have to allow time to show her the results.

&

Rulon — August 31, 1861

At long last, Rulon found himself discharged from the physician's care, and not a moment too soon, as Garth Von strode up to the hospital, evidently bent on taking a rest from picket duty.

"Outta my path, Shenandoah sissy," growled the man, shoving Rulon as they both tried to use the door.

Rulon backed out of the way, assessing the threat. The man clearly was unhappy, but was he dangerous? Figuring caution was the better part of valor on this occasion, he took his departure and discovered that his company had moved away from the headquarters. Ren Lovell had left word that he had custody of Rulon's belongings, including his horse, so he was obliged to trudge on foot over a considerable part of the muddy countryside to rejoin his outfit.

When Ren Lovell saw him at evening, he greeted Rulon with a touch of deliberation. "Got rid of your contagion, have you? You still look a little swollen up."

Rulon shook his head. "That's your imaginings, Lovell. Mayhap I've grown plump on hospital gruel."

"Did it spread any?" He pointed downward. "A couple of the men made bets on it."

Rulon was unwilling to discuss his fears or be the butt of jokes, and put Lovell off with a few curt words. "That's none of your business. I'm sound now."

"You seem a tad bitter, Owen." Lovell laughed, showing his

dimples. "I didn't bet on your misfortunate contagion, by the way, and you haven't missed any fightin', if that's what worries you. Not so you'd notice, anyway. We've had a minor fracas here or there, but this rain has kept us from doin' more than simply keeping the Federals out of our land."

Rulon relaxed his guard and dropped his prickly attitude. He said, "I come across Von down to the hospital. "What's his story?"

Lovell made a face. "He says he has boils. He won't ride. I reckon we weren't getting enough killin' action for him."

"Boils? On his butt?"

"That's what he says. I'm not surprised a bit. You know the man doesn't keep himself clean." Lovell rearranged a few papers on his desk. "Captain Yancey was happy to let him go for a while. Von's an unpleasant man when he's not busy."

"He's unpleasant most any day."

Rulon took advantage of the evening to borrow pen, ink, and paper to write to Mary. It had been a very long time since he had sent her a letter. She must be frantic with worry.

Septemb'r 2, 1861

He paused to reflect. Did he have the date correct? It didn't matter, he supposed. He bent over the paper again.

Near Fairfax C-H
My dearest love Mary,
You have been in my thoughts constantly during the Past month as I lay sick in the Hospital. I am recover'd now, and enjoying Good helth, but I fared very poorly for a long while with the Mumps swelling sickness. first in one side of my Jaw and then the other. I will not harow your thots. with a descripshun of my pains. Suffice it to say I had many agonies to get thru before the physician would Release me.

Such a lot of dying, Mary. The Hospital was not only for the Ill but the Wounded and Dyeing from the big Battle. I shudder now to think of it.

I will leave off talking of unpleasantries. Insted I will tell you that My heart was full to Bursting when I read of your good news. Are you well? Do you lack for anything? You must ask my

Ma to bring you fresh eggs to eat. She will do that if you Say I asked.

Did Ben marry the Allen girl? He was very set on running away with her to Staunton to elope. Did he get his wish?

Is Peter behaving himself? He gave Ma the flutters with his talk of Enlisting. I hope he waits a while. I think this war will be longer than we at first thot. The Yankess do push back, although I reckon we will win out.

That is enouf news and questions for now. I miss your dear person and think of you every day.

Receiv a kiss from yor husband who adores you and wishes to see you soon

Rulon

Chapter 15

Mary — September 1, 1861

One Sunday after church services, the Hilbrands family was surprised by an afternoon visit from Dr. Meem, a prominent physician in the area. He asked to speak with Mrs. Owen, and Mary agreed to entertain him in the parlor.

"We are most honored by your visit," Mrs. Hilbrands said, and turned to lead the way into the room.

"Mama," Mary said so low that the visitor could not hear. "He wishes to speak to me."

"Nonsense," retorted her mother in the same fashion. "You cannot be alone with the man."

And so, Dr. Meem sat down to converse with the two ladies of the house, senior and junior.

As soon as he had taken a bit of refreshment, the doctor put down his cup and cleared his throat. "Mrs. Owen, I have been appointed as director of a new soldier's hospital that is to be built upon land donated by Colonel Rinker. We will have a need for ladies from Mount Jackson to lend a hand with some of the tasks suited to their station and nature. Your name has been presented as one who might wish to give such service, since you have a husband, I believe, at the front, serving his country?"

Mary bent her head, basking for a moment in the recognition of her married state and of Rulon's sacrifice. At last she smiled and lifted her eyes to give the doctor her assent, but her mother's voice cut across her train of thought.

"Certainly not. My daughter is in a delicate condition. It is not fitting for her to be among those of the opposite gender while she is, um, that is, while she remains, um, so indisposed."

"Mama! I am perfectly able to nurse the poor men who have given so much to our country. When will the buildin' of the hospital be finished, Doctor?"

"Next spring, madam. It will—"

"I forbid it, daughter. Think of the odors, the contagion. You can scarcely hold food upon your stomach as it is."

"I am told that the sickness will go away soon, Mama. I will manage."

"No." She gave Mary a stern look, then turned to the doctor and said, "My daughter is unwell on many days. I am sure you will understand, Dr. Meem. She cannot help you." She arose. "Good day to you, sir."

While Mrs. Hilbrands showed the unhappy doctor to the door, Mary could hardly hold her temper in check. She stood beside her chair in the parlor, quivering with indignation that the decision had been so rudely taken from her power. When it was clear that her mother would not be returning, Mary went after her.

"How dare you speak for me?" she said, almost overcome with rage. "That was unconscionable. Mr. Owen would want me to help in any way possible."

"You forget yourself, Mary. You live in my house, under my roof and your father's protection. That husband of yours has no concern in the matters of my household. He was happy enough to leave you in my care, and I shall do as I see fit to keep you safe." She took a step away, then half turned and threw a cruel thought over her shoulder. "He is young and reckless. You cannot trust him. He is likely going to take up with the sort of women who follow the soldier camps."

Mary dug her fingernails into her hands and bit the inside of her cheek until it bled. She would not faint or carry on for her mother's benefit. She watched her go, with a bleak question sitting in the pit of her stomach. *What if Mama is right?*

☙

Ben — September 18, 1861

When Ben received more than one letter one drizzly afternoon in camp, he took the mail into the tent and sat on his cot. He looked at the first envelope, addressed to him in his mother's familiar hand, then shuffled the paper to inspect the second. The handwriting looped and dipped in a grand fashion, clearly a feminine characteristic, but was unknown to him. Perhaps the ladies of Mount Jackson had got up a campaign to write to lonely soldiers? If that were so, would this missive be from some lonely maiden lady, hoping to receive a note of gratitude from a male person?

As he examined the writing on the sturdy envelope, he spotted a miniscule set of initials in an upper corner, the sight of which sent a jolt of surprise through his soul.

E. R. A.

His head buzzed in shock. E. R. A. He knew a person with those initials. Ella Ruth Allen.

Miss Ella Ruth Allen had cruelly cast him aside like a dried corn husk. She had not wanted him. She had soundly rejected him. Had she now drawn the short straw in the bolster-the-spirits-of-the-lonely-soldier letter-writing assignment? Well, she could go whistle for any reply from him!

He turned the envelope over and over in his hands, thinking of going outside the tent and throwing it—unopened—into the cooking fire, but as he handled it, curiosity grew to overcome his ire. Had she written under the pressure of civic duty? Had she come to miss having him around to abuse? Or might she possibly have had a change of heart?

A seed of hope began to grow in his chest. He told himself not to build happy expectations on an unopened envelope, but his fingers refused to break the seal. He stared at the letter. Perhaps he should save it until he had read the news from home. Yes, he told himself. That was the best course to take. Let his mother's loving words buffer him from whatever unpleasant surprise Ella Ruth's note had in store. He put the letter beside him on the cot and opened the one from home.

Ma wrote that all at home were well except Julianna, who had a touch of grippe. She was glad he had found the time to correspond at last, and that he must take all good care with his wound. Then she recounted the outstanding events in the county since he had left home, including a tidbit about Peter stealing his horse—*his horse*—and enlisting from Edinburg.

"The scoundrel," he muttered. *Brownie, a war horse?*

She wrote that both Mistress Mary and her mother, Mrs. Hilbrands, were awaiting a happy event, and that James was overseeing the crops as well as the horses, due to Peter's hasty departure. She mentioned that his father had chafed sorely at delays in raising his cavalry company that caused him to miss the action at Manassas Junction, but that he and his troopers finally rode off, much to his satisfaction.

Ben imagined how sad that parting must have made Ma feel, even though there was not a hint of reproach against his father in her words. He knew she was strong, but she surely drew part of that strength from Pa. They had always been so close-knit, not like squabbling couples he'd seen in Mount Jackson.

Finally, Ma urged him to remember his prayers and to seek out church services as often as he could, and said that she bore him great affection. She signed it "your mother, Julia Helm Owen." A line from Marie had been added at the bottom of the paper, then the letter was finished.

Ben tucked the sheet back into the envelope, rose to put it into his knapsack, then glanced at the other letter lying on the cot.

The letter marked with E.R.A.

The letter he was sure had come from Ella Ruth.

The letter he should chuck into the cook fire.

He picked it up, and almost turned toward the tent flap to follow thought with deed, but knew it would be cruel of him to fail to acknowledge her efforts, whatever they might have produced in the way of words.

Sighing and steeling himself against further heart-break by way of Miss Ella Ruth Allen, he sat and opened the envelope.

Glancing down the page, he spotted imperfections, smudges in the ink. He brought the paper close to his face to puzzle out the cause. Oh lordy, those were tear splotches.

He dropped his hands to his lap. Ella Ruth crying? Pouting, giggling, feigning anger, arching her eyebrows. He was familiar with all those wiles. He had never seen her in tears.

After a moment spent in reflecting on their last harsh encounter, Ben lifted the letter and began to read.

Benjamin,

Many a time you have chided me for coming late to an appointment. It is true. I have an intolerable habit of running behind times in all my endeavors in life.

So too, am I late in realizing the truth of what you tried so expressively to tell me. We are at war. Men must fight for their country else their liberty be taken from them. You have gone upon that endeavor.

Oh Ben. I have done wrong. I have taken your trust and love and ground them to pieces beneath my foolish heel. I know this now, and I have come to acknowledge this at a later date than gentility demands.

My heart is broken at the grievous hurt I caused you. I am contrite. I scourge my spirit daily at remembering my unwise action and unreasonable pride. I was lost in impossible dreams that cannot, and should not, be included in my daily walk.

Can you find it in your generous soul to forgive me? I cannot expect that you will do so, but I am compelled to ask this boon of you. I hope that I may ever call myself your friend, however imprudent I have been.

Ella Ruth /

From a partial stroke of her pen at the conclusion of her signature, Ben surmised that she had nearly added her surname, then decided against it. This was an intimate apology, not a formal one. He held his breath, assessing what that could mean.

Was she begging to resume their friendship at the point to which it had arrived? That was unclear. Perhaps she only felt a good dollop of remorse and wished to be Christian friends. She seemed to be suffering under a great weight, at the very least, and wished his forgiveness to get out from under it.

He expelled the breath. Her petition required an answer. He was too wrung out at the moment to reply. It would have to wait for another day, and for a much clearer head than the one he possessed at this time.

Ella Ruth. The golden girl he had hoped to woo and win. He recalled his ultimatum. He had offered her his heart and his life, then said, "But you must take them now, or you must leave them alone."

She had chosen in haste, and now she wanted to repent of throwing him over. His brain refused to hand him a fitting response. Did he want the girl back, or was he done with her?

A few moments spent in a muddle did him no good, but the call of the bugle broke him free of the need to make an instant decision. He put the letter away and sprinted to do his duty.

Rulon — September 24, 1861

Rulon continued to write in his mumps journal, but now he made notes about things he experienced, some of which he would share with Mary in his letters.

On September 12, he noted that the regiment had been reorganized that day. The extra companies that had been added over time were transferred to other regiments and ten companies remained. The Harrisonburg Cavalry troop was kept, and continued with the designation of Company "I".

Later that month, a greater change came about when the regimental commander, Colonel J. E. B. Stuart, ascended to the rank of brigadier general and rose to command of the brigade.

He discussed the changes with Ren and Owen later that day over supper.

"Where is Colonel Jones from?" he asked about their new commander.

Owen answered. "He brought in the Mounted Rifles, Company 'L,' from Washington County. My sister married a fellow from Abington, where they raised the company. He has a crooked leg."

"The colonel?"

"No. My sister's husband. He couldn't get into the fight on account of the leg."

"Ah."

Ren spoke up. "I'm going to miss those Company 'K' fellows from Rockingham County. It was comforting to fight alongside folks we knew."

"They have spunk, I will say," Rulon said, nodding. "Any kin of yours in that group?"

"No, but their captain is brother to ours. I reckon it will be hard on them to be separated."

"Why do they call the colonel 'Grumble' Jones?" Rulon asked.

"I hear tell it is because of his irritable nature," Ren replied, and got to his feet. "We'd best keep our behavior on the impeccable side. Who is on guard duty tonight?"

Owen answered. "I'm your boy."

"Finish up and see to it," Ren said, and strode away.

Rod — September 27, 1861

The stars must finally have aligned for Rod Owen, for in late September, when the breezes blew chill and the sun shone less each day, he came upon a young cavalryman with his back turned to him who was grooming the stolen horse Brownie.

"Son?" Rod queried, not sure this strapping lad was his offspring, but certain that the horse was his.

The boy pivoted and faced him. "Pa?" he said, his voice a bit defensive.

"My boy." A wash of relief caused Rod to abandon any preconceived plan to harangue Peter for his misdeeds. He opened his arms to embrace him, and Peter met him in like fashion.

"Pa," Peter said when they had broken the embrace. "I reckon it was wrong of me to take Ben's horse, although he wasn't goin' to use it for a while. I had the need. I figured you would come to know that, in time."

"You should have waited for your birthday before you enlisted, son. Surely there is war enough that it would have lasted until then."

"I didn't want to lose my chance."

"You grieved your ma."

Peter hung his head for a moment. When he raised it, he said, "I reckon that's true. I did write an apology to her. Your name was on the letter, as well. I had half a notion you would linger a mite longer at home, instead of leaving Ma to her own devices."

Rod felt a moment of ire at the hint of reproach his son had cast upon him at leaving his wife. It was true. He had left Julia to carry on, but was it not expected of an honorable man that he would defend his family and his country? There were capable boys at home to give her every aid. Instead of answering the charge, he turned the topic. "I told your ma I would get you sent home for being underage."

"No. Don't do that." Peter yanked up his shirt, unbuttoned his undershirt, pulled it aside, and revealed a lengthy red scar from which the scab had already fallen. "I've been bloodied in battle. I won't leave the defense of my land to lesser men."

"I'm sure a word to your captain—"

"He knows my age, Pa. He don't care. He said I was a valiant fighter and he wished he had a dozen men like me under his command." Under the truculent manner, Peter's face shone with an expression of satisfaction.

"Hmm," Rod said. "I didn't know about your injury."

"Ma knows of it. I wrote in the letter that it was a trifle."

"I'm sure you did." He wondered what argument was left to him with the boy. Clearly he had won the good opinion of his company commander. Peter's reasons for coming into the cavalry were much the same as his own—the defense of family and country, mixed with a youthful exuberance he himself now lacked.

"I ain't goin' home until the fight is won," Peter said, setting his jaw.

"You always were a stubborn lad," Rod said. "Much like me, unfortunately. If you give me your word to be cautious in the face of the enemy, I won't press the matter."

"Cautious? I can't promise that, Pa. I can promise to remember my mother and sisters, and to defend their honor with all my body and soul. That's all I can promise."

Rod's sigh lasted for several seconds, it seemed, all the breath leaving his body as though in terrible resignation. The boy would not be moved. As his father, his emotions warred in his breast. Love. Concern. Pride for the man his son had become in a few short weeks.

Life was a muddle of a knot, and he couldn't always make out the right way to cut through it. Should he leave the boy alone? If he let the issue die of natural causes, what was he to tell Julia?

He could only say he had found the boy, and determined that the war situation was desperate enough that the army needed Peter more than the farm and his kin did. He knew that was the truth of the matter, even as his heart urged him to carry the boy home to his mama, where he would be safe from harm.

At length, Rod said, "I reckon that's all I can ask."

૭૦

Mary — October 31, 1861

Mary held her belly and bent double, gasping at the force of the kick the creature inside her had dealt. Surely this child was a boy. No female could be so unruly.

She straightened with care, then grasped the supportive back of the chair beside her. Two weeks gone since she had last written to Rulon, and no letter had come back in that time. Was he even alive? Perhaps he was too busy to think of her. Or . . . perhaps those cruel words Mama had flung at her were true, especially with the seemingly confirming whispers she had heard of "camp followers" setting up tents— No! Those boys joking and laughing outside the store, what did they know? She wouldn't pay heed to them. She couldn't.

But the black thoughts continued. Rulon had needs. What had he called them? She searched through her swirling mind to remember their wedding day. *Lustful yearnings.* Yes. Very powerful yearnings. The two of them had spent a good deal of time assuaging his yearnings before their honeymoon days were spent. How could he set those urges aside now?

Another strong message from her babe demanded her attention, and for the moment, her body's needs prevailed over thoughts about Rulon's.

When the child had calmed himself, Mary thought about Rulon again. How could she turn *his* thoughts to *her*? How could she make him recall her attempt to brand him with the remembrance of her bared body pressed against him in the light of day? *What a foolish gesture*, she thought. A vain and feeble bid to claim his affection forever. Men's thoughts wandered. She had heard of a woman whose husband had strayed quite publicly, shaming the woman to such an extent that she had taken sufficient poison to end her pain. That had caused a terrible scandal. The man had buried his wife and fled north, taking his paramour with him, but leaving three poor children orphaned and at the mercy of relations.

Lust is a vicious drive, she tortured herself. She envisioned Rulon in the arms of a painted harlot, and cried out in despair. How could she return his thoughts, his allegiance to her? Had he not taken vows? Did he not give them uppermost value in his life?

She paced the room, their room, where he had whispered words of affection as he took her body beneath his own, entangling her in his needs, opening her to lustful emotions of her own as he spilled his seed within her. She paused to endure another attack from the babe. Rulon had planted this child that hurt her so sorely. When the kicking had passed, she thought, *I have given you body and soul, husband. What more must I do to ensure your fidelity?*

She spied a likeness of her parents that hung against the wall. Should she have a likeness made, wear a low-cut dress to entice him into remembering their nights of passion together? She had nothing of the sort in her wardrobe. Perhaps that would have an opposite effect, and drive him to seek relief. Should she turn in profile, to show him an outline of what he had left behind? She bowed in shame at the thought of revealing her condition so blatantly to a photograph maker. She sighed, then straightened and made a decision. She would have a likeness made of her face and hope it would be sweet and enchanting enough to give him thoughts of home and respite from battle.

The child brushed gently against her insides, giving her what she took as approval. Yes. She must be the sweet wife Rulon claimed to love, and show him that side of her in the likeness she would send. Having settled her mind on a course of action gave her the first peace she had felt for some time, and she went to the door with a new sense of resolve.

Chapter 16

Ben — November 4, 1861

On November 4th, General Jackson addressed his brigade. Ben stood on a hill with the rest of the troops, trying to keep his emotions in check. Old Jack, who now held the name Stonewall Jackson, was headed for the Shenandoah Valley to take command there, but the brigade that also bore the nickname would hold the hard-won line before Washington.

The General said he was not making a speech, but was there to bid them farewell. After making more speech than Ben had ever heard from him, he stood in his stirrups and exclaimed, "In the Army of the Shenandoah you were the *First* Brigade, in the Army of the Potomac you were the *First* Brigade, in the 2d Corps of this army you are the *First* Brigade. . . ."

Ben swallowed down the lump in his throat as the General went on.

"You are the *First* Brigade in the affections of your general, and I hope by your future deeds and bearing you will be handed down to posterity as the *First* Brigade in this, our second war of independence. Farewell!"

The hush extended for a moment only, then the men around him raised cheer after cheer. Ben joined in until his throat felt raw. General Jackson briefly waved farewell and rode away at a gallop.

The man next to Ben groaned. "I wish I was a-goin' with him," he said. "I'd cotton to seein' my Sara right about now."

Ben turned to him and nodded, remembering the strange letter he had received a few weeks ago from Miss Ella Ruth Allen. He'd done nothing about it. What was there to do? Not knowing what the girl expected of him, he'd put it away and forgotten it.

Now the pangs of homesickness hit him like the concussion from a cannon. He'd wanted a future with Ella Ruth, but now his future lay with fellows like the man beside him, Tom something.

He searched his memory. Tom Grace. He was in the company from Hardy County.

He went back to camp, disheartened by the departure of the general he had come to respect. The rest of his company appeared to be out of humor, as well, so he decided to stay out of the way and write a letter home.

Instead of "Dear Ma," he stared at the words "Dear Miss Allen." No. He had no idea what to say to Ella Ruth. He thought about crumpling the sheet, but paper was in short supply in camp. Perhaps he would figure out what to say to the girl at some future day, so he put the paper back in his rucksack and pulled out another piece to write to Ma.

&

Mary — November 5, 1861

Mary entered the front door of the house, having taken the morning to go to the photographer's studio to have her likeness made to send to Rulon. She had not even had time to close the door when Ida's voice came down the stairs in a screech.

"Mama needs you. Come here at once!"

Mary's warm sense of worth and contentment vanished in the instant. What could be wrong with Mama? She hastily shed and hung her wrap, and trudged up the steps.

The second floor was a complete hub-bub. Her sisters yelled or wrung their hands, according to their nature. Mary followed the loudest noise, which came from her parents' room. Ida flapped about, urging their mother not to worry, that Mary would arrive soon. Mama lay on the bedspread, fully clothed, gritting her teeth through some paroxysm of pain, her eyes tightly closed and her face set.

Well, she was here now, and what was she supposed to do about this unusual situation? Had Mama fallen? Broken a limb?

Mama's fingers gripped the chenille bed covering. Her head quivered.

Mary gazed at the mounded fabric covering her mother's abdomen, and was astounded to see it move of its own accord; a sort of cramping or squeezing seemed to be taking place.

Then the idea of what was occurring hit Mary like a slap upon the side of her head. Mama was in the throes of giving birth to her

149

baby. What was she to do about it? She had not had the same experience yet, and could not imagine herself dealing with the event.

She went to the side of the bed, stooped and took Mama's hand, then asked, "What arrangements have you made? Who is to attend you?"

"Char— Mrs. Bingham," Mama gasped. "Send Ida." She panted, worn out from such a small bit of talk. "Hurry!" Her voice came out low and strained, a harsh gargle.

Mary almost drew back at the venom in the command. Instead, she swallowed and looked at Ida. "You heard her. Make haste."

Ida left the room, looking back over her shoulder, and Mary saw tears brimming in widened eyes, a demonstration of emotion so unlike the saucy girl. How long had Mama been lying here in pain? Guilt at being absent swept through her. How was she to know this day had been set aside for a birth?

"Mama, is there anything I can do to relieve your pain?"

"No," her mother answered in the same harsh voice. "Bring my clean nightgown." Her hand flew up, indicating the wardrobe on the other side of the room.

Mary pushed herself around the bed and found the required article, which lay apart from the other clothing on top of a stack of clean sheets and towels. Was this all designated for the birthing? She picked up the stack and went back to Mama's side, laying the pile upon a nearby chair.

"Am I to help you change?" Mary's voice shook. Such an intimate act was beyond the limits of her sense of modesty. Mama could not wish it of her, for her thoughts on the subject were even more extreme.

"No!" she barked. "Unless." She waited for some reason, and Mary saw that the belly was in the grip of another contracting squeeze. "Unless she doesn't come in time," Mama finished her thought in a rush.

Mary fervently hoped Mrs. Bingham would do so. She had no idea of the stage of Mama's laborings. Was she to the point of expelling the infant? How was that done? Momentary panic froze her mind. How did babies arrive? Up to this time, she'd only known that a midwife came, assisted Mama in whatever the process had been, and left, after many hours behind a shut door.

She quailed to think of the only path she knew about by which a man delivered the seed of his loins to his woman. A baby didn't— It was impossible. The inlet was too small, too delicate, too sensitive. Her mouth dried. A baby would not fit. She squeezed her limbs together.

Her babe gave a kick as if to refute the silly notion. The purveyor of the activity would never deign to quiet himself enough to tunnel through—

"Mary," her mother grunted. "Is Charity here?"

"No, Mama. You must hold on."

Mama responded by gripping Mary's hand as though it were caught in a loop of rope drawn tight by a runaway horse. She made no other sound but a low moaning from time to time that rasped against Mary's heart, laying it open to pain and humility.

In ten more minutes, Mrs. Bingham arrived, bustling in and taking charge.

Mary sighed in relief to see the woman, and was on the verge of removing herself from the scene when Mrs. Bingham said, "Mary, help me with your mother."

She turned, cringing. Mama would not welcome her assistance.

"Hand me the nightgown," the woman said.

Mary went right to the pile on the chair, eyes half-closed in an effort to maintain her mother's dignity. She heard the rustle of clothing, a sharp gasp from Mama, a word of comfort from Mrs. Bingham. When would this be finished?

A hand brushed her sleeve. The nightgown was wanted. Mary handed it over, eyes averted. Mama groaned, muffled it, tried to keep another outburst contained.

I would not keep the pain to myself, Mary thought. *I believe I will scream when my time comes, if I need to do so.*

She berated herself. How did she know what her reaction would be to childbearing? She might be a perfect ninny. On the other hand, it was possible she could follow her mother's example of stoicism under travail.

The baby kicked, and she muffled her own outcry. There now. She would be silent. Strong. Brave.

Brave? What was there of bravery to stifling a great ordeal?

She ventured a glance over her shoulder. Mrs. Bingham had peeled the bed clothes back and spread a new sheet on top of the old. Mama lay upon it, clad in the nightgown, in a curled position. Her shoulders heaved as she panted.

"How bad is it?" Mary asked.

"Bad?" Mrs. Bingham gave Mary a quick glance. "It's good, girl. She's nearly ready." She looked at Mary again. "You'll be doing the same in a few months." She raised an eyebrow. "I can't believe how fast little Rulon Owen grew up."

Mary's face went hot in reaction to the comment. Mrs. Bingham knew what Rulon had done with her. Her fingers twitched. She had to get out of this room!

Mrs. Bingham chuckled. "There, there. No sense getting hot and bothered. Your ma needs you close by."

Did the woman know her every thought?

"Hand me a towel."

She did so, catching a glimpse of white limbs as Mrs. Bingham raised the hem of her mother's gown and tugged it obscenely high. She turned away. What was the woman doing?

"Mary. Another towel." A brief moment later, "Come over here."

Mrs. Bingham's sharp command brought her up short. She shuddered, and went to the woman's side with the towel.

She caught herself before she said more than "Ah!" at the sight of her mother's knees apart, white flesh spotted with blood, and the junction of her limbs bulging with a strange distortion that seemed bent upon emerging. The child!

Mary shut her eyes, trying not to faint. She felt her body quivering as Mrs. Bingham put herself in the middle of the action, holding the infant's head and crooning words of encouragement. In making their appearance, babies did violate that sacred area. She wondered how it could survive the onslaught to be of use again.

But this was Mama's fifth child. Five times Papa had put—

She wrapped her arms tightly around herself and squeezed the fruit of her own actions. She would not think of Papa. Parents did not— Surely not so late in life.

But the evidence lay between Mrs. Bingham's hands, coming forth from Mama's body. Her parents *had* done that.

Enwrapped in Rulon's arms, she had thought of what they did as a special act reserved for young people. Mama could not possibly take pleasure in it. She deemed it shameful. No wonder she hated Rulon so. She had no notion that such an act could be glorious and pleasurable. Poor Mama.

Mama screamed, and Mary jumped. With a squishy sound, the child popped onto the towel on Mrs. Bingham's hands. She swiveled and gave the baby to Mary, who almost dropped the burden.

"What am I to do?" she squealed.

"Wipe the face," the woman replied, busying herself with other matters. "Clear the mouth. Make sure it's breathing."

Mary stood still for a moment, overcome with the responsibility of making sure life began.

"Now, girl."

She looked to the task, noticing that she had a new sister, and gave a moment of thought to her father's wish for a son. Not this time. Would there be another? She doubted it as the baby took breath and wailed.

ℴ

Rulon — November 28, 1861

28th Nov'br, 1861
Near Fairfax C-H
My belov'd wife,
The days grow shorter. The army is quiet, and long evenings of Idleness beside the fire strech before me. I think of you and the preshus burden you carry under yor heart. Several other fellows in The Troop have left their wives in a Delicate condition. Not long ago we discussed what Names our young'uns should carry. If it be in accordince with your Favor, I should Like for ~~my~~ Our Son to bear the name of my Father, Roderick Owen. He is a stalwart man, and worthy of such Respect and Honor. If it should be within my Pow'r, I will be there for our Child's birth, but I do not kno what God or the Fates has in store for my appointments at that time.

I can only think of You, dear heart. My arms ache to hold you again, even more so since you had the Likeness made and sint to me and I can gaze upon your sweet Face once more. I kiss the

Likeness a dozen times a day, pretendin it is you, my Darling. Alas it is not. There is no warmth of flesh Beneath my fing'rtips, no sweet breath coming from between The lips portraied with such realism. I yearn for the day when I can gaze upon the true Face and not the likeness, kiss the dear lips of flesh and Blood, and explore the delights that entranced Us in days of yore.

Receev a kiss from me upon your brow and upon your lips. Extend it to our Son, residing in warmth and comfort within his mother's woom. How I wish I could be by yor side, to hold you close and sooth your burdens and wipe away yor despair. I am yor true love, and my body and vig'r are yors alone.

Ever, yor Rulon

&

Mary — December 14, 1861

Wondering what Christmas would be like during a war, Mary tried to be cheerful for the sake of her younger sisters, but the absence of her husband and the unsteady gait caused by her increased weight pulled her spirits downward. Although no word had been published of conflicts with the Federal army, the men defending Virginia and the Confederacy had not come home during the cold weather, as her father had said they would. This was a grave disappointment, but with the excitement of a new baby in the house, Mary was putting the best face possible on her outlook for the holidays.

Papa brought the mail home at noontime, and there was a letter for her! She snatched it away from his hand, and opened it in the kitchen with the aid of a sharp knife.

"My belov'd wife," Rulon had written. Mary could have burst into tears at the swell of emotion this brought forth, but if she did, she would wash out the ink, so she restrained herself and commenced to read of her husband's desire that she name the child for his father.

"Mama wants her dinner right away," Ida said as she entered the kitchen. She paused to look at Mary's rapt attention to her mail, and said in a nasty tone, "Stop lally-gagging around with that moon face and dish it up. I'm giving you fair warning. Don't you dare be as demanding as Mama when you drop that brat."

It was all Mary could do to keep from slapping Ida's insolent face, but she gathered her wits without a retort and folded the letter to tuck it into her apron pocket, out of sight. When would this war be over so she and Rulon could get their own place?

When dinner was finished, Papa had returned to the store, Mama was placated, and the dishes were washed and put away, Mary retired to her room to read the rest of Rulon's letter. She put her hand into her pocket as she sat, but her fingers did not find the precious envelope. She stood, digging deeper into the material, but her letter was not in evidence.

Horror rising in her throat, Mary clung to the bannister as she made her way as quickly as she could back down the stairs and into the kitchen. Where had she been standing? There, beside the food safe. But she could see nothing on the floor. Of course. Sylvia had swept. She went to the dust bin. Nothing. Had the letter been kicked underneath the food safe or a cabinet? How was she to find it if it had? As big and ungainly as she was now with her belly full of child, she would never be able to get down on her hands and knees to look. Even if she did get down on the floor, she would never be able to get up again.

Sobbing now, Mary tried to get the broom underneath the most likely hiding spots, but she could coax nothing from beneath them. Again and again she tried to maneuver the broom straws to her advantage, but it was not to be. Wherever the letter had gotten to, it was as good as lost.

&

Rulon — December 31, 1861

Dec 31, 1861
Below Fairfax CH
Dearest Mary,
It is the last day of the year as I rite to you. We have past a joyful Christmas in our tents on the Cemetery road. One fellow got his father to send him a cask of brandy to celebrate the Holiday, which he shared out to the company. I admit I took a sip of the stuff, but being only lately recovered of my good health, I felt it the better part of good sense to forbear imbibing a greater amount.
We received presents gathered by ladies of the Lutheran church in Richmond. shirts, blankets and shoes were much

appreciated by the boys and me. A blanket made of wool was my portion, which I gratefully accepted. The minister brought us the gifts, adding small Testaments for each man. For myself, I am happy to have The Word about my person.

Our corporal, Ren Lovell, says this place is unhealthy, and I believe that to be true, as there has been much sickness in the regiment. We have even suffered a number of deaths unrelated to wounds received on the field of battle.

Our Captan is one whose health has not been good. He was away from the company for ten days earlier this month, and has just returned yesterday. Ren says the rumor is he has been taken with a typhoid fever. You must join your prayers with mine for his rapid recovery.

Sweet Mary, we did not speak much of our Christian Faith before we joined together in wedded bliss. This was a sore neglect on my part, as I was to be the head of our union and your guide in spiritual matters. I regret not discussing this with you. I will state that I have an abiding Faith in the goodness of God and His Holy Son, Christ Jesus. It is my hope that yor faith is in Him, as it is good to be equally yoked in Christ. I count my parents as a good example of being equally yoked. Pa has led the family in nightly devotions as long as I can remember, with Ma at his side. If it is agreeable to your dear self, I wish to do the same when we are once more united. How I long for that day of reunion. May the new Year bring it about.

Yor own Rulon

After he had taken his letter to be posted to Mary, Rulon kissed his wife's likeness, wrapped up in his Christmas blanket, and lay staring into the embers flickering in the fireplace they had built for the tent. When sleep did not close his eyes, he wondered what he had forgotten to do. He grunted softly as he remembered professing his beliefs to his wife; perhaps he should end the day with prayer.

He hoped Garth Von was asleep as he hoisted his legs over the edge of the cot and knelt beside it. For once, he was unmolested as he asked for safety for his wife, the coming child, his captain and the cause of the Confederacy, then tacked on a postscript concerning himself.

By the time he got back onto his cot, the cold of night had deepened, and he shivered until his body warmth filled the blanket cocoon and he relaxed into sleep.

�

The prick of a well-honed knife point just below his chin brought Rulon awake. He held himself rigid as Von's low chuckle reached him.

"Thought I didn't see, did you?" He swore, then spit out, "Think you're better 'n me, with your Shenandoah pathway to heaven? Want to be a martyr, boy?"

Then he was gone as though he had not been poised to slit Rulon's throat. The tent flap rustled and cold air entered, but it could not chill Rulon's blood more than it already was. He got up and went through his pack until he had his pistol in hand, loaded and primed.

Owen Leoyd mumbled, "What's the matter, Owen?"

Rulon licked his lips and cleared his throat before he got out an answer. "Von." He took two quick breaths before adding, "I'd like to relieve him of that hog-sticker someday, and cut a boil or two off his butt."

Owen chuckled. "Good luck to you. He sleeps light."

"Mayhap I should learn the trick," Rulon muttered as he lay down with the pistol at his side.

In a few moments, the flap twisted once more, and Von came in, cursing the cold, the lack of a wind-proof privy, and Rulon. The man made no further attempt toward violence, however, and when he began to snore, Rulon let his grip on the pistol relax.

Chapter 17

Ben — January 26, 1862

As soon as his sodden company entered the camp near Winchester and erected a tent, Ben found his pent-up emotions over being half dead from exposure to the cold needed an outlet.

Ma would frown on any communication that had the least bit of complaint. He was sure of that, so writing a letter home was out of the question. He pulled out a sheaf of letters he had received from Miss Allen, all unanswered. Perhaps it was not too late for him to write to her. Would she censure him on account of his lack of civility in replying?

He wasn't sure. All he knew was that he had to write to someone who cared for his welfare. Perhaps Miss Ella Ruth would welcome some kind of word from him, even though it be full of an excess of frustration.

He began reading again the letters she had sent to him. The first, which he had wondered if she wrote as a civic exercise, was quite intimate for a first communication. It was the one in which she had begged his forgiveness for her rejection of his love.

A second letter had followed, and she had not again petitioned for a restoration of their friendship. Indeed, she had been bold enough to write as though he had agreed. He had wondered at the time he received the note why she had been so sure he would accept a renewed friendship with her, and had put off replying, just as he had put off answering the first letter.

By the time the third missive had appeared, Ben's feelings in the matter had become quite soothed, but still, he did not find the time to answer her almost brazen remembrance of a certain tryst within a potting shed where he had tried mightily to seduce her, and she had withstood his advances. He read again her mention of how close she had come to giving in to his caresses.

He hesitated before he reread the fourth letter. He had received it just before the regiment's trek to Romney, and he had not had time to formulate a reply, although he knew at the time that he would have to do so soon. Almost a month had passed since then. He could not forget the words she had written professing to love him, and telling him how she had pressed each and every letter she had written to him to her lips in multiple places so that he might feel the warmth of her affection. Even now, he could almost feel his fingertips burning as he held the sheet of paper. He wondered if the married fellows in the company received such astounding letters from their wives. He had not dared to bring up the subject to the men, and then all desires had been squelched in the snow and sleet of their expedition.

He thought very carefully for five minutes on how he should begin his side of the correspondence, then threw all caution to the wind and began as he felt, calling her his darling Ella Ruth.

He filled two sheets of paper, put down his pencil, and began to re-read the letter before he sealed it. He almost blushed to see his words of yearning instead of complaint. Let the snow fall. Let the wind howl. He had warmed to his subject, and did not regret a single word of affection. Although his pride had taken a severe blow when she had refused to marry him, he knew now he had never ceased to love Ella Ruth. For all her follies and foibles, he wanted her more now than ever, and looked to a day when he could flee warfare and begin a new life as her protector and husband.

80

Rulon — February 13, 1862

Rulon found the inclement winter weather almost intolerable. Coming off a three-day picket assignment, he wiped down the bay horse as best he could under a makeshift shelter. After feeding his mount, he ran to his own shelter.

Ren was in the tent. Rulon entered to find him moving a chamber pot to catch a drip coming from the ridge.

"If we had tar, we could stop that leak," Rulon said.

"If we had tar, it would still be raining and the stuff wouldn't stick," Ren answered.

Rulon had no response. He felt the shirt that three days ago he had laid out on his cot to dry. It remained damp along every seam. He wiped his nose and made a derisive sound. What did he expect? With the air so saturated, the moisture in the material had little chance to evaporate.

"Any word on Leoyd?" he asked Ren, who had sat down to shuffle through paperwork.

"He's fortunate. The doc pulled him through the worst of the fever. That typhoid is nasty stuff. Doc is sending the captain home."

Rulon stood up straight, shocked. "You don't mean it."

"I'm afraid so. Herring is in charge until he returns." He shook his head, and added in a softer voice, "If he does."

Rulon absorbed the somber news. He felt bad asking, but with the change of leadership, he felt he had to broach the subject uppermost in his mind. "Do you reckon I can get a furlough?"

Ren shook his head. "Herring won't let you go with so many men laid up."

"Mary is nearing her time. I've got to go home and be with her."

"I'm sorry, Owen. We need every able-bodied man out there with their eyes open."

"And rain running down their collars. It's brutal detail. The Yankees aren't leaving their cozy tents."

"Spring will draw them out."

"Spring," Rulon said, and snorted. "I'm not sure I believe in it anymore."

A few days later, Rulon slogged through eighteen-inch deep mud to saddle his horse for another three days on duty away from camp. He spent twenty-four hours as a vidette, mounted almost all that time and hidden in a copse of trees keeping watch on a Yankee camp. For hours he shivered and wished for the fire he knew General Stuart had forbidden. Of course he knew a fire was impossible so close to the enemy, but the cold did suck the soul out of a man.

He worried about Mary. Centreville seemed so far away from Mount Jackson. He worried about catching cold and dying before he could see her again. He worried that the mumps would return.

After he returned from the patrol, he worried over how to impart to his wife the devastating news that greeted him. Captain Yancey had succumbed to the typhoid fever. He shouldn't tell her.

She would be concerned about him catching the fever. At long last, he kept his explanation of the situation brief, and sent Mary his wishes for every good prospect in her coming ordeal.

After he sealed and posted the letter, he worried that he couldn't recall if he had used the word "ordeal." He should have been more positive, giving her his assurances that she had nothing to fear. After all, his mother had birthed ten children without dying. No, it was better that he hadn't talked any more on that subject. His mention of the captain's death was enough for her to deal with.

౩

Mary — February 19, 1862

On a chilly day in February, Mary sat at the dinner table at noon, more for appearances than to actually take nourishment. She was so large in the belly that the mere thought of trying to fit food in with the child gave her qualms of anxiety. When would this torture be over? She waddled when she walked. Her arched back ached. Every little occurrence irritated her. A great sense of heaviness lay upon her soul, and she had not heard from Rulon for longer than she cared to think about.

Since entering what Mama had called "confinement" a few weeks ago, she had naturally not been to church services. Mama had tried to bring Mr. Moore around. Mary refused to see him, begging off with so much force that her mother had given up trying to persuade her that she must needs prepare her immortal soul for her coming journey through the Valley of the Shadow of Death. She could scarcely stand to be in the company of family members. Entertaining a visitor, even the minister, was more than she could support. Her only desire was to build a cozy nest in her bedroom and retreat into it.

"Mama, Mary won't eat," Ida complained.

Her mother turned to Mary and gave her the eye. "Mistress Mary, your babe will not be strong if you neglect your duty. Eat the pumpkin, at least. Your sister is quite proud of her dish."

Mary sighed. Ida had a tiresome streak that strained her forbearance. "I will make an attempt," she said, and took one bite of the mushy vegetable. Then she felt a heavy flow of liquid pass from between the juncture of her lower limbs. Alarmed, she choked, sputtered until the pumpkin lay upon and beside her plate, and cried out, "Fetch the doctor. Something has gone wrong."

A spasm crushed her stomach, and she bent as far forward as she could to contain it. "Oh Lordy, I'm dying," she gasped when she could breathe.

"Good heavens, daughter, what is amiss?" asked her father.

By this time, Mary was in the throes of another cramp, and could only shake her head. She had somehow pushed back from the table, but without arising. Looking down, she spied a stain on the carpet that looked vaguely pink. Could she have commenced to bleed? Blood had more of a crimson hue. What had rushed out of her body?

She felt herself swaying, and her father was there, stopping her from falling.

"Ida, go bring the doctor," he commanded.

The next thing Mary knew, she was ensconced on her bed, and Sylvia was bathing her face with a cold cloth. Her dress felt odd, and she glanced at the skirt to discover that it clung damply to her limbs. Perhaps she had lost control of her bodily process. No, there was none of the stink of that fluid in the room. Her instinct told her it was appropriate to be lying upon her bed, but she didn't want the dress to soak the bedclothes, and she begged Sylvia to help her remove it.

After that task had been accomplished, her focus narrowed to one thing, the cramping in her belly that caused her such pain and forced her to groan and shriek in terror. The loss of self-control frightened her. She had never been given to vapors and screaming fits. Why was her throat giving voice to all manner of sounds? Her belly again contracted in a mighty spasm and she let loose a horrid moan. Bending forward, she cradled the offending portion of her body with hands and arms that were powerless to rip the agony away. Was this the dreaded childbirth?

"Yes," said the doctor when he arrived an hour later and had persuaded her that he must give her an examination or he might pronounce an incorrect diagnosis. When he had finished, his conclusion was that she was indeed laboring to bring forth her child. He would send for Granny Pankwurst, the midwife, to attend her. Did she want him to notify Mrs. Julia Owen to be present?

Mrs. Owen? Rulon's mother? Yes, yes, she nodded, over and over, until the doctor left the room. Another agonizing moment gripped her. She screamed. She seemed to make an outcry each time a spasm came. Where was her mother's stoicism, the tightly gritted teeth that permitted no utterance? She knew herself to be a failure, an unworthy daughter who had no self-dignity or control.

"Mama, Mama," Mary keened when her mother came in and sat beside the bed, tight-lipped and unsmiling. "Mama," she sobbed when she went away to suckle her new child.

She craved a tender touch, a soothing hand upon her sweat-beaded brow, but she knew there would be no such approving gestures from her mother. She had done the unthinkable deed in this very room, and was thus to be punished for marrying, for breeding, for having an absent husband.

Ida came into the room what must have been hours later, bringing Granny Pankwurst. Just then Mary let loose an ear-piercing wail, and the girl covered her ears and hid in the corner by the door.

"Here now," said the midwife. "None of that caterwauling noise around when I deliver *my* babies."

Her babies? Mary didn't understand. This was Rulon's baby, *her* baby. She was the one undergoing this terrible pain to give birth. She wanted to protest, but she had no energy.

Then the woman demanded that she stand and stride about the room. What did she mean? As it was, Mary could scarcely bear to lie here now. How could she be expected to walk? But walk she did, half carried between the wizened old woman and a protesting Ida: shuffling, doubling over, clutching herself when the pains returned and she sank to her knees in agony.

When she wanted to sit, the midwife forbade it. When she panted, the midwife told her to stop, to breathe naturally. She wanted to shout at her, to send her from the room, but she had no energy.

Then the woman told her to get onto the bed, which was what she had wanted to do all the while she had been forced to ambulate. But once she had crawled upon it, belly pressing deep into the mattress, the woman pushed her over onto her back. She then sent Ida from the room, which surely pleased her craven sister. Oh horror! The midwife wanted to inspect the place only Rulon and the doctor had ever viewed.

The midwife pawed at her knees. Mary resisted. The woman slapped her upon one lower limb. Mary cried out at the ignominy. She tried to hold her limbs together, but she had no energy, and the woman succeeded in violating the privacy of her sanctuary.

"Rulon!" she wailed, guilt flooding her senses. She had allowed an invasion into the intimate place they had shared. The doctor had been persuasive of the need; this detestable woman had forced her to give way to her will. But where was Rulon? Her mind ceased to give her answers for a time, then she remembered that he was at war, off where lewd women followed the soldier camps to ply a trade both ancient and sordid. Was Rulon partaking of their filthiness? He should be here, beside her as she offered up the gift of a child to him from her very loins.

As the woman probed between her limbs, Mary sobbed at the robbery of both her dignity and her guardianship. Had Rulon matched her betrayal with one of his own? How could she know? He surely would not tell her if he had broken his vows. She whimpered his name in despair.

The midwife mocked her. "Leave off hollering for your man. He ain't nowhere around."

Yes, the fact was that he was nowhere around. Rulon could be dead and buried, for all she knew. Was this child to have no father? Would she die from shame if this perverse woman kept peering between her limbs? If she did, the child would die within her, having no chance to come forth into the world.

The interminable pain came again, wearing her out, scouring her body until she had no bones to bear her up.

The midwife finished her probing and left the room, carrying away the only light. Mary sensed that she was alone. Was she dying, then? Had the woman abandoned her? Another spasm beset her. *Rulon, can having a child be worth this pain?*

A cool hand touched her brow. She started, unaware that anyone had entered the room. A soft voice assured her, "Mary. You're doin' fine, girl. The babe will arrive soon."

Mother Owen. She had come. Would she be able to remove this awful burden of pain?

But no. A soothing voice and a cooling hand were all she could offer, and Mary's disappointment ran bone deep.

No one could save her. She must go through this all alone. She alone could enter the Valley of the Shadow of Death. What outcome would she find in that dismal place? Would she cheat Death, or would it cheat her? Her and Rulon? Her and Rulon and the babe?

Finally, the wicked old woman returned, elbowing Julia Owen quite cruelly, Mary thought, but her mother-in-law gave no protest. She simply sat at Mary's head and spoke comforting words.

"Hold on to my hand, Mary. Listen careful and do as the midwife tells you."

Mary could do no more than nod as the sweeping, all-encompassing torment came again.

Later, Mother Owen said, "Allow me to rub your neck, girl. Your shoulders have had quite a workout, bending and stretching so."

The tender fingers brought momentary relief before the onslaught of the next wave of affliction.

Then, when Mary was grunting and panting and holding apart her own limbs, a great despair upon her, Mother Owen whispered urgently, "It will soon be finished. Push on that babe. Push for your life, girl."

Some other creature cried out, high-pitched and protesting, wailing more robustly than she could find energy to do.

"A boy child," stated a self-satisfied voice.

Mary wanted only to sink into a mass of jelly and limp skin and cease to labor. She had worked so hard, harder than she ever had in her life up to this time. Her belly hurt from straining. Her back bore unremitting pain. Her special part burned as though torn. Her breasts ached from tension. Her arms yearned to hold the caterwauling creature she knew was Rulon's son. Her son. Their son.

∽

Mary watched the midwife pack up her belongings and leave the room. Sweet relief enveloped her. She would never see that woman again, if she could possibly help it.

"Here is your babe," Mother Owen said, and lay the sleeping infant, who she had wrapped in a soft blanket, in Mary's arms. "What name will you put on him?"

Cradling her son, Mary crooned to him, "Roddy, sweet little Roddy, my precious boy." She undid the covers enough to check something and sighed with satisfaction. "Ten wee fingers. Ten wee toes. A miniature likeness of your papa."

"Roddy, then?"

"Roderick Rulon Owen, but he is so tiny. Roddy will do for now."

Mother Owen smiled and resumed her seat in the shadow beside the bed.

Mama bustled into the room, carrying the baby Eliza. "Now that the excitement has ceased, let me look at little Randolph. I suppose you will do him the indignity of shortening his name to Randy?"

"No, Mama. His short name will be Roddy. His long name is Roderick."

"Roderick! You want to name him after that strutting rooster of a man?"

"Good morning, Amanda."

"Julia!"

Mary looked at Mother Owen, expecting some sort of outburst in defense of her husband. She herself certainly felt offense at her mother's characterization of the man. She liked Father Owen.

"He's not such a bad sort," Mother Owen said, a little smile quivering at the corner of her mouth.

"I beg your pardon. I did not see you there, and meant no offense to you."

"You meant every offense to Mr. Owen," she rejoined, but in a mild tone.

Mama turned back to stare at Mary. "I prefer the name Randolph, in honor of your father."

Mary took a deep breath and steeled her spine for the encounter. "He is named Roderick, to give honor to my husband's father. The next boy can bear Papa's name."

"I must protest. You live in your father's house."

"Mama, I will not be dissuaded. Mother Owen, please go to the minister to record the name as I have said it to you."

"You cannot dishonor your father."

"Amanda," Mother Owen said, her voice indicating rising ire. "Leave the girl be. You did not bring the child into the light. She did the job, and a fine job it was."

Mama rounded upon Mother Owen. "She herself is a child, play-acting at being a wife. Now she pretends to be a mother, as well? I won't have it."

Mother Owen's eyebrows went up. She patted Mary's shoulder. "Amanda, we've been friends for many a year. I cannot speak any plainer than this. Mary is a wife, woman, and mother. She ain't acting at it. She earned the right to name her own babe with her labor and blood. If you can't reckon with the broad fact of it, I'll move her and the boy out to the place."

"You would not."

"She bears the Owen name. By rights, she should be with us. Mary stayed here because she wanted to sooth your feelin's, so Rulon told me. She's welcome on the Owen farm."

Mary watched as the starch went out of her mother's spine. She sagged against the chest of drawers, her face going pale. At length, she said in a strained voice. "I may have spoke out without thinkin'. Mary, I bear you no ill will. Name the boy as you please. Don't leave us."

"Mama." Mary couldn't say more for the lump in her throat. She had never seen such a transformation.

"That's sensible, Amanda. It's high time you give the girl the affection you've been withholding these long months, heaping on her head your disapproval of my son."

"It's not himself—"

"I reckon. You didn't cotton to his haste. It was better that they married than take other paths." Her eyes softened. "They had so little time together, Amanda. Mayhap it's all they get."

"No!" Mary felt her throat go raw. The two women turned to her, distress written across their countenances. Realizing they thought she had not faced reality, she added, "Don't speak of it now. Don't haunt my wee boy's dreams with that sad vision."

They looked at each other, her mother, Rulon's mother. Eliza began to wail. Roddy woke up and whimpered. "Let us be reconciled," Mary begged, bouncing the boy gently.

Mama extended her hand toward Mother Owen, who took it

and gave it a squeeze.

"We will say no more of this," said Mother Owen. "We will be good Christian neighbors. This upset in our country can't last forever. Rulon will come home and make his family complete. At that time, we all must leave the young'uns be."

"I will say no more, "Mama said.

Mother Owen gave a slight nod. "See that you keep your resolve."

Mary sensed the balance shifting in the room. What had she just experienced? Mother Owen had gained the upper hand, and Mama had willingly allowed it.

"Mary," Mother Owen said softly, turning toward her, "I'll go see Mr. Moore now. It will be as you wish."

◈

Not much time had elapsed after Mother Owen left that the wee babe awoke and began to sniffle. Then he started to cry, a long wail at first, then robust and alarming demands for attention.

"What does he want?" Mary asked her mother.

"He is most likely hungry, if he has not wet himself" she said, and approached the bed. "You must give him suck."

Mary touched her bodice above her swollen breast, self-conscious in the presence of her mother. "Will it hurt?" she whispered.

"I do not recall any pain," Amanda said, her words clipped. "Merely put him to the teat. He will know what to do." She hoisted Eliza into a more comfortable position, nodded once, and left the room.

Mary slowly unbuttoned her bodice, making shushing sounds all the while to try to appease her squalling infant. She wanted to join him in his howls, but that would never do. She must now be the adult lady she professed to be, and give her child sustenance.

Roddy did not know what to do when Mary brought him to her breast. He rooted around, whimpering, but did not seem to know what to do with his mouth, which Mary imagined was supposed to clamp around her tender nipple, or something of the sort. She tried guiding his efforts, but he would not take it into his mouth, preferring to cry instead.

After a while, she had joined him, weeping in frustration and pain. Even when she tried to squeeze out liquid, none appeared, and she only succeeded in making herself sore.

Was he only wet? She discovered that he was not, but could not ease his distress.

After at least an hour of the most humiliating effort that Mary had ever experienced, the baby had exhausted himself with crying, and fell into a fitful sleep. She sat with him resting on her lap, weeping silent tears, her shoulders shaking convulsively.

A rap sounded on the door, and immediately thereafter, it opened. A dark woman not much older than herself appeared in the doorway. "Pardon, ma'am," she said. "The lady says I am to nurse the boy baby for you."

Mary endeavored to compose herself in the face of this stranger. "My mother brought you here?"

"I comes from Mount Airy," the girl explained. "Your mama have rented me."

"Rented you? To feed my child? I don't even know who you are."

"Marse Meem call me Pansy, ma'am. I's a wet nurse." She gestured to her bosom. "I has milk, ma'am, for the young'un."

Mama's repentant spirit has not lasted for long, Mary thought as she felt Roddy stir against her limbs. Their voices must have disturbed him, and he worked himself awake and resumed his wails.

Embarrassed, Mary held him out to the Negro girl. "Feed him," she said, barely able to restrain her own wails as the girl took him and went to the chair beside the bed.

As her baby began to suck greedily at the dark breast, Mary sank into her pillow and turned away, trembling with shame that she could not fulfill her most basic role as a mother, that of suckling her own child.

Chapter 18

Mary — February 26, 1862

A week later, Mary got herself out of bed, lit a candle, pulled on a dressing gown, and took on the task of writing a letter. She had neglected her correspondence with Rulon for some time, and it pained her to admit her sloth. But if truth be told, she had been under a great strain of late, what with her baby's birth last week and all the turmoil afterward. Now it was past time for her to catch her husband up on those matters.

Biting her lip, she began:

26 February, 1862

My darling Rulon,

I send news which I hope is agreable to you. On Wednesday last I was delivr'd of a helthie baby boy. Yor wishes prevailed over those of my mother, and I have named the child Roderick Rulon Owen. Yor ma recorded the name for me so my moth'r could not have her way.

I hope you do not mind that I put your name to the boy along side that of yor father, as you had asked for. I call the baby Roddy, as he is much too tiney to bear yor papa's long name at present.

Sister Marie brought baby Roddy the most cunning rattle, whittled out by Carl, I believe, or perhaps James. I fear I am distracted by dificulties I have experinced folowing the birth.

I hope to use the rattle to appease Baby when he cries from hunger. I continue trubled with ~~diffacultyies~~ failing in ~~giving him su~~ feeding him properly. He is not patient with me. Mama brings in a wet nurse to feed the boy, but it distreses me sorely to see Baby fed by a slave girl rented from Mount Airy. Such a scene harows me with guilt that I cannot do my duty as well as he demands. He is a very robust child. I promise I will continue my efforts to feed him.

Dearest husband, please take all mesures to avoid harm's way. Altho we do not hear of battels with the foe as yet, I pray The Telegraf does not return to bringin in horible casualty lists like we read last summr. They were most distresing. I prey for you nite and morning, for my bosom aches with fear over yor well-being as the seas'n for war approaches.

Plese excuze my poor spelling. I cannot seem to make my brain fathum the proper letters I need to express myself to you.

Accept the kiss I place upon this X as tho it was put upon yor brow by my own lips. It is ment to convey all the love of my heart to you.

Yor wife,
Mary

She finished, tongue sticking out from between her bitten lips, and paused to place a kiss upon the mark. Then she shook sand over the ink. She carefully poured it back into the shaker, folded the paper as though it were an envelope, turned it over, and affixed Rulon's last known address.

She heard Roddy stirring in his cradle at the foot of her bed, and hurried her task as he began to cry.

Mary sealed the improvised flap shut with a few drippings from her melting candle, wishing she had a grand signet ring to press into the wax seal. She shrugged, used her thumb to smash it flat instead, then winced at the momentary burn.

"There," she said, satisfied that she had finished the long-pending task. "I have suffered long, husband," she said to the letter as she quickly moved it through the air in order to cool the seal. "The baby is crying. I had better go try to feed him with these poor, chapped breasts, or Mama will interfere again." She stuck her burned thumb in her mouth to alleviate the pain, and leaving the letter on the table, prepared to attempt to nurse her son.

છ

Julia — February 28, 1862

When Julia had finished her town business at the Hilbrands store on Friday, she began to pull herself up into the buggy for the return trip home, but something stopped her, and she put her foot back on the ground.

She looked in the buggy. Her egg basket, now heaped with parcels, lay on the floor of the vehicle. Had she forgotten some task, an item she was to buy or sell? No. Had she neglected to ask for the mail? The envelope addressed to her in Rod's firm hand that seemed to burn a hole in her pocket belied that notion.

Her grandchild. Oh lordy, she had forgotten to pay a visit to Mary and the baby!

Taking herself in hand, she walked around the block to the Hilbrands' home and let the knocker fall on the brass plate. Ida bade her enter, and she soon knocked on Mary's door.

She found the girl in her bed, in tears, her bodice open, and the baby lying across her limbs squalling in counterpoint to his mother.

"Ah, Mary girl! What's this?" She picked up Roddy and put a finger into his mouth. "Shush, sweet boy. Shush," she crooned.

"I am a failure," Mary wailed. "I cannot feed him." She covered her face. "Mama rents a wet nurse."

"There, there." Julia tried to sooth both mother and son.

Mary put her hands across her bosom and gasped out, "I've tried so hard. Mama says they are too small, which prevents the milk from coming."

"Nonsense," Julia said. "I am small, and have not lacked milk for my young'uns." She bounced Roddy as she commenced walking about the room. "You are anxious. That is causing the stoppage." She returned to the side of the bed. "Have you been up? Hasn't it been two weeks now since he came along?"

Mary shook her head. "I am to stay quiet until I cease passing blood."

Julia raised her eyebrows. "That will take a time. You must arise and go on livin'. Activity will stimulate the milk. The baby's cries should also help."

"They swell," Mary said, sniffing. "Nothing lets loose."

"May I see them?"

Mary allowed her to view one breast, then the other.

"There is chapping, but perhaps no fever. May I touch?"

Mary drew a sharp breath. She let it out slowly. "Must you?"

"I think it's needful," Julia replied, and put out her hand to check for a raised temperature in the skin. "Ah, yes. This one requires a warm, wet cloth applied here for fifteen minutes at a time, once an hour, until you feel relief. Do not nurse from it until the redness goes out of it. I would not recommend a mustard plaster, but perhaps a warm poultice once a day." She explained which herbs should be mixed for the application. "And you must get out of bed. You will only wither, lying in bed all the day. That is not healthy."

Mary began to cry. "Why doesn't Mama tell me these things?"

"She is not forthcoming in such matters," Julia explained. "You know her reticence about physicality. You must bear affection for her in spite of her foibles."

"I do love my mother. Whether she returns the feeling is in question."

"Then now, girl. You know she loves you. She is goin' through her own child-bearin' cycle, and a surprise it was, too. Give her time to return to normal."

"She is usually affectionate and kind. I have missed that in her."

"We have all, none more so than your pa." Julia smiled. "You may have noticed that menfolk need affection more than women."

"Papa? He's busy with his work."

"Don't you go to thinkin' that he has no need of your mother's time and care."

Mary shuddered. "He's my papa."

"He's a man. Like your own."

"Please, Mother Owen."

Julia laughed. "I have embarrassed you. I beg your pardon. At times I speak too plainly for my own good." She stooped and helped Mary out of the bed and into the chair alongside it. Then she gave Roddy to her. "Put him to the breast and think of a pleasant scene." She continued with advice in a soothing voice. "Lean back against the cushion. Feel its softness enveloping you. Here. Try this with your fingers." She showed Mary how to guide her nipple into Roddy's mouth. "It will soon be second nature to you, if you will heed my words. Remember to be calm. Don't think about difficulty. Think of pleasant views."

"He is sucking," Mary said. "He has not done that before."

"Relax," Julia advised in a low tone. "Rain coursin' down a window pane. Water squeezed from a sponge. Sippin' warm milk from a cup." She could see Mary lowering her hunched shoulders.

"That's the way, girl. Give the babe of your strength."

"I am not strong," Mary murmured.

"More than you suspect," Julia answered. "More each passin' day."

80

Mary — March 4, 1862

Mary cowered in the cellar of the house, arms wrapped around her baby. Another shell whistled overhead and exploded in the distance. Ida shrieked in her ear, and Mary elbowed her sister in an attempt to quiet her. Sylvia and India huddled together. Mama sat in the corner, covering Baby Eliza with her shawl.

Poor Papa. He must be taking cover in the storeroom, Mary thought. She was glad the little girls had come home for dinner. She wondered how long the school would remain open. She shuddered at a boom that was too close at hand. *God, help us,* she begged. *Help Rulon.* She wasn't sure where he was now. She had lost track of all the different armies while these invaders were threatening her baby's life. *God, please don't let them kill my baby.*

Dust drifted down from the ceiling as a shell thudded into the ground nearby. Sylvia and India joined Ida's outcry, and now Roddy also raised his voice.

"Hush, hush," she said, trying to sooth him.

Mary could hear little Eliza greedily sucking from her mother's breast, unheeding of the bombardment. *Why is it so easy for Mama to give nourishment and at the same time, she prohibits me from doing so?* she wondered. *I will not let her rent the wet nurse again.*

She had been putting the warm herbal compresses upon her sore breast, as Mother Owen had advised, and the infection had now gone. It was time to be the strong mother Rulon's mama thought her to be.

Defiantly, Mary opened her bodice, brought Roddy to her breast, and concentrated on remembering what Mother Owen had told her.

"You must relax," she had said. "Do not pay heed to your bosom or to pain. Think of a pleasant scene, a meadow with sheep grazing, or the mountains beyond the river. Think on the flow of water. Be peaceful in your soul, and milk will come through to the boy."

Roddy opened his mouth, latched onto her nipple and began to suck. She thought of the flowing river, nurturing the land with needed moisture. She thought of rain gently falling on the bean crop in the garden. She thought of Sylvia pouring a can of water onto the base of the azaleas. She felt an unfamiliar sensation, and looked down to discover that her son was gustily drawing liquid into his mouth, a drop dribbling from the side of his lips. A patch of darkness marked her bodice above the unused breast. Her milk had let down, and she was nursing her child as easily as ever her mother had.

Almost sobbing with relief, she took a moment to say a grateful prayer, and to bless her mother-in-law for her kindness and wisdom. When another bomb burst overhead, she scarcely noticed.

80

Rulon — March 6, 1862

The Yankee cavalrymen came out of their winter camps.

Nearly every day they accosted the Confederate pickets in fierce skirmishes. One evening, Rulon limped into the tent, dropped his saddlebags and weapons on his bed, and spread his hands before the warmth of the stove.

Owen Leoyd came in behind him and said, "Holy Hepzibah! You're dripping blood all over the floor."

Rulon examined his arms and didn't see any wounds. "Where, man?"

"The back of your right leg. You don't feel it?"

Rulon snorted. "I'm so cold I can't feel my own nose." He looked over his shoulder and winced at the sight of the blood on the limb Leoyd had indicated.

"That needs to be tended. Do you want to see the doc?"

"I'd rather not. He'll likely take the leg off." Rulon unfastened his uniform trousers and kicked them off, then rummaged in his saddlebag. "My Ma sent me a bandage for Christmas. I hoped I wouldn't need it anytime soon." He held out a knitted roll to Leoyd. "I'd be obliged if you'd do the honors."

175

Leoyd acquiesced and splashed a small amount of spirits on the wound, at which Rulon gritted his teeth to avoid crying out. Leoyd held the edges of the gash together until he'd wrapped the knitted bandage around Rulon's calf.

"The cut's not deep, but it surely dripped a fair amount. Too bad it spoiled your fancy trousers."

"Don't you speak ill of my mother's fancy work," Rulon said, grinning to defuse his words. "She cared enough to make it pretty for me. I count her a true Virginia patriot, even if she did come from up North."

"Your ma's a Yankee?"

"No, no. She hasn't been that for a long spell. One summer when she was a slip of a girl, she went down to Shenandoah County to visit a cousin, and never returned home."

"Uh huh. What kept her in the county?"

"Her stay was prolonged on account of my Pa's persuasive words on behalf of his bright future and overwhelming manliness. When he asked if she would be his bride, she told him 'yes' and never looked back."

"A Yankee, huh?"

"Not anymore." He looked ruefully at his trousers, then donned them again. "I'll ask that you don't share the facts of my heritage with Von. He already thinks I'm not worthy of fightin' for Virginia."

"He's mighty peculiar, for sure" Leoyd said. "I don't think he's right in the head."

"I will give him credit that he fights the Yankees like a devil from hell," Rulon said. "However, I never want to be in front of that blade of his when he's not set on toying with me."

Leoyd raised his eyebrows. "You think he's playing with you? He's got some kind of grudge against you, Owen. I don't know what caused it."

Rulon shook his head. "He took a dislike to me from the moment he first saw me. I reckon it's mighty awkward to have to sleep with one eye open and not even know why."

"Huh," said Leoyd. "Let's go grab whatever's left of supper."

On the way to eat, someone thrust a couple of letters into Rulon's hands. While he ate, he opened Mary's to read.

In only seconds, he was on his feet, whooping and hollering, his wound forgotten and the contents of his plate scattered on the ground.

One of the men looked up and asked, "What ails you, Owen?"

Rulon tried to calm himself enough to answer, but the powerful emotion Mary's words had evoked prevented him from giving a coherent reply for some minutes.

"I'm a papa," he finally gasped. "I have a son." The strength left his legs as the enormity of that responsibility swept through him. He sat with a whoosh as the air left his lungs.

The troopers of Company "I" gathered around, pounding him on the back and offering congratulations. All except for one, who eyed him with a resentful air.

ॐ

Ella Ruth — March 11, 1862

Poppa stormed into the parlor, bearing aloft an envelope.

"What is the meaning of this?" he said, his voice raised and angry.

Ella Ruth patted a wrinkle out of her skirt before she replied, striving to put on a coquettish smile. "Why, Poppa. I have no idea. Pray tell, what do you have there?"

He approached on stiff legs, his face crimson, and waved the paper in the air. "This, young lady, is a letter. It is addressed to you. It comes from that young man you professed to love, then cast aside. Why does he presume to write?"

Ben wrote to me? She felt her legs begin to tremble, then stilled them with an effort. *He finally wrote?* It had been several months since she first assayed to forge a tie with him, but when he hadn't responded to any of her missives, her hopes of hearing from him had diminished almost to despair.

"Poppa, I cannot say," she replied, trying to be arch, and finding herself failing miserably. Her stomach clenched.

"I fail to see why he would think you desired a correspondence with him." He stared back at Ella Ruth, pursing his lips and gripping the letter in two hands at the level of his watch chain.

After a long moment, she put out her hand and said in a meek voice, "May I have it?"

Poppa seemed startled by her request. "What? You may not." He held it out of her reach.

177

Ella Ruth raised her chin. "Perhaps he has sent me news of the progress of the war. Or a warning about the advance of the enemy. I must have it."

He considered. "I hardly dare think a lowly private soldier would be in possession of such information." He narrowed his eyes. "Did you write to him?"

She raised her chin even higher. "What if I did? It cannot matter to you. We are at war, and it behooves the women of this county to support our brave soldiers."

"Ella Ruth, you are not to encourage this young scoundrel. I forbid further contact with him."

She rose and attempted to snatch the letter from his hands, but he held it above her head. She cried out, "Poppa, you cannot deter me from having affection for Benjamin. If you had only bent your will the tiniest little bit, I would have been a bride and out of your hair long ago."

He snorted. "You were ill suited to be the bride of a farmer. You still are, even in these hard times."

She smiled, feeling her lips quivering the slightest amount. *I will not cry*, she decided. "You think poorly of me, Poppa, but you shall not forbid me to love this man."

"Love. What do you know of love, daughter? You imagine the emotion makes the world revolve. I know it helps, but does not do the job alone."

"Such a cynical Poppa."

He looked down at her, his heightened color fading. "I'm a realist. Our world is undergoing a tumult that may crush us, and you only think of that Owen boy."

"Man, Poppa. He's a soldier."

"Not even of the age of majority." He turned and strode around the room.

"I don't care. He's done the work of a man for years."

He stopped before Ella Ruth, waved the envelope in her face and said, "And he's tried to seduce my daughter into dalliance on more than one occasion."

"Poppa!" She felt her face grow warm. "What a thing to say to me." Her stomach twisted in dismay at the insult.

"Don't deny it. I have eyes." His voice began an upward march into renewed anger. "I've seen you come back from meeting him, your face flushed and your eyes filled with stars. He's not the right sort of man for my daughter."

"Oh Poppa. If you only knew him as I do." More than her lips trembled now. Her entire body vibrated with emotion. "He wanted only to marry me." She inhaled.

"I won't have it," he said, his voice hard and brittle. He tore the letter to bits, dropped them into a tin wastebasket beside a table, and left the room.

Ella Ruth let her breath go in a rush as she dropped to her knees beside the basket, feeling a sob clog her throat. *Poppa, what have you done?*

଼

Julia — March 11, 1862

Julia waited on the porch of the Hilbrands' home while James knocked on the door a second time. He stepped back, frowning. She placed a hand on his arm to forestall any complaint. She had no idea why it was taking so long for the family to respond, but surely someone would answer sooner or later.

At last, Julia heard footfalls approaching, and the door opened as though it were jerked backward. Ida stood in the opening, hair disheveled and apron rumpled. She held a squalling child on her shoulder.

"Go away," Ida said. "I'm too busy to entertain." She patted the baby and moved side to side in a futile attempt to sooth the child.

Julia couldn't determine if the babe was Amanda's girl or her grandchild, Roddy. She put out her hands to give aid, but Ida wasn't ready to accept help, for she turned away, kicking the door shut behind her.

Feeling anger rising up in her, Julia was on the point of snatching the door latch and pushing the door open again, but James grabbed her by the upper arms.

"Whoa, Ma. Ida is a mite overwrought. She won't welcome your help." He cocked his head. "She's ornery enough to see it as interferin'."

Julia sighed. He was correct. Even so, she took the slight to heart, feeling as though she had been stung by a passel of wasps.

She looked up. James gazed at her, his dark eyes reflecting his concern. She patted his arms as the anger drained away. "You're so right, son. She's prickly as a bundle of nettles. We'll go."

She wanted to see Mary. She wanted to hold Roddy. Now was not the right moment. "We'll go," she repeated, and stepped off the stoop.

Chapter 19

Rulon — March 13, 1862

March 13, 1862
In Camp, Warrenton Junc. Via.
My Dearest Wife,
My joy upon hearing our blessed news new no bounds when I recved your letter the past week. I wood have ritten you at the time to thank you for producing a fine heir, but events with the Enemy prevented me taking pen in hand.

The Yankees have come up in such numbers that our general Johnston decided to remove the army from the thret. As a consequence, many suplys had to be destroyed, along with a mountain of private soldiers baggage. Oh Sugar, the smell of bacon burning about drove us mad. Also grain was set afire to keep it from the Yankees hands. Flour broken from barr'ls and heeped on the ground resembl'd a strange snowfall. I warrant we will rue the day we had to waste these provisions, but we had no way to carry them off from Manassas Junc.

My little Wife, I miss you with all my heart. Conserve your health in all ways. Kiss my Dear Son upon his brow and tell him of my boundless affection for him.

I remain, yor husband,
Rulon Owen

80

Ella Ruth — March 15, 1862

For several days, Ella Ruth barely left her room, trying to find a way to read Ben's destroyed letter. Putting the pieces together was like trying to assemble a picture puzzle. At first, she thought she would make up a paste of flour and water and affix the mangled bits onto another piece of paper. After only a moment, she knew that wouldn't work. Ben had written on both sides of the paper. She wanted to read all that he had written, especially when it became evident from the first few words that he had forgiven her, and wanted her friendship.

She tried laying the pieces out and simply turning them over, but they were so small and lightweight that the slightest breath sent them fluttering to the floor, and all her labor was for naught.

Despairing, she stared out the window, seeking solace in the sunlight bathing the tops of the trees. She stared so long that her eyes became dry, and she blinked to moisten them.

Dear Ben. His letter deserved to be read so that she might answer.

She sniffed. She reached around to pick up her handkerchief to wipe her nose, and her elbow bumped the window pane.

The window pane. Glass. If I place the pieces on a sheet of glass, I can cover them— She stopped. How was she to get two sheets of glass? Poppa would scarcely buy them for her, if indeed, any were to be had. Where was she going to obtain glass?

It was not long before Ella Ruth decided that she would remove two of her window panes and use them to encase the pieces of paper. No matter if a little cold seeped into the room. She could sacrifice a bit of comfort for a desirable outcome to her letter dilemma.

After the midday meal, she hid a table knife in the folds of her skirt, told her mother she was going to take a nap, and mounted the stairs as quickly as she dared. She locked her bedroom door and surveyed the windows of the chamber. It wouldn't do for her maid to discover that she had cannibalized her window panes, so she chose the casement that had the least use, and regularly remained covered by the thick draperies that had hung in place for ages.

She laid an old pillowcase on the floor beneath the window, and began to attack the putty that held one pane of glass in the frame with her purloined knife. Was Mama likely to discover a knife was missing? She decided not to let that fret her. *Who counts silver anymore? There are larger issues at hand.*

Soon she had chiseled a quantity of putty from the bottom of the frame. Her hands quivered from the effects of the unaccustomed labor, and one was red and abraded. She determined to find another solution than hitting the base of the knife with the heel of her hand to dig out the stubborn putty.

After looking around in her room, she found a wooden figurine that would serve to hammer on the knife handle, and then the work went more rapidly and with far less pain.

At last the moment came when one window pane was free, and she carefully pried it loose from the last remnants of the putty keeping it in the frame. *Ha!* she thought. *I will not be defeated, Poppa.*

She took the glass to her dressing table and wrapped it in a towel, then went back to work on a second panel.

The putty in this frame had hardened unevenly, and at one point, she held her breath as the knife blade skittered across the glass, fearing that the pane would shatter. It chipped a bit on the edge, but that probably was acceptable, as long as she watched where she held the glass later.

At last she had two sheets of glass free and out of the window frame. Now, what was she to do with the putty? If she put it in the wastebasket, Lula would find it as she cleaned the room. No, Ella Ruth must dispose of it herself.

She gathered up the pillowcase and hid it in the back of her armoire, behind a pair of shoes. Lula would not be cleaning in there. Later, she would think about how to get the putty safely out of the house.

But first, she must clean the glass.

She poured a small amount of water into her wash basin and wet a face scrubbing rag. Then she rubbed the surface of the glass with it. *My goodness, how dirty the glass is!* Lula must not have washed the lesser-used windows much. She would speak to her about—

No, I won't. I can't let her know I've taken the glass.

When the panes were clean and she was at the point of laying the paper puzzle of Ben's letter down on the first sheet of glass, someone knocked on the door.

She squeaked involuntarily and almost dropped the glass.

Remembering that she was supposed to be napping, Ella Ruth let the knocking continue for a moment while she hid the glass, then answered in what she hoped was a sleepy voice.

"What is it?"

Lula said, "Miss Ella Ruth, you have a caller."

"Who is it?"

"It's the preacher man, Mr. Moore."

Ella Ruth groaned. The man probably wanted her to sing in the choir. "Send him away. I'm tired."

"No, miss. I ain't gonna send away no preacher man. That'd be scandalous."

This time, Ella Ruth sighed. "He won't bite you."

"He's the preacher!"

She supposed she would have to appease the man, and her maid, for sure. "All right. Let him know I will be down shortly."

"Yes, Miss Ella Ruth. I surely will."

Mr. Moore did not want her to join the choir. He wanted to counsel her about her soul.

After the formalities had been seen to, he said, "Your father is concerned for your welfare. He says you have fallen under the influence of a, ah, I believe he said 'a reprobate,' Miss Allen."

Ella Ruth felt her eyes widen. *Poppa can only mean Ben, but surely he isn't a reprobate.* "I'm sure I don't know what you mean, Mr. Moore." She refused to call him *sir* after such a beginning.

The minister tugged on his coat by the lapels, clearly nervous. "He, ah, claims you received a letter from an undesirable person."

Ella Ruth fixed her gaze upon him. "Do any of your parishioners fall into those categories? Reprobate? Undesirable?"

"I don't believe so, Miss Allen."

"This person my father brands with those pejoratives comes from one of our oldest county families. My father is mistaken." She got to her feet. "There you have it, Mr. Moore. You cannot think the son of Roderick Owen is some wanton beast."

He hastily rose. "No, Miss. A fine family, indeed."

She wanted to know if Poppa had mentioned that he had destroyed the letter before she had a chance to be "influenced" by it, but decided not to prolong the interview.

"Good day, sir. I'm sure you have other calls more pressing than this little misunderstanding." She hurried the minister to the door, shut it almost before he was clear, and hurried up the stairs. A puzzle awaited her.

80

Determining which of the pieces of paper constituted the first page of the letter was more difficult than Ella Ruth supposed it would be. After an hour's work, however, she finally had assembled the page on one sheet of glass, placed the second sheet atop the first, and was ready to begin reading.

She had scarcely begun when the supper bell rang.

She made an unladylike sound, and then got to her feet and looked around for a place to hide the letter in its glass encasement. She finally decided it could be hidden under the bed if she arranged a few carelessly-dropped items of clothing in front of it. She added one slipper behind the clothing, just in case, and firmly shut the door behind her as she left the room.

Supper went on forever. She sustained herself through the hour by repeating to herself time and again the salutation with which Ben had begun: *My darling Ella Ruth.*

That was not the greeting of a polite correspondent replying to an acquaintance. It most certainly was the heartfelt greeting of a friend. She remembered the tingle of pleasure that swept through her upon setting her eyes on the words. She was understating the case. Ben wrote not as a friend, but as a lover.

Momma asked her something. Ella Ruth had to beg her pardon and ask her to repeat the question. It was a matter of passing around the biscuits, and Ella Ruth felt her face warm. Poppa was looking her way with a wary expression. She would have to lend more attention to the business of supper if she were to get through it with good grace and no suspicion.

Afterward, Momma wanted a family hour of music, and Ella Ruth had to endure hearing Merlin sing "Lorena" as though he were on the battlefront, pining after a girl. She wondered if he were going to join the army, or if Poppa had pressured him to complete his university education first. What a shame it must be to her brother to remain home when all his friends had enlisted straight away. Ben had been eager to serve.

Ben. Ella Ruth repeated to herself his greeting. *My darling Ella Ruth.* She was his darling. No matter what he thought, Poppa could never take that from her.

Suddenly the music ended, and Momma went about kissing everyone goodnight. At last! Ella Ruth fled to her room, shut the door, and leaned against it. Had Lula turned down her bed and removed her discarded clothing from the floor?

Yes. She had. However, the slipper still masked the letter sufficiently that she thought it safe to assume that her secret had not been discovered. She would have to find a better hiding place tonight. That could come after she read Ben's words.

Setting the glass sheets on her dressing table, she remembered to return to the door and lock it, slipping the key into the pocket of her dressing gown. She placed the lamp where it would shine upon the paper puzzle, and bent to her task.

Ben most certainly had feelings for her. His words warmed her, body and spirit, and when she had perused the first side of the first sheet, Ella Ruth very carefully rotated the sheets of glass to read the back side.

Although he told her a great deal about the grueling campaign he had survived in western Virginia, he spent time reminiscing about moments he and she had spent together.

He had not yet written a word of love for her, but the undercurrent ran deep, and she pressed forward, reading Ben's account of one time when he took her inside the mill after everyone had left. She recalled the air being hazy with dust from the day's wheat grinding. She had sneezed again and again, and he lent her his handkerchief, tying it around her head to filter what she breathed.

Was that the action of a reprobate? No. He cared for her then, and she imagined he cared for her now.

She sat back with a sigh when she came to the end of the first sheet of the letter. She wondered how long it would take to piece together the second half.

Before she disassembled the puzzle, a thought came to her. She might wish to read Ben's words again. Perhaps she should take the time to write out a copy of his missive.

This prompting sent her on a mental search for suitable paper on which to transcribe the precious words. *I can't use writing paper. I dare not use up what I have on hand.* Would parcel paper serve? The kitchen storeroom had a supply. Though it was coarse paper, it surely would take the impression of a lead pencil.

By now, the house had fallen into rest. She rose from the dressing table and carefully opened her door. She would have to be quiet as she descended the stair and went into the kitchen.

Careful! That is the squeaky tread. To bypass it, she

supported her weight on the railing with one hand so she could take a large step while holding her candle with the other hand.

What was that moaning noise? She froze, listening. It could only be the wind. Funny, she had never noticed wind howling around the eaves before. But then, she was accustomed to being asleep at this hour.

Ella Ruth finally got safely to the bottom of the stair and listened before she ventured toward the back of the house. No sounds. Lula slept in an upper room, and the other house workers did, as well, so she needn't worry about disturbing anyone on the ground floor.

Unless Poppa was up doing some kind of business accounts.

She looked toward his study. *Good. There's no light showing.* She took a great breath and stepped around the newel post. Something ran over her foot, and she scarcely kept from screaming.

Shivering, she stood on tiptoe, trying to regularize her breathing. Had it been a rat? Lula had complained of vermin in the storeroom, and now she was headed right there.

It's only a small creature, she told herself. *One of God's creatures, so it must have a purpose.* Still, she shivered almost uncontrollably. She dearly wanted to fly up the stairs and retreat to her bed, but that would not do. She *had* to get paper if she were to preserve Ben's precious words.

Coaxing herself forward, step by step, she made it into the kitchen proper and held her light aloft to make sure she found her way to the storeroom without mishap.

Then, as quickly as she could, she pulled open the door, searched for the parcel paper, found it, ripped off a lengthy piece, and hurried back up to her room in such a rush that she didn't even care if the stair tread made a noise.

She stood with her back against the closed and locked door, breathing, breathing, breathing, until her heart and respirations returned to normal. Then she sat and carefully began the task of transcribing Ben's words.

She had no idea of the time when she finished the task with the first page, but it was far too late to begin her puzzle work for the second sheet of the letter. Reluctantly, she hid all her tools and the paper away underneath her shoes in the back corner of her wardrobe, changed into her nightdress, blew out the candle, and slipped into bed.

৪০

Ella Ruth — March 17, 1862

The next night, after meticulous labor had resulted in Ella Ruth reading and preserving the sweet words found on the second sheet of Ben's letter, she sat up from a dead sleep. *Ben mustn't send letters here*, she thought. *Poppa will only destroy them.*

She lay back down on her pillow, worry creasing her forehead as her eyebrows pinched together. She hadn't ever received a letter before, and didn't know how delivery was accomplished. Poppa knew, but she could hardly ask him about the subject. Momma would suspect something strange was in the air if Ella Ruth were to approach her. Who could she ask about letters?

Mrs. Julia Owen would know, but Ella Ruth still had a nervous fascination with the mother of her Ben. She imagined that such an accomplished woman would take no notice of her problem. But perhaps the *other* Mrs. Owen would.

She thought about that for a while. She hadn't seen Mistress Mary in the store for ever so long, but then, perhaps it was time for her confinement. She was having a child. Rulon Owen's child.

Ella Ruth thought about how it would be if she were carrying Ben's child, and felt an odd tingle in the pit of her stomach. Would she ever get the opportunity? This horrible war threw such complications into her life. Would she never be able to marry Ben, join with him in conjugal bliss, bear him a child?

She wanted to weep at the thought of never. That was not acceptable to her. She would begin prayers every night and every morning to ensure that Ben returned to her. *Fervent* prayers. God would surely heed prayers offered with all the fervor of which she was capable.

But first, she must think of a way to ensure that their courtship by correspondence, if such it had to be, was not interrupted by her father's heavy hand.

She went to sleep with that problem foremost in her thoughts, trusting that her brain would arrive at a solution by morning.

When Ella Ruth awoke at daybreak, she determined to go to

188

the store and see about Mistress Mary's situation. Perhaps she had given birth by now and would return soon. If not, perhaps one of her sisters would be amenable to the idea of keeping letters aside for her. Mrs. Hilbrands occasionally took a turn behind the counter, but Ella Ruth discarded the notion of approaching her. She seemed . . . prickly. Certainly not welcoming of unorthodox ideas.

After breakfast, Ella Ruth had another problem. How was she to get to the store? Poppa had not announced plans to go anywhere today, so she couldn't conjure an excuse to accompany him to town. Momma wasn't thinking of going out. Merlin never took the buggy if he was off to see a friend.

She wandered into the kitchen to see if the cook Sadie needed supplies, but found no answers from that quarter. Sadie was occupied with making the noon meal. As she took a jar of applesauce from the storeroom shelf, she shrugged off Ella Ruth's suggestion that she might need to go shopping. She opened the jar with a flourish as Ella Ruth's mouth began to water at the smell of the ham in the oven. With no options left, she removed herself from the kitchen.

Fuss and feathers! How am I to get to Mount Jackson?

As she sat in the parlor, idly flipping through a year-old copy of a magazine of ladies' fashions from New York, an idea came into her head. It was a rather unheard-of concept, but it would not leave her, so she let it free and examined it.

She could walk.

She swallowed.

Walk?

She had never walked the distance from her home to Mount Jackson, but surely it could be done. She had seen darkies and farm lads trudging along the road when she had passed by in the buggy, thinking nothing of their feat. Surely it wasn't difficult to put one foot in front of another and traverse a mile or two, even three. She enjoyed robust health, and had no impairment to her limbs. So what if the way was dusty? She could accomplish her objective with a little persistence. Indeed, she must.

Another thought came to her. What if Mary, or her sister, if it came to that, required coaxing to come to an agreement? She only had enough coins to post a note to Ben if she could make arrangements. What else did she have that she could use to sweeten her request?

A jar of applesauce.

Ella Ruth threw down the magazine and rose, excited that her problem was melting away after she had put so much mental energy into solving it. She would not let Poppa's attitude defeat her, now that Ben had come around to the point to responding to her letters. Ben loved her. She knew it. Nothing must become an obstacle to seeing their tenuously renewed friendship blossom into the full flower of courtship.

She hurried toward the kitchen, then slowed her pace so the cook would not become suspicious of her motives. She would say she had come for a tumbler of water. Yes, that was reasonable.

She entered the warm room and surveyed it.

Sadie had her head and arms extended toward the oven, preparing to remove the ham. She saw Ella Ruth and frowned. "What you doin' back in my kitchen, child? I won't feed you nothin' this close to dinner."

"Pay me no mind. Sadie. I'm parched, so I've come for a drink of water."

The cook cast a skeptical eye at Ella Ruth, then said, "Humph," and turned her back to complete her task.

Ella Ruth walked to the storeroom for a tumbler and removed a jar of applesauce from the shelf as well. She concealed the jar in the folds of her skirt, quickly filled the glass with water and drank it, then hurried out of the room.

She hid the applesauce in her room, knowing it was too close to the noon meal to leave. It would be counted odd if she did not show up.

When the bell sounded, she went downstairs and ate as fast as she could without drawing undue attention to herself. Unfortunately, she could not think of an excuse for leaving the table early, and had to sit, enduring the family small talk until her mother rose, the signal that everyone was dismissed to go about their activities.

Ella Ruth retrieved the applesauce, professed the desire to take a turn around the garden to see if anything had sprouted yet, and fled.

She crossed the river on a footbridge her brother had built last summer, climbed out of the bottom to the Valley Pike, and began her journey. After walking down the side of the pike for what seemed like forever, Ella Ruth looked behind her and realized that she wasn't all that far from home. The road stretched endlessly before her, white in the sunlight. The jar of applesauce she clutched felt like an andiron at the end of her arm. Why hadn't she thought to bring a basket?

She paused to catch her breath opposite the lane that led to the Owen farm, and ease her toes within her shoes. Was that dull pain from a blister rising?

She began to wonder if her plan had merit. What if she couldn't arrive in town before the store closed? She inhaled resolutely and set off once more, ignoring the pinching of her shoes. She had to achieve her goal.

Resting again sometime later, Ella Ruth wished she had thought to bring a basket *and* a container of water. Her mouth felt dry as the dust that covered her skirt and bodice. She was sure now that she had not one, but several blisters on her feet. She might make it to town and interview Mary or one of her sisters, but *how* was she to make it home again?

What would Ben do? *Silly girl, Ben would have a horse or a wagon to travel this great distance.*

She set her mouth in a grim line. She would walk until she reached the next fence post, and then go on to the next one. Accordingly, she began to walk, limping, but making progress along the pasture fence bordering the road.

After an interval of halting advancement that sapped her strength to the very limits of her constitution, Ella Ruth arrived in Mount Jackson. She dusted her dress, straightened her aching back, and walked with as much dignity as she could muster on blister-ravaged feet down the street toward the store.

She entered, then felt like crying when she espied Mrs. Hilbrands at the counter. Was all her labor for naught? She lingered beside the door, mastering her emotion before she decided what to do. A baby wailed from a back room. Was Mistress Mary here after all?

Mrs. Hilbrands made a resigned face and left the counter. She encountered one of her daughters coming out of the room, but it wasn't Mary. It was the next one, a selfish twit named Ida.

Ella Ruth caught a fragment of the girl's side of the conversation, something expressing dissatisfaction with tending the child and a question of when Mary was going to return to help with the work.

"Perhaps next week," the mother said curtly, and hurried to take care of the youngest offspring.

Ella Ruth turned and left the store. Mary lived at the Hilbrands' home, and must be there now. That was just around the block, and she hurried as fast as she could to get there, glad of the turn of events. Mary was much easier to talk to than the other ladies of the family. She could make a social visit of the occasion and still achieve her end.

One of Mary's younger sisters conducted her upstairs into Mary's room, where Ella Ruth cooed at the baby, and presented the jar of sauce. After what she adjudged was a decent period, she asked Mary if she would accommodate her desire to receive mail at the store.

"Brother Ben has replied to you, then?" Mary asked, a conspiratorial smile creeping onto her face.

"He has. But Poppa— My father is still opposed to our friendship." She hung her head. "I've been put to a great deal of trouble to rescue his letter from the trash."

"Oh my. Were you obliged to iron out the creases?"

"Oh Mary, if it were only so easy as that! I had to piece together the fragments after Poppa tore it to bits."

Mary frowned. "Do you truly love Brother Ben?"

Ella Ruth slapped her hands to her mouth to keep from crying out.

Mary must have seen that her question had caused Ella Ruth anguish. She nodded once, then said, "I will assist you. Now you must write to him that he is to direct your mail to Papa's store." She paused and patted Ella Ruth on the arm. "I wish you happiness, friend. I may call you *friend*?"

Ella Ruth nodded, not yet able to speak.

Mary gestured to a writing desk. "You may use that paper, but I have no stamps."

"I have enough coins to post the letter."

"Then you must get to the task." Mary put down her babe and went to the window to shut off a rising breeze. She turned away before she did so and asked, "You are footsore. How are you to return home?"

Seeing that Mary understood how she had arrived, Ella Ruth shook her head. "I haven't a plan."

Mary turned back, called out the window, "James! Hold, please. Wait there," and dashed out of the room.

Ella Ruth's heart throbbed with relief when Mary returned and told her James Owen would convey her home on the back of his horse. "You are a dear," she whispered as she finished sealing the note and handing it over.

"I said it before, friend Ella Ruth. I wish you happiness."

Ella Ruth hugged Mary, took her leave, and made her way carefully down the stairs to thank another kind soul for helping her in this time of dire need.

Chapter 20

Ben — March 20, 1862

When Ben first read his mother's letter exhorting him to attend church every time he had a chance, and to curb in himself the carnal nature of mankind, he felt his ears burn. Anger rose in his chest. Ma had no call to give him such advice. He wasn't a little child sitting at her skirts, owing her his attention and paying heed to her words. He was a man now, a soldier with a man's responsibilities for killing or being killed. He had precious little opportunity to attend prayer services when his time was spent on the battlefield or building roads over the muck and mud so wagons could bring provisions to the brigade. He was a man. With time on his hands this evening. With temptation in the form of perfumed and painted women calling to him from just beyond the camp.

He was on the point of casting Ma's letter into the fire and joining the fellows who were brushing the mud off their coats with the prospect of an evening's pleasure when his eye fell upon a word in Ma's fine handwriting. Disease.

He scoffed, but with a sense of unease as he recalled her words. Ma was a forthright woman, but she did have a sense of delicacy and had never come right out before and mentioned in such searing detail the dangers of partaking of forbidden fruits.

He reread the portion where her warnings had become particularly pointed. ". . . many cases of syphilis in the Soldier's Hospital . . . suffering . . . go mad . . . treatment almost worse than the disease."

Was Ma helping in the hospital, exposed to the results of man's corruptible nature?

He'd never heard the proper name for French sickness before, but Ma knew it, and had warned him against venturing into a path that might bring such a vile retribution upon him. A thought chased through his mind that curdled the contents of his stomach. Pa had gone to war. Had he—?

"Impossible," he muttered. Pa would never sin against his wife. He was a man of honor.

Where did that leave him, Ben? Where was his honor if he was contemplating lifting the skirt of a camp follower for a moment of relief?

The feeling of sickness caught him so quickly that he almost lost his supper. He fought the nausea, swallowing over and over. His thoughts swirled in a dizzy array, but one swam to the top of the whirlwind. He'd made up his mind that when he got a chance, he would ask Ella Ruth to be his bride. Did he want to take home an evil sickness to pass to her?

Sweat drenched his brow and ran in rivulets down his cheeks. He took out his handkerchief and mopped at his face. What would Ella Ruth think if he came home to her bearing the burden of worldliness? He could not stomach the thought of tainting her in such a manner. If he sinned in this fashion, he would lose her forever.

The dampness of the handkerchief seemed to freeze his hand. Ma was right. He needed to get his appetites under control. He needed to go to church. He needed to get right with God. Above all, he needed to forestall any barrier between himself and Ella Ruth.

❧

Peter — June 10, 1862

The fight had moved into the Shenandoah Valley, and Peter's cavalry regiment fought up and down the road that summer, as General Jackson's army chased Yankees. The enemy chased back, and the competing forces alternated driving and being driven.

On a retreat through Mount Jackson, skirmishing with Frémont's cavalry, Peter wished times were different and he could stop off at the farm for a visit. That would have to wait, as they were hard-pressed by vengeful Federals eager to take action against the Confederates for a defeat in the last battle.

A few days later, close by Harrisonburg, the Yankees got an unexpected benefit from a relatively minor engagement. A regiment of New Jersey cavalry led by an English adventurer attacked the Confederate cavalry, and in the fight, Colonel Turner

Ashby's horse was shot from under him. He rose to lead his men on foot, and fell almost immediately, pierced by a Yankee bullet. He died almost instantly.

Jun 10, 1862
In camp at Brown's Gap, Vir.
Der Ma,
I wish I cood have pressed my lips to your browe when last I past the Farm, but Alas! the yankees drove us throu and we went up the Valy to a acursed place. You no dobt herd of our misfortunate encounter near Harisonburg. We are distrawt at the loss of Col. Ashby. Where will we find another leder of his dash and skill?

The boys are very loe of mind at his passing, as am I. We do not know who will become our comander. Pray for us to get a good'un.

I will leave off whinin, altho I coud speak my grief all the day.

I hope to be able to see you next time we pass nearby. If not, I will wave my hand in fond greetin. Does Pa ever stop by? I see him from time to time, but not often.

How big is Rulon's little Baby now? Do you see him or does the Hilbrands family keep you away from him? I recall Rulon wanted Mistress Mary to live with you at the farm. Will she be moving there, now that she has presented an eir?

I must close now. I am told we will be on picket duty tonight.
With a heavy heart but most Affectionately,
Your son, Peter

Rulon — June 17, 1862

June 17, 1862 in Camp near Charles City C-H, Va.
Mary love,
Our company has returned from a great Adventure, riding clear around the entire Army of the Federals. This is McClellan's bunch of invaders. The boys were ready for patrol duty, as we did not engage in the late affair at Seven Pines, although we stood in readiness to support the infantry.

What a time we had! It began when about a thousand of us were ordered to move to Kilby's Station, where we were bid to cook three days' rations, but given no further orders. You may imagine our surprise to be woke up in the middle of the night and told to be mounted in ten minutes! Oh Mary, what juices flowed in our veins at the prospect of a fight! I swear to you the very horses felt their oats that night.

When we started off, from the direction we took, we thought we were marching to the Valley, and I had hopes of catching a glimpse of yor sweet face, but soon it became apparent we were going to observe the enemy close to hand, and do our utmost to gain intelligence and cause what trouble we could behind their lines.

Our spirits were high, despite the grave danger of our situation at times. Col. Fitz Lee took us on a little jaunt down a side road in hopes of cutting off a squad of Yankees, which exployt ended up with us crossing a swamp with some difficulty. Most of the enemy fled, and we took only one prisoner.

Another day, Col. Rooney Lee's 9th Reg't got into a close fight with sabrs and pistols, but prevailed. The Yankees took off and our colonel begged to be permitted to make a pursuit, and gaining consent, we were off on the road to Old Church.

I have been doing a bit of tracking under the instruction of old Mister Vernon Earl. I do not recall if I told you of him before. He is a hunter from the Blue Ridge who has good skills that he is imparting to me. He has taut me how to find the spots where animals go besides where the human animals pass. We've been looking for the latter, of course. Mayhap I will have a use for the animal tracking after this war is done.

On one occasion, our Col. put me to work practicing the knowledge I have gained from Mr. Earl. I am happy to report that I did not lead us into a swamp, but with only one mistake on my part, we ended up on the trail of a patrol of Yankees, of which we captured a great lot.

There is so much more to recount, but my paper is almost used up, and I have other words to say to you. Mary, how I miss you. How I miss the little son you have borne me, even though I have not seen him with my own eyes. I wish you could get a likeness made of the boy to send to me. I would keep it upon my heart at all times. I treasure the one you sent to me of yor dear person. I kiss it every night. Oh my love. I dream of the sweet day when I can return home to you, greet you with an embrace, and lay with you once again cradled in my arms. Do you not dream of the same? Do not be shy in riting affectionate words to me, my darling. I hold sacred yor trust. Feer not. My body and soul are yors alone.

I figure we are going into battle again within a short time. I am informed that when the spring and summer come, with them arrives a new season of battles. General Lee will not hesitate to move on the enemy. I will do everything in my power to remain whole and safe.

With all the tender feelings of my soul,
Yor husband, Rulon

☙

Mary — June 24, 1862

One morning, Rand Hilbrands came into the store with his arms full of letters and packages. "Ida, come take this parcel," he said, glancing in her direction.

Mary, who was closer to him, put out her arms to receive it, but he gave it into Ida's charge instead.

"Here is a letter for you, Mistress Mary. From your husband, I suspect."

Mary took it, relief sweeping through her breast at having evidence of his good health in her hand. "Thank you, Papa. We have no customers in the store. May I go to read it?"

"Can I prevent you from doing so?" he replied in a jovial manner. "I hope it is good tidings."

"Thank you, Papa," she said, and hurried into the back room where Roddy slept in his cradle, his breathing even, except when he made an occasional little snuffling sound.

Mary sat, unsealed the envelope flap, and took out one sheet of paper, written on both sides to the very margins. Rulon had been on a grand adventure, he said, and recounted some of the events. He seemed to have a liking for the art of tracking. Mary shrugged. That was a man's concern.

She caught her breath. He missed her. He spoke longingly of Roddy. She had not thought of sending a likeness of the boy, but must now certainly see about having one made of him, because Rulon wanted to have it.

Oh my, she thought, her heart leaping. She had just read his words of how he treated her likeness, and what effect it had upon him. Hungrily, she scanned the next sentence. "Oh my love," it read. She scarce could breathe for the tightness in her chest. How long had it been since she had heard his voice whisper those words to her? The next bit caught her by surprise, and she froze.

Rulon longed for her to be in his embrace, to lie beside him, in his arms. And then she read, "Feer not. My body and soul are yors alone."

She began to weep. Rulon had remained true to her. His letter clearly expressed his devotion. She had fretted and worried herself sick of mind for no reason. Her self-afflicted pain had been a misuse of her energies, and she regretted the waste of contentment while she had been engaged in doubting her husband's fidelity.

Conscious of her precarious location, and fearing to awaken her babe, she wiped her eyes and breathed slowly until her tears were under control. She reckoned she must make every effort to put doubt out of her mind. She must aid Rulon in being true. He desired her to use words of affection in her letters. Her mind shrank at the idea of putting her private thoughts on paper. She hadn't been a wife long enough to be comfortable in saying such things as he had included in this letter. He was a bolder creature than she. Even though he had taught her to relish certain intimacies, she certainly would not speak of them. Must she devise a code? Perhaps she would give thought to that notion. For now, it sufficed that Rulon bore bountiful affection for her and honored his vows.

Chapter 21

Rulon — August 30, 1862

Rulon had a great surprise upon the field of battle at Manassas late on the third day. He had been detailed as a courier for General Stuart and was carrying orders to General Robertson when he encountered his father.

"Pa!" he shouted, reining up. "Pa!" he tried again to get his attention.

His father turned his head, and seeing Rulon, spurred his horse in his direction.

"Son. Be safe. This fight is vicious."

"I will. Have you seen Ben or Peter?"

"Peter is in the thick fighting near the plantation house. I haven't caught sight of Ben. God speed, son," he said, and was off, leading his company in a different direction.

"Lordy, lordy," Rulon whispered in a demi prayer, relieved to see Pa was whole, but now concerned about Peter. The rascal would manage to go into the hottest part of the fray. Nothing would prevent him seeking glory.

Then Rulon could put no thought to his brother's pride, as he was on the move again, looking for the brigade colors that marked the spot from which the General directed his regiments. He had orders to deliver.

෩

Julia — September 2, 1862

After a year of war, Julia had grown used to the exercise of scanning the casualty lists published by the newspaper after the big battles. She would never become accustomed to the clutching sense of dread that accompanied the perusal.

Carl came home from town in late afternoon and handed the list to her, folded with such sharp edges that he must have run pinching fingers over the fold several times to leave a tight crease.

"Did you read it yet?" she asked.

He shook his head, eyes cautious. Albert stood half behind him, clutching white-knuckled hands together.

She held the sheet for a moment, then turned away from her sons, the dread closing her throat already.

She took a seat at the table. Marie came into the room, followed by Julianna. Julia said, "Sit down, daughters." Her quavering voice startled her.

Marie sat on one side and Julianna on the other. Julia heard Carl and Albert go outside, but they hadn't closed the door, and she could feel their eyes boring into her shoulder blades. She didn't know where James and Clayton were.

Marie twisted a handkerchief. Julianna folded her arms on the table top and put her head down on them. She squeezed her eyes shut.

Julia unfolded the paper and looked at it. The list was neither alphabetized nor ordered by unit, which meant she had to read each name. She did not want to see any name ending in Owen. She ran her tongue across her bottom lip. She struggled to take a breath.

She exhaled and began, drawing her forefinger slowly down the first column as she read the names. She noticed that her finger trembled, and she paused to get herself in hand.

Marie made a small sound.

Julia looked at her, then back to the paper. Her heart pounded in her ears. She slowly began to read again, her lips forming each name.

Near the bottom of the third column, her finger stopped. She shrank back, a cry arising from the depths of her soul.

"Mama?" moaned Julianna.

Peter. The entry said Peter Owen. It gave his regiment and company.

Julia whispered his name once, disbelieving the printer's ink under her finger. Her hands convulsed, opening and closing above the sheet before her. Her ears buzzed. *I dasn't faint. I dasn't!*

Shadows moved in front of her as the girls peered at the spot her finger had marked. Julianna whimpered and sat back. Julia forced herself to focus her eyes on her daughter. The girl's face had gone white as alabaster. She appeared about to topple to one side.

Julia found the strength to thrust out her arm and grasp her daughter's wrist. She heard a chair's legs scrape against the floor. Marie was on her feet, pacing, tears streaming down her cheeks as she sobbed.

"Ma?" Carl put his hands on her shoulders.

All she could do was point. She had no voice to speak his name again. Gone. The boy was gone.

Carl must have located the awful bit of news. She heard his sharp inhalation, and Albert's "Who is it, Carl?" as he came around her side. Carl's hands had slipped off her shoulders. The boys whispered to each other, then Albert choked off a sob.

Julianna had gone limp, leaning backwards, almost off the bench. Julia knew she couldn't hold her upright from her chair. She somehow got her feet underneath her, levered herself upright, and pulled the girl back to lean on the table, all the while chills ran races along her spine. Peter was dead. She had no time to mourn while her other children were in such sore straits.

⁊

Julia — September 12, 1862

For days, Julia navigated the paths of her everyday life with her heart torn to shreds. Peter was gone. Peter, whose reckless spirit had led him to seek the adventures of war, was no more. She couldn't fathom it. Yes, she had been forced to lay a babe in a grave before this, but to have a half-grown child wrested from her? It was unthinkable.

She wondered if Rod knew of the loss. The two of them had been in the same regiment, so it was possible that he had found out. She longed to have his arm around her shoulders, to gain solace from his sturdy body held next to hers, but that was impossible just now. She would have to travel this path of sorrow alone.

No. She wasn't alone. She had children beside her, children who were grieving the taking of their playmate, older brother, and friend. Tease. Rapscallion. Jokester. He was all of those. But he was also a hard worker.

Had been. Not now. Julia felt her soul was stripped to pieces.

Peter would never again come up behind her and tie the tails of her apron strings where she couldn't reach them. He would never again curry the buggy horse and put it into harness for her. He would never again object to her swift kiss on his cheek at night.

Peter was gone, dumped into a hole on a battlefield and covered over with a few spades of Virginia earth.

She sank into a chair, ready to weep, knowing she should comfort Julianna, who went about the house like a ghost. Marie sobbed in her room at night. Carl wore the face of a martyr, white as alabaster. Clay and Albert huddled on the fireplace hearth in the evenings, shoulders drooping, each one looking at the other then away, too proud to cry.

She had no strength. Peter. The dark-haired child who'd come along after two little tow-headed boys. How was she to do without him?

She rested for a few moments, imagining him dashing into the thick of the battle, then shied away from following that thought. She must not mope here. It would lead her into dark avenues. She gathered her resources into a tiny ball of resolve, and rose to get a basket and go outdoors to take the clothes off the lines. She hoped the open air would sooth her battered soul.

ଚ୍ଚ

Rulon — September 20, 1862

Rulon's regiment had pressed forward into Maryland as General Lee sought to gain an advantage by invading the North. One evening, shortly after the bloody days at Sharpsburg, he got a letter. He leaned on his horse to rip it open, having recognized Mary's hand.

September 4, 1862
Dear Husband,
I scarce can hold a pen to write these words for the great sorrow enwrapping my soul. Your sister Marie came to see our dear child and me. Soon after coming through the door, she commenced to weep as though she would perish from grief, bringing the most fearful news. Your brother Peter is no more. His name was writ on the casualty list from the second fight

about Manassas railway junction. No one knows where his erthly remains are laid to rest. I am terriby distracted by the evil news of your brother's demise.

Your mama is beside herself with mourning, Marie tells me. She herself is almost in the same state. I endeavored to tell her to be brave so she wood be fit to help your mama bear her burden. After a time, she cried her final tears and agreed to do what she could. We must now find or make black material for mourning clothes. However, I do not kno of a weaver left in the county.

Dear husband, I pray you are well and can take the terribl loss of your broth'r in stride. We hear many reports of your bravery and skill in fighting the dred foe in Maryland. I tell Baby Roddy about his Papa every night before I lay him in bed. Do not put yourself in Harm's Way. My love for you is unending.

Yor faithful wife,
Mary Hilbrands Owen

Halfway through his reading of the letter, he felt himself sliding down the withers of the horse, and then he was sitting on the ground, distraught and trying to hold himself together. Peter dead? It did not seem possible.

"No," he groaned. "No, not my brother. Dear God, why Peter? Why not me instead?"

Ren found him there, and led the horse away so it wouldn't do him damage. He returned and squatted beside Rulon.

"Ill news?"

"Oh God in heaven," Rulon cried out as though he petitioned the Lord for a different outcome. "It's my brother. Gone. Dead."

He felt Ren's hand touching him lightly on the shoulder. "I'm sorry, Rule. That's a terrible loss." The voice was so quiet Rulon could barely hear it.

He crumpled Mary's letter in his two fists, crying unashamed tears.

Ren stayed still and silent for a time, then arose. "You'd best take a mouthful or two of rations, man. You may not think it will help, but it will keep you from wasting in this hard time."

Rulon shook his head. How could he think of eating when his rascally brother would never take sustenance again? "My poor ma. She don't deserve this."

Ren gave a little snort. "No mother does, but you know the truth. Our men are dying most every day. Some poor mothers who don't get any notice are left to wonder why their dear boy don't write home anymore."

"That don't help the pain, Ren."

"It's fresh, man. Don't dwell on it for more than a little space. You've got your duty."

Rulon remembered the picket he was supposed to relieve. "Give me a minute. I'll pull myself together."

"You will do. Ridin' by your side these months past, I've learned you've got the mettle."

"I—" Rulon scrubbed his eyes with the backs of his hands, almost tearing the letter in the process. "God have mercy on his soul," he muttered, then got to his feet. He carefully folded the letter to finish later, and tucked it into his jacket. "Oh Mary," he groaned. "Don't let the boy come to any harm."

 જી

Ella Ruth — September 21, 1862

Weeks after Ella Ruth heard of Mrs. Owen's loss of her son, her parents invited Doctor Allen and his wife to Sunday dinner. The dinner conversation between the two brothers centered on the conflict just past at Sharpsburg, and the influx of wounded men into the new soldier's hospital just outside Mount Jackson. While the ham was served, Dr. Allen mentioned that he was looking for ladies from the town to volunteer several hours a week to come nurse the new patients. "My own dear wife helps as she has time, but the children do need her at home."

Mrs. Doctor Allen nodded and murmured a bit about how the little ones kept her quite occupied.

"Brother Joseph," Ella Ruth's mother said in a tone firm enough to catch the doctor's attention. "What kind of topic is this for the dinner table?"

"A war time topic, my dear," the doctor said. "These soldiers need care. Our country owes great thanks to these young men. What better way than to tend to their needs?"

Did Peter Owen die because no one was there to tend to his needs? Ella Ruth gave a little shudder, imagining Ben lying on a field strewn with the injured and dying. *Mama should let Uncle have his say.*

"Perhaps you should speak to Theodore on the topic after we dine. He can offer you several helpful ideas, I am quite sure. That would be more proper, don't you agree?" Mrs. Allen turned to her husband for support.

"Uncle," Ella Ruth surprised herself by speaking up. "What are your requirements for nurses?"

"Miss Ella Ruth, they need only have a pair of willing and able hands, a compassionate heart, and spare time." He wiped a dripping of sauce off his chin with his napkin. "We will give any needed training to the nurses as they work."

Ella Ruth let the conversation go on as she thought about his answer. She certainly had spare time, and her hands were capable, if not willing. Did she have a compassionate heart? Perhaps not. She wanted to be compassionate, but either it was a trait she lacked, or she had not been taught about compassion.

Was that the same thing as kindness? She thought of herself as kind. She always treated her maid Lula kindly. She never struck her, or spoke harshly to her. Was not that being kind? Was it compassionate? Perhaps so.

Or was compassion sympathy? She inhaled, contemplating the muddle in her brain. She was only confusing herself, putting too much thought into the affair. Why did it matter in the end? The doctor needed more hands to aid the soldiers in the hospital. She felt a chill run up her spine. Should Ben be wounded during his next encounter with the enemy and enter a hospital, would it not be her fondest desire that he have competent nursing care from some kindly woman? Yes, indeed it would.

"Dr. Allen," she blurted out, interrupting her father in mid-sentence. "I should like to serve in the hospital."

"Daughter, that is impossible," her mother said, drawing herself into a stiff posture.

"No, it is not. I have very little work to do here at home, no purpose in my life. This is what I will do as my thanks to our fine soldiers."

Her mother made a sound of protest, but her father jumped into the conversation with, "You see how it is, Louisa. She has set her mind to do this thing, and she will not be dissuaded." He turned to his brother. "It seems you have a volunteer, Joseph. Be sure she is treated well."

And that, Ella Ruth thought, *is that. I shall be an excellent nurse.*

☙

Julia — October 4, 1862

On a Saturday morning, Julia entered the kitchen to begin breakfast, and found a folded sheet of paper propped against her large mixing bowl. Immediate dread flowed down her spine as though an icy finger had stroked her bare skin. She sank into her chair, holding the paper where her blurred eyes could see the words on the outside.

To Ma

"No," she moaned, knowing what must be inside. "No." This time, the word escaped her throat as a sob.

Almost as though her hands were controlled by another person, they unfolded the paper.

Ma,
I kno you will take this hard, but I am hon'r-bound to take Peter's place. We lost so many good men at Manassas, and now that the Yankeys have been fot at great cost at Sharpsburg, Gen'l Bobby Lee needs me.
Do not dispare. I will be as a ghost in the mist attacking the foe. I sware to you I will return.
Your son, Carl

☙

Rulon — December 31, 1862

31st day of Decemb'r 1862
Culpepper C.H.
Dear Wife,
You will have heard about the Yankees bringing war to us in Fredricsburg. They did not prevale, due to much delay in bringing the fight across the river. Our regimn't was not much employed in the battle at Fredricsburg but We afterward

embarked upon a bold raid across the Rappahannoc and into the realm of the foe. Nearly two Thousand of troops in three Brigades under Gen'l Stuart's own leadership made the raiding party. We rode as far north as Dumfries before we went in other directions to impede the enemy's designs and give him pause. Near a place called Greenwood Church, our Regmt had a encounter with some boys from Penn, who turned tail and ran when we charged into them. The command routed, at which we pursewed them for about two miles, taking many prisoners.

Gen'r Stuart captured a telegraph house and made fools of the Yankees in Washington, getting information that helped him decide where to attac next. Our Brigadeer Gen'l, Fitz Lee, took a party and pulled down the rail road brige over a creek.

We coold not attac Fairfax C.H., as the enemy seemed to know of our activities, but we have returned to safety in this place.

I hope our little son and yor dear person had a plesent Christmas celebration. I wish I coold be there to hold you in my arms and see the New Year come in. This war must end soon. The Yankees surely by now see our determination to be a country separate from them. They cannot carry on this conflict much longer.

If you see my mother soon, give her a kiss for me. Receev a special kiss from my lips as if it were placed upon your brow and all other places. I miss my sweet Sugar.

Yor Husband,
Rulon Owen
1st Virginia Regiment, Cavalry

Chapter 22

Rulon — February through May 10, 1863

Despite sorry weather, in February General Fitz Lee's Brigade moved from their winter foraging in King William and Caroline counties back to Culpeper Court House to relieve Wade Hampton's Brigade on picket duty. Across the upper Rappahannock, the Federal troops sheltered for the winter, but Rulon's regiment picked away at the Federal videttes and lines of communication, in company with the other three regiments of the command.

The successful cavalry raids brought a response once the weather warmed a trifle. Rulon found himself tagged for courier duty during one of the encounters, and wrote to Mary of the recklessness of the task, dashing about the battleground taking messages from one commander to another. He embellished the patriotic elements of the duty while toning down the danger.

For the rest of the month of April, Rulon was occupied with picket duty and riding in support when a picket post at Rixeyville was reported under attack.

On the way back the next day, Ren said, "I reckon false reports will wear a body out quicker than a nice fight."

"It surely gets the blood up to no good purpose," Rulon replied. "My horse is about beat to death."

At the end of the month, though, Hooker's army crossed the Rappahannock. The 1st Virginia Cavalry struck the Federal advance on the Germanna Ford road, but Rulon's company was ordered to guard another road, and while there, captured enough prisoners to send good information to General Robert Lee about the Federal commands opposing them. The regiment rode all night through the Wilderness on winding roads, then were put into a fight the next day, without rest.

Moving through the woods, the column came to a standstill when they came in contact with the enemy. After a courier had come from General Stuart several times, bidding Colonel Drake to hurry on to Chancellorsville, and the colonel had sent him back with the ill tidings that they could not fulfill the order, Colonel Drake sent Rulon with the courier to emphasize the futility of the dispatch.

Soon General Stuart came up with a brigade of infantry, and although the soldiers were deployed in front of the regiment, the enemy was firmly entrenched in an old railroad cut and could not be dislodged.

General Jackson's corps later rolled up the Federal flank, and the Yankees retreated toward Chancellorsville.

Although the enemy was on the run, matters turned deadly serious when General Jackson rode out in front of his lines on a reconnaissance and was mortally wounded by his own men on his return.

Caught out of position during the battle, Rulon's company joined General Rooney Lee's Brigade in chasing the Federal cavalry south led by General Stoneman toward the James River. The pursuit lasted over eight days and nights, and although no major battles ensued, they skirmished with the Yankees nearly every day.

When General Stoneman's cavalry eluded capture, the 1st Regiment camped at Orange Court House.

Rulon threw himself onto the ground after he saw to his horse. "I declare I am dead of hunger," he said to Ren.

"Did you find any more crackers in your saddlebags?"

Rulon snorted. "I'm not a magician. I ate the last one two days ago."

Ren expressed his disappointment in sharp words.

"I can hear your stomach growl from over here," Rulon retorted, and tore up a handful of grass. He looked at the bright blades. "Do you reckon it's edible for humans?"

"Cats eat it. And goats. Horses graze on it." He sat beside Rulon and picked a blade of grass. "Why not us?" he said, and stuck the grass into his mouth.

&

Ben — May 13, 1863

Word spread through the Confederate Army like wildfire that

General Jackson had died. Some said losing his arm had disheartened him. Some said being shot by his own troops had put him in a mortal state of grief. After a time it was understood that the great general had died from pneumonia. That did not erase the sense of gloom that overshadowed his command.

My darling Ella Ruth,

I hope this finds you well and happy as can be expected, given the circumstances.

You cannot imagine the pain we endure in the Brigade. I do not know your feelins toward the General, but his death has thrown us into despair.

The heart within me seemed to break when the news came that the dread day had arriv'd. We hoped and prayed that God would spare Gen'l Jackson to lead us agin. I suppose God wanted him more than we did, but oh! The grief cuts us sore and deep.

The Yankees have so many men they seem to come from a deep well. We are drafting schoolboys and greybeards. Some come with no weapons, no shoes. I suppose they dragged them off a hill hideout in Tennessee. North Carolina sent good fighters early on, but the recroots now are reluctant to stand. Pray for the Cause, sweet girl. Pray with fervent heart that we will overcome the foe, and soon. We cannot go on like this forever.

Ben added a few lines about his plans for expanding crop production on the farm after the war, then continued.

I reckon you have had every good thing in your life. My hope is that as you consider becoming my little farm wife you will hav no regrets. Be assured that I adore you, but you will need to learn many tasks that will dirty your hands. My ma has felt great satisfaction in doing hard work for her family. You will feel the same joy as you learn the work.

He ended the letter expressing his fervent love, and then, signed it simply,

Ben

ಐ

Mary — May 15, 1863

Dear Husband,

My, how my arms do ache! We made soft soap today from the winter's ashs. Mama sent India to the store in my place so I could pitch into the labor. I hope Papa did not take offence at having a jun'r worker instead of his right-hand Mary.

The fire roared, the kett'l bubbled and splash'd, and Roddy lern'd how to hold up his dress to toddle toward the center of the excitment. I could not let harm come to yor son, so I fashn'd a pen of chairs and blankets in the hedge of the garden. He is a smart creature for merely 15-months-old, and found a way to dig out between the bushes. I was forev'r putting him back in place and piling dirt up to keep him contain'd. Mama became so alarmed that she sent Ida to the store and India returned to tend the boy.

This made more work for Sylvia and me, but at the end of the day, we had poured out a quantity of soap for bars. I enclose one, wich I hope did not leek on the paper, as I wrapped it in the last oilcloth I could find.

I must hide my pleasure to see Papa treating with his grandson. With only girls in his projeny, havin a boy about the place is a novelty. I hast'n to add it is a joy to him. He looks for trinkets in the store to bring home to Roddy. I am ever cautining Papa about small items, for the boy still puts everything to a taste-test before he plays with it. I do not want him to choke, as a child did in New Market the past week. The moth'r is inconsoalable. She blames the Yankees, passin down the Valley again, for scaring the baby into swallowing his sugartit. I keep Roddy out of their way when they come thru town.

Yor Mother had a siege of sickness amongst your kin during the winter. All have recover'd and pray for an end to this conflict. Rulon, my prayers are constant on yor behalf. Keep safe, dear Life, and return to me whole and strong.

I take Roddy's hand in my own to make his mark
X
All our love,
Mary

ৰু

Rod — May 17, 1863

My dear Julie,

I am well. The cough that playged me during the cold spell has gone away. When I lost my good horse I had a rough time finding a remount, but finally acquired a sturdy bay mare that is coming along well.

When you rote me Carl had gone into the army I was not much surprised. I have kept my eyes open for him. He was in a regular horse company, but Jeb Stuart gave John Mosby permission to form up a company of partisans under the Act thet Congress passed. As soon as he could, Carl joined Mosby's Men.

How I wish I could see you and comfort you as you continue this year of mourning. If it will give you peace, Peter's captain told me of his valor upon the field of combat. He fought with bravery and honor. Cap'n Thomas said our boy passed quickly and painlessly in a charge against the foe at Portici Plantation. I hope that knowledge will suffice to give you pride in our son and comfort at his loss.

We have been much exercised in determining the position of the enemy as their army moves. It is fortunate that we have good forage for the horses now. I'm sure yor prayers have been effective, little Wife. Thank you for keeping our sons and me and my men in them.

Give the girls a kiss for me and embrace my sons at home. Receive a kiss upon your brow and an especial sincere hug from yor husband,

 Roderick Owen
 Cap'n, Owen Dragoons

ৰু

Rulon — June 5 through 9, 1863

The ranks of the cavalry had swelled considerably with new recruits and the return of a couple of brigades, and Jeb Stuart called for a general review of the entire command for June 5.

Such a hullabaloo, Rulon thought as the 1st Virginia Cavalry Regiment passed in rigid order before a group of ladies and invited guests. The invitees included 10,000 Texans of Hood's

Division, who were neither quiet nor politic in their assessments of the Virginians. *Things might get rowdy tonight.*

The regiment avoided much of the shenanigans planned for them by Hood's veteran scrappers by marching across the ford on Hazel River and riding until two the next morning to Jeffersonton. Rulon dismounted as though his legs were made of apple jelly after the extended ride. He planted the side of his head against the saddle blanket and breathed deeply, trying to get enough air flowing to clear the dust from his lungs.

"Imagine walking that far," Ren Lovell said, his crooked smile a pale imitation of the one he used to turn on Rulon. "I'll go see if the Captain has orders."

Rulon hadn't shifted from leaning against his horse when Ren returned.

"Don't unsaddle. We're going on picket as soon as we get some grub into our bellies."

"I'd rather sleep," Rulon muttered.

"Do it quick, then. We're riding at sunrise over to Waterloo Bridge."

Rulon fished a portion of a hard tack cracker out of his saddlebag, just in case he had a yen to put something the army called food into his mouth, and led the horse to a lane. He tethered it to a tree and lay down nearby.

Owen Leoyd shook him awake before the sky had lightened. "Time to go, Owen," he said, the old joke worn thin by now.

Rulon stirred, opened his eyes, and got to his feet. The inside of his mouth made him think he'd ingested sand during the night. He took a swig of water from his canteen, swished it around, and spit. He found the cracker and put it into his cheek to soften until he could chew it. A roast chicken would taste better about now. He wondered if there were any chickens in the county. He shrugged off the thought. He didn't have any money to buy one if they were to be had.

When he was ready to mount up, Ren came by and said, "General Lee's stove up with rheumatism. Colonel Munford is taking the brigade until he comes back."

Rulon groaned. Every commander had a distinct leadership style. He was too tired to deal with Munford, so he hoped Old Fitz got well in a hurry.

Rulon drew a short straw and paired with Garth Von at a picket post. The surly fellow proceeded to pare his fingernails with his knife, and Rulon determined not to blink while he was in the company of Von.

Shortly after noon, Rulon's eyes sprang open when he heard carbine fire from a position closer to the bridge. Surprised he was still alive, he drew his weapon and looked around. Von had gigged his horse out of the trees toward the fight, and Rulon followed, gnashing his teeth at the thought that he had slumbered.

The other men from "I" Company joined the skirmish with a small detachment of Yankee cavalrymen. When the enemy had been driven off, Ren assessed the squadron and discovered that Private Whitmore had been injured.

Rulon promptly volunteered to take the man back to the surgeon at Rixeyville, and Ren let him go.

"Coward," Ren whispered as he bent near.

Rulon shook his head and mouthed, "Von."

Ren raised an eyebrow, but nodded and waved Rulon and Whitmore off in the direction of the regiment's headquarters.

A few days later, a buzz went around the brigade. The Yankee cavalry had crossed the Rappahannock and attacked Stuart's main encampment near Brandy Station. "Boots and Saddles" blared from multiple bugles, and men ran around the camp as though demons chased them. Although the distance to the battle wasn't that far, moving the men and horses of the Brigade effectively was a daunting task for a newly designated commander.

Colonel Drake wanted the 1st to leave first, but Munford had other ideas, and with all the hubbub, the brigade didn't arrive on the field until about four o'clock.

The 1st was ordered forward, and Rulon drew his sabre and galloped forward at the charge, yelling at the top of his voice. He heard Ren scream, "Give 'em the sabre, boys!" Desperate to drive back the Yankees, the men of the 1st Virginia called on all the boldness and dash they possessed.

A melee of men swirled around Rulon as the charge disintegrated into small fights in isolated pockets. He found himself in the midst of fierce action with his weapon, clashing in individual contest with one Yankee after another. One almost slashed his arm with a thrust but he parried at the last moment and the man went off his horse instead. Rulon incapacitated the man with a quick thrust of his own, not pausing to wonder how he did this so callously, as he had done at the beginning of the war. It was wound, or be wounded, kill or be killed, and the clash of sabres around him, the smoke and dust clogging the air, the screams of downed horses, the rattle of balls, and the roar of artillery reminded him that combat of this sort was intensely personal.

When he had a second to catch his breath, Rulon wondered how the brigades encamped around Stuart's headquarters had been caught with their pants down. Then he had no more time for thought, as another foeman rode toward him.

Then the Yankees began to retreat, their bugles calling them back from the field. Rulon engaged one last holdout, then the man turned and galloped off.

Rulon pulled his horse around in response to his own regiment's bugles, his heart still racing with the effects of the chaos and excitement, and saw Garth Von dismount and slit the throat of a downed Yankee officer. Von looked about, lifted the man's head by his hair, and with his bloody blade, carved a circle around the top of the Yankee's head, then sliced the scalp from the man's cranium.

Rulon fought back the urge to vomit, but Von wasn't finished.

He stuffed the ghastly prize into his saddlebag, then slit the officer's trousers up the front. He let out a keening yell of triumph, then mutilated the man's crotch. Lifting the remains, he ran to his horse and mounted.

Rulon lost his battle against nausea. Retching, he kicked his horse away from the scene, back toward the regiment, putting a fair amount of distance between himself and the man he had thought of as merely crazy. Ren's assessment had been correct. Von was evil.

❧

Rulon — late June through early July, 1863

After the sickening events at Brandy Station, Rulon kept as far as he could from Garth Von as the regiment rested in camp at Rixeyville. He invited Owen Leoyd to join him for an entertainment.

"Come on, Leoyd. Company 'B' is putting on a race."

"They ought not to wear out the horses," Leoyd said, his face set in solemn lines.

"Oh, these critters have plenty of go in them."

"Critters? Where did they get racing hounds?"

"Not hounds. Come on. You'll see."

Rulon led the way to where the men of Company "B" had gathered in a flat area. A small patch of tent canvas lay on the ground, with the men shouting encouragement.

"What are they yelling about?" Leoyd asked.

Rulon dragged him into the circle. Several tiny dark objects scurried across the canvas, guided by splinters of wood held by the men closest to the fray.

"Fleas? They're racing fleas?" Leoyd scoffed at the sight, and would have turned away but for Rulon's hand on his sleeve.

"Don't matter what they're doin'. At least we're away from Von."

At that, Leoyd sat right down on the ground and observed.

Within days, the army was on the move, sending out pickets to warn of the approach of the enemy. They found them near Aldie, and the 1st held the road, fighting dismounted from behind stone walls.

After the skirmish, the 1st was on picket at Mountsville, but had to battle to keep the position. This continued until General Fitz Lee took command of his brigade again.

"We're heading east," Ren told the squadron. "General Bobbie Lee took the infantry boys over the river into Maryland. We're to do damage behind the lines."

The cavalry brigades destroyed canal boats, captured wagons and supplies, burned bridges and tore up railroad tracks as they advanced into Maryland and Pennsylvania. They skirmished in Westminster, and fought their way out of an encounter with overpowering numbers at Hanover.

"Stuart's lost, ain't he." Rulon observed to Ren when they reached Dover, Pennsylvania at daylight after riding through the night. "I don't see any sign of Early's army."

"Maybe so, but I see plentiful forage hereabouts."

"I hope Stuart lets us find provisions," Rulon said. "My

stomach thinks my throat's been cut."

"They don't like us here."

"We don't like them in Virginia, either. It's time the Yankees learned that turn-about is fair."

After filling their bellies, they were on the march again by night.

"Jeb heard that Dick Ewell's in Carlisle," Ren said.

Rulon only groaned in reply. He'd managed to keep himself on his horse, but several men had gone to sleep and fallen from theirs.

Stuart sent Fitz Lee's brigade to lead the advance on the town, but it was full of Pennsylvania militiamen who refused to surrender.

Garth Von muttered, "Burn the Yankees out," and after a second attempt to convince the militia to surrender, Lee proceeded to bombard the town with his horse artillery.

A courier came with orders for the 1st to burn the Carlisle Barracks, then join the rest of the cavalry on the way to Gettysburg.

"Gettysburg?" Owen Leoyd asked. "What's going on there?"

"Jeb found Bobbie Lee," Ren replied. "Bobbie Lee found Meade. I reckon it's going to be a big fight."

∞

Rulon — July 3, 1863

Rulon crouched in a farmer's field behind a fence, trying not to yawn. It was a good thing General Stuart had ordered the 1st Virginia to get into this fight dismounted. He didn't think his horse could take another step, much less gallop into a fray. He squelched another yawn behind his hand. His brigade hadn't arrived until the wee hours this morning after riding long miles from Carlisle, and here it was after noon. He'd not slept since arriving. Who could, with the Yankees flinging shell and shot at the Confederate cavalry for the last hour? They had stopped the ruckus only a few minutes ago. The air lay flat and calm around him, without a human sound to interrupt the flow of nature.

Ren coughed at his side. "Get ready," he said.

"I am ready," Rulon replied, a bit irritated by the wait. "Were those boys using Spencer rifles?"

"Yes, and the next brigade probably has them, too." Ren dug in his cartridge box. "Damn Yankee repeaters."

Then the bugle sounded, and Rulon was up and over the fence, yelling as he fired, reloading on the run, trying to beat back the Federal skirmishers in his path so the cavalry could take yonder intersection and sweep around the Yankee flank to their rear.

A barrage of cannon fire began and Rulon tripped and fell flat. The sound was wrong. It came from behind and to the left, and it was distant. It shook the earth beneath his belly, however, rolling thunder replacing the calm of moments before.

Rulon got to his feet and continued across the field, the 1st driving the Yankees down and across another fence line. But now, he heard screams of "Come on, you Wolverines!" The Yankees pushed back. Hampton's brigade came up from behind on horseback, and the 1st was signaled to withdraw and let the mounted troops take over the fight.

What a furious affair! Men fought with carbines, pistols, sabres, all the while screaming invective at each other. As he backed out of the battle, Rulon saw horses collide along the fence with a crash so hurtful that he imagined bones snapped. One horse went end over end and the rider screamed in agony as he was pinned by half a ton of horseflesh.

Now the Yankees were on three sides of them, and Hampton bled from a sabre cut. Frantic bugle calls summoned the men to withdraw, and so they did. No one came after them. The Yankees must have had enough, too.

෧

Ella Ruth — November 16, 1863

Christmas was coming in about a month, despite the war dragging on and on. Ella Ruth sat down after a long stint helping her Uncle Joseph with a wounded soldier, arching her aching back in an attempt to work the kinks out. If she was going to send a gift to Ben, it would have to be done soon or he would never receive it in time.

She knew he had survived that awful fight in Pennsylvania last summer. Thank the Good Lord he wasn't in General Pickett's division. Since July she had received a few letters from Ben, and the last note said he was somewhere in Orange County, below the Rapidan.

"Miss Allen," Uncle Joseph called to her. "I need your assistance."

With a sigh, Ella Ruth went back to work in the surgery room. What could she send to Ben?

Her answer came several days later as she read a letter to a young man whose bandages on a head wound made it impossible for him to see. His wife talked about a likeness she had sent to the soldier, and after she read that part, she glanced up to see him fumbling in his pocket to be sure he had the cherished item.

"Ain't she the most comely woman you ever saw?" he asked, moving the likeness where Ella Ruth could view it. She hoped he could not see her widened eyes at the sight of a very homely creature, but she made polite sounds and went back to reading.

Something about the man's devotion to his wife stirred Ella Ruth's heart. No matter what the girl's appearance, the remembrance she had sent was important to him.

Would Ben take such pride in my portrait? she wondered. A soft emotion swelling in her breast told her that he would. That was settled, then. She would take her pearl earrings to the photographer's studio to barter for a likeness of herself for Ben's Christmas gift.

Chapter 23

Rulon — May 13, 1864

Dear Wife of my very soul

We had a skirmish two days ago that causes my heart to quail within me as I think on it. Our Cause has lost its noble Cavalier to mortal wounds. Oh my love, JEB Stuart is gone. I am as desolate as tho another of my brothers has died. We all feel as low as can be. There is no one to take his Place. The spirit of every man in the Cavalry is broken to peaces.

My heart hangs heavy in my bosom today. We are in camp. It has been silent as a toomb. A short while ago, I listened as a comrade began playin' the tune "Lorena" on his banjo, and another fellow started in singin' the words. My dear Mary, I about fell to weepin' for the melancholy of the sound.

My sweet Sugar, I am so lonely for you and the brillunce of yor smile. I yearn to feel yor dear love encircling me to comfort my body and soul.

These days have been long and burdensome. Besides our Great Cavalier, many of our comrades have fallen. Mary, my love, I long for the day when this war will end and I can return to yor sweet embrace.

Rulon

∽

Julia — May 16, 1864

Julia heard an insistent thumping on the front door, and ran to answer it, her heart in her throat. *Are the Yankees back?* To her immense relief, a Confederate officer and several infantrymen stood outside.

"Yes?" She looked at the man's uniform. He appeared to be a lieutenant.

"Am I addressing Mrs. Owen?" he asked.

Julia raised her chin a fraction. His manner was too brusque for her taste. "You are. What is wanted?"

The lieutenant consulted a paper in his hand, then looked up. "Do you have a son, James Owen, living here?"

Julia nodded, very slowly, her throat so constricted that she had no voice.

"I have papers for his conscription."

She cleared her throat and inhaled. "He's the man of the house now."

He glanced at the paper, then back at her. "That may be, ma'am, but his country needs him in the army."

"I've sent four sons and a husband, and one gave his life defending his country. Isn't that enough?"

The man's eyes softened, but he straightened his shoulders. "No, ma'am. The Yankees are in the Valley again. We need your son."

A chill swept through her. "How long does he have before you collect him?"

"No time, ma'am. I'm to bring him with me."

She sucked in her breath. "Y'all can wait here. I'll gather his necessaries." She half turned away, then stopped. "You won't be needing my twelve-year-old, will you?" She turned back to hear the man's answer.

"No ma'am. Not today." His gaze fixed on hers, and a bit of dizziness swept through her.

How long will this warring last? Will it come down to sending Clay and Albert to the front?

She closed the door, ran through the parlor into the kitchen and opened the back door. She saw Albert hoeing weeds in the kitchen garden.

"Albert!" she called, her voice sounding as rough as though she gargled vinegar.

The boy paused at his work and looked up.

"Go fetch James. Give him a tight hug, while you're at it."

"Ma?"

"He's been drafted." Her voice broke.

Albert gave her a horrified look, dropped his hoe, and sprinted off into the fields.

Julia held back her tears and went up the stairs to put together a bundle for James.

ॐ

Ben — May 19, 1864

May 19 or 20 1864
My beautiful Friend,
I know not what the day is. We have come through such a terrible fight. If you have heard reports of "The Bloody Angle" in the newspaper, I was there. I saw many of my comrades reduced to lifeless corpses by forces that overcame our best made brestwerks. I must tell the truth that I was scared more than at any other time of my life. In the rain our weapons would not fire. Only by the grace of the Great God am I alive to rite to you. The fact is, the Stonewall Brigade is no more. we are so reduced in numbers that a small Brigade has been patched together from the leavings of the 33d and two or three others, Colonel Terry of the 4th Va, commanding.

My sweet heart, we are somewhere near what I think is the North Anna river. Mercifully, Grant's forces withdrew so that we could quit the vicinity of Spottsylvania, and before that, the wilderness.

I suffered a wound of no consicuence, which I will beg of you to kiss into wholeness when I return to the Valley. Before that may occur, you must agree to marry me. I beg this boon of you, sweet Ella Ruth. I can no longer go without a promise from you that you will be my own bride. I look at yor likeness ten times a day unless we are marching or fighting. It has a place of honor in my pock't over my heart. Each night I kiss the representation of yor lips in hopes that you will feel a ghost of mine upon yors. I beg again that you will give me yor heart and hand.

I close with a prayr that you are well and have enouf to eat and cloths to warm you. I kno what privation is. My heart fails me to think you may as well.

Accept a kiss and my everlasting love.
Yor Benj'n

ॐ

Mary — May 30, 1864

Mary read Rulon's brief letter again. *I wish I could be there to comfort him,* she thought. *He does sound very low. What can I do to brighten his spirits?*

A customer came into the store, sniffed at the scarcity of goods on the shelves, asked for eggs—of which Mary had none at that moment—and settled upon purchasing a jar of pickles that Mrs. Moore, the minister's wife, had exchanged for goods the previous week.

Mrs. Bingham and her three daughters brought in several loaves of fresh bread. The baker's wife traded for groceries, such as there were, and left with two of her daughters in tow, each carrying parcels. The youngest, Jessie, lingered behind, cradling her two parcels in one arm.

Mary smiled at her, and spoke. "Did you forget something, Miss Jessie?"

The girl ran the fingers of her free hand along the edge of the counter. "I wondered . . . I was wondering if y'all had heard anything of James."

"James Owen?"

"Yes, ma'am."

Mary almost giggled at being called *ma'am*. Most of the older matrons of Mount Jackson still called her *Miss Mary*, even after she'd been wed for three years with a little boy hugging her skirts. Instead, she put on a sober—but she hoped comforting—face and said, "We haven't yet. He's not been gone so long. I'm sure Mother Owen will bring word as soon as she receives a letter." Mary now smiled at the girl, recognizing the faraway look in her eyes. *I didn't know she was interested in young James.*

Jessie bent her head as though she made a curtsy, said, "Thank you, ma'am. You're most kind," and hurried out of the store.

Well, well. I hope the lad comes back, for Jessie's sake.

Mary arranged the vegetable display so that it seemed to hold more items, then cleaned a dusting of flour from the counter. Foodstuffs were so dear nowadays. She couldn't believe the cost of the peck of flour she had sold today. Of course the value of Confederate bills was inflated, but the war's cost wasn't only in lives lost.

As she sorted potatoes, she wondered how the Owen brothers were faring. She could only judge Ben's welfare from the aspect of Miss Allen's face whenever she dropped by the store, which wasn't often. He never had cause to write to Mary, and Mother Owen didn't impart news about him. She felt a twinge of sadness when she ran Peter's name through her mental countdown. His loss was still sorely felt on the farm. Carl? Carl was with Mosby, whose men seemed to lead a charmed existence. She actually had no idea where James had gone. She supposed he was with the infantry somewhere in eastern Virginia.

Father Owen had come into the store once when his company moved down the valley. He'd latched onto Roddy right away, and left with great reluctance, she'd judged.

She knew about Rulon's movements from his letters, and from the last one, he was well in body, but not doing well in his soul. She couldn't help sighing. *I must write something that will give him cheer*, she thought. Perhaps it was time to quit being a shy sister and let him know exactly what she planned for their reunion—behind closed doors—when this war had been won. An unfamiliar yearning filled her, a stirring that had long been dormant.

Mary closed her eyes. Yes. The time had come. She breathed deeply. Then she opened her eyes, went into the back room, and sat at the table. Writing paper was precious, but she determined to use as much as the task required to take Rulon's mind off his present sorrows.

✎

Ella Ruth — June 17, 1864

Ella Ruth stood on the edge of the road and eagerly attacked the letter she had only just picked up from the Hilbrands' store. Ben had written at last.

It began "My beautiful Friend." She smiled. Ben had so many ways of telling her how closely connected he felt to her. Her skin tingled to know that he counted her as his friend.

From there on to the end of the paragraph, his tone became so somber she wanted to weep. She had devoured news from the battle front, and had indeed heard of the Bloody Angle, where so many valiant Southern men had lost their lives. She had not found his name on the casualty lists, thank the good God, but from his words, he suffered nevertheless from the indignities and slaughter the Yankees had heaped upon the men of Virginia on home soil.

Sweet Ben, you are well away from the fray, she thought. Then she gasped to read he had been wounded, and clutched the letter to her bosom. How like him to discount the severity of his injury. He might have his heart half torn from his body and he would say, *it's of little consequence.* She shuddered, and resumed reading where he begged her to restore him to wholeness, upon condition of marrying him.

Her heart bounded with joy. She and Ben had skirted around the topic of a marriage ever since she had regained his trust. She knew from the top of her head to the tips of her toes that they were destined to marry one day, but he had not come right out and asked her until now. This very day. Actually, several weeks ago, but what did that matter? He was asking her to be his bride. No. He was *begging* her. She wanted to skip down the street, yell her news at the top of her lungs, and scandalize the entire neighborhood. Ben wanted to marry her!

She rejoiced that the sacrifice of her earrings had been for such an excellent reward, as he treasured her likeness as much as the wounded soldier in the hospital had done with that of his wife.

I will be Ben's wife! The very idea made her want to sing.

She read the final words with a bit less joy. *Privation.* Such a nasty word. She would not venture to recount to Ben the hardships on the home front. They would dishearten him at a time when she must instill joy into his heart as his letter had, overall, done in hers.

I will be Ben's wife, she repeated to herself. Nothing could take away the glory of that bright future promise. She took a step that, oddly enough, resembled a skip. How she wished the day were here when they would wed. She desired no friends or strangers to gawk at them, only their parents and families surrounding them with love and gladness to wish them well on their most happy day.

"Accept a kiss and my Everlasting love. Your Benj'n." She sighed and put the letter to her cheek to receive the kiss she imagined Ben had bestowed upon it. Maybe he hadn't actually done that. For all his sentimental talk, Ben was, after all, a man. In her experience of soldiers in the hospital, she had observed that men didn't always follow through with certain actions,

---

especially if other men were close by. She had no idea how much privacy a soldier in camp could command. Perhaps they were crammed together like peas in a pod, arms constrained by the shoulders of comrades in arms.

"Even if you didn't kiss the letter, I will pretend that you did," she murmured to a far-off Ben, and hurried down the street, planning what she would write to tell him she would, indeed, marry him.

Rulon — September 19, 1864

The battle had scarcely begun when Rulon heard bullets whizzing past his ears. Garth Von, riding on his left, rolled out a string of swear words. Most of the invective was directed at him, Rulon.

What did I do? he wondered, parrying a Yankee trooper's sabre blow with his own blade. He slashed at the next trooper to approach, Von's curses ringing in his ears.

" . . . your foppish feather!" Von screamed.

Feather? This animosity is about my plume? Rulon swept a different Federal cavalryman off his horse.

" . . . think you're a stinking officer!" Von added.

Dumbfounded, Rulon froze, but his horse shied, taking him just beyond the reach of the blue-coated Yankee whose sabre swished past his ear.

When he finally got his horse under control, Rulon found himself staring at the distant hills full of troopers and infantrymen as the heat of the battle moved elsewhere.

An artillery shell screamed overhead, and Rulon ducked reflexively. Wheeling around, he looked for Garth Von, but the man was not in sight. He rode toward his comrades gathered around the company's ragged guidon.

My feather. He envies me for that? It didn't make any sense that the man hated him so for want of a feather of his own.

He thought of Mary's father, presenting the stylish hat with such pride and pompous words. By now the hat was so bedraggled that he only wore the thing to keep the sun off his head. There was no fashion to it now. And the feather. *Great lands! That feather would make the ostrich weep.*

The company had been ordered into reserve. Rulon spotted Von in the midst of the pack, but rode silently back into position, keeping distance between himself and the man.

After an hour of waiting, Company "I" was put back into the battle. The squadron rode together, Garth Von among the men strung out in the line. Von hung back a slight bit, and Rulon, sensing danger from the scowling man, did so as well so he could keep the man in view.

A bugle blew for the charge, and Rulon put spurs to his mount. Again, bullets pinged around him. He felt a tug on his sleeve, but no pain. The ball had passed through the fabric. Then a horse shrieked and a man yelled obscenities as he fell. Rulon didn't dare turn to check who had lost his horse, for they were among the Yankee cavalry, slashing and parrying and being driven back. Soon they were retreating over ground they had held previously.

When they bivouacked that night up the valley at Fisher's Hill, Rulon looked around at the diminished company. Owen Leoyd was among the missing.

Overwhelming sadness tore at him. He'd fought beside Leoyd, rode around McClellan at his side, endured three-day vidette duties with him, and learned tricks from him that kept him alive.

It wasn't long before Rulon learned that Garth Von had survived the battle.

Von flew at him, a fist cocked. "It's your damn fault my horse is kilt, Owen," he raged. "Your damn swooping feather makes the Yankees think you're an officer."

Rulon fended him off, dancing backwards. "Hold on. The captains never said I was doin' wrong to look like a cavalier. Why do you object?"

"The damn Yankees shoot at officers," Von answered, adding extra invective. "Anyone ridin' near you could be kilt."

Rulon snatched the now-bedraggled plume off his hat and stomped on it, but he knew the damage had been done long ago.

Von took a swing and missed as Rulon retreated. "You made me a camp dog," Von said. "I should have shot you dead the day you rode in wearing that ridiculous getup, thinking you was the King of Prussia."

"That's enough," Ren roared, coming up to the argument with

a bandage around his sleeve. He pushed his way between Rulon and Von, and turning to Von, said, "Save that ire for the Federals. You'll need it. We've lost a fair amount of men, so go catch yourself a loose horse." He turned to Rulon. "Stay out of his way. They're coming for us tomorrow, I'll warrant."

§

Julia — October 7, 1864

When Clay burst into the front room, screeching like he'd been attacked by a lion, Julia dropped the shirt she was patching.

"Ma! Mr. Bates rode through. The Yankees are coming down the pike." He rubbed his neck. "They're takin' the stock and burnin' the crops and harvests. Ma, they will surely burn the barn."

Julia stood. "Son. Quiet down. Let me think." She walked to the fireplace and put three fingers to her forehead. She tapped them, one at a time against skin and bone, thumping multiple times, the sound echoing like a horse crossing a bridge until her brain engaged and an idea came to her.

She took a breath and looked up. "Here's what to do. Get Albert and Marie." She looked at her youngest child, who had followed Clay into the room. "Anna, you go with them. Clay, all y'all drag out the corn sacks. Tie them closed. Put as many sacks on the backs of the cattle as they will tolerate. Tie them on secure. You don't want to spook them with shiftin' loads or they'll run off from you."

She laid a hand on his shoulder to steady his quaking frame. "When you finish up, take your brother and drive the cows up the mountain. Stay till the Yankees pass. I reckon you'll be there a few days, so I'll rustle up provisions for your stay." She squeezed his shoulder. "Go, you two. Get a wiggle on!"

Clay hesitated. "Mr. Bates said they're a mean bunch. They burned his house."

Julia set her jaw. That would not happen here. She shooed her son away and went to the kitchen. She fried the last of the pork skin to make cracklings, boiled eggs she'd been collecting from the last laying hen about the place, and wrapped corn pone in brown paper she had saved for stationery. No matter. Rod hadn't received but half of her letters. She would be spared the trouble of making ink from ground walnut hulls and stove soot. She never could achieve the proper fluid mixture to get it to flow smoothly from her nib anyhow.

She gathered the food and stuffed it into a carpetbag that would have to serve. She ran with it to the barn. Far to the south, smoke wreathed above the windbreak trees marking the lanes of their neighbors. The Yankees were coming.

The boys drove the dairy herd across the road and into the fields, riding after them on nearly the only horses left. Julia called after them, "Muffle that clatterin' bell or take it off." She and her daughters watched them go into the trees and down the creek bed, heading toward the Massanutten. She hoped her sons remembered the way to the hidden spot Rod used to take them to when hunting. It was their only hope for saving the herd and the corn.

She turned and stared down the pike. The smoke now billowed in black shafts in the distance. The Yankees were coming.

Julianna began to sob, tears coursing down cheeks smeared with corn silk and pollen from her labors.

"Stop that, child," Julia scolded, wiping the girl's face with her apron. "Show them your spirit, not your fear."

The three of them stood in the lane, waiting, watching as the Union soldiers advanced down the pike, marching unevenly as they came. Men broke out of the main body to torch the fields on each side. On they came. The Yankees were here.

ॐ

As the Union troops drew near enough that the soldiers started looking their way, Julia spoke in a low voice. "Girls, get to the house. I'm goin' to put a chair in the doorway and set down in it. Marie, bring me that Sharps rifle your pa left behind. Then you two stay upstairs unless I call you."

"Yes, Ma." Marie's voice quivered, but she turned her back and walked away to fetch the weapon.

"Mama, I'm scared." Julianna appeared to be keeping her tears in check, but her voice shook worse than Marie's had done.

"You will both be fine, Anna-girl. Just do as I tell you, mind?"

"Yes, Mama." She walked backward down the lane for a few

paces, then turned and ran toward the house.

Julia walked backward herself for a few steps, then turned her back on the oncoming Union soldiers and strode toward her home, trying to give her daughters confidence in her, even if she barely felt any herself. The girls must not see her knees or her hands shake. Mothers must be brave in the face of danger.

She let the sight of the burning fields and the knowledge that her barn would likely be destroyed build indignation, then irritation, and finally anger in her. By the time she saw the Yankees coming toward her home, she sat in her rocker, holding the rifle down at her side, hidden by her skirt and apron, and she was in a righteous rage. Let a Yankee try to disturb her home. He would think twice before he attacked a southern woman's abode again.

"Mama!"

Marie hardly ever called her "Mama" these days. Something must be wrong to bring her down the stair in disobedience to instructions.

"Marie?"

"I tied Sheba in the barn. She'll burn up, Mama."

"Stay here."

"I can't leave her to die!" Marie slipped through the small space between Julia and the door jamb and set off toward the barn.

"No! Come back, daughter."

Marie glanced over her shoulder, but kept going.

Julia, faced with approaching soldiers bearing torches, didn't know which she should do first, drive the Yankees away from the house and her daughter upstairs, or get Marie and the dog out of the barn. She turned to gauge how close the soldiers had come. One man was intent upon torching the trees along the lane. She ground her teeth. Those trees broke the wind. They didn't bear any fruit. This was an unruly bunch. Three more soldiers brought their firebrands straight toward her. Her indecision past, she arose, kicked the rocker backward into the room, raised the rifle, and pointed it at the nearest man.

"Drop your torch. My home won't burn."

"Now ma'am," the soldier under her eye said, "we've got orders to take your crop."

"There's no crop here. Move yourself back."

"Ma'am. You do yourself no good turn holding a weapon on us," he said, his voice a little shaky as he looked down her barrel.

She raised her voice a mite. "Git off my property. Turn around and go!"

"We can't do that, little lady," another man said, approaching the first. He edged out of her vision, then broke into a run toward the barn. The third soldier joined him, and the tree-burner came closer by the second.

Julia could feel the heat coming from the trees. The snapping of the fire reminded her of pistols cracking in the distance. She couldn't contain all the men, couldn't leave the first man unguarded to deter the others.

"Marie!" she screamed, knowing she dared not turn her head. "My girl's in that barn," she told the man under her gun, knowing she was pleading, hating herself for doing so.

"Sam!" he barked. "Let the girl clear out."

As the man spoke, she noticed several stripes on his uniform sleeve. She had picked a sergeant to threaten. Was that good, bad? He had some part of decency in him, judging from his last words.

"You can destroy the barn." Her voice sounded strident, but she couldn't do anything about that. "Leave me my home and my girl."

She heard the report of a rifle and Marie's shriek, then a wail. She almost looked in her daughter's direction, but kept her eyes on the sergeant. If Marie had voice, she was alive.

"Your men will shoot a defenseless girl?"

The sergeant flicked a glance in the direction of the barn. "She's whole, ma'am," he reported, looking relieved, but at the same time, disgusted.

"Just tormenting her, then?"

"No ma'am," he said in a low voice. "He shot the dog."

Julia heard herself crying, out of control, losing herself in pain.

"Ma'am, you need to lower that rifle and go inside," the sergeant pleaded. "We have to be about our business."

Marie was thrust against her then, momentarily throwing off her aim. The barrel of her rifle dipped, and the sergeant took the opportunity to escape toward the barn.

"Mama. Sheba." Marie sobbed, then leaned against her, gasping and scrubbing the tears from her eyes with balled fists.

"Inside," Julia managed to say, and shoved the girl behind her. She backed through the doorway, waving the barrel of the rifle from side to side. Once clear of the doorway, she slammed and bolted the door.

"Mama. Why didn't you shoot them?" Marie asked in a broken voice.

Julia took several breaths, fighting the weakness of her knees until she got the rocker upright and sank into it, laying the weapon across her lap.

"It's not loaded," she said, her voice sounding like a raven's caw.

Chapter 24

Rulon — October 9, 1864

The base of the hill bristled with dismounted men waiting for action behind stone fences. Under a sky lightened by dawn, Rulon watched the skirmishers from the brigade move forward across the meadow toward Tom's Brook. Behind him on the hill, wheels squeaked as artillerymen dragged the guns of the battery around, bringing them to bear on General Custer's cavalry. Rumor said the Yankees were finally going to fight back.

The 1st Virginia and other regiments in the brigades had harried Custer's retreating troopers for the last few days. The Union general had not turned his men and given them tit for tat, but had continued down the Valley, relying on his rearguard to keep General Rosser at bay. Yesterday, it seemed that Custer's patience had finally grown thin enough to let his boys give them a fight, but they had only engaged in a brief skirmish along the Back Road.

A shell whistled overhead from the rear. The battery had sent a message amongst the horses lined up in the distance, hazy through smoke. On a hill to the north, an echoing gun boomed to hurl disdain their way.

Damn the Yankees! It wasn't enough they had put in the ground all the decent men he'd served with the past years? Now they had busied themselves burning barns, mills, crops, and even the occasional abode, making his country a barren wasteland under a pall of smoke. How could God allow it?

He heard a groan, glanced at the fellow crouching beside him, then discovered he had made the sound himself. *Rulon, find your mettle*, he chided himself, but still groaned again. He knew he'd lost a great deal of courage the day General Stuart had been mortally wounded at Yellow Tavern. He ground his teeth to keep from crying out again at the waste. The glorious General gone. He bowed his neck under the pain.

That same day, he had lost his well-trained bay horse, shot from under him as he parried a sabre thrust with the stock of his rifle. Although toppling with the dying horse had saved his life, the loss was much to bear. He'd kept the horse healthy longer than he would have thought possible. Now his mount was a plow horse, ill-fitted for battle.

He took a deep breath to settle himself, then regretted it as he went into a spell of coughing to clear smoke from his lungs. When he had finished, he shivered as though a ghost had stepped on his grave. *Has God turned His face away from my country?*

Gone were the men who had ridden alongside him, fought beside him, shared a tent, tended fire, cooked rations. First Owen Leoyd had fallen, then Ren Lovell. *Good old Ren.* He shook his head. He doubted he would have survived his first days in the Troop without him. All were gone save one. Garth Von.

He almost let loose with a mighty curse, but managed to restrain himself at the last moment. He hated the loathsome, evil man.

Thinking about Von, one hand went to his head, to the once-fine hat Mary's father had presented to him with great ceremony. He jammed the filthy head-gear tighter onto his head, glad that he'd stomped the plume into the dust. If he had known the trouble it would bring him, he would have torn off the feather the second he left Mary behind. He remembered the strong emotion on her face as he and the company paraded through Mount Jackson in their splendid array, horses lined up just so, backs straight, heads up, off to beat the Yankee foe.

Oh Mary. He bent his head to mask his face. He missed her above all else. Even though they'd been here in the Valley since— when had it been? August? It was so hard to account for the days, let alone the months anymore. Even though the cavalry had passed through Mount Jackson what seemed like countless times, going up, going down, chasing or being chased, he had not been able to so much as rein in his horse and throw a kiss to his wife. War had robbed him of that simple pleasure. War occupied his every waking moment. Only at night could he spare Mary a thought, touch her likeness, and dream of the future. Would there be a future?

A great weariness swept him. How long had it been since he

had eaten a home-cooked meal? Slept on a mattress tick filled with soft goose feathers and down? Held Mary in his arms?

He took a shallow breath, wary now of the smoke filling the countryside. He despised the mindless carnage, the cold and the heat and the dying, and being apart from his wife. He hated the war.

But much as he hated Garth Von and the war, he hated the Yankees more. They had given provocation from the first, invading his native land with their immense armies, but now their actions went beyond the pale as they proved themselves to be ravishers of the land.

As the sky brightened more, Rulon could see in the countryside below where smoke hung low over still-flickering flames. Damn Phil Sheridan! For the last three days, the Yankees had carried out their general's orders to burn, to ruin, to destroy.

How many houses had gone up in smoke and flames? Did Mary have a place to lay her head? Anger curled up from his toes, much as the smoke curled upward from the hay stacks off to the right. Pillagers! Vandals! Whatever provisions they could not use for themselves, they were leaving in ashes so Early's men and the Valley's inhabitants would starve.

Rulon thought of his little boy, the son he had never met. As though it rose upward, caused by friction through resistance from his clenched muscles, white heat seared his belly. The Yankees were starving his son! Surely God did not intend for this to happen? Sheridan and his minions could only be fiends from the deepest hell.

Smoke danced before his eyes, burning them. His stomach churned with fury as he waited for Yankees to come so he could kill them. The hardship to his baby would be avenged.

෨

The charge came suddenly, as Custer's men, their throats raising a cry of challenge, came out of the smoke at a gallop, sabres aloft. Rulon expected the men around him to mount at any moment to counter the Yankee charge, but instead, they remained dismounted, ordered to make a stand behind this stone wall to defend the line.

Is Rosser mad to keep us dismounted? The company, indeed,

the whole brigade, would be swept before the fury of Custer's cavalry.

But the command had come down the line, and Rulon obediently shouldered his weapon. The 1st Virginia held the left flank, and if they were turned . . . He didn't want to think about the consequences.

Somewhere to the front, cannon boomed. Where were their answering guns? He looked over his shoulder. The battery stood silent, men lying broken around the guns. As he turned back to the front, a cry went up at the end of the line. Custer's troopers came on at their front, approaching with blood in their eyes, but the canny cavalier also had sent another unit to flank them. It was breaking through. It threatened what remained of the battery. It threatened them.

Rulon shivered. Fear flooded into his throat. The Yankees were in front and behind him.

A man or two threw themselves onto their mounts and rode off to the right. The bugler sounded retreat, and they kept on going. Soon, the trickle became a torrent, as the Yankees beat them back from their position.

He fought to find his horse, the nag he'd liberated after he found it chomping grass in a meadow. He reached it at last, threw himself into the saddle, and followed the others. Cannon boomed behind him and he pulled the fleeing horse to the left to avoid a shower of canister. He wondered if he would ever see Mary's face in this life again.

"Owen! Mind your back!"

Rulon did not know who screamed the warning. Mr. Earl? He pivoted in his saddle in time to grab hold of Garth Von's arm above the wrist with both hands before the man could stab him in the kidney.

The knife now veered toward his ribs, but Rulon jerked the arm sideways. In doing so, he unseated Von, but the man's falling weight served to drag him off his own mount. He fell heavily onto his side, still gripping Von's forearm. A shell ripped the air above them.

It had come to this: close combat with a supposed comrade under fire of the enemy.

He held on, struggling to best the man, sensing that if he did not come off victorious, it would mean the death of him.

Von got a foot up and kicked, aiming his holey boot at Rulon's jaw.

He twisted away, and they rolled, fury driving both of them, fueling a desperate engagement that never should have come about. All because of a feather.

Von clawed at Rulon's eyes with his free hand. Rulon evaded the gouging fingers and butted his forehead into the man's breastbone, felt it give. Von howled, cursing and exerting himself to rise, hauling Rulon to his feet as well.

Hampered by the need to keep the knife away from his gizzard, Rulon attempted to swing the man, to shake him until he dropped the wicked blade. He thought he was succeeding when the world exploded into scarlet and black, reducing Von to bits while shards of metal pierced his own chest and belly in multiple places.

A massive force threw him onto his back against the unforgiving surface of the road as shattered bone splinters and gouts of blood spattered him. He thought that he clutched the man's arm still, but its lightness refuted the notion as implausible. The knife dropped from the hand at last, and he heaved a sigh of relief, even as he slipped into the timeless world beneath the blare of battle.

༺

Rulon — October 12, 1864

Rulon awoke with nightmares haunting his memory. Drenched in sweat, he endeavored to put the cursed visions into a deep pocket of his brain, but they escaped to torment his wakeful moments. It seemed he had been traveling in a wagon, but he wasn't the driver. He was inside, lying down on a rough pallet of burlap, trapped within canvas sidewalls that blocked the light of the sun but encased him in heat and misery.

Other unfortunate souls lay next to him, moaning each time the wagon took a bump on what must have been a very primitive path. He was horrified to discover that the loudest voice crying out was his own as pain, no, agony thrust a thousand spears into his chest and belly with each jolt. Finally, darkness came upon him.

Later, he battled the sensation that someone took him by the feet and pulled him toward the rear of the rickety vehicle. Another person lifted his shoulders seconds before he would have fallen headfirst to the ground. The two carried him a distance while he writhed in distress.

Rulon fought to subdue remembrance of the nightmare, but it only skipped forward. He found himself half-lying in a muddy ditch. Was he dead? No. Pain refuted that notion. He moved slightly and his head slipped downward on the muck and splashed into water, which immediately entered his nose. He sputtered frantically, trying to raise his head out of the murky liquid, but seemed to have no ready muscles in his torso. That part of his body cried out to die to escape the constant attacks from sharp instruments. In a moment, he discovered that his arms were whole, and succeeded in using them to raise his face above the surface of the water.

He opened his mouth and sucked air into his lungs, greedy to prolong his life. Yes, that was it. He wanted to live. Despite the immense pain inhabiting his body, he was not ready to die.

"Mary," he whispered. "I want to live."

"Shush, shush," she replied.

Stillness enveloped him at the sound of her voice. He opened his eyes to a dim space lit by one candle. Alas! He was dead after all. Mary's shimmering face hovered over him. She must have called him to join her in death.

He struggled against the thought, the despair that encompassed him at the notion. No. That wasn't right. He'd received no word that Mary had passed to Eternity. As far as he knew, she was alive. Did that mean—?

He tried to sit, found it impossible, struggled to focus and hold on to the spot of candlelight through the great wash of pain.

A glass pressed against his lips, forcing them open. A bitter liquid assailed his tongue. He struggled against swallowing, but a soft voice whispered, "Take the laudanum, dear husband," and a soft hand stroked his throat until he did so.

Could it be true that Mary had come here to nurse him? Where was *here*? How had he escaped the watery grave? Soon he felt himself slip into darkness, soothed by soft whispers of "There, there. I'll be here when you wake."

🕸

Mary — October 12, 1864

"Papa. We must have the small house. Rulon cannot abide all the noise here."

"What would you have me do?" her father asked. "Boot the Yankee company out on their ears?"

"They will go soon. Everyone says they are pushing up the Valley."

Mr. Hilbrands stroked his chin. He patted his stomach beneath his store apron. "It will be filthy."

"I will clean it somehow. He must have quiet. Have you seen the—" She broke off, afraid she would lose her supper if she thought long upon the horrible wounds in Rulon's body.

He patted her shoulder, nodding. "I marvel that he yet lives."

"He came home to me." She looked at her father, and began to shake. "I owe him a pleasant place to die." Her voice broke. "Roddy will be fatherless! Oh Papa!"

He wrapped his arms around her, holding her tight. "There now. I'm sure we can find someone to clean up the mess." He smoothed her hair. After a while, he held her at arm's length and peered down at her. "You go see to your husband now. He is still strong at the core. He's Rod Owen's son, after all."

Mary sniffled and wiped her eyes with a soft bit of worn fabric. Yes, and Mother Owen's as well. Perhaps she would not need to find walnut husks to dye her dress black. Perhaps she could bring him through this nightmare.

🕸

Rulon — October 15, 1864

Rulon came out of blackness and into pain. Thrashing against whatever held his wrists immobile, he opened his eyes to slits, looking about for relief.

He spied purple fabric. Maybe it was a skirt. Where had he seen it before? He thought perhaps it had something to do with his wife, but couldn't look up far enough to see if she was encased within it.

"Rulon, husband," he heard. "Calm yourself. Are you in pain?"

He made a noise. Was he whimpering? He closed his eyes.

Dear God, he begged, *don't let me cry.*

He felt a light touch on his shoulder. "I will return shortly, dear husband," came Mary's voice. He knew it now. How long had it been since he had heard her speak his name? Was there a burr of tears overlaying the sound?

Soon he heard a rustle of cloth. Mary must have sat beside him. She put a spoon between his lips and tilted rancid liquid into his mouth. She did it several times, and he swallowed, under the power of her urgings.

It was laudanum again. He hated the taste. At the same time, he yearned for the stupor and surcease from pain he knew would come soon. Mary took his hand, and he clung to it before the drug began its work, beset all the while by the stabbing knives of the injuries, feeling every chunk of the foreign objects lodged in his body. He recalled a moment of twilight when a surgeon had reckoned him to be a dead man and had barely closed the wounds with a score of stitches. He had not wasted a pain-killer or a slug of liquor on the patient.

Rulon remembered receiving the stitches. No man should have such a memory.

He waited to sink into the numbness of the narcotic slumber, anxious for the agony to be gone.

"Papa?"

Whose was that tiny, piping voice? It called him "Papa." Who could it be?

"This is your son, my husband," Mary whispered, as though she guessed his perplexity. "We call him Roddy."

Tiny fingers touched the back of his other hand, no more than a feather's stroke.

His boy. His son!

Rulon struggled to open his eyes. Through slits he saw him, dark curls framing his cherubic face. The wonder of creation that began so long ago. His son.

"Roddy?" he whispered, aware that moisture seeped down his cheek.

"Please Papa. You must get well," the small voice quavered, then the boy reached up and kissed Rulon's cheek.

"Come, child. Leave your papa to rest," another woman's voice said.

Someone in a brown dress took the lad by the hand and led him from the room.

Rulon closed his eyes. He had made that wondrous creature, he and Mary. Out of their union had come the miracle that was their son.

Would he live to take Mary into his arms again? He tried to squeeze her hand, but felt the effects of the laudanum overcoming him at last. Even as the pain faded, he felt robbed of that expression of affection between them.

Chapter 25

Ben — October 19 through 20, 1864

Why is it always my leg? Ben wondered, fighting to reach something to tie around the wound. This wasn't like the inconsequential leg injury he had suffered before. This one was bleeding to beat the band, and he had to stop it.

He discovered his belt would do to wrap around the leg above the flow. Now he had to get out of the field before the Yankees renewed their attack, pressed forward, and captured him.

He struggled to his feet, bearing his weight upon his rifle. The leg was not broken, he was relieved to discover. He looked around him. A body or two lay in the field below, but the losses weren't great this time. His company had left him, it appeared, as he was the only one of his fellows still here. Perhaps the shot had come from one of his own comrades?

Hunched over, he dragged his unresponsive leg and the rest of himself toward a hill covered with broken apple trees. Not the best cover, but perhaps it would serve until he located his company or someone who could take him to a surgeon to stitch him up. Once he achieved the shelter of the trees, he would allow himself to rest and survey the ground.

Fortunately, the rails of the fence surrounding the orchard were missing, so he didn't have to make a struggle to climb over. He found a spot high on the side of the hill where he could keep watch for anyone passing, and sat down with his back against a trunk. He promptly fell asleep.

Night came before he awoke. He could see campfires of the Federal troops off to the north, but the hill impeded his sight to the south. How far could the company have retreated before it stopped to regroup?

He checked his leg by moonlight. The bleeding seemed to have ceased, and he loosened the belt so the flesh would not die. Good. The wound was crusted over, and the flow of blood did not begin anew.

Where was he? He couldn't be far from Mount Jackson, or maybe his own home, but he had lost track of his precise location. Who still had an apple orchard that hadn't been entirely cut down for fuel? A rich man, he presumed, with enough slave hands to keep shivering soldiers at bay.

It wasn't possible that he was on the Allen farm, was it? What a comedown if he were to be lying in an orchard owned by his girl's father. He sighed, turned to get a better position, and went back to sleep.

He awoke at dawn, ravenous and in pain. He wondered if he had been moaning. He hoped not. He didn't want some darkie to come upon him and drag him to the Massa for trespassing.

He attempted to rise so he could move on south, and almost made it, but weakness and pain prevailed and he had to sit in a heap and husband his forces for another try.

Before he could do it, he heard a pistol clicking to full cock behind him.

"Do not move," came a voice. Feminine. "I will shoot you if you do not raise your hands."

He did so. "I'm wounded," he ventured. "You a Yankee?"

"Damn the Yankees to hell!" the voice replied, breaking a bit on the expletive. "Who are you?"

"Benjamin Owen, Company, Company. . . . I don't rightly know what company I'm in anymore. Was in the 33rd Virginia Infantry Regiment, but I've been sent hither and yon until I give up knowin'."

"Wait. Wait! Did you say 'Benjamin Owen'?"

"I did."

"From Allen's Infantry?"

"Yes, in the beginnin'."

"Ben?" Skirts rustled as the woman came into view. She laid the pistol down and dropped to her knees. "Ben?" she shrieked. "Oh, my Benjamin."

She was crying now, but underneath the mob cap, Ben recognized the gaunt features of Miss Ella Ruth Allen.

❧

Ben — October 20, 1864

"Jerusalem crickets!" he said as she fell upon him. "I scarce can believe it."

She held him tightly, rocking him back and forth, crooning his name.

"Mind the leg," he petitioned as her knee slid across his thigh. He gritted his teeth to avoid crying out.

She pulled back. "You are hurt? My poor Benjamin. Let me look."

"I'd druther you didn't," he said. "I told you I was wounded at the outset. Get me to a surgeon."

"I do not know where one is to be found who is not engaged in treating others," she said. "However, I have worked at the hospital under my uncle's eye. I can help you."

He wilted under the force of her assurances, and the pain, besides. "Go ahead. I can't bear the pain much longer."

Ella Ruth began by trying to open the hole in his trousers that had been cut by the Yankee ball sufficiently wide enough to assess the wound, but could not get a good look.

"Ben," she said, a bit timidly. "You will have to shuck your britches."

"The devil you say!"

"I cannot see the wound. I am sorry, but if I cannot see it, I cannot find the ball to remove it."

Ben shook his head. "No. Get me under a roof and bring me something to wrap about myself, and I'll decide then what course to take."

"You are so stubborn," she declared, sighing.

"I've quit bleedin'. Help me rise, and shelter me in the shed or the stable." He held up his arm to be steadied by her. "Besides, you have no instruments here."

"All right. The old nursery shed is closest." She picked up the pistol, uncocked it, then helped him rise. "Lean on me, Ben. I can bear your weight."

"I doubt it."

"Yes I can. I have had lots of practice walking men about in the hospital."

She grunted a bit when he slung his arm around her shoulder

and leaned on her. Despite his sleep, he was exhausted, and panted with the exertion of forward movement.

"Are you still in pain?" she asked a bit later as she bore him slowly along.

"A mite," he lied through gritted teeth, trying to use the rifle as a crutch. "Some little bit," he amended after a few more steps. As they neared the goal, he finally admitted, "More than I'd like to say."

"Oh Ben," she wailed, then tsked several times with her tongue. "Do not tell me lies. I must know your state before I endeavor to fish out the ball."

"You're not a surgeon, Ella Ruth."

"No, but I have seen many balls removed from wounds by my uncle and other surgeons. I believe I can do the task." She propped him against a work bench used in former times to prepare apple grafts. "Hold onto that rail," she commanded. "I shall return in no time at all with assistance."

"Leave me the pistol," he said. "It looks heavy."

"It is heavy, and I can shoot it," she said, and kept it with her as she hurried off.

Ben sank into a semi-dazed state while he waited for her to return. Perhaps she would think better of her plan and bring someone else to perform a surgery on him. Or mayhap she would find a vehicle to cart him to the hospital, if it wasn't within Yankee lines now.

After a time that seemed interminable, Ella Ruth came back with her arms full, but no one else accompanying her. Hadn't she mentioned seeking someone's assistance? Instead, she carried two tattered but clean-looking blankets, a handful of kitchen utensils, a roll of bandage, and most of a bottle of whiskey. She had donned an apron to cover her skirt and bodice, and the handle of the pistol poked out of a pocket.

"Where are your pa and ma? Did you tell them I'm here?" he asked, concerned that she had not brought anyone back with her to help attend to his wound.

Ella Ruth made a face. "They removed themselves to Charlottesville, but I refused to accompany them."

"You did what?" He felt a fever rising as he spoke sharply to her.

"You must be quiet, Ben. Your face is looking very pale. I fear you have lost a great deal of blood." She placed the items in her arms on the bench, then spread one blanket on the floor of the shed. She cocked her head to one side, then said, "No, I believe it is better if you lie on the work bench so you are high enough to tend to." Moving the items to the floor, she retrieved the first blanket, shook it with a snap to free it of dirt and straw, and spread it upon the bench as best she could with him leaning over it. Breathing rapidly, she surveyed her work. "Ben, you must get atop the bench with my help alone. We do not have any male darkies about. The ungrateful wretches all ran off to the enemy when the Yankees started up the Valley this year."

He groaned, half from disbelief that she persisted in her notion that she could tend him, and half from pain.

She glanced around the shed. "Oh, that stool will help," she said, going to a corner of the building and bringing it back. "Darling Ben, I knew I must be here if you came through. How else could we marry? Besides, Uncle Joseph had need of me at the soldier's hospital." She put her arms around Ben's chest and assisted him in mounting the stool and climbing onto the bench.

Ben's head felt as though he had already drunk the whiskey, as a profound lightness was affecting his reasoning. He must be crazed to think about letting this girl do an operation on him. But what recourse did he have? She seemed to be the only person about the place, and mayhap her uncle's skill ran in the family.

"Are you here alone, then?" he managed to ask. That would account for her fondness for keeping the pistol with her.

"No. One of the darkies, my maid Lula, stayed to care for me. She was rather mortified that I refused to go as a refugee with my parents, but I'm very glad she decided to stay with me. She is making you a bit of gruel."

"You are a caution, girl," he said, and that was all he could whisper as he lapsed into blackness.

80

When Ben awoke, his leg throbbed abominably, but he seemed not to have any fever. His stomach grated against his backbone, he was so hungry. Lying on the bench, covered by the second blanket, he felt vulnerable, and struggled to rise, but gave

247

up the attempt because of the pain it caused.

He looked around. He was alone. His rifle and accoutrements lay heaped in a jumble by the wall. What was that cloth? As he was puzzling out the question, he recognized the patchwork handiwork on the fabric. Jerusalem crickets! His trousers!

He groaned. He did not recall having removed them. That could only mean Ella Ruth had done so. Embarrassment flooded his thoughts and his hands clutched at the blanket. He had quit wearing underclothes when the last pair to his name became holey enough to let the breezes through. Had Ella Ruth been so fully caught up in her self-appointed task that she had accidentally or willfully gazed upon his parts?

Her bold actions in the last few hours confirmed to him that her streak of doggedness, her obdurate, unyielding nature had not changed. Gaining her way was of great importance to her. Whatever he wanted could go hang.

But yet, she may have saved his life by her persistence. Removing a poisonous lead ball from a wound was of equal importance to modesty, wasn't it? He chewed on that notion for a few moments. Would Ma be scandalized or practical about the matter? She had always appeared to have a direct conduit to God and His ideas of proper conduct. What advice would Ma give him, if he were to have the courage to ask for it?

The unseemly viewing had most likely taken place. He had an uncomfortable sense that this fell into the "offense to God" department. As soon as he could get around, even before he sought to rejoin his company, he would have to seek out a minister.

These circumstances accelerated the need for their wedding to take place as soon as may be. Otherwise, he could not make the matter right and assuage these overwhelmingly guilty feelings.

As he was musing on where he would get money to pay for a ceremony—which most likely cost more nowadays than the two dollars Rulon had paid over—Ella Ruth came through the shed door, bearing a bowl covered with a cloth.

"I'm sorry I don't have a tray for your food," she apologized. "The pewter was melted down ages ago for munitions, and Momma took the silver with her."

Ben eyed the bowl. "No matter. I'm starving, girl."

She came to the bench, propped him up, and handed him the food. "It is only corn gruel, but we do not have much in the way of provisions. Does your wound pain you?"

He paused between shoveled spoonsful. "Yes, a mite."

"I have whiskey left over from cleaning out the injury. When you have finished eating, I will give you a portion to dull the pain."

Ben wanted to finish eating before he got onto the tricky subject of clothing removal and its consequences. When he had scraped the dish clean, he handed it back to her. At least his stomach felt better for the food, if not for the nerves.

As she helped him lie back on the bench, he racked his brain for a suitable opening to the topic. He couldn't merely blurt out a question about how much of him she had seen. Perhaps he could approach in a sideways fashion.

"I'm obliged to you for tending my wound," he began. "I reckon I need the limb for later."

"Indeed," she said, giving him a smile.

"As soon as it can bear weight, I must take myself back to the army." No, that wasn't right. The pain must have muddled his brain, and he'd completely gone astray from speaking of the obligation they had to marry.

He noticed that Ella Ruth had stopped smiling.

"Remember what I promised you? You were quite insistent about the matter."

"Of course." What, exactly, was she thinking about amongst all the things they had written about?

"You are here now. You are injured, which is unfortunate, but my hope is that you will recover, given time and rest."

"I am agreed with that notion. I don't want to be reported absent without leave, though. I'm not a deserter."

"Then do not desert me."

He thought about her words for a long time. How had this conversation gone off from his planned topic of discussion? The silence stretched on. It was his turn to speak, and Ella Ruth was clearly waiting for him to do so.

"I don't intend to desert you." He had to get back on track. He swallowed. "I do have a question."

"Ask it, Ben."

He cleared his throat. What a fix he was in. The words he needed didn't appear as he had hoped. Where had his gift for fine words gone? All his charms had gone missing. Finally, he blurted out, "How much of me was uncovered and in your sight durin' the wound-tending?"

Oh, shame! He'd gone and done what he had determined not to do. He covered his eyes with his wrist, then let the arm fall to his side.

"Darling Ben," Ella Ruth said, after a very long time. "I caught sight of all of you." She stopped, and he could see her throat moving in a swallow of her own. When she continued, her voice had acquired a huskiness that he found no less disturbing than her words. "My work with Uncle Richard obliged me to nurse men with injuries in every possible place. I suppose I have no reputation at all, anymore." She inhaled deeply before she went on. "You may find me unattractive, now that you know I have seen other men's most intimate parts."

Certainly not. Even in her gaunt, war-worn state and well-laundered attire, she was lovely as could be. A yearning for her began to grow, but he squashed it in order to set matters back on an orderly course.

"I've compromised you, girl."

"I just told you—"

"We must be wed, and soon."

"I have washed those men."

He shuddered. "For the honor of Virginia."

"As I have you," she said in a halting voice.

"No," he moaned.

"Yes. There was blood everywhere."

"We have to marry now. Today. Is Mr. Moore in the town?" He struggled to sit up, and his agitation gave him the strength to achieve that end.

"Ben, lie quiet."

"You must send the woman for the minister."

"He is gone, Ben. He was arrested by the Yankees for preaching against them."

"The Dunker preacher?"

"Dead."

"The German—"

"There is no one, Ben. We cannot have a church ceremony."

"But you saw—"

"I do not care." She lifted her chin a slight bit. "I have pledged myself to you, as you have to me. I promised to marry you, but we cannot have a regular ceremony. Let us make marriage vows to each other, Ben. That will put things right."

"Ella." He could hardly speak for the pain in his soul. "We must marry. Bring the judge."

"He went for a soldier."

"The mayor."

"He is gone."

"There is truly no one around?"

"Only the armies."

He clutched at a straw. "Can an officer—"

"I do not know, Ben." She shook her head. "General Early has gone south, and I will not be married by a Yankee."

That prospect alarmed him. He could be captured and sent off to a prison. Exhausted, he let himself sink back onto the blanket. He had to make Ella Ruth his wife, but his options seemed to have run out.

Chapter 26

Ella Ruth — October 20, 1864

Ella Ruth leaned forward and laid her forehead on Ben's chest. He put an arm over her shoulders. *He is in such a weakened state. Does he know how much blood he lost?* She thought not.

She turned her head slightly until she could see a part of his face. He was not looking at her, but at the roof above them. Such a puny roof. It leaked abominably, and she feared for his health if she kept him hidden here in the shed.

I need to move him to the house. He won't last in this rain and cold.

How was she to manage that? Would Lula help her? Could she count on the woman's loyalty if the Yankees came up the Valley again, or would the servant reveal Ben's presence? Lula had been a trifle uppity the last time Ella Ruth spoke with her. *Best not to take the chance.*

She took a deep breath and expelled it slowly. How many more obstacles to keeping Ben safe did she have to overcome?

Her mind skipped to her main concern. How were they to marry?

All the answers she had given to Ben's half-frantic questions were true. There was no religious or civil authority left to say any words over them, to sanction the union they had promised to make.

She felt a welling sadness rise from her middle. She wanted what Mary Owen had. The husband, even though he be horribly wounded. The child. The name. She no longer cared about the external appearances, the magnificent clothing and pomp of a church ceremony. She only wanted this man, her Ben, to hold her close, to caress her, to make her his woman.

What did words matter? They could say words, whisper to each other vows of fealty and devotion. She would promise whatever he wanted, if he would give her his name and his child.

A thought came to her mind, an image from her early childhood. The darkies had held a celebration she did not understood at the time. Now the meaning came clear to her, vivid in its import. Denied a Christian marriage ceremony, the slaves had devised their own.

"We will jump the broomstick," she murmured against Ben's shirt.

He lifted his head. "That's the Negro way."

"It's the only way," she whispered. "The only way left to us."

She saw that he would shake his head, and stopped him with a brief kiss on his cheek. "We can have a minister when this awful war ends," she whispered. "In the meantime, I will become your wife in the same way our servants have done."

"Ella—"

She cut him off. "Poppa always looked on such unions as legal. He considered the couple married. He wouldn't sell off one or the other and put them apart."

Ben rested his head on the bench, stared at the roof again. "We must do right."

"This will be right for us," she answered. "You want to marry me. I want you . . . to marry me," she added in a husky voice. "This is our solution."

"The minute Mr. Moore comes back—"

"We will have words said in the regular way," she promised, kissing his cheek again to seal the bargain.

৩০

Ben — October 21, 1864

The next day at noon, Ella Ruth brought Ben a plate heaped with applesauce, what could be mashed potatoes or maybe turnips, and one little piece of meat of an indeterminate origin.

"Did you eat today?" he asked her.

She tilted her head and smiled, shrugging one shoulder in a coquettish manner.

"Well then, we will share," he said, and cut into the meat substance to divide it.

She tried to refuse, but he stared her down until she opened her mouth and accepted a bite from his fork.

"You really are a caution, Benjamin," she said in the old voice full of lightness and charm. "You need the nourishment to overcome that terrible injury."

He knew what she said was true, but seeing her face, so thin and drawn, tore at his sense of the right way to treat a lady, and his notion of who should go first in matters of polite society.

When he had consumed what he deemed was his fair share of the meal, he gave the leavings to Ella Ruth, and insisted that she finish the food.

She did so under protest, and then set the plate aside.

"I must change the dressing on your wound," she said.

His heart pounded with anxiety. "I don't reckon it's been bleedin' or nothin' of the sort," he said. "You don't need to bother."

"I know more than you about treating a variety of wounds, Ben." It was her turn to stare him down, and she did it with relish. "I will mind your sensibilities, but the flesh must be inspected for infection." She began to lift his blanket.

He cringed.

Noticing it, she said, "Benjamin! Your brother Rulon recently took a number of wounds from an exploding shell. He's struggling to survive from the effects of putrefying flesh. You don't want that sort of problem, do you?"

"Rulon's hurt? Lordy, I must go to him!"

"You are much too weak for that. Besides, the Yankees are still in the area. I cannot get you to Mount Jackson."

"Cannot, or will not?"

"I cannot. Truly. Please trust me, Ben. Have I not proven myself to you by now?" Tears started into her eyes, and she appeared to be on the verge of weeping.

"There now, don't you go to cryin', sweet girl. He made a hand sign of resignation. "Look at the wound all you want, but don't take any notions of, of—" He stopped, unable to speak further.

Ella Ruth took a shuddering breath. "I will be circumspect, my love."

She raised the blanket enough to get a good field of vision of the wound site, and proceeded to take off the bandage she had applied previously.

Ben looked down his body at her busy hands, noting that they did not stray into forbidden areas. Since that issue was settled, he thought about the news Ella Ruth had sprung on him. Rulon was fighting for his life. The notion brought a sweep of nausea upon him. His next younger brother was gone. He couldn't bear to lose his big brother, too.

A sharp pain interrupted his worries about Rulon. "Ow!" He should have kept an eye on Ella Ruth's ministrations. She seemed to be probing his flesh with some cold metal implement. No, she was *cutting* his flesh! "Ella! For the love of—"

"Shush, Ben. Act the part of a man. I must remove this infection or you could lose the leg." Her look was stern, but quite concerned, and he gritted his teeth so hard he was afraid he would break them.

"Go ahead," he muttered. "Give me warning when you're fixin' to cut me again."

"I'm sorry. It must be done. I wish I could give you a tumbler of liquor to dull your senses, but I cannot spare it. It is all I have to wash your wound afterward." She held up a bottle of amber liquid.

He nodded his understanding.

She returned to her work, and after a bit said, "Prepare yourself. I have one more cut to make."

He thought perhaps he blacked out for a while, because when he opened his eyes again, the blanket covered him. Ella Ruth wadded up the waste and put it into a basket. Then she turned to him and placed her hand on the blanket, uncomfortably close to his parts.

"Now you must rest. Tonight I will take you into the house. It's too dangerous to leave you here. You could be discovered."

"Ella?"

"Yes?"

"I owe you a debt of gratitude for takin' me in and usin' your healin' arts on me."

She stared at the ground, nervously working the fingers of the hand on the blanket against her thumb.

"Your devotion to me is clear. Will you forgive me for my doubts?"

She nodded. "With all my heart."

"I reckon you gave me that already."

"Yes." She joined her hands together before her mouth, and

oh horror, a tear slid down her cheek.

"Don't weep, girl. We'll find a minister."

She sniffed and bowed her head, not saying anything further before she turned and left with her basket and his dinner plate.

හ

After nightfall, Ella came back to the shed and whispered, "Ben. Are you awake?"

He was nearly asleep, truth be told, but got himself in hand enough to answer, "Yes, mostly."

"Good," she said. "Swing your limbs over the side of the table. I will assist you."

"Why?"

"I'm taking you to the house. The Yankees are about, and I don't want them to discover you."

Alert, now that she had reminded him of his dangerous circumstance, Ben struggled upright and did as Ella Ruth had bid him.

She took his arm and guided him onto the stool, then down to the ground. "Mind your wound," she murmured. "Let me bear your weight."

He looked around for his gear, but could see nothing in the dimness.

"Have no fear," she said. "Your rifle is safe in the house."

"I thank you," he whispered, wrapping his arm around her shoulder and venturing a step. Pain shivered up his leg, but he could hardly cry out and bring the enemy down upon them, so he bit his lip and bore the pain as well as he could while Ella Ruth tugged him toward the house.

He stumbled a time or two, both from weakness and from encountering unknown obstacles in the path, but they made good progress, and soon approached the house.

"Shh!" Ella Ruth cautioned, standing still.

Ben stopped, now clutching the girl for all he was worth in an attempt to keep his balance.

"Now go," she muttered, and tugged him forward.

Ben stumbled again, stepping on a rounded object that must have some length to it, as both feet found it.

"Careful. It's only a stick," she said, a little catch in her voice.

"I will make it, if we haven't far to go," he replied.

"Just a bit more," she promised, and soon they did arrive at the back of the house.

Ella Ruth pulled on the latch and opened the door to the darkened wash room. The kitchen showed no light either. They paused so she could close and bolt the door. Then they passed through the wash room and into the kitchen.

"Here," Ella Ruth said, pulling back a chair and easing Ben into it. "You must rest, dear husband."

Husband? Figuring his ears had stopped up to the extent that he had misheard her, he put a finger into one and wiggled it around.

Ella Ruth lit a candle, placed it on the table, took his hand from his ear, and said, "Ben, we've stepped over the broomstick. We're now husband and wife."

Even as he groaned in disbelief, he recalled the rounded stick near the back of the house. "I stepped *on* it," he whispered. "That's not the same as jumping over it."

She held herself rigidly erect, grasping his hand with hers. "No matter. You crossed over the broomstick. You are my husband, according to the rites of the servants." She paused, then took a breath and continued in a softer tone. "If you need words, I will say words to you, words of fealty and devotion, words of love and adoration."

"You can speak them later, once I've rested," he said, his mind reeling with the notion that they were married. Pain dulled his senses. He longed for sleep, could barely keep himself awake, but he would have to deal with Ella Ruth's conviction sooner or later. "If you're set on this rite, I'll come up with words to speak. Right now, I have to sleep."

❧

Ben — October 22 through November 6, 1864

Ben awoke the following morning with words in his brain that led him to believe that he had been mulling over the state of affairs during the night.

Ella Ruth had ensconced him in her parent's bed despite his strenuous objections. The girl would not be denied, which he already knew from sad experience, but at least he had put his mind to ease once he had spoken his doubts.

Now he felt a mite off. When he took stock of himself, he discovered that his leg had swollen up to a tremendous extent, and he feared infection and fever had set in.

Jerusalem crickets! He didn't have time or inclination to be laid up in bed for an extended period. He had to get back to his company.

He tried calling out for Ella Ruth. The weakness of his voice frightened him. He tried again, and this time he achieved some volume. She came quickly, worry written upon her face as she examined his leg.

"Ben, you must lie still. I'll bring an herbal powder for the wound. We must bring down that swelling and the fever. Bear with me, and I'll pull you through this rough spot."

At times in the days that followed, Ben doubted he would survive. At others, he wished for a surgeon to cut off the limb. But at the end of a fortnight, Ella Ruth's faith and labors were rewarded. Ben had come through the daunting hours of intense pain and weakness and finally felt he had regained his strength.

"Darling Ben," his miracle worker said as she spooned a thick soup into his mouth.

"Yes?" he asked between swallows. He could pull off the task of feeding himself, but at the moment, he enjoyed the luxury of lying in bed without pain at last.

"You must begin to walk around more."

"In due time," he said, not wanting to exercise at the moment.

"I will assist you."

"As ever." He noticed the brightness of her blue eyes against the dark hollows around them. Could she be starving? She should be eating this soup. Heaven only knew where she had acquired the ingredients. "Ain't you tired? Hungry?"

She gave a small shrug with one shoulder. "A little."

"You've gone without food and sleep to serve me."

She made a face of denial.

"Come rest beside me. I'll feed you what remains of the soup." He moved over to make room for her and took the bowl from her hand.

She raised an eyebrow. "Do you have any fever?"

"No. You have cured me of the infection."

She sat on the bed. A bird cawed outside the window. "I own I am a mite tired."

"Lie back. Eat."

He fed her the soup remaining in the bowl until she had taken it all and ran her tongue across her bottom lip in search of any lingering sustenance. The sight sent a stirring through his nether regions. He reached across her to put the bowl on the small table beside the bed and sensed the warmth of her breast beneath his arm.

His body responded with a yearning so sharp he barely could contain it. He sucked in a breath and held it. Had she spoke the truth when she had insisted he was indeed her husband? Could a step over a stick make it so?

He used the breath to ask, "Ella? You are truly my wife?"

She nodded, and he read conviction in her eyes, and yes, a spark of hunger.

"And I am your husband?"

"Please," she said.

Chapter 27

Ben — November 7, 1864

Ben awoke at daybreak, his heart hammering, and his breathing—ragged, labored—took a long time to regularize.

What have I done?

He looked at the girl in his arms. She had murmured words to him, binding words of love and devotion and marriage. He dimly recalled some such pledge had come from his mouth in response. The details were hazy, but he had spoken of his undying adoration and claimed her as his wife.

Then he had done so in a carnal manner.

What have I done? his mind screamed. His heart replied that she was his own bride, but his innermost being cried out that he had sinned against Heaven and against Ella Ruth.

"No," he moaned, and felt her stir.

"Ben?"

He stiffened, felt his arms tighten around her. "I'm here," he muttered.

"Husband," she sighed.

He dared not speak. The idea that stepping over the broomstick was a legal and lawful marriage ceremony had lodged deep in her brain, convincing her that they were man and wife. He knew they were not. How could they be? They were not slaves.

He breathed slowly, deeply, trying to loosen his grip on the woman whose favors he had taken with such relish.

He shuddered. Slaves. Perhaps they were. Slaves to passion. Slaves to carnal actions. Slaves to the Eternal Pit. He had dragged her down to damnation.

He groaned, and she was instantly awake and aware.

"Are you ill?" Her voice was sharp.

"God forgive me. I have sinned."

"No." She sat up. "Look at me, Ben." She took his face between her palms to make sure he did. "Do I have the aspect of a sinner?"

She did not. Her countenance was radiant, peaceful. Could she be right in her conviction?

"We crossed over the broomstick. We spoke the words. We are wed, as perfectly wed as Mistress Mary and brother Rulon. Is that not so?" Her eyes bore into his.

He had to nod. He must not let her doubt her status. He knew the truth. He had violated her trust as much as her body, and he was damned to enter Hell for his sin.

₭

Julia — November 20, 1864

Owen Farm
Mt. Jackson, Via.
My dear husband,

How I long for your company. Instead, I am putting up three left-behind fellows who need nursing before they can go back to their companies. Yes, they should be in the soldier's hospital or in Staunton, but capacity having been reached, we are obliged to provide room, board, and bandages.

I do not let Marie or Jule anywhere near these young men, for they are a low sort of person from another state not known for gentility. I hope to see the last of them off in the next week, food being in short supply from the time of Sheridan's burning.

I fear it will be necessary to send the girls into town, perhaps to stay with Rulon and Mary. I hesitate to do so, as Mary has her hands full nursing Rulon. Husband, his wounds are grievous. At first, I despaired for his life, but Mary would not let him die. If I had the surgeon who ill-treated him in my rifle sights, I cannot say what I would do.

Surely you do not wish to hear blood-thirsty threats from your wife, so I will cease such talk, but my anger does not abait when I remember how my son was dumped in a ditch to die! I am weary of war and of trying to cope with a dire new situation nearly every day. When will it end, dear husband?

Ben is with Gen'l Early's army here in the Valley. Carl still rides with Mosby. James is besieged at Petersburg. He is certain Gen'l Lee will bust them out this coming Spring.

I pray for you and our sons every morning and every night. If Heaven has ears, surely the Father will give heed to our noble

cause and bring this conflict to a close.
   Craving to feel your arms about me, I remain,
   Your loving wife, Julia

ဢ

Ben — November 24, 1864

Ben stood in the entryway, holding Ella Ruth tightly against his chest. She had been trying to put on a brave face, but he could tell from the riotous rhythm of her heart that she was profoundly affected.

"It won't be long before I'm back," he swore. "We'll find a true minister to unite us when warring is done."

"Ben," she sighed into his shirt. "There is no need. We are wedded as firmly as though we had said words in the church." She tilted up her face and planted a kiss on his lips. "I wish you would believe me."

He wished he could. He cupped her cheek in his hand. How she had changed since that fatal day. Her face radiated joy. She took pleasure in fetching and carrying for him, even though he knew his health had been restored, except for a slight limp. No more the heedless coquette, she had become the little wife she believed herself to be. His little wife.

Hating to erase the happiness from her brow, he had prolonged his stay as long as he could and still feel his absence was honorable. However, yesterday he had stated his intention to rejoin his company, which he figured to be wintering in a gap in the Blue Ridge.

Now the moment of parting had come and his heart ached, even as it beat wildly in anticipation of traveling back to the regiment.

"You will write?"

"Must I send letters to the store?"

"No. While Poppa is gone I shall take delivery here. Don't forget to begin with 'Missus,' or I won't know to whom you've addressed your note."

He smiled at the bantering tone in her voice. "You are a little scamp." Becoming serious, he tapped her on the nose. "That could be dangerous for you. Don't be surprised if I use the Allen surname." He saw the beginning of a frown on her lips, and hastened to add, "Just until the war is over."

"Then I may claim your name?"

"I promise." He felt a bit of unease at giving the vow, but shook off the doubt. They would be wed by proper authority as soon as he returned, and then she could call herself "Mrs. Benjamin Owen" to her heart's content. He sealed the promise with a long, yearning kiss.

"I must go, my love," he said at last, squeezed her gently, and turned on his heel.

80

Ella Ruth — December 3, 1864

Ella Ruth woke and faced the day ahead with a sigh. Ben had scarcely been gone a week, but she missed his grin, his warm presence beside her in her parents' bed, his tantalizing scent of manhood. She had waited such a long time for the caresses that had carried her away to the realm of womanly fulfillment.

She could hardly believe her good fortune when she had come upon him so unexpectedly in the battered orchard. She had gladly nursed him back to health, clinging to the promises they had made to marry when next they met. But she had not foreseen the impediment to their plans of a lack of ministers of the gospel.

The old Ben would not have cared. How many times had he urged her to give him her favors just one time? As many times as she had refused him. However, the Ben she had kissed last week and sent back to Jubal Early's army cared very deeply about the risk of carnal temptations.

She sat up. That didn't matter now. Poppa would acknowledge her marriage, wouldn't he? He had never denied the Negro servants their ceremonies. Ben's reservations would be overcome when he returned and they would be united in connubial bliss once more.

As she dressed, she considered if there were any changes in her body that would indicate coming motherhood. She knew the signs to watch for, but so far, there were none. Perhaps the handful of encounters she had teased out of Ben after that first night were not sufficient. When he returned, she intended to keep him to herself for a very long honeymoon. She had no desire now for a trip to Europe. Anywhere private would suit her, even a barn or a ferny dell. All she wanted was Ben's arms around her and the delightful exertions of marriage. She smiled to herself. Sooner or later, a child would come.

&

Rulon — December 31, 1864

Rulon looked down at the puckered scars on his stomach and chest and grimaced. How would Mary react to his unsightly body when time came for them to change their relationship from casualty and nurse to man and wife?

They lived in their own house. No one but the little son was around to impede them. The boy went to bed early, but would the awful mess of wounds cause his Mary's heart to shrink?

She had seen the wounds, true, but as his nurse, not as his lover.

He had fought back from the brink of extinction, holding fast to the longed-for reward of Mary's arms about his neck and her ready response to his embrace. Ever since he had returned home, his enemy had been the exhaustion that came hurtling out of the corner of the room to ensnare him after each attempt to begin an everyday activity. He had husbanded each gain in strength as a victory over the specter of death and defeat.

He had won the ability to feed himself. How sweet that was! He could draw himself to a sitting position, even swing his limbs over the side of the bed without pain lancing through his vital organs. He had advanced to being able to take short steps to sit in the armed chair Mary had dragged up the stairs from the kitchen. His greatest victory thus far was the ability to use the chamber pot by himself.

Be that as it may, he still was a prisoner of the second floor of the house. Two days ago, he had ventured as far as the stairs, but fell and tumbled down the steps to the landing. Mary would not permit a second try at escape now. He gingerly twisted his torso. The ache was still in his ribs. Descending the stairs was a victory yet to be gained.

Christmas had come and gone, celebrated here in this cell. He had not had anything to give to his son. Mary had produced a tin whistle and told the boy it was from Papa and herself, but Rulon felt the sting of uselessness.

He suppressed a groan as he lay back and drew up the sheet. He had never thought about how well his body had worked until his vitality had been stripped away in that horrible moment on the battlefield at Tom's Brook. Now he struggled to make it perform simple tasks.

All he wanted on this New Year's Eve was enough strength to hold Mary and make love to her. He'd been resting all day and thought he was ready, but how would she receive his advances? Would she reject any attempt to begin a connubial interlude because of concern, or would she be repulsed by his scars?

An hour ago, Mary brought the boy in for nightly devotions, then tucked him into bed in the next room. He'd listened to the murmur of their voices as she told him a Bible story. It had sounded like Abraham and Isaac, because Roddy asked about the ram in the thicket. Mary told him about miracles. Rulon wondered when his own miracle would come and *he* could tell his boy the stories. Ma had been their family's storyteller. Maybe that was Mary's role.

He sighed. After the boy had quieted, Mary returned to the kitchen downstairs. Had she turned left or right at the foot of the stairs? He didn't even know the rooms of his dwelling place.

The light behind the curtained window faded. Sundown. How long would Mary remain below, tidying up her house? Was she putting away Roddy's toys? Papa Hilbrands had found a toy bugle for the boy, which he tooted endlessly, except when he used the tin whistle. From the sounds during the day, he also galloped around the parlor on some sort of horse.

Rulon smiled. A horseman like his papa.

Was that Mary's tread on the stairs? He held his breath, listening to be sure. Yes. She paused on the landing. Gave a little cough. She wasn't coming down sick, was she? He'd have to— Have to do what? She was the nurse and he, the patient.

No. Not tonight. Tonight he would become a husband again.

Excitement thrummed through his veins. Mary came through the door, carrying a lamp. She set it on the washstand, then left the room again.

"Mary?"

She was back almost before the words died, carrying two mugs. She smiled. "These aren't Mama's fancy glassware, but

265

they'll do for raspberry wine."

Raspberry wine? Strength flowed to where he'd hoped it would.

"It's New Year's. I thought a little celebration was in order."

Indeed. He felt a grin rise.

She handed him one of the mugs. "Roddy wanted a taste when I brought out the bottle, but I told him Papa would have to approve. He seemed satisfied to wait until you speak to him."

She drew the chair forward and sat at the bedside, her knees pressing against the mattress tick. He heard the rustle of the corn husks as she adjusted her position.

"I don't mean to keep you up until midnight," she said, smiling with a hint of mystery. "A toast and a wish will have to do to ring in the New Year together."

"Together," he muttered, feeling the burn of desire.

"Our first New Year's." Mary's smile quivered. Perhaps it was a trick of the light. Perhaps she bore a strong emotion. "Shall you make the toast?" she asked.

Rulon cleared his throat and extended his mug toward Mary's. "To our family," he said. "To being together again."

"To our family," she repeated. "Together," and tapped her mug against his.

Rulon lifted the mug and took a swallow. The wine was sweet, as he'd expected. *No sweeter than Mary's lips,* he imagined. He looked over the rim at her.

She sipped the wine sedately.

"A kiss?" he proposed.

"Of course." She leaned close and pecked his lips. Before he could put his hand behind her head, she withdrew.

"Mary." The word came out sounding rougher than he had intended. She didn't seem alarmed, and he went on. "I want a true celebration."

"Of course." The huskiness in her voice told him all he needed to know.

She stood and took his mug and set it, with her own, on the washstand. She didn't come back right away, but stood blocking the light of the lamp, wisps of her hair creating a halo around her head. Something occupied her attention for some while.

He finally decided she was undoing the buttons of her bodice.

That would take time. Women used too many fastenings.

She turned at last, doffing pieces of attire. When she approached the bedside, he caught his breath. She was clothed in naught but lamplight.

"Husband," she said as she slipped under the bedding.

He kissed her as he had dreamed for so long of doing. She responded with verve. But before he could accomplish his goal, the daunting enemy, exhaustion, overtook him. His disappointment was mirrored on Mary's face.

"Are you unwell?" she whispered as he groaned and turned onto his side.

He trembled from the weakness that encompassed him, could not give her an answer.

"Rulon!" The sharpness in her voice pricked him.

"I'm well enough," he muttered, "but I have no strength." He watched fear and concern battle on her face until she cradled him in her arms and rocked him as she would a babe.

"There now," she crooned. "You must rest."

Rulon could only cling to her, disheartened by his body's betrayal.

Chapter 28

Rod — March 1, 1865

Rod held the torch to the flooring timber at the end of the bridge, grumbling to himself, because the air was so damp due to the continuous rain that nothing was catching fire. General Rosser wanted this bridge down. Sheridan was on the march again, and even if the cavalrymen's actions only slowed him down a bit, it was something.

He looked up when Wylie called him.

"Captain, it's slow to burn," Wylie said.

Rod thought a moment. "Hmm. Take your knife and pare down the wood, but leave it hanging," he said. "Make it like kindling."

Wylie did as he suggested, and Rod took out his knife to follow his own suggestion. The wood finally blazed up, and Rod and his men retreated down the covered bridge, leaving dancing fire in their wake.

He heard a shot, and dashed toward the south end of the bridge, heart pounding. *They're here!* He and Wylie made it to the road leading out from the bridge as a volley of firing sounded to the west.

Evans rode up with Rod's horse in tow and said, "They're swimming the river, captain. It's Custer."

Rod flung his torch onto the bridge and mounted. His horse reared from the excitement, and he brought it under control with difficulty. While he worked to settled it down, he shouted, "Cut them off when they come up the bank."

He and his men rallied to the other horsemen, and fired a second volley at the Yankees emerging from the river. The Yankees kept coming across the river through the water. Now they were also on the bridge, fighting the blaze.

An eerie, high sound from many voices echoed in the void under the bridge's cover. The Union horsemen charged across the burning timbers and into the open, still yelling.

"Back, back," Rosser yelled, gesturing to the woods, and Rod rode in that direction, urging his men to follow.

They'd done all they could here, but the numbers were on the enemy's side. It was time to retreat.

ℊ

Ben — March 1 through 2, 1865

Even though several months had gone by since Ben had left Ella Ruth, he continued to sleep badly, haunted by guilt. He'd been attempting to pray every night since he had been caught in the trap of lust. It wasn't any good. God already knew of his great transgression. He felt the disapproval and sorrow from the heavens every minute of the day, and all night long.

As he lay one evening staring into the stars, he finally came to the conclusion that he must confess his sin to someone who could guide him through the process of making amends for his act of ultimate robbery. Who could help him? Mr. Moore? He and the minister had never hit it off well, so he didn't really want to approach him. Besides that, he didn't know if the Yankees had let the man loose yet.

Perhaps he could speak to the Catholic priest who came around whenever they camped near Harrisonburg. Ben wondered if the man would refuse his assistance unless he converted to the faith. Who else might be suitable to help him cleanse his soul? He could think of no one. Would he have to venture toward repentance all on his own?

He supposed a first step would be to write to Ella Ruth and beg her forgiveness. He wondered what her response would be. She had been the one who had planted the seed of the idea, who had insisted they were married by virtue of them stepping on and over a broomstick in the dark. She sincerely believed they were wed. He knew they were not. Did that leave Ella Ruth blameless? His mind quivered to think that perhaps not. Perhaps her soul was in as much everlasting peril as his own.

He bore the ultimate blame for giving in to his passion. Under her coaxing, he had done so more than one time. Now he had to own up to the fact that they had sinned against each other, and against God.

269

He groaned, thinking about how far he had wandered from grace. Ma would be devastated. What a blow it would be upon her God-fearing heart to know that her son had distanced himself from his Creator in such a tawdry fashion. Could he bring himself to write to Ma, to beg her forgiveness, as well? Would that give him any relief from the chains of sin he felt tightening around his soul?

He felt the Testament digging into the small of his back. He needed to move it into a pocket, he thought, then refrained from doing so. Perhaps he needed a goad, a reminder of his fault, until he took steps toward making his soul clean.

After a long period of thinking, he arose and went to the campfire that had burned down to embers. Ella Ruth had given him a pocketbook with a sheaf of writing paper within. In addition, a lead pencil was affixed under the flap. He drew the object out of his pocket, and by the puny light of what remained of the fire he wrote,

My darling Ella Ruth,

I hope you are well, as I am not. Great sorrow weighs me down every day since we erred against our Maker in committing the sin of lust and acting upon our passion. We should not have done so, my dear girl. I forever regret that I was driven by unseemly appetites to rob you of virtue, and I cannot forget my wrong.

I cannot return to you that wich I stole. I can merely ask your forgivness for what I did to you. I pray you to grant me that favor, at leest - To forgive me as I forgive you.

I am weary of battle. The yankees have more men than we. They have provisions were we have none. We run short on munitions. They have all they need. Even so, I fight on for my dear Country until the end, whether it be the end of the fightin or the end of me.

I love you as man has never loved a woman before. I despise the thot that I have become a low sort of man, unable to keep myself strait with God. I beg your forgivness. Set my mind at ease so I mite petition God for His Grace and Forgivness.

Keep this note from the sight of strangers.

Your unworthy suitor, Ben

A bit of an old hymn ran through his mind as he signed and folded the letter. "Prone to wander, Lord, I feel it, prone to leave the God I love." Yes. He had left God, had run away to an enticing episode of carnal satisfaction, blinded by thoughts and acts of fleshly desire. How had he sunk into such depravity? How could he rise from it again?

He started writing a letter to Ma.

Julia Owen
Owen Farm outside Mount Jackson, Via.
Dear Ma,
I hope all is well with you. We are retreating before an overwhelming host, but my dread is that I won't be able to send this note before we come into another battle.
It pains me to tell you that I have done wrong. I sinned in givin in to lust. I let my pashun carry me into the forbiden gardin with a girl I know. She is also known to you, but I will not divulge her name unless forced by circumstances. How I regret my sinful acts!

Unable to formulate more words at the moment, he tucked away the pocketbook and, having made a start to his atonement, slept soundly for the first time in months.

The next morning, he gave the letter meant for Ella Ruth into the hands of the adjutant, hoping he could find a way to post it, but because he had not finished the one to Ma, Ben kept it in his pocket book.

Later that day, he found himself trudging south up the Valley, falling sleet threatening to freeze upon his face. Ole Jube Early had sent his larger force of infantry toward Lynchburg, but Ben was marching with his company to Waynesborough, a bit east. Sheridan would chase after one of the ragtag armies. Ben hoped he would go to Lynchburg.

He stole a glance over his shoulder, wishing for a sight of a long-gone comrade's countenance. So many had been cut down in the months behind them. Now Sheridan was chasing the Confederates with a vengeance. All the armies could do was march to a place of resistance, somewhere they could stand their ground against Federals who wanted them dead.

"Company, halt," came to his ears. They had approached the outskirts of the town. Here on the west side, a little ridge rose before them. Would that do for a defensive ground? He didn't pretend to know strategies or tactics. Those were up to the colonels and captains to figure out. He was merely cannon fodder, a foot soldier doing his best to keep a hold on a little piece of the Southern dream. What was that dream? He could scarcely remember the long discussions at the home table about freedom of conscience and state's rights, and fighting for home and country.

Virginia was his country, and when it had joined the great secession, the Confederacy had become his country. But how much longer could he arm his weapon, raise it to his shoulder, and fire upon other men?

Now the order came to dig rifle pits. Weariness overtook him, but he dropped his gun and haversack, received a pick that was passed to him, and advanced to the appointed line. Heave. Swing. Heave. Swing. Heave. Swing. The rhythm caught him, and he continued blindly to heave and swing until told to stop.

How long could this defense last? Rain sluiced down his face. He could hear the roaring waters of the South Fork of the Shenandoah behind him. If the Yankees overran them, they were stuck between the enemy and the river without a place of refuge. What was Jubal Early thinking?

He hadn't been thinking well for a while, Ben mused. Even General Lee thought so. The General had been stripping away bits and pieces of Early's command, until now their strength was about 1500 or so, he'd been told. How could they stand off Sheridan? The Yankee general had more than ten thousand troops with him. Ten thousand!

He was told to pack the dirt beneath his feet and prepare to defend his pit. Yes, they said "dirt." It wasn't dirt, as any fool could see. Tromping the mud with his almost bare feet, Ben felt it squishing between his toes, clammy clay. He wondered if it held good fishing worms.

Fishing? Well, the river wasn't so far off. If he weren't a soldier priming to fight off a hoard of enemy invaders, he would go fishing. Or swimming. No, the river was too high for either leisurely pursuit.

Jerusalem crickets! When had he last had leisure? Time to himself for reflection? He had spent the last such moments sinning as though there was no tomorrow! Maybe there was no tomorrow for him. Maybe his sin had doomed him to Hell forever. He had to finish the letter to Ma, to confess his sin and express his regret, to seek forgiveness.

Someone, possibly Ma, had told him in the dim past that Jesus had died for his sins. Why then did he feel so forsaken for having been with Ella Ruth? The moments should have been sweet. Instead, the Jaws of Hell yawned open beneath him, and he couldn't shake a sense that his time was running out.

He knew the Federals had caught up to them when a shell screamed overhead, followed by a bee's swarm of balls. He ducked into the rifle pit and steeled himself for the fight to come.

"Oh dear God, forgive me," he whispered, popping up from the hole to fire his rifle at the attackers. "Lord Jesus, forgive my trespasses. Come and save me from my sins!"

The battle soon became a thunder of artillery pieces interspersed with the rattle of rifles in a frontal assault. Then a bugle sounded to the left of the line of breastworks.

That's not our bugle.

Shortly afterward, a hoard of yelling men broke from the trees on the left flank, firing rifles they didn't have to pause to load. *Spencers. Repeaters. Seven-shots.* At the same time, artillery shells pinned Ben's company in place. Surely Hell could be no worse than this.

A man next to him shrieked briefly and lay still. Another lifted his rifle and shot toward the Yankees approaching on the left. A ball caught him in the face, and he fell into the pit at Ben's feet.

"I'm not staying here to die," said another soldier, and slithered out of the pit on his belly toward the river. He crab-walked a few feet, stopped, then began again to move toward the rear. After he was out of rifle range, he stood and ran. Other men copied his thinking, and soon, the field was full of men running to the rear.

Emboldened by mass escape, Ben tried the same moves. He knew he had miscalculated the distance the Spencer rifle could shoot accurately when he felt himself being lifted off his feet by a round striking his body.

When he hit the ground, Ben lay unmoving on his side in a crumpled position, wondering why he didn't feel any pain in his leg, as he could see it had suffered a wound. He tried to dig his other heel into the ground to get himself onto his back, but it would not obey his thought.

A man from the regiment knelt beside him for a moment, grabbed him under the arms and dragged him toward the line of trees bordering the river. He gave him a drink from his canteen, and said, "Lie still, Owen."

"Help me up," Ben begged. "Take me with you."

The man tried to lift Ben, then swore softly. "Here's another hole." He lowered Ben to the ground.

"Where? I don't feel it."

"Here on your side." He checked Ben's opposite side. "Didn't go through. Is your spine broke, Owen?"

"I can't tell."

The man gave him another drink, then picked up his rifle, said "Lie still" again, and ran into the trees.

Ben craned his neck to where he could see his side and noticed his blood spilled steadily from the hole. Not much blood, it appeared, but he had nothing with which to staunch the flow. No part of his body below the hole in his side made response to his mental commands to move. Melancholy gripped his spirit as he felt a subtle weakness overcoming him, rising from his waist upward.

So I am to die, he thought. *Have I any valor left?*

He took Ella Ruth's likeness from his pocket, kissed it tenderly, struggling against tears, and laid it on his breast above his heart. He dug out his pencil and pocket book and added to his letter to Ma.

Waynesborough battle
Ma,
This note is short. My life is forfeit, as I am sorly wounded and bleedin my strength away. I am griev'd to leave without seeing you again. God has struck me down for my sin. Treat Miss Ella Ruth All'n with kindness as she was to be my wife.

If my seed took root, guard her as you woud your own child. I do not know how her pa will treat her if she is increasin with a poor man's bastard. It is to late for me to make it right.

I feel life ebbing. My last hope is this note will be found and sent to you.

With tender affect'n
Your dying son, Benj'n Owen

Knowing he was spending his last bit of strength, Ben folded the letter with clumsy fingers, put it into the pocket book, and placed the leather case on his chest beside Ella Ruth's likeness. His hands dropped to his sides. He whispered, "Jesus God, forgive my sins," and said no more.

⋯

Rod — March 3, 1865

When Rod Owen was rousted out of his blankets with orders to report to General Rosser, he wondered what news had come. Once the regimental commanders and several other company captains had been gathered, he found out. A scout had come early in the morning with word that General Early's command at Waynesborough had been almost entirely captured. The general and some of his staff had escaped across the Blue Ridge, but about 1,100 men under guard of the Yankee cavalry would soon be passing through Staunton toward Winchester.

Rod wondered what Rosser was going to do about the situation.

The cavalry general sheltered underneath a spread canvas, on his knees, drawing a map in the mud. "We won't leave those boys in Yankee hands," he said. "With so many prisoners, they'll likely take this road. We'll hound them on the flanks, and attack here, near Harrisonburg, tomorrow night." He shook his finger at his commanders. "They'll be on the alert. They know I won't rest while my countrymen are held captive." He pointed to a pair of company commanders. "You will hold the fords here and here." He drew the fords across the line designated as the Shenandoah River. "Keep them bottled up until we get those boys free." He looked up. "Owen, you're my spy. Take a squad to mingle with the prisoners. Incite them to revolt and escape when we attack. If you find your boy, get his cooperation to help you. Be cautious. I don't want you to join the prisoners permanently."

"Yes sir," Rod said, feeling the tingle of anticipation that danger always raised in his belly.

Rosser got to his feet. "The Yankees need to think we have a larger force, so we'll ride past them, double back, and pass 'em again." He pointed to three other captains. "That's your duty," he said, and took a lungful of air. "Boots and saddles, gentlemen."

Rod went back to his company, sorting out in his mind who best could join him in the delicate business. How he wished Rulon were in his company. He would keep a cool head.

No matter. He would take Evans, Wylie, and Court. He could risk no more than the four of them.

By now, the company was awake and the men were cooking rations over small fires. He snorted. What passed for rations. The days of full rations had ended long ago, when Sheridan burned the Valley.

Rod pulled his chosen few aside, gave them instructions, and left the lieutenant in command of the company. Then he pulled a worn coat over a linsey-woolsey shirt and wool pants, and they set off on the mission.

Once they found the army and their prisoners, it wasn't difficult to slip in among the dispirited captives and spread out. What was difficult was reanimating the men, trying to give them heart enough to agree to revolt when the attack from Rosser began. More times than not, he and his men encountered negative shakes of the head and little support for Rosser's plan. These men had lost all nerve and only wanted to get to a Federal camp where food was available.

Worse still, Rod couldn't find Ben. Few of the men knew him. Those who did know him had no news. The prisoners were too tired, too disheartened to care. Feeling sick to the depths of his soul, Rod stuck to his task, but when night came and Rosser with it, the captives made no attempt to break free. Rod and his men got away only because they carried pistols and made judicious use of them to extract themselves from the tender guardianship of the Union soldiers.

80

Rod — March 4, 1865

Chafing that the mission had not succeeded, but even more

because he hadn't found Ben among the captives, Rod and his three spies rejoined Rosser's command. The general decided to give up the rescue effort and turned to follow Sheridan, who had continued toward Petersburg.

"He's joining Grant, blast him," Court said.

"We'll slow him down some," Rod answered, swinging up into his saddle for another day's hard ride.

When the Owen Dragoons entered Waynesborough, Rod found that a complement of citizens had buried the dead in the rifle pits behind the fortifications they'd defended. His belly crawling with dread, he went to the town hall and asked for information about the casualties.

"We kept the effects from the lads," the clerk said. "Some had very little, but one boy had time to write a letter. What's your name again?"

"Owen. Roderick Owen. I'm looking for my son, Benjamin."

"Owen. Where do you hale from, captain?" The man rubbed his ear.

"My farm's outside Mount Jackson, Shenandoah County."

The clerk's face went solemn, and he shook his head as though to clear a bad memory. "I'm sorry, captain. We kept a few things from a boy—"

"What do you have?" Rod kept himself from grabbing the man's lapels by a strong effort.

"There's a pocketbook with a few notes addressed to Ben or Benjamin Owen, and a likeness of a young lady."

Rod's legs quivered. He felt a peculiar weakness sapping his vitality, as though he were gushing blood from his heart.

"What is your wife's name, sir?"

"Julia." Was that faint voice his own?

"I'm so sorry, sir." He retrieved a parcel wrapped in a cloth from a cubbyhole and handed it to Rod. "We took these from your son's body. There's a letter for your missus."

Rod cleared his throat several times before he could manage a "thank you." He took the parcel, left the hall, and struggled to his horse on legs so weak he barely made the short distance before clutching the saddle to keep himself from falling.

"Sir?" It was Evans, his corporal.

"Ben," Rod whispered in a hoarse voice. "He's gone." He

heard the man swear, but had no strength to reprimand him for his language. He was sucked dry. His voice had crackled like an old corn husk left on the ear too long. He thought of Julia. This news would kill her. He must not send her word until he could be with her.

He unbuttoned his shirt and tucked the parcel inside. It was too soon to look at the last remaining vestiges of Benjamin's life. He had spent too much time in this town, and Rosser needed him to harass Sheridan. Duty called.

He swallowed with great effort. Honor. Duty. At least he still had those. He clucked to his horse. He was still at war. With Sheridan. With Grant. With the Federals.

Chapter 29

Julia — April 7, 1865

Julia heard a noise outside and looked through her kitchen window. Someone trudged down her lane from the Pike. The man didn't wear a blue uniform. She could be thankful for that. However, he could be a straggling soldier come to ask for food. She grabbed her rifle and moved toward the back door.

Should she wait until the man knocked, or stand where he could see her? Show that she was armed?

She called to the girls to go into hiding, opened the door, and took a step out onto the stoop.

The man hesitated when he saw her, then set down his gear and began to run toward her.

Julia felt a shiver of fear. What compelled the man to do that? She lifted the rifle into view.

The man stopped, raised one hand in surrender and called, "Ma?"

That was confusing. Who would call her that? She saw the man bore a bandage about his left shoulder. Perhaps he was playing on her sympathies.

"Who are you?" she asked, leveling the weapon.

"Six little beans!" he spat out in disgust.

Julia dropped the rifle, running, running, running down the lane to her son, her James, her boy who wore Peter's hair but had come home. His arms were out, ready to embrace her, and she gladly flew into them, bumping against him with a thud that drew a groan from his body.

She cried out in wordless wonder, kissing his neck, his scruffy chin, his lips, his eyes, her arms about him, enfolding him against her breast.

"Ma," he protested. "Mind the shoulder."

She stood back then, holding his forearms and taking in the sight of him.

"How bad?" she murmured.

"Not so bad if you don't bump it," he replied in a strangled voice.

"Oh my dear son," she said, sniffling. "I beg pardon. Come. Let's get you under a roof."

∾

Rod — April 13, 1865

Rod led his horse up the lane, his heart thumping from equal parts relief, joy, and dread. The war was over. He'd never leave Julie again. He had a burdensome task ahead of him.

He figured if the telegraph wires were up, news had spread of the surrender, and she must be aware he would be on the homeward road.

The kitchen door opened. Mayhap she had been watching, or heard his step crunching on the gravel of the lane.

She stepped through the door, halted, put the rifle in the corner and ran toward him.

He dropped the reins and strode toward her, then quit all pretense of age and dignity and broke into a run.

His heart stopped when he saw her smile. He would wipe it from her face with his tidings. But for a moment, he could savor the sweetness of her welcome and hold her close before he broke the news.

She came into his embrace smelling of soap and wind, nuzzling into the space below his jaw that fit her like a glove. He knew his beard scratched, but she made no protest as she laid her lips on his cheek, then settled into his arms for a long, hungry kiss.

He gave what was due and more. Sorrow drove him as much as longing. His heart shrank that he had to break hers.

"Rod," she murmured when he let her breathe. "Is it truly over?"

"The fightin' is done," he answered, and she looked up at him. Did she sense that he had more to impart? Was this the best time and place to tell her Benjamin wasn't coming home?

He felt naked out in the air. Better to tell her indoors, where she could weep unashamed and away from prying eyes.

He should put up the horse. He looked toward the barn. No

barn. No wellhead. No stock pens. No stock.

He set his jaw. This is what it meant to be the loser in the conflict.

"Albert," she called, startling him.

He looked down at his wife. She had already adjusted to losses around the farm. He would have to make an effort. He retraced his steps, brought the horse to where his Julie stood.

The boy came. He gave him an embrace, then handed him the reins.

"What more?" she asked.

He nodded to the house. "Indoors." The huskiness in his voice disturbed him. He had to be strong.

"Rod?" Julia asked once they were inside the main room.

"Julie." He swallowed the lump tightening his throat. "Sit."

She eyed him, then did as he bid her, but sitting upright, not relaxed.

God help him. He did not want to say the words. He looked into her eyes and dug in his shirt for the parcel he'd kept close to his heart for the last few weeks. He had not looked at it. They would have to do that together. He steeled himself and unwrapped the cloth.

The bundle contained three items, a leather pocket notebook, a folded frame that probably contained a photographic likeness, and a letter folded over and addressed to Julia.

He looked over at her and caught deep fear that shadowed her eyes. She already knew the items meant something very bad.

He cleared his throat. His voice came out more ragged than he would have liked when he said, "We chased Sheridan through Waynesborough after the fight there." He paused to clear his throat again. "Julie, Ben wasn't among the prisoners Sheridan sent north. A fellow at the town hall gave me these." He held out the letter to her, and she took it, her face set and as white as he had ever seen it.

She read the note, her breathing irregular, her hands shaking. She stopped once and laid the paper in her lap. She bowed her head and pinched the bridge of her nose, then took the paper up again.

He watched her read it, his soul shivering. Ben. What had he written that harrowed her up so badly? Unable to watch her pain, he looked at the other items he still held. He opened the picture frame and drew in a sharp breath.

Theodore Allen's daughter. Miss Ella Ruth. He hadn't known they had reconciled after their quarrel, but it had been a long war. If he had carried her portrait . . . the situation between them must have been serious.

He opened the pocketbook. It contained writing paper, and several letters, all from Miss Allen. He flipped the latest one open, ashamed to read a private message, but astonished to see her greeting.

"Dearest husband," she had begun. He closed the paper.

Julia sat with her head bowed again, the letter resting in her lap. From what he could see, she wasn't crying. How could she not cry? His own grief had gnawed at him, causing tears to fall in the dark when he could mourn privately.

She looked up. Her eyes had dark hollows around them, as though the news she read had caused them to sink into the sockets.

He held out the likeness and she took it. "Miss Allen," he said. "Somehow, they married. I'll pay a visit and inform her." He huddled against his crossed arms.

She whispered something so low he bent toward her and asked, "What's that?"

"Ben thinks they did not wed." She traced the curve of the girl's cheek.

He straightened up, rubbing the back of his neck. Then he held out Ella Ruth's letter. "She calls him 'husband.' That's as far as I read."

She shook her head, refusing to take the letter.

He watched her swallow, breathe deeply, and shut her eyes against the pain.

"Julie?" He wanted to offer comfort, and didn't know how.

"You must be tired," she said, her voice quivering just slightly. She rose and stepped into his arms.

He held her gently. "Bone deep," he answered, his shoulders sloping downward as renewed grief dropped its load onto them.

℘

Ella Ruth — April 14, 1865

Ella Ruth went to answer the knock on the front door, since Lula was busy in the kitchen. She didn't expect anyone in particular, but when she opened the door, she put her hand to her mouth. The formidable Mrs. Owen and her husband stood on her porch and stared at her with grave eyes.

A moment later, she remembered her manners and stepped back, uttering polite words bidding them to enter.

Mr. and Mrs. Owen had never been to her home. She watched to see if Mrs. Owen would look around in admiration of— of what, exactly? The furniture had grown almost shabby over the duration of the conflict.

But no, Mrs. Owen never turned her head. She gazed straight at Ella Ruth, which was a bit disconcerting. Mr. Owen's head was more bowed, like he had the weight of the fall of Petersburg on his shoulders. How did a man bear surrendering to a victorious foe? Not well, she supposed, as she ushered them in silence toward the parlor.

Something must be wrong with Ben, she thought. Why else would his parents visit her?

She felt her limbs go numb as she tried to gesture toward the sofa. *Something is very wrong with Ben*. She sank into a chair as they took places on the sofa opposite her. Her heart became a block of ice.

"May I get you a refreshment?" she asked, her voice shaking. Shaking terribly. Shaking as though she spoke into a windstorm.

Mr. Owen moved his hand to dismiss the thought of food or drink.

"Miss Allen," he began. He bowed his head. It seemed like hours passed before he raised it again. "Miss," he began again and stopped. "Daughter Ella Ruth," he managed to say at last.

She knew for certain then, and her heart cracked as she lurched upright, a moan starting in the pit of her stomach and rising through her chest and up into her throat to emerge as a cry of grief so terrible she could not stand the sound of it. She collapsed back into the chair, limp as the babe she would never carry. The sounds coming from her body hurt her ears, yet she could not stop them. They came in waves of agony more desolate than could be borne.

Mr. Owen was on his feet, coming over, then stopping as his wife rose unsteadily and dropped to her knees beside Ella Ruth.

"Go ahead," she whispered. "Let it out." Mrs. Owen's voice also shook, but she remained dry-eyed.

Doesn't she care?

Ella Ruth's keening continued, the sound hollow as a wolf's at a distance. Surely her heart must burst due to the bubble of anguish that rose in her midsection, pressing against her lungs, shredding her dignity, killing her soul.

Her mind managed a few thoughts. *Ben. Gone. I won't see him again. Ever.* "Nooo," her wail began again, rising to the rafters, a howl so primal she drew up her knees and curled into a ball.

She would have fallen to the floor and remained there for the rest of her existence, screaming in an overabundance of woe if not for Ben's father, who gathered her up in his arms and muttered to someone, who stuttered a reply. *Lula.*

He carried her, lightly as she imagined Ben would have done had he been here to do the task, out into the vestibule and down the long hall to her parent's room, where Mrs. Owen stripped back the bed covers so Mr. Owen could lay her tenderly upon the sheet. Lula sobbed in the background, rooted to the floorboards, immovable.

"Water," Mrs. Owen said to Lula, a bit sharply, as though to get her attention. "Bring her a glassful."

By now Ella Ruth's cries had subsided to moans, but still came, unrestricted, from her lips. *I must die*, she thought. *I must join Ben.* Her eyes streamed now.

"No," said Mrs. Owen.

You're reading my mind.

"No. You're speaking aloud, child."

She had no sense of having spoken. *I am losing my mind.*

"It will return," Mrs. Owen said, her voice soft, but the sound grating as though her throat were raw. "The first shock will pass. You will be clear in your mind . . . someday." Mrs. Owen's voice broke, but she still did not shed a tear.

Ella Ruth stopped moaning, but the flood of tears continued. She tried to put up her fist to dash them away, but her arm would not move, and they slid down her cheeks and onto the pillow. She looked from Mrs. Owen to Ben's father. He held his hand over his eyes, and she knew he was hiding his own emotion. Mrs. Owen's eyes were filled with affliction, but not tears.

"Mama." Pain washed over her again. Mama wasn't here to blunt her sorrow. Mama was in Charlottesville. She didn't know about Ben.

Mrs. Owen patted her hand. "There, there."

Ella Ruth's muscles finally moved, and she gripped the woman's hand. *She's kin, my mother-in-law.*

"Mama," she cried again, and Mrs. Owen enfolded her in her arms. Ella Ruth sobbed and wailed and cried anew. Hours must have gone by while she grieved, but Mrs. Owen never left her alone. She pressed a drink of water upon her, whispering soft words of comfort that seemed to come from a deep inner well. And yet, she did not join Ella Ruth in crying.

At last, exhaustion came, and the tears dried to crusts on Ella Ruth's cheeks. Mrs. Owen called for a cloth and warm water, and bathed Ella Ruth's face.

Relief touched Ella Ruth when she felt the cloth on her skin. *Mary was right. Mama Owen is not hard to know. Mary loves her. I will too.*

୫

Mary — April 14, 1865

Father Owen left. Mary closed the door, went back into the parlor, and stared toward Rulon. He sat on the sofa, stunned, shriveled beyond anything she had yet seen. She wondered how she would get him back upstairs. He had come down on his own power when she told him his father had called in, but this news, this brutal news obviously had chopped him down to mincemeat.

He looked up. There was no light in his eyes. They appeared sunken, anguished beyond her understanding. His gaze quickly dropped to his lap where his fisted hands pounded upon his thighs.

His sense of loss was too great for her to comprehend. She had no brothers. She had come to know that Rulon had fought, teased, joked, wrestled, and loved Ben from the time of his birth. They'd worked and played side by side on the farm, teaming up against their younger brothers to teach them the lessons of life and the ways of boys. Now that bond with his next younger brother had been severed. He had every appearance of a devastated soul.

Since she had become involved in Rulon's life, she had learned that sisters were different. She supposed she loved them, but Ida was a handful, and prickly as a pincushion. Mary's relationship with her next younger sister was not the same as Rulon's had been with Ben.

She sat gingerly beside him. He still thumped his legs, as though beating some understanding into a willfully heedless body.

"Rule?"

He turned to her, his eyes deep pits of despair. Still he kept up the thumping, looking away again, shaking his head now from side to side. Then he opened his mouth and cried out, "Bennnnnn," so dolefully that Mary thought her heart would break at the pain he expressed. She thought of Roddy, perhaps awakening from his nap to the eerie sound, but Rulon's need superseded that of her child, and she leaned in to put an arm around him.

He shook her off, his face set in a grimace of stone.

Her arm fell away, unwanted, unneeded. Her heart shrank at the rejection, but she struggled to bring reason to bear on the situation. *He is hurt. Perhaps he wants to be alone just now.* She didn't want to leave him, but she rose and went away, trying to understand his need for isolation. *I'll check on Roddy,* she decided. *It won't do for him to become frightened.*

Chapter 30

Mary — April 22, 1865

A week later, in an attempt to ease Rulon's grief, Mary decided to wear a dress that had sweet memories for them, the dress with the lavender skirt that she wore the day she married him. The dark shade would keep their mourning, although the light bodice would not. She hoped he would forgive her the lapse when he saw her in it, if it brought to mind happier days.

A happy surprise will do him good, she thought, searching through the wardrobe when he was asleep. She did not find the outfit there.

Hoping it was in the attic, she got up into the small space, but did not find it. However, Roddy took delight in holding up his toy sword and prancing around the attic as though he rode a horse.

Curbing her smile at the antics of her son, she wondered if she had left the dress behind at Papa's house. Mary sighed, remembering the fuzzy state of her mind when Rulon had returned in such dire straits. Yes, it probably still occupied a place in Ida's wardrobe.

"Come down now, Roddy. We must go wake Papa." She brushed dust off the boy. "He will have charge of you while I run an errand."

"Papa will play with me? Yippee!" he crowed, and dashed down the stair ahead of her.

"Quiet, dear son. We must wake Papa slowly, lest he become startled."

"Papa, Papa, Papa," Roddy whispered with enthusiasm.

Mary shushed the boy and took him into the larger bedroom of the two in the house.

"Rulon," she said softly as she passed through the doorway. She put a finger to her lips for Roddy's benefit, and approached the bed. "Husband? Will you wake?" When Rulon opened his eyes she continued. "Could you tend to Roddy for an hour? I must go do an errand."

Rulon raised himself on an elbow. He smiled at the child. "He gives me joy, Mary. I don't mind playing nursemaid for a spell."

She smiled, grateful that in the last two days Rulon had found his strength returning. A week ago, what a horror to learn of another great loss! It had laid Rulon low again, a setback to all the progress he had made in healing from his injuries. But yesterday he was much improved, and she took heart that his grief had taken on a yearning, almost accepting aspect, which helped soothe her own pain. Brother Ben had treated her kindly. She would miss him terribly. How Miss Allen must feel!

Once Roddy was safely in Rulon's charge, Mary hurried to the home of her childhood, watching out for Yankee soldiers, and went straight into her old room to search the wardrobe.

She found Ida in the room, sitting before the mirror, hunched over something she held close. She appeared to be in an unusual state, moaning softly to herself.

"Ida! What are you up to?"

Ida shrieked, jumped up, and backed away, trying to hide the object in her hand behind her back, but Mary was too quick for her, and snatched away a piece of paper.

Ida's red face turned petulant. "I'm only exploring the delights that entranced you," she blustered. "I deserve a few delights."

Mary looked at the paper and froze. A letter. Her letter. The lost letter from Rulon. Horrors! Ida had stolen it.

"'My body and vigor are yours alone'," Ida sneered. "They can't be anything special, now that he's all full of holes."

"You read my letter." Mary's ears rang, and she grabbed the back of Ida's chair to support herself.

"Perhaps he is missing his Things," Ida taunted, pointing downward. "Is that why he's so cross?"

"You read my letter and kept it from me." Mary's toes gripped the insides of her shoes.

"You don't know, do you? Six months, and you haven't even bothered to lay with him." Ida's mouth twisted in a smirk.

"What sort of tramp are you?" Mary asked in a low voice.

"I am not a tramp."

Mary spoke the worst insult she could think of. "Are you servicing Yankees?"

Ida cried out at the accusation and came at Mary with her nails bared.

Mary socked her in the eye. "You shame yourself," she hissed as Ida fell backward on her hind end. She turned and left the room.

She ran down the stairs, amazed at the rage that would not abate. Shaking out the pain in her violent hand, she hustled down the blocks, heedless of any Yankees standing about. Just let them try to molest her!

What Ida had said was true. She had not lain with Rulon. They had tried, but bitter circumstances prevented their union.

She stormed into her own house, shaking, wishing she had torn out Ida's hair, but knowing it was better to get away from the wayward minx. Shivering, she escaped toward her room, found Rulon alone, and stood in the doorway holding the letter she had never finished reading.

"I wore him out," Rulon said in a sleepy voice. "He's taking a nap."

She began to cry, almost certain he had all his manly parts, but ashamed that she had not been more attentive, more loving. Perhaps he now had no interest in her. After all, it had been months since that distressing attempt on New Year's Eve. In truth, his distressing weakness had frightened her. She had not wanted to press him with her needs, but perhaps he no longer wanted her. She gulped, hiccoughing now, then sobbing again as Rulon rose and came toward her.

"Mary?"

"Do you want me?"

"Mary, Sugar," he sighed, wrapping his arms around her. "Hush, now. Hush."

She leaned into his chest, wetting his shirt. She thumped his shoulder, away from his wounds. "Do you want me?"

"I do," he whispered into her hair. His arms tightened.

"She stole my letter." She shook it until the paper rattled. "I had not read it through." She listened to the horrible breaking of her voice. *How can he care for such a ninny?*

He didn't ask who she meant. "My precious Mary. Come. Sit. I will read it to you." He sat in the rocking chair, holding her on his lap, and took the paper from her hand. "My beloved wife," he

began, and read it to the end, his voice trembling with emotion. He ended with, "Ever, your Rulon," and held her closer than before.

Mary turned her head and stretched up to kiss him on the mouth. "Show me," she whispered against his lips.

No dunce, he did.

🙾

Rod — April 28, 1865

Rod stalked around the room, slapping one fist into the other. "Carl should be home by now."

Julia glanced up from her ever-present mending. "Husband, he may have gone south. You told me about the army in the Carolinas." She paused, then said quietly. "He's stubborn enough to not give up."

He turned on her, scowling. "He may be rotting in a grave and us without a whit of knowin'."

"Could he be a prisoner?"

Rod looked at his wife. She had sounded hopeful, as though being in prison was better than being dead. He immediately repented of his scornful thought. Even if his son was in prison, he was still breathing. Not like Peter. Not like Ben. Alive.

He stood still and let his ire drain away. It wouldn't help his thinking. He had to admit to himself that anger never did. At last he was ready to consider the possibilities with rational purpose. "His name hasn't shown up on a casualty list." He said it almost like a sigh.

"No," Julia agreed.

"If he went south, there's no way to know until he comes home."

"Yes."

He wished Julia would cry, mourn Ben's death as the Allen girl had done. It worried him that she hadn't shed a tear yet. It couldn't be doing her any good.

The Allen girl. He had to stop thinking of her by that name. She counted herself an Owen now. He shook himself. His mind seemed to wander off too much lately. He wondered if grief did that to a body.

Carl. "If he's a prisoner, we won't get word."

"They wouldn't keep him now that the war's done, would they?"

He didn't know. He shook his head.

"Then we wait." She looked down and took a stitch.

She seemed so calm.

"One thing I learned about the Yankees," he said, "is they keep records. Good records. If he's a prisoner, there will be a record of him in Washington City." He rubbed his thumb across his forefinger. "I should leave this week."

"No!"

He jumped at the harshness in Julia's voice.

"I can't wait around forever."

"We wait and give the boy time to get home. If he doesn't come in a month's time, you can go."

Simple. Direct. His Julie's mind was working clear and true, even in the midst of this trouble. He moved behind her, put his hand on her shoulder. He gave it one pat. She placed her hand over his. The warmth eased his anxiety. For Carl. For her. If her mind was working, her tears would come loose sometime.

ଚ୍ଚ

Mary — May 10, 1865

Mary stood on the corner, watching the Federal cavalrymen parading themselves down the street like they owned Mount Jackson outright. She shivered. Men ought not to take upon themselves such self-righteous airs.

When they had passed, she stepped into the street to cross, but hesitated as one horseman wheeled and gave her the eye, then smirking, joined his fellows in their haughty procession.

"Yankees!" she said, spitting into the dust. The action made her half ashamed of herself, but she had been through just about enough turmoil for a lifetime. She didn't need to feel insulted every time she put a foot outside her door.

She finished crossing the street, slowing her pace so as not to show a shred of fear. *I won't give them the satisfaction.*

She walked a block, then turned a corner to a blast of laughter coming from Fletcher's Tavern. She stopped. Did she dare to walk past the door where a bunch of soldiers had congregated in plain daylight to drink spirits and behave in outrageous ways? She crossed her arms against her bosom, shivering again. She's heard whispers of women being assaulted when they ventured into the streets of Mount Jackson at night. Did the same danger present itself here? She decided to be on her guard and take another route to her destination.

Another peal of laughter unnerved her, and she backed around the corner, chest heaving as she took in great gulps of air. *Oh Rulon. I wish you were strong and whole again.*

❧

Julia — May 16, 1865

The rap on the front door startled Julia. Strangers used that entrance. Someone at the front door almost always meant bad news or unwelcome company.

She got slowly to her feet, abandoning her mending. Everyone in the family but Carl was accounted for. Was someone here to tell her that he, like Peter and Ben, would never come home?

She moved toward the door on limbs that felt as heavy as pig iron bars. She opened the door. Ella Ruth Allen stood on the porch, dressed from bonnet to hem in black. Only her white face broke the somber color of the trappings of grief.

"Oh!" Julia said, and swung the door wide.

The girl stepped inside and put out her black-mitted hand, seemingly unsure what manner of greeting to offer.

Julia took it, pressed it between her two hands, then led her deeper into the room.

"I don't know how to call you," Ella Ruth said in a whispery voice. "Your comfort when you came— You are Ben's— I am Ben's—" She sank into the chair Julia offered.

"I reckon we're beyond the stage of formality," Julia replied as she sat.

Ella Ruth nodded. "We cannot be formal. He was . . ." She faltered, looked at her hands, clenched them until they went white, pulled her back straight and erect, and looked at Julia again. "You are my mother-in-law."

"Ben thought not."

"He is . . . was mistaken." Ella Ruth stopped speaking for a moment, and Julia allowed her time to compose herself and gather her thoughts.

"There was no one to marry us. Mr. Moore, the mayor, even the Dunker preacher, they were all gone." Ella Ruth's voice had a tinge of desperation. "We even considered a military officer, except I would not be married by a Yankee." She paused again. "Ben agreed. He was in danger of capture every moment he was away from the army."

Julia asked a question that had been burning a hole in her soul. "Why was he with you? Did he desert?"

"Never! He was shot in battle. I kept him safe while he healed."

Julia let the anxiety leave and replaced it with unease of another sort. "You could not marry, yet you claim kinship to me."

The statement hung between them for a moment. Ella Ruth broke the silence with a sigh, then said, "Poppa's slaves. They used a wedding ceremony that he recognized as binding. Ben and I jumped the broomstick."

"Jumped the what?" Julia entwined her fingers and rubbed her thumbs together.

"Broomstick. It's an old custom among the servants," Ella Ruth said. She looked thoughtful, narrowing her brows briefly. "Actually, Ben stepped on the broomstick. He was not sound enough to hop."

Julia nodded. "I see. That made a marriage?"

"We also said words. Vows. He loved me."

"And you loved him?"

"I love him still," she said.

Julia sensed the girl's deep conviction in the matter of her marriage being as real as though they had been church-wed. She let the conviction come across the space between them and into her own soul, felt the comfort it brought. The girl had married Ben. She basked in that surety. Then she remembered a phrase from his letter. She unclasped her hands and placed them in her lap.

"Will there be a child?"

Ella Ruth's face crumpled and she made a sound of woe. Then she said, "No," in an agony-wracked voice. She choked back a further sob.

Another silence wrapped around them, and they sat in its embrace.

At length, Julia spoke. "I will call you 'Daughter'. What will you call me?"

Ella Ruth came off her chair and to her knees before Julia. She grasped her hands. "Will you be 'Mama Owen'?"

"With all my heart," she answered.

Ella Ruth buried her face in Julia's lap and began to cry. When she raised her tear-streaked face, she said, "Poppa and Momma are taking me away to Charlottesville. I may never see you again."

"You cannot know that," Julia said. "Charlottesville is not so far from here."

"Perhaps not." She sniffed and delicately touched the tip of her nose with her knuckle. "I will not remarry," she stated flatly. "I will always be Ella Ruth Owen."

"You will always be my daughter," Julia replied. "Daughter Ella Ruth."

&

Julia — May 21, 1865

Julia heard the sound of running footsteps coming from the direction of the lane. She stopped grinding corn and looked up as Albert ran in, yelling like the Yankees were still warring with the neighborhood.

"Ma!" The boy stopped, panted, went on. "Somebody's riding in, mighty confident like."

She pushed back a loose lock of hair. "Confident, you say? Does he look like a Yankee?"

Albert hung his head. "I mostly just saw him a-coming before I ran in, Ma. But he's riding real straight and sure of himself."

"Get your pa," she said, walking to the corner and grabbing the Sharps rifle. "No Yankees will set foot in this house."

Julia walked through the doorway with the Sharps in firing position and watched as a horseman in a mud-covered gray coat came down the lane from the pike. *That man rides bold*, she thought. *Bertie spoke the truth.*

"Hold up right there," she called out. "Put your hands where I can see 'em, and get down off that horse." She could see now that he was a young man. Maybe a Confederate cavalier on his way home? Best she found out before she lowered the weapon.

He halted the horse and raised his hands but made no other move than to laugh. "You always did look fine with fire in your eye, Ma."

She sucked in her breath, almost disbelieving the sight of her son's familiar grin. "Carl?" She took a step, lowering the rifle barrel toward the ground. "Carl! Is it really you? Lawsy, boy, we almost gave up on ever seeing you again."

Her eyes started to tear up, and she swiped at them with one hand. "Get off that horse and hug your ma."

He dropped gingerly to the muddy ground and approached with long strides. "Ma, I'm home." He grabbed her—rifle and all— and swung her into the air.

As he lifted her, she caught sight of a wince that he tried to cover. That, coupled with the dried blood on his face, sent her into a tizzy of worry over his health.

Carl set her on her feet at last, and brushed at the mud he had transferred to her dress. "I'm sorry about the mud, Ma. I had a little trouble with some fellers down the road a piece, and we wrasseled around a bit. Here, let me put that rifle aside. I reckon you don't want to put a ball into me."

He took the rifle from her nerveless hands and began to walk toward the front of the house.

She followed him, trying to stop him so she could get a clear view of his face, but he kept walking. "You're not hurt? What's the meaning of that blood on your chin, then?" She watched him lean the rifle against the stone wall and took the opportunity, when he straightened up, to get close.

"Here, let me look at you." She grabbed his arm, and turned him so she could inspect the source of the dried blood. As he squirmed in her grasp, she noted that he appeared to be not much damaged, beyond a split in his lip and several bruises. She moistened the corner of her apron with her tongue and dabbed at his face.

"Ma!" he protested. "It's just a little cut."

"And it needs tending to," she insisted, then hugged him again.

"Look here!" Rod's voice. Threatening. He could be so formidable.

Julie looked at him, feeling her smile spreading wide as a

rainbow. Before she could speak, Carl turned to him.

"Have I changed so much, Pa?" He grinned under his camouflage of smeared mud.

"Rod, it's Carl. He's home at last." Julia swiped at the mud on her face with the apron.

Without a word, Rod wrapped his arms around Carl. After a long embrace, he held him off to look at him, and shook his head. "By gum, you sure got your growth dashing around with Mosby. We thought you were dead, boy, not hearing from you, nor seeing you home yet."

"Your pa was set on going to Washington City to ask after you." Julia could not stop smiling.

"I took the long road home. The Colonel disbanded the Rangers about three weeks into April, but me and some thirty others wouldn't leave him, so he took us south to join up with General Johnston in the Carolinas. Before we got there, we learned the General had surrendered, so Colonel Mosby cut us loose and made us go in to get paroled." He paused a moment, rubbing at a patch of mud on his nose. "They won't give him a parole, Pa. There's a price on his head!"

"I reckon there's mighty little justice around now, son. Your colonel won't get fair treatment since Booth shot the President. There's rumors Mosby had a hand in it."

"Somebody shot Jeff Davis?"

"The other president, Abe Lincoln."

"Is he dead?"

Rod set his jaw and turned his back on Carl. Julia reached out for him, but he walked off toward Carl's horse.

He picked up the trailing reins and came back. "Yes, and it brings hard times upon us. There's no mercy in the boys running the country now."

"Mosby had no part in it, Pa." He turned toward Julia. "Ma. I rode with him day and night for over two years." He pivoted back toward Rod. "He done no such a thing."

"I reckon," Rod said.

"He didn't. That's all." Carl's stomach growled. He looked at Julia. "Sorry my gut's so ill-mannered." He glanced around the ruined dooryard. "It sure don't look like Phil Sheridan left much hereabouts. We heard about his orders to burn the Valley, but we laughed. Not one of us believed he could do it as long as Jeb Early's troops were on home ground. How did he do it, Pa?"

"They sent in two and three times our number, son. All we could do was pester them around the edges some."

"Well, here I am now. I'll help rebuild the place. This ground will still grow food—if we can get seed."

Julia watched Albert come out of the shadow of the corner of the house. "Here's your brother, Bertie. Home safe."

Carl said, "You can't be Bertie. He were a little bitty sprout when I left."

"I ain't a sprout now. I been growing." His face bore a frown. "I go by Albert," he added, his voice a touch heated. "I'll be fourteen nigh on to Christmas time."

"You aged a right smart bit, Albert. Been doing most all the chores, I reckon."

"You left 'em to do."

Carl nodded. "I figured you three boys could handle the farm. When Peter died, I was obliged to take his place in the fight."

"I reckon." Albert looked at the ground and kicked the mud.

"I didn't know James would go, too."

Julia said, "They drafted him." She moved forward and pulled on Carl's arm. "Come in and set, boy. Doubtless you're weary, riding all day. I'll finish the pone we're having for supper while you tell your pa what shape the Valley's in south of here. He's been seeking news of the state of the Valley ever since he got home."

"Now Julie, the boy's just got here. I can quiz him later while he eats." Rod turned to Albert. "Take your brother's horse out back and put him in the pen behind the barn. See if you can find some grain. That animal's come far."

"Yes, Pa." Albert took the reins and led the horse around the corner of the house.

Julia got her rifle and went inside. She restored the weapon to its place behind the door, then went back to grinding corn. Carl and Rod came into the house and began to converse before the fire, something about buttons and uniforms and Yankees who had knocked him around.

She asked him, "That's where you got the cuts and bruises and the mud?"

"I reckon, but they didn't hurt me none."

He eased his body to a new position, and she figured he would be plenty sore tomorrow. She'd best give him the bottle of liniment before bed.

Rod's reaction was typical of his attitude nowadays. He slapped his thigh and spat out, "Yankees!"

Julia dumped the batch of cornmeal into a bowl with the rest she had ground. Pone was getting old, but at least they had corn to make it. Carl and Rod kept up the buzz of their talk as she mixed the meal with a bit of leavening and poured water over it.

As she mixed the bowl's contents with her large wooden spoon, Carl turned toward her.

"Ma, where's Marie and the little girl? Ain't they supposed to help you?"

Julia shook her head at his characterization. "Your little sister is nigh on to twelve years old, boy. We kept having birthdays while you were away." She looked over at him. "You've had a couple yourself. Ain't you about nineteen now?"

"Closer to twenty, Ma. I ain't a young'un no more."

Julia looked at the week-old stubble on Carl's face. He had grown into a man. "I see you been over the mountain, son." She laid down the spoon and began the task of forming corn cakes between her hands. "To answer your question, I sent the girls to Mount Jackson to Rulon's place. Mary's not feeling well. She's got Rulon to tend to, so they're helping out with young Roddy. I wrote you Rulon got hurt bad. Did you get my letter?"

Carl nodded.

"There's a mite more food in town," Rod said. "Your ma has her wits scraped down to a nubbin to find us enough to eat since Sheridan paid his call."

"I sent Clay in with the girls," Julia added. "He got himself a job at the livery. I only have to find victuals for your pa, James and Albert."

"And Benjamin," Carl reminded her.

Julia stiffened. The boy didn't know. She didn't fault him for bringing up her deepest sorrow, but his words caused pain to well up out of the place where she'd hidden it away. It swept over her with such force that she thought she would fall to the floor. She saw Rod take a step toward her. Silence hung in the room like a curtain made of combed cotton fibers, thick and heavy and oppressive. Then Rod spoke, his words muffled and measured.

"Benjamin fell at Waynesborough. I had no way to get word home. Your ma only found out when I got here."

Carl sagged on his stool and dropped his head against his hands. Julia felt her ears ringing hollow, filling her skull with a soft buzzing. She thought she should sit before she fell, but Carl was getting to his feet, turning to face Rod and her.

"I'm powerful sorry," he said standing stock still. "Benjamin was always such a lucky cuss, full of life, and all. It don't seem right he's gone." Carl bowed his head, took a deep breath, and began again. "Ma, I know he was your favorite son, and I don't hold it against him. He was the favorite of everybody."

She felt herself toppling, her face going slack like she was blacking out. Carl took two steps and had her in his arms, holding her up, patting her on the head and shoulders. She clung to him, struggling against the dammed emotions she needed so badly to unleash. She felt as though a serpent wrapped around her ribs so tightly she could scarcely breathe.

"There now, Ma, you cry. It'll do you good."

She wanted to cry. She hadn't been able to do it since Rod had brought her word.

Rod's arms came around the two of them. "The boy talks sense, Julia. You ain't cried since you got the news. Let tears come and wash out the grief you been carrying around." His voice became gruff as he said, "I reckon I already done my sorrowing."

The remembrance of her husband sobbing over the loss of his sons cut through the snake binding her heart. The tears came in a great torrent that let her heart expand. She wailed. She cried out. She drummed her fists against Carl's chest.

Her men waited, suspended, as her sobs tore the air. After a long, long time, she quieted, wiped the tears from her cheeks with her apron, and stepped out of the men's arms.

Exhausted, yet strangely renewed, she said, "I reckon that'll have to do for Benjamin. The living need their daily bread." She went back to the table, wiped her hands, and went to work again on her supper preparations. Carl was home. Rulon was on the mend. The family was now as whole as it could get after the terrible conflict. Somehow, they would survive.

ജ

Mary — May 24, 1865

Mary sat on the edge of the bed, facing away from her husband. She found her voice and asked, "Rule?"

After a moment, he answered in a voice burred with sleep, "Love?"

In truth, she'd been sitting there for some time, endeavoring to find more courage than she thought she possessed. Butterflies flitted through her stomach. *Will he be pleased?*

Exhausted with the emotion she'd been wrestling all afternoon, she felt the need to rest her dithering head, to lie close to him. She rose, pulled the sheet free, and slipped beneath the covers. Rulon turned on his side and laid his arm across her body, just under her bosom. The warmth from his skin heartened her, and she asked again, "Rule?"

A sigh escaped her lips before she could tumble any more words out, and she sensed him coming awake.

"I'm here."

Let him be pleased. She turned toward him, lightly touching his cheek. "Husband." She paused, choking back her joy until she knew his mind. "Rulon. I am . . . increasing."

His arm tightened, drawing her closer, pulling her against him. "Sugar," he murmured against her lips. "My sweet Sugar."

The End

About the Author

Marsha Ward is an award-winning writer and editor who has published over 900 pieces of work, including four previous novels in the Owen Family Saga, numerous newspaper articles, and sections in books on the craft of writing. She is a member of Western Writers of America, Women Writing the West, and American Night Writers Association. Born in the sleepy little town of Phoenix, Arizona, Marsha grew up with chickens, citrus trees, and lots of room to roam. She began telling stories at a very early age, regaling neighborhood chums with her tales as they snacked on her homemade sugar cookies and drank cold milk. Visiting her cousins on their ranch and listening to her father's stories of homesteading in Old Mexico and in the Tucson area reinforced Marsha's love of the 19th Century Western era.

After many years in the big city, Marsha now makes her home in a tiny hamlet under Central Arizona's magnificent Mogollon Rim. When she is not busy researching, writing, or mentoring fellow writers, she loves to travel, give talks, meet readers, and sign books.

Connect Online with Marsha Ward

Website: http://marshaward.com
Author Blog: http://marshaward.blogspot.com
Character Blog: http://charactersinmarshashead.blogspot.com
Facebook: https://www.facebook.com/authormarshaward
Twitter: http://twitter.com/MarshaWard
Smashwords: https://www.smashwords.com/profile/view/marshaward
Amazon: http://www.amazon.com/Marsha-Ward/e/B003RB9P9Q/
Newsletter signup: http://eepurl.com/vBKEj

Made in the USA
San Bernardino, CA
24 May 2015